THE QUEST

—BOOK 1—
SAVING MANKIND

STEVEN P. HORNE

ISBN 978-1-941907-73-3 *(paperback)*

ISBN 978-1-941907-74-0 *(eBook)*

Published by Firebrand Publishing

This book is dedicated to Gene Roddenberry and George Lucas for lighting the spark and to Vicki Dummett for her patience, support, comments and love.

CHAPTER ONE

The sun had barely risen and was not boding well for a sunny day in early March. The temperature was nudging the freezing mark. The snow clouds looked full and ready to unload another round of wintertime whiteness over the countryside surrounding Dome 17. All in all, it had been a typical wintery day, and since the wars (WW3, 75 years ago and WW4, nearly a half century ago), they had all become bleak and dreary. Most of the folks missed the days when there was sunshine during winter. It kept their hopes up. There had already been four straight days of the fluffy downfall accumulating inches, less than a week prior, but the city was used to heavy snowfall and all the snow removal and de-icing equipment sat ready for service. Despite the preparation in place, the citizenry was not looking forward to more snow. It just meant that there were driveways and sidewalks that would have to be shoveled. With the Dome ordinance, requiring all driveways and sidewalks be cleared by the landowner or the Dome-road crews, that just meant a lot more work needed to be done before the average Joe could get to his paying job.

Sara Kingston, 53, began the same daily routine she had done for the last 19 years, three months, 15 days, 7hrs, 55 minutes. She had only 8 months, 14 days and 5 minutes until she could retire. Not that she wouldn't miss the job; she enjoyed being able to help people in their time of need, but it did not fill the entire void in her life, the one that had gotten much larger, since her husband Jeff's sudden passing, two years prior. Coming in to work, did remind her daily, of the shortness of life, and she was thankful she was still alive, but she was beginning to feel the oppressive nature of the increasing loneliness, that was invading her life. She leaned over and switched on her computer, printer, and her foot heater.

"Must be getting old when I have to have a heater at my feet," she said to herself.

When she turned around to sit down, an alp of a man stood in front of her. He was 6'4", 235 pounds, wearing a snow camouflaged combat uniform including a white knit cap. There was a black knife hanging from his web gear on his left chest, two grenades underneath it. There was a pistol in his left armpit and another on his right hip, strapped to his right thigh. He had an impressive rifle slung down, across his chest. There were dirt, smoke stains and smudges on his face and uniform. His right arm had a steady trickle of blood from a tear in his coat, just above his right elbow.

"Where is Star Trek?" he said, almost a command, spoken by someone obviously used to being obeyed.

Sara was at a loss as to how to respond. "There's no one here by that name sir," she said, almost meekly.

"Bull shit," he responded, with a slight increase in volume and intensity. "I just brought him in by MedEvac and dropped him off out back. They would not allow me in, so they sent me around here for some reason."

Sara, calmly sitting at her desk, entered 'Star Trek' into the computer.

"I'm sorry sir, there was no one registered with that name," she said, turning the monitor around so he could see for himself. At the same time, she reached under the counter and rapidly pressed the security panic button three times. The man was becoming more upset and agitated by the minute. *Oh great,* she thought, *just what I need to start my shift.*

"Um Sir," she said, "if you could just have a seat over there, I will try to look into this for you." She gestured towards one of the cushioned seats, off to the left.

"I don't need to sit down, I need to find Star Trek," he again stated, this time a little louder and more forcefully.

"Please have a seat sir, I'm working on it," Sara replied, struggling a little to remain calm and professional, turning the monitor back around so he would again be able to see it.

A moment or two later, a slightly out of breath security officer hurriedly came around the corner, obviously prepared for the worst.

"What's going on?" he asked.

Skip Johansen stepped back and looked at the man standing in front of the check-in counter. "Sean? Sean McCann? Sergeant Major Sean McCann? It's me, Gunnery Sergeant Skip Johansen, second platoon…What's up?"

"Skip, thank God someone is here I can talk to. I'm looking for Star Trek and they do not know anything about it. Hell, I just brought him in via MedEvac, so I know he's here," McCann said, with a trace of exasperation in his voice.

Skip took a couple of steps closer, threw his arm over Sean's shoulder and pulled him closer so he could speak into his ear privately.

"She doesn't know who Star Trek is, so she can't look him up, ya know. So, to answer your question, just give me a minute and I will get this fixed," Skip whispered into Sean's left ear.

"Sara, could you please look up Coulter, James Tiberius, Lt Colonel DSF17 commanding officer?" asked the officer that just came in.

"That was all he had to say, Jesus, who the hell names their kid after an ancient TV show anyway, for Pete's sake?" she said with more than a little aggravation in her voice. Thirty seconds later she said, "Coulter, James T is in, oh my, SFU4.

"You sure?" Skip asked.

"It's all right there," she replied, turning the monitor screen around so Skip could see.

With his arm still around his shoulder, Skip said, "Sean, come with me. There are a bunch of things that are going to have to happen to you, before you go in to see him. So, we need to get started." The seriousness of his voice was quite clear.

"What's going on? Sean asked, worry entering his tone a little.

"Well, he's not dead. It's the best I can tell you right now," Skip said. "He is in SFU 4, SFU stands for Seriously Fucked Up. Four is the highest level. It's saved for patients that are alive but just barely. We have very specific protocols that have to be accomplished before anyone is allowed back there. No exceptions! Even for family members. Come with me and we'll get started." Skip took him by the left elbow and escorted him down the hall, turning right at the second corner, stopping in front of the second door on the left.

Skip gave him a set of instructions, which included removing every single weapon on his person and securing them in the provided locker that he could lock.

"You will remove all your clothing and deposit them in the provided bins. You will push the green button first. When the lids on all the bins are closed and the green light goes out, you will push the blue button. When the door opens completely, you will push the yellow button and immediately step through the door. When that door has closed behind you, the overhead light will change to red. Thirty seconds later you will be wet down. Be sure to run your fingers through all scalp and body hair. Ten seconds after the water stops, you will be coated with anti-bacterial soap. After the soap application stops, you have two full minutes to scrub every inch of your body with the brush provided on the wall. After the two minutes are complete, a freshwater rinse will begin. Be sure to run your fingers through all body hair again, thoroughly," Skip continued his instructions, while the latter nodded.

"When the rinse cycle is complete, the wall in front of you will open. Pass through and stop, you are to stay on the pad on the floor. At this point, just stand there. Be sure to close your eyes and mouth and raise your arms above your head. A very fine mist will be sprayed all over your body. When the mist stops, stay put. You will continue to stand on the pad until you are verbally told to step off. Be sure to keep your eyes shut during the ultraviolet and infrared light sequence. I will give you further instructions at that point. Are we clear on this? Is there any part of what I just told you that you do not under-stand? Do I need to go over anything again?" Skip said again, as though he had been reading from a script.

"No, Gunny, I got it. When will I get my arm looked at?" Sean asked.

"When you are through with the sterilization procedure, besides its just a nick, and it has already stopped bleeding. What got ya, shrapnel?" Skip asked.

"Ricochet, when everything was over, wouldn't ya know it."

"Ain't that the way it always is when the jobs done that's when shit happens. You'll have to fill me in a little later, meanwhile, let's get this show on the road."

Twenty minutes later, Sean was putting on a paper gown, pants and slippers when Skip came through the door with a PA in a sterile outfit, ready to bandage up his wound. Skip raised his hand in a STOP gesture.

"OK, just let me tell you what's up, then you get to ask questions," Skip started. "He's still alive but pretty bad off. Right now, they have told me that he has two fractured hips and two fractured upper thighs. Both shoulders and upper arms are fractured. He has a partially collapsed right lung, six fractured ribs all on the right side and multiple good-sized lacerations. He also has a pretty noteworthy, closed head-injury, they are trying to decide whether or not he is going to need to have his skull opened to treat that right now. Fortunately, he has two of the finest surgeons in the Dome system. Dr. Heather Dunkirk, she's a board-certified orthopedic surgeon and she also double boarded as a human robotic surgeon. J.T.'s got a lot of recon-structive stuff that is going to have to be done just so he will be able to walk around. The other Doctor is Dr. Li Meng Sun.

She's also double boarded in neurosurgery and robotics / brain injury," Skip said, trying hard to put a positive spin on things.

"Ok," Sean started, "Where are his parents? They were part of the whole thing… are they safe?"

"Yep, they are and when we are done with your arm and this little conversation, I will take you to them. Shannon is with them, before you ask. She knows you are okay. Meanwhile, let me get out of the way, you have a couple of shots and some stitches coming your way, so let's get the show on the road."

"Thanks Gunny, I owe ya."

"I'll settle for a couple of beers and a complete debrief of today's mission. I am still active reserve, so my clearances are all still valid."

"You got it," Sean said as he sat on the treatment table, trying not to look at the multiple needles he was about to have stuck in his body. "I'd rather get shot and blown up than get shots," he muttered under his breath, but loud enough for the PA to hear.

"You already did get shot or blown up, that's why you are here. By the way, your friend is in great hands," the PA offered. "If I were in his place, those are the docs I would want to work on me. I've seen their work, there's none finer."

"Thanks," Sean replied, "that's good to know. Do you really have to give me all those shots?"

"Yep, so suck it up, Sergeant Major, they won't let you in to see him without them. They are not as bad as you think." He emptied a syringe in him and said, "There that is the first one," and ten seconds later, "There's the second."

"You do those pretty well. I barely felt either one," Sean said.

"Now we have to get to the stitches," the PA replied. "I can do it with or without anesthesia, your choice."

"Does that involve needles?" Sean asked.

"Yes, to both, anesthesia and sutures, the only upside is that with anesthesia, that will be all that you feel, you won't feel all the pricks from the suture needle."

"Ok, well, in for a penny, in for a pound," he replied.

Sean stifled a minor yelp when the PA administered the anesthesia. "That shit burns, you didn't say anything about that."

Ten minutes later, the bandaging was done. "Keep the bandage clean and dry for three days. Then you can leave it open when you are doing things that won't get dirt on the wound, cover it if you do. Take all of the antibiotics until they are gone, not doing that is just asking for some unpleasant things to happen. Do you think you will need any kind of pain medication"? he asked. "I would be surprised if you do but acetaminophen should be able to take care of it. Stitches out in 7-8 days. Call me if it gets red or starts to drain."

"Thanks doc," Sean said as he hopped down off the treatment table.

Sean wandered through the tiny maze of hallways, dutifully following Skip, all the way around SFU4 suite to the conference room. Skip went through the door first, while Sean was still lagging behind. As soon as he entered, he saw Sean's wife and Coulter's younger sister, Shannon. She was with Dr. Dunkirk, a tall, very attractive, redhead, and Dr. Sun, a demure appearing Asian woman with a short stature, long black hair pulled back, and an enticing pair of eyes.

Dr. Dunkirk had on a form-fitting white silk blouse and a navy-blue skirt that stopped a couple of inches above the knee and a mid-thigh length lab coat with her name embroidered on the left upper chest, above a pocket that was stuffed with pens and the other things she needed for her job. Dr. Sun was wearing a set of light blue surgical scrubs and a similar lab coat. Seated on the sofa were the Coulters. Dr. Frank Coulter, a PhD in advanced computer engineering and physics, carrying a bit of weight around the waist and a head of slightly thinning, salt and pepper hair and his wife of forty-one years, Dr. Helen Coulter, a PhD in advanced physics and nuclear engineering. She was still a very striking woman, in good physical shape with a full thick mane of luxurious silver hair. They were obviously deep in conversation, trying to take in everything they were being told about the status of their only son. They were surprising the physicians with their depth of knowledge and understanding of all the information they were being given, as well as the poignant questions they asked about the proposed therapies, surgical interventions and ultimately, his survivability.

Dr. Dunkirk asked J.T.'s parents about his history and general overall lifestyle.

"Doc, I think I can help in that regard. I've known Star Trek for seventeen and a half years," Skip interjected. "He takes no meds, had a questionable reaction to bee stings about six years ago on a mission, has had both bone forearm fractures with surgery to fix it five years ago during a mission I am not at liberty to discuss. He has no vices, will have a beer once in a great while, usually with the troops after a successful mission, does like a glass of red wine with a steak when he eats out or attends a unit cookout. He has a very strict daily regimen that never varies. He rises at 0430 then runs five miles on odd number days, six miles on even-numbered days, all in thirty minutes give or take thirty seconds."

"He then spends however long it takes to shoot hundred rounds from a pistol with the right hand, then hundred rounds from the left hand. Monday, Wednesday and Friday, he works out on his upper body, while Tuesday, Thursday and Saturday he works out on the lower body," he continued.

"Then he has breakfast. At 8:30 a.m. he does one hour of either Kung fu, Karate, Muay Thai, Savate, Krav Maga and other hand to hand combat disciplines. On Tuesday, he returns to the range and practices with each of the weapons the squad carries on any particular missions, so he is able to train his men better. He usually has an early lunch while doing reports on the unit, studying intelligence reports on possible threats, then planning responses for each scenario. The afternoon and early evening are devoted to his educational studies. Last I heard, and I may be a little off since I was detached from active service with the Unit six months ago, best I can recall, he has six bachelor's degrees; chemistry, sociology, literature, philosophy, psychology and earth sciences, seven or eight Masters in Math, physics, computer science, electrical and mechanical engineering, and chemistry," Skip said and paused, before continuing.

"He was working towards his third and fourth PhDs, nuclear engineering, Astro-metrics, aeronautical engineering. I just don't know if he has finished or not. He has a photographic memory and almost total recall."

Skip took a breath and looked at the faces of everyone in the room. Helen's and Frank's smiling faces radiated pride in the accomplishments of their son. Shannon shook her head while mumbling something about him always having to show off. The look on the faces of Dr. Dunkirk and Sun were ones of awe and disbelief.

Dr. Dunkirk was the first to speak. "That's amazing. Does he have a wife or girlfriend, or does he have interpersonal issues with a particular woman?" she asked.

"No, he doesn't have any problems with women. He is just very focused on doing the best job he can because he takes the security of this Dome personally."

With that, the two doctors asked if anyone had any questions. Helen wanted to know when they could see him.

"My suggestion is that you all go home, get something to eat, get some rest but stay by the comm system so we can update you whenever we have something to say. We can't let you physically see him because of the possibility of infection. He has some very severe injuries and the surgical corrections he is going to undergo are each going to take at least ten to hours per surgery. Therefore, at the very least, it is going to be at least three days," Heather explained.

At that point, Sean walked through the door, saying, "Three days what?"

Shannon ran over to him, launching herself into his arms and sobbing.

"I was so worried. Are you OK?" she asked as she gently felt the bandage on his arm.

"I'm fine, babe, just a scratch," he replied. "Three days what?" he asked again.

"Till we can see him," Helen said as she came over and gave him a very heartfelt hug. She knew her daughter had chosen a fine, strong, good man as her mate and that gave her peace of mind, even though she barely approved of what he did for a living.

Frank came over and offered his hand, then thought better of it and also gave him another heartfelt hug.

"How's the wing?" he asked.

"Ricochet, just a scratch, didn't happen until everything was pretty much over," Sean said.

Frank was tempted to say "Bullshit" but held his tongue around his wife and daughter. He would get a truthful answer later, over a scotch, preferably Tullamore Dew. J.T. had introduced him to it a number of years ago.

"Now let's all follow the doctor's orders. Besides, I'm starving and dying of thirst," he said with a slight annoyance in his voice. They all gathered up their belongings and coats and headed out the door.

Skip leaned close to Heather's ear and said in a whisper, "There's a bit more info I didn't wish to share with the rest of the group, but we can discuss it in private."

Turning, she said, "Certainly, at your convenience."

"It's not going to make a difference in what you have to do for him. More of a personal thing," Skip said, trying to clarify his comment.

"Oh, how about ten minutes in the coffee room?" she asked.

"Works for me," Skip replied.

"Folks, I need to get back to things. Dr. Sun and I have a lot of planning and discussing to do, so we are going to take our leave. We both promise to keep you informed. You'll just have to trust us. If you call us a lot, we will probably not be able to speak with you, because once we get started, we can't stop until the procedure is completed. We hope you understand, but that is just the way it has to be," Heather said with empathy, but a strict matter-of-fact tone, removing any debate from anyone.

Heather and Li gave everyone a hug and a gentle, reassuring pat on the arm or shoulder as they left the conference room.

Skip decided it was also time to leave, so he shook hands with everyone and said directly to Sean, "Call me if there is anything you need. Where is everyone going to be staying?"

Shannon popped up immediately and stated that the family was going to be staying with family at her and Sean's place. There were murmurs between Frank and Helen, but both realized that there was not going to be any discussion about the matter, so they resigned themselves to staying with their daughter. Well, Frank thought, *I'll get a chance to get the whole story out of earshot of the women, plus Sean always had some nicely aged Tullamore Dew to sip.*

CHAPTER TWO

S kip walked to the employee breakroom and fixed himself a cup of coffee, with just a little sugar and cream. Military coffee had cured him of ever being able to drink coffee black.

He shuddered at the memory of his first cup of coffee as a corporal, just transferring into the Dome Security Force, unit 17. He had walked into the Unit office and presented his orders to what looked like a brand-new shave tail lieutenant standing behind the counter.

"Corporal Ivan Johansen reporting as ordered, sir. Guys call me Skip, Sir."

"J.T. Coulter, 1st Lieutenant and unit XO. Welcome aboard, Skip! Would you like a cup of coffee?"

"Thank you, Sir."

"I'll take one too, black, nothing in it."

"Yes sir, right away, Sir."

When he went to get the coffee, he noticed that there wasn't anything to put in the coffee, so he was going to have to drink his black. He carried the cups across the room to the office the XO was sitting in.

"Come in and have a seat, Skip," the XO said. "How long have you been in the DSF?"

"Two and a half years, Sir."

"Any specialties or skills that we need to be aware of?"

"Well Sir, I can shoot the eyes out of a gnat, at 500 yards, Sir."

"Well, Skip, we'll just have to see if you can back up your mouth with actions."

"Any time, any rifle, Sir. The Lieutenant will notice I did not say weapon Sir. I lost a whole month's pay to the unit Gunny, Sir."

"Oh, really, Corporal."

"Yes sir, we had the same conversation and when we went to the range and he handed me a really old 45 caliber pistol and told me to have at it. It was a really long month, but it did teach me to be very specific when making bets, Sir."

The XO chuckled, somewhat stifled, but out loud, none-theless.

"I can well imagine. Had kind of the same thing except, it was my grandfather, and I ended up washing his car and truck all summer. You're right, it was a long summer. But I still intend to see what you are made of and whether or not your mouth can be backed up."

"Any time Sir, I know what I can do, Sir."

There was a strength and confidence in his voice that impressed J.T, as J.T would tell him later.

"Very well then, Corporal. We will meet at the range at 0445 tomorrow. I will provide the rifle and ammunition."

"Um Sir, where is the range, Sir," he asked.

"Tell you what, meet me here at 0415 and we will go to the range together."

"Aye, Aye sir."

Skip was waiting at the front door of the Units' office at 0410 the next day and was surprised to see that J.T. was already there.

"Cup of coffee, Skip?" J.T asked.

"No, thank you Sir, don't need caffeine when I am trying to shoot, Sir," he replied.

"Look Skip, when it is just you and me, you can call me Lord or Master. No, just kidding. J.T is fine."

"Military decorum will be maintained at all other times, you understand? It's a discipline thing. Can't have the troops thinking they do not have to show the proper respect for an officer. So, are you ready?" J.T. asked. "Would you like to sweeten the pot, so to speak? Say $5 bet between shooters?"

"You gonna shoot against me, Sir? I'll take that wager, however we will keep this between us, right, Sir?" Skip queried.

"Wouldn't have it any other way," the XO replied. "Mount up Corporal, I'll drive since I am a Lieutenant ,and you are not. Besides I know where we are going, and you don't."

"Yes sir. Lead the way, Sir."

"I always do," J.T. replied as he sat down in the driver's seat of a non-descript four-wheel drive, open bed truck.

"Buckle up for safety, Skip, hate to lose you less than 24 hours after you have just reported in."

The ride was short but quick and filled with a few tight turns that made Skip glad he had taken J.T.'s advice to buckle up.

"J.T. you are not going to rattle me with your driving, but you may break a couple of bones before we get there." Skip was bordering on a whine as he spoke.

"Corporal, are you impugning my character as an officer and a gentleman?"

"No, Sir, just stating a few concerns, Sir."

J.T. slid to a stop in front of a non-descript one story building. He stepped out from the truck, walked around to the bed and retrieved two obvious rifle cases and a large knapsack that he threw over his left shoulder. As he walked towards the front door he asked, "Ready to get your game face on, Skip?"

"Yes sir, I am," he replied.

"By the way how many missions did you go on at your previous Dome command?"

"Three sir,"

"Over what time frame are we talking about?"

"Thirty months, give or take a few days."

"What was the average enemy combatant count, seen at each of those missions?"

"You mean how many bad guys, sir? Alive or dead, Sir?"

"Skip, we average 2.3 missions per month, usually with 25-30 combatants per event. We do not take prisoners, so these are end of action body counts. How did your teams stay sharp with so few missions?"

"We had once a week training missions, usually the same as the week before. We ran the hostage house with pistols once a week for scores," Skip replied.

"The problem was they never changed the scenarios inside the house. The first one was a bad guy with a knife, the second were two bad guys with a child hostage. And so on. You only had to run through it two or three times and you knew what to expect and where to shoot. The Major liked having his numbers being universally high. We had a Gunny, the same one that bet me my monthly paycheck, who went in on a Sunday night and changed the scenarios and presentations in the hostage house. 73% of the men shot less than 45% and on average, killed 57% of the hostages. The major had him busted to staff sergeant and transferred to a different dome," Skip continued.

"Well Skip, we don't do things like that here. It is my sworn duty to keep each member of my unit razor sharp, thoroughly cross trained, and to involve each team member in the planning of every mission. Do you have any idea of the casualty numbers in your last unit?"

"35% or thereabouts, Sir."

"Care to guess what ours is?"

"No idea, Sir."

"We have had two dead and six wounded in the last two years, and remember, that is with an average of two missions per month. Well-trained troops do not make mistakes and are able to complete the mission with the only loss of life being the enemy. You have fallen in with an elite bunch of scoundrels, Corporal. Congrats."

J.T. turned to the door and unlocked it. As he opened the door, he reached around and flipped on a bank of lights.

"Come on in," he said. "The hostage house is on the left, the long rifle range on the right, and the pistol range is behind the hostage house. Let's head over to the rifle range. Both weapons are centered at 250 yards. You will see before you a console. This console is set up to the range and provides temperature, wind direction, wind velocity and barometric pressure. Since we average 25 to 30 enemy combatants per mission, you will be given a clip of 32 rounds. The first two rounds are to center the weapon. You will then fire as rapidly as you can, and we will tabulate the numbers. Outer ring is one point, inner bullseye is ten. Any questions?"

"Yes sir, sitting, kneeling, or prone?"

"Prone."

"Prone it is, Sir."

"Spoken like a true shooter. You may proceed."

Skip went over to the table and opened one of the cases. Inside was a perfectly preserved AR 15.

"How old is this weapon, Sir?"

"125 years or so, belonged to my grandfather."

"It's a fine weapon Sir. Looks like it has been well taken care of, shown a lot of love."

"It has, and there are only three people that have ever fired it."

"I'm honored, Sir."

"You can prove that by doing your very best today, you understand?"

"Yes, Sir." Skip moved to the console on the left, checked the console and adjusted the sights.

He slammed the clip home and racked a round into the chamber. Checking the safety, he reverently laid the weapon on the floor, trying his best not to scratch it or get any dirt or dust on it. He got down on his belly and stretched out, spreading his legs and turning his toes outbound. He then reached for the rifle, feeling its weight in his hand, softly stroking the wood grained stock. He began to murmur some unintelligible sounds at the weapon, obviously getting comfortable with it. Shooting with such a weapon as this was like making love to a beautiful woman. He had to caress it just so, stroke it, whisper softly to it, until he felt that he knew the weapon on a personal level. J.T. was impressed with this ritual. It told him volumes about the man, and his approach to shooting. It was very personal and intimate, traits that made for an excellent marksman.

J.T. kept his position directly behind Skip, looking straight down the range. He slowly brought the range binoculars up to his eyes and said, "whenever you are ready, Skip."

Skip gave a little wiggle, getting settled in, put the earplugs in both ears, flipped off the safety, and pressed his cheek to the stock. He slowed his breathing and then caressed the trigger. The kick of the rifle hit perfectly in the sweet spot on his shoulder. He repeated the ritual, without deviation, until the bolt lock opened and he felt as though all was right with the world.

He gently laid the rifle down and was about to get up when J.T. told him that was only the first part of the competition.

"Reload, corporal," J.T said and handed him the next clip. Skip laid the rifle down and stood up.

"Remove the first two rounds and load the weapon." He picked up both consoles and showed them to Skip.

"You will take the first shot at the target on the left and the second shot at the target on the right. You will alternate targets until the clip is empty. You have five minutes total to complete the shooting. Tell me when you are ready to begin," J.T. said.

Skip repeated the ritual he had done at the beginning of the competition. When he was done, he said, "Beginning now."

Four seconds later, he squeezed off the first shot and continued with a shot every seven seconds until the bolt lock opened the second time. He laid the rifle on the ground and stood up.

"Your turn, Sir."

"In just a second," he replied.

J.T. flipped a switch and there was a whirring noise and fifteen seconds later, two targets stopped right in front of both of them.

"The best you could have done on both trials, total points, is a max of 600. When I push this button, the computer will tabulate your score, you ready?"

"When are you going to shoot, Sir?"

"Don't be impertinent, young man. Are you ready?"

"Yes, Sir."

The final tabulation popped up on the screen. It was 599.

"That is outstanding, Sergeant!"

"That's Corporal, sir."

"Not any longer, Staff Sergeant."

"Sir?"

"Skip, the unit needs an overwatch squad and I need someone to be in command of that squad. By definition, that commander has to be a better marksman than anyone on the squad. It instills respect and trust when a commander can do the same job as his troops, but better than any of them. I have decided that I have found just that person and he has passed my test and that is all that matters, Sergeant."

Skip's face wore a look of surprise, but he quickly maintained a straight face.

"Now you can decline this promotion and I will accept your choice, but do not forget, I am your superior and I have a very long and vengeful memory but don't let that sway you," J.T spoke with quite a serious, no bull-shit tone.

"In that case, Sir, I accept your proposal, although, I should point out that I have no command experience or training, neither do I have the faintest idea as to how to do this job."

"Skip look, remember that I told you that I always involve every man in the unit in the planning of each mission?"

"Yes, I do."

"Well, when we are planning a mission, you will need to figure out where you can place the squad with the best field of fire, providing the rest of the unit with the greatest amount of coverage and protection."

Skip nodded.

"Overwatch should get most," J.T continued, "if not all of the kills on every mission. Is that going to bother you? You will decide on the squad's training standards, weaponry loadouts, and your squad membership. You will transfer anyone in and out of your squad as you see fit. Our command structure will not override your choices or decisions, OK?"

"Just onequestion, Sir."

"Shoot."

"Did I win the $5?"

"Are you always going to be a smartass sergeant?"

"No Sir, but this was about money as well as honor, Sir."

J.T. had handed him a $5 spot that day.

Skip snapped out of his reverie when he noticed the two doctors approaching.

"There you are. We have been waiting for you in the Doctor's lounge for the last twenty minutes."

"I believe I said I would meet you in the coffee room. I can't get into the Doctor's lounge," Skip replied.

The two doctors looked at each other sheepishly.

"We didn't realize," Dr. Sun said. "Look I really have some things to get done before our planning session and I was thinking that with the massive amount of tissue damage he has, he will probably develop Rhabdomyolysis. So, I thought I would get Frank Collier in on things and maybe even get him on preventative dialysis. This should help improve his overall kidney function and help with perfusion."

"Great idea!" Heather said, thinking to herself, *I should have thought of that. Get on your game girl, this is the Superbowl of cases, it is going to require you to be always on top of your game.* "Anyway, Skip, you had some info about Colonel Coulter."

Skip replied, "Like I said, I don't think this is going to be anything that is going to affect what is going on with him right now, but it is a significant aspect of his personal life that he does have to deal with."

"OK, go on."

"It has to do with his love life or lack thereof. I am not sure how to say this but, J.T. is still a virgin," he said hesitantly. "Thirty-five years old and he has never been with a woman. The reason for that is that, well, how do I say this? He is really, really well endowed. I mean like a horse, literally. He once told me that every time he gets to the point that he is about to be intimate with a woman, and she sees him get undressed, they basically tell him there is no way in hell they are gonna have relations with something that big. They get dressed and leave and he never hears back from them."

Seeing the doctor's blank face, he continued, "I thought you might have noticed, what with you examining him and all. Hell of a problem, ain't it? Most men wish they could have this kind of a problem. Kinda puts the shoe on the other foot, ya know what I mean?"

Heather was at a loss for words. Being an orthopedic surgeon, she never really had a need to examine that part of the man's anatomy.

"TTThanks for the info," she stuttered. "I need to get back to work. We'll keep you posted."

She reached out and put a gentle hand on his forearm and said, "You're a good man and a great friend. I hope I can say the same things about people I call my friends."

She turned and strode off, wiping a tiny tear from her eye.

At Sean and Shannon's house, everyone was just finishing up with having a sandwich and some potato salad, with some chips. Sean leaned his head towards the den, in a manner that only Frank could see. Frank raised an eyebrow in acknowledgement and slowly moseyed over to the den. Sean slowly made his way to the den also.

"Tullamore Dew, Dad?"

"I thought you would never ask. Three fingers if you don't mind. I think I am going to need it," Frank said.

"It's not really that bad, Frank."

"How can you sit there and say that when J.T. is in, what did they call it, SFU? For gods' sake!"

"That's not what I meant, and you know it. I was there, remember, I pulled him from the wreck," Sean said with more than a little irritation in his slightly raised voice. Not at all the way he had intended for it to come out.

"Everything OK in there?" Helen called from the dining room.

"We're fine, mom, just frustrated, that's all. Sorry for yelling," Sean replied.

"We're all worried and concerned," Helen offered.

"I know," he replied.

"So," Frank said, "start from the beginning. I reserve the right to interrupt for clarifying questions. Begin," he said with a wave of his hand.

"Ok, Dad," Sean said and began his narration.

"About four weeks ago, they got some early intelligence that there was a mole in the Dome system that was feeding info on train schedules and the supplies that they would be carrying. It seemed that they were informing a rebel militia group, run by a *Colonel Merriweather*, who was a self-proclaimed Colonel. He was then arranging his 'REBEL' militia to intercept and rob these shipments. To date, there have been five robberies, with a total loss of life set at eighteen. The casualties were mostly civilians and professionals, like engineers, chemists, computer guys, etcetera. J.T. had the idea to stage a train shipment that contained a lot of things that this Colonel Merriweather just couldn't pass up, like uranium rods for reactors, gunpowder and metal to make bullets, VIP's and six ranking members of the Council. They hoped that this self-acclaimed colonel would think that they could be used for ransom purposes. So, it was arranged for the train to come from Dome 7 to Dome 17. The train system was drilled 250 feet below the surface to avoid damage in case of a wartime attack. This meant that there could be a straight shot to any point without having to go around anything, including most rivers and small lakes. The only issue between there and Dome 17 was the fault line at Bonner's Creek. So, it was decided that since the rail line would rise up into the mountain range, exit the range and cross over the fault line with a moveable suspension trestle and then back into the mountain range and back underground.

This seemed like the perfect place to set up an ambush. It was believed that Colonel Merriweather was aware of the bridge and would feel that this area was the only place where the train was vulnerable to attack. It was also believed that he was not intimately aware of everything in the area, like mines, booby traps and reinforced sniper positions and multiple previously constructed, protected fields of fire. Both entrances, on each side of the ravine, had foot thick, reinforced, steel blast doors, which opened only from the inside the mountain, electronically, via cables. This was all designed by J.T, back when it was being constructed nearly eleven years ago.

We thought that Colonel Merriweather would think this was the best unprotected area and the most opportune time to attempt an assault and robbery of the supply train. J.T. designed the inside of the mountain so there are two sets of railroad tracks on each side of the mountain range. Side by side. One is a 3/4th mile long siding-track, the other is the regular railroad track. Inside, there are living quarters for 50 people.

So immediately after approval of J.T.'s plan, half the unit was sent out to provision the tunnel and set up mine fields, remove a lot of obstructions that could be used for concealment, and open up fields of fire. Afterwards, they then moved a 4-car train, complete with engine onto the track inside the same section of the mountain that the train would be coming from. Over the next five days or so, that section of the fake train was super-reinforced so it could withstand a prolonged assault. The trestle was also reinforced. The plan was to deploy the unit on the same side as the arriving train. The arriving train would pull on to the siding and the spare reinforced train would hook-up to what was left of the original train. J.T. was going to be flying an ARSPD (armed recon single pilot drone), to see where the attacking force was located, as well as provide airborne command and control, in addition to whatever combat air support he could provide.

The drone was armed with 2-16 rocket pods, one on each wing and a forty-caliber machine gun in the nose with 650 HE rounds. J.T. was flying at about 1500 feet when he finally saw the first evidence of a column in the distance. He radioed the unit with the direction of the column, coordinates, anticipated arrival time, and some other instructions. They armed all the mines and the antipersonnel explosives; the snipers took positions, and the trains were hooked up.

The train unit took up their positions in the phony train and the steel door was opened. As the attacking force approached, the diversionary train exited the mouth of the entrance to the mountain and headed for the stopping point where they were to wait for the opposite mountain range to open and the suspension trestle to be activated and extended. As they sat there waiting, the attacking force attacked with a mounted brace of machine guns on two separate jeeps, surrounded by improvised armor that was not really designed to stop any serious firepower, just designed to stop infantry rifle fire. It was obvious they had no idea what was coming. As the foot soldiers dismounted their 6x6 transportation, they spread out and began a rush towards the stationary train. After most of the dismounted troops had been pushed into position, the anti-personnel mines, like the claymore mines of the early 21st century, were set off. This wiped out about two-thirds of the attacking force before they could take two more steps. The quasi-armored jeeps then moved up into position, while the sniper units opened fire on the jeeps from hidden, protected positions. This stopped the jeeps in their tracks. The machine guns mounted on the back of these jeeps were effectively forced to stay in one spot and due to size, weight and heat, they were not able to be physically lifted off their mounts and moved to more secure positions. The gunners hunkered down, unwilling to stand, and continue to press the attack.

Some of the squad with hand-carried automatic weapons scattered rounds across the entire face of the mountain in hopes that with spraying bullets, a stray round would take out a sniper and, or at least, silence them. The rest of the hidden Unit troops now opened fire on the remaining, still viable, rebel fighters making short work of most of them. The rebel command-and-control vehicles moved forward, using LAWS (light anti-tank weapons), most of which were over sixty years old. Their job was to try to disable the engine of the faux train still sitting there, waiting for the suspension trestle to move into position. The last of the mines were detonated, again being fairly accurate where needed. At this point, the rebel reserves came in to play, mostly using grenade launchers.

The architects that had designed the defensive positions certainly earned their pay that day. A few minor ricochet rounds and flying stone chip injuries were the only injuries inflicted on the stalwart defenders. There was a lull in the fighting when out of the sun came an aerial assault from the armed drone being flown by J.T. Diving with the sun at his back, blinding his opponents, he unleashed a barrage of rockets aimed at all the remaining vehicles, hitting most of them with deadly accuracy. J.T. pulled the drone up and did a loop-d-loop maneuver, to bring him back into position, with the sun still behind him, for another attack. As J.T. dived again, he opened fire with his machine gun, moving like a scythe through the remaining troops. As he finished his gun run and was beginning to pull up, a lone rebel stepped out, firing a rocket-propelled grenade and was successful in hitting the tip of the right wing. This caused an immediate control problem for the drone, pulling it around to the right, all the while causing it to lose altitude.

There was no way for J.T. to bail out from the armed drone. He was strapped in so tight that he literally almost became a part of the drone. There was no parachute. If the drone is hit, the best the pilot could hope for is a controlled crash and that was what J.T. was fighting for, in the last two minutes of his flight. Using overcorrection, J.T. managed to get the drone almost level, even as he rapidly lost altitude. He jettisoned the two rocket pods, which lightened the overall weight and allowed a modicum of lift to be salvaged.

J.T. fought to stay aloft. He battled to keep the drone as level as possible, even as the angle of his descent increased. While this was going on, he scanned the countryside, looking for a place to set the drone down. The ground was rapidly coming up, and you could tell he was expending the last of his adrenaline augmented strength, fighting to exert some small amount of control over that untamed beast of a drone.

He finally picked a spot about 500 yards ahead. It appeared flat for the most part, although it, like the rest of the battlefield, was covered with snow. While that would have provided a cushion and melted ice water to cut down on the possibility of fire after the crash, it also hid objects like rock outcroppings and tree stumps. As he raced towards the ground, he gave a violent, tremendous, backwards yank on the yoke, bending it, succeeding in bringing the nose up a little bit, keeping the drone from nosediving into snow covered terrain. As the drone plunged and scraped across the frozen snow-covered landscape, J.T. was jarred and banged around like he was riding a prized, half ton Texas longhorn bull.

The straps holding his chest and his hips tore loose, allowing him to be thrown around even more violently. The left side of the nose of the drone hit a hidden rock outcropping, hitting the fuselage frame on its left side and breaking the wing off. The nose mounted machine gun broke loose from its mounts and hit him squarely on the right side of the chest and shoulder. His ribs snapped on the right side of his chest. He coughed painfully, and blood pooled in his mouth. As the drone cartwheeled, both hips wrenched, and the upper thighs of both legs broke. Because his restraining straps were gone, the drone landed on his left shoulder.

The drone finally stopped, but it was all on top of him, pushing his face into the snow. He was struggling to move his face into a position where he could breathe. As he lay there, the fear of being smothered welled up in him, but he struggled to remain focused. He could hear voices but did not recognize them. He heard a 3-shot burst and felt a body hitting the drone's frame.

Sean went to him at the same time he yelled instructions to other people on how to lift the frame off him. When the frame was finally lifted off him, J.T. gently rolled over and saw Sean.

"Sean, I knew you'd come and get me," he whispered with a great deal of effort. "Be sure to tell everyone I love them."

Just then, the merciful blackness of unconsciousness sucked him down into the void.

Sean put him in a MedEvac fifteen minutes later. While in, Doc Horner had two IVs started, a thoracic dart was stuck in the lateral right lower chest to re-inflate his traumatic collapsed lung, and bandages were applied to almost all his cuts. Morphine, a steroid, and an antibiotic injection had all been administered on the way to Dome 17 emergency ward.

"What happened to the rebels?" J.T.'s father asked.

"We finished off the remainder of the rebels. I personally finished off Colonel Merriweather after I interrogated him and got the names of three other spies. Those names have been sent to command via the XO, Major Stein. As you know, the train continued to Dome 17, unimpeded, and unbothered. We had a total of three minor injuries, not counting J.T. No KIA's. J.T.'s plan worked absolutely brilliantly. You should be proud."

"I am. Can I have another Tullamore Dew? I need it," Frank said, a little choked up and a little misty eyed with pride, love and concern for his only son. Not to diminish how he felt about Sean, because he viewed him as another son, but he wasn't blood.

CHAPTER
THREE

The meeting between Heather and Li took two hours longer than planned, not counting the multiple interrupting pages dealing with patient care. There were six separate surgeries that needed to be planned out, supplies ordered, roles delineated, and the order of completion decided.

Heather was not sure about number six, but Li had done some research on a project she was into, about Intracranial Information Implantation, and given the obvious intellect of the patient, she had thought that, implanting electrodes into J.T.'s brain while he was in a coma and the bulk of his body's energy was going to be focused on his healing and this would allow his brain to progress along with his chosen course of education. If it worked, he would have advanced his learning to the end of three different PhD studies and maybe even a fourth. The trouble was, he was in a coma and could not give consent, so it was going to fall to the two doctors on the case to discuss this with his family. Fortunately, the family was readily available, and it was very fortuitous they were in town. Heather picked up the comm link and said, "Sean McCann residence."

Five seconds later, Shannon answered, "McCann residence. Shannon here."

"Hey Shannon, this is Heather at the medical center."

"Has something happened to J.T.? Is he dead?"

"No, no, nothing like that. I was just calling to see if I could arrange a meeting with you, your mom and dad, later today, to go over our proposed plans and get all the permissions, forms signed, and questions answered."

"Okay sure." She held the device away from her mouth and yelled, "Mom, Dad, Heather's on the line." There was a rush and a rustling in the background before Frank came on the line.

"Is something wrong? Has he died?"

"No, no, nothing like that. I was just wondering if all of you could come to the medical center today, say around 3 p.m.? There are a number of things we need to go over before we can proceed."

"Do you have anything planned for this afternoon?" he yelled to his wife. Heather heard her negative reply.

"Frank, let's set it up for 3 p.m. in the conference room, where we were yesterday, okay?" Heather asked.

"That sounds great. We will see you then."

Heather hung up. *I need to remember that they are preparing for the worst when I call*, she thought.

Heather called Li and brought her up to speed. She also reminded her to bring the literature she had on III (intracranial information implantation). Both of the Coulters were quite intelligent as well as being inquisitive, insightful and were scientists. She imagined that they would be interested, as well as concerned.

————————

Heather had a number of urgent things that cropped up between the time she hung up and when 3 p.m. rolled around. So much so that she was twenty minutes late.

The meeting started without Heather, in the 25'x35' foot conference room; a comfortably appointed room, with lots of long sofas and love seats. Visitors and family members of patients were allowed to rest or even sleep there. There were a few areas that were much more private.

Li went over the muscle implant modules she was going to put in and fielded questions from the family. They wanted to know where the implant would go, what it would do. Would it ever need to be replaced, or plugged in to recharge? Would J.T. be able to feel them? Li did an outstanding job describing the procedure from her end, answering all the questions and, in general making the Coulters feel confident in the procedure.

Heather breezed into the room effusively apologizing for being tardy. Li brought her up to speed on what she had already covered. Heather dived in, beginning with how she was going to address the hip and thigh implants first. She told them that with J.T.'s incredible physical workout regimen; she was going to use some extra strong customized implants for the hip sockets, trochanters and, in addition, she was going to use complete femoral rod implants. This was rarely done, but the location of the fractures really left her no other choice. She planned on doing both surgeries in the same time frame to minimize the anesthesia risk. Heather also told the family about him being placed on dialysis and that he was doing much better because of it. She then discussed the same information about the bilateral shoulder and rib fracture reconstructions. This was not usually done, but allowing the fractures to heal on their own would dramatically reduce the ability of his lungs to expand. That would restrict his ability to rehab himself after all the surgeries had healed. He would then have to get back to the active lifestyle he had set up for himself, not forgetting his role, as commanding officer of a DSF unit that protected thousands of residents in and around Dome 17.

Heather had chosen to have some aluminum or titanium alloys molded into the shape of ribs with a flexible polymer substance that was going to be used to replace the cartilage at both ends of the ribs, the attachment to the breastbone and the spinal column. That would allow the chest to contract and expand with breathing. She was going to top things off with lining the interior of the chest cavity with a 6th generation Kevlar derivative material that would give him some chest protection from projectiles, like bullets, since he seems to frequently be in a position where he could get shot.

There were the customary questions about healing rates, chance of infection and other questions about deformities. Heather handled them all with calm, frank, and confident answers. She hung no extra crepe nor added any bullshit; it just wasn't her style. Besides, it tended to keep the family's expectations at a reasonable level, which in the end, made her look like a miracle worker.

As her first attending physician always said, "Happy patients do not sue nor complain to the licensing board."

Now it was time for LI to bring up the III.

"There's one more thing I would like to bring up," Li began.

"I am doing some research in Intracranial Information Implantation. It has been hard to find subjects we could demonstrate useful improvement in information use. Your son is obviously quite intelligent, and he currently is working on three PhDs at once and I thought he would be a perfect candidate," Li continued.

"We would be able to accurately measure the amount and quality of implanted information if we used III on him," she concluded.

Frank was the first to speak. "I have read a few papers on computer assisted information implantation and frankly, I think. J.T. would be a perfect candidate. He definitely has the intellectual capacity."

Helen said, "I would love to help with the information programming."

Shannon wailed, "I am always left out of things and J.T. always seems to get to do the coolest things."

Frank said, "Well Shannon, I will see if we can arrange to have you in a plane crash, break most of your major bones and have a closed head injury so you can get all the things planned for J.T. But don't forget, you are the one that is going to be providing us with grandchildren. Doesn't look like J.T. is headed down that road anytime soon. Mother, when was the last time he had a girlfriend?"

"Three years, two months and a couple of weeks. I liked her, but she didn't really seem like the marrying kind. Come to think of it, none of his female friends, I won't say girlfriends, because there never seemed to be the intimacy you would expect with a girlfriend. I just don't understand. J.T. is really a catch. Did you know he is quite the chef? What woman wouldn't want a man that is a fabulous cook?"

Heather felt herself blush.

Listening to J.T.'s family reminded her of the frequent conversations that were held in the past, by her family, concerning her lack of a steady beau. Li popped up and said that she used to hear the same thing from her family but now, it was about when was she going to start a family. Everyone chuckled at that. Heather added that she felt as though she was sitting around the kitchen table at her parents' house.

"Well dear," Helen said, "when were you planning to?"

"Oh, I'm not looking at this point. My career takes up a lot of time and there are a lot of people that depend on me, so that part I have put on hold for a while."

Frank threw in, "Don't take this the wrong way, but you are not getting any younger."

Helen slapped him on his upper arm. "You are so rude."

Everyone got a good laugh out of the banter. Heather and Li then laid out all the forms, re-explained each section and handed Frank the pen and pointed out where to sign. The mood suddenly became more somber as the reality of things sank in.

"We trust you two," Frank said, as he signed the forms. "You have our son's life in your hands."

"And we promise to take the very best care of him we can. We swear," Heather said with all the confidence she felt through her entire being.

As she and Li gathered up the papers, she said, "Li and I have a bunch of things to wrap up, so we have to get going. We will keep you informed as much as we can. Whenever we can. If the two of you," she said, pointing to Frank and Helen, "can figure out where J.T. was in his studies, we can pick up where he left off, then try to work out a compilation of the required information and just for the heck of it, why don't you add in any recent publications on different aspects of each of his courses. Maybe you can even find updates on work that is currently being done around the globe and add that in too. Who knows what he could discover or build? You will need to have this ready to go in ten days."

"Did we mention we would be using the immersion tanks for 8-12 weeks after we have finished the surgery? It cuts down on infection possibilities and promotes more complete healing."

The parents agreed and said their goodbyes as Heather and Li exited the conference room.

"Shannon, you will need to take us over to J.T.'s house so we can get started. I feel so much better now that there is something I can do to contribute," Frank said.

"Me too," Helen added. "So, let's get started."

The whole family piled into Shannon's sedan and took the short trip over to J.T.'s house. Shannon had the emergency key, so she could let everyone in. The home was a wood and brick ranch with shutters that were painted white and a deeply intense red front door. Shannon shut off the alarm and walked through the nicely appointed, immaculately cleaned and maintained front room, with a large wall mounted TV with 112" screen. There were pictures scattered throughout. There was a hallway that ended in a master bedroom, with a bathroom. On either side of the hall there were three bedrooms with 2 ½ bathrooms. The den was off the left side of the family room, loaded with books arranged on a redwood bookshelf, taking up the entire right-hand wall. There were diplomas hanging on the wall opposite the bookshelves. In between the two walls was a huge mahogany desk with a large computer centrally located. There were stacks of reference books flanking the computer on both sides. The deep forest green carpet gave the room a warm, relaxing ambiance, making everyone feel comfortable and relaxed, just as it was intended to do. Two plush, red leather covered recliners were separated by a small coffee table with a Tiffany lamp in the center, and a remote for the TV and stereo system.

The kitchen was just what you would have expected of a man that took his cooking very seriously. In the center was a very large island with a deep sink at one end and an 8-burner gas range on the other. The top was beige and black swirl quartz, two inches thick. Suspended over the center of the island was an arrangement of shiny copper cookware. J.T.'s cutlery collection was on a butcher block against the wall, next to the containers that held all of his cooking utensils. The mixer, food processor and microwave oven stood to the other side.

Helen had picked the right-hand stack of books, mostly referencing ion/plasma propulsion, cold fusion reactors, and negative polarity magnet propulsion theory. The left-hand stack was all about aeronautical engineering, spacecraft design and space exploration theory.

"All this, plus what we can dig up that is currently being studied and researched somewhere else, will probably make his brain explode," Helen commented.

"We have our work cut out for us and a short period of time within which to accomplish that."

Shannon was in J.T.'s bedroom, looking through his dresser and then into the bathroom, looking through the drawers, looking for something even she did not know what.

"Shannon," her dad called, "what are you doing?"

"Just looking around. I don't get invited here very often," she replied.

"Well, come here and help your mother and I look through these textbooks and see if we can find anything that indicates how far he is in that book," her father commanded.

"Yes sir, be right there." She opened the closet door and moved the clothes around, peering inside. She closed the door after seeing nothing but different types of uniforms and shoes and boots. "No books in here," she announced as she came into the den.

"Here, take this stack. If you find a book that is obviously being used, thumb through it and see if you can find evidence of where he left off. If you can, bend the page to mark it and put the book in this stack over here," her mother said. "I am going to go through the drawers and see if there are any reference notes or scratch papers."

Three hours later, the three of them were exhausted, so they gathered all the books and information they could find and went out to Shannon's car, heading home.

During the ride, Frank laid out the tasks that needed to be done. All the information they had, or would need, had to be found online or at least on a computer, because that was what was necessary for the data to be able to be transmitted into J.T.'s brain via III. They had a lot of labor-intensive work that would need to be done in time for hooking up to the implants.

Both Frank and Helen were scientifically curious as to whether J.T. would absorb any of the information implanted, if it would be usable, or if it would make a difference in what he would be able to do with the information. Since he was obviously interested in space travel, they added some theoretical studies and information on suspended animation/hibernation that he may be able to do something with. It gave them quite a vicarious thrill to know that they had input into what their only son was learning, what he was possibly capable of doing with that information, or how that information may end up changing the course of man's destiny. Since they were both scientists, being as accurate, honest, and unbiased as possible were all traits that were part of their core, even into their DNA. They both took this situation with the right amount of seriousness. Helen decided she was going to be the one that decided which information referenced nuclear/ cold fusion issues, while they would interact and collaborate on the Astro-metrics and aeronautical engineering as well as the ion/ plasma propulsion, and the negative polarity magnet propulsion theory, since they both had advanced degrees in physics.

CHAPTER
FOUR

I t was 9pm. Dr. Heather Dunkirk sat at her kitchen table. On the table were multiple anatomy and surgical technique manuals. She rubbed her eyes and ran her fingers through her full, rich, red hair. She was tired, and the stress of the Coulter case was beginning to weigh heavily on her mind. This was the biggest, most complicated, and surgically varied case she had ever been involved in. In fact, she had been unable to find any textual references to a surgical case this extensive anywhere in the text and online literature.

A fleeting thought: *Have I bitten off too much?* Had crossed her mind and was immediately dismissed.

Heather reviewed all the applicable surgical literature on each of the proposed procedures. She cross-referenced the different anatomy books as well as her notes concerning the overall condition of the patient, the MRI and radiographs of all the injuries, his current lab status including his kidney function, which was stable and doing well, thanks to the early start of dialysis by Dr. Sun, and blood coagulation studies. His cardiac status was excellent. Even though there was a question of a cardiac contusion with the rib fractures from his crushing chest injury, it had not panned out. Lung function impairment was to be expected with a crushing chest injury, but fortunately he had not developed ARDS (adult respiratory distress syndrome) or pneumonia, both of which were a significant concern, prompting her to move towards the surgeries a little faster than she would have liked. Given the total complexity of the case, she had very little choice.

You got this girl! She thought to herself. *You've been preparing for a case like this all your life. You can do this.* She rubbed her eyes again, closed her books, got up from the table and headed to bed. 7am was going to come early, and she needed to be sharp and on point. As she undressed and slipped into bed, she remembered what Skip had said about J.T's endowment. He wasn't lying because J.T was really well endowed. With that, she turned off the light and got comfortable.

6:15 a.m. the alarm went off rousing her from what had been a really good night's sleep. She was refreshed and relaxed, and the tension she had been carrying the night before at the kitchen table was gone. She knew she was up to the task. She strode into the bathroom, turned on the water and stepped in. The warm water took the chill off a bit as she soaped herself. She then put her high-end shampoo on her head and worked it into her thick mane of hair. As she rinsed the second round of shampoo out of her hair, she thought of the upcoming task facing her. She had repeatedly reviewed the anatomy texts and the surgical techniques she would be using in about two hours. She then remembered a dictum taught to her by her mentor and chief attending physician during her 5th year of residency, "Never perform a surgery unless you are able to handle anything that could go wrong."

She pondered all the different things that could go wrong today, from drug reactions, strokes, myocardial infarctions and the most common problem of orthopedic surgery, pulmonary embolism where a blood clot forms, usually in the lower extremities because of inactivity, then breaks off and goes to the heart, brain, or lungs. They already had protocols and therapies in place and were active to prevent this, but there was always a chance.

She stepped out of the shower and dried her hair, then bent forward, and wrapped her hair in a towel, before reaching for a second towel to dry off her body. When she was dry, she stepped in front of a full-length mirror and did a half pirouette, looking herself over. *Not bad for 33, you go girl*, she thought. She then went to get dressed where she put on her special underwear. Not that they were sexy, but they were comfortable, and she was going to be standing continuously for the next ten to twelve hours. She finished dressing and headed out to her vehicle, still mulling over the task that was before her.

Heather parked at the medical center doctors' parking lot. Entering through the *doctor's only* door, she headed down a long corridor, quiet this time of the day. The antiseptic and cleanser smell of the hospital filled her nostrils. It was familiar, comforting and reassuring to her. She made her way to SFU 4, stopping at the nurses' desk, and requesting Coulter's chart. The charge nurse handed it to her.

"Are the latest lab results on the chart?" she asked.

"Yes, Doctor," was the reply. "I put them there myself, a few minutes ago."

Heather flipped through the labs, noting the new values, especially the coagulation studies and the kidney function tests, then looked at the previous lab values looking for any noteworthy changes. She was particularly pleased to see a small improvement in the kidney tests, a credit to Dr. Sun's decision to get him on early dialysis. Another issue that could be relegated to the back burner. Heather handed the chart back to the charge nurse, asking her if she had seen Dr. Sun recently.

"Yes, she came through about fifteen minutes ago, headed for the doctors' lounge."

"Thanks," Heather replied, as she made her way to the lounge.

After swiping her ID badge in front of the lock, she pushed her way inside, scanning the room trying to find Li. Li was sitting at a small table in the corner with a cup of tea in front of her and a whole raft of papers spread out on top of the table.

"Hey Heather, grab a seat," Li said.

"Let me get a cup of coffee and a donut. I missed breakfast on my way in this morning."

After she had put everything on the table and sat down, Li said, "I'm glad you stopped in. I need to talk to you about the placement of the muscle modules. I've been thinking that we should place the modules external to the spinal column above the gluteal crease. There's a good fat pad there to cushion the modules. Plus, there is ease of access if something goes wrong and the modules need to be replaced."

"I completely agree. An intrapelvic placement would cause more issues than we need to deal with at this point."

"My thoughts exactly. I am glad we are on the same page."

"You ready to get the show on the road?"

"I am."

"Me too. I have a couple of things to do so I will see you in the OR."

"Okay," was Li's reply as she took the last bite of her donut and the last swig of coffee.

Normally before surgery, Heather would stop by the patient's room, give some words of confidence, and answer any last-minute questions. But this was different, as J.T. was being maintained in a medically induced coma for both pain control and systemic stabilization. Still, she stopped by J.T.'s bed and reached out to take his hand.

"I'm the one who's going to put you back together. I got this. We are going to get you back to normal, so just hang with us. You have a lot of people in your corner supporting and pulling for you."

She gave his hand a squeeze. She had always felt that people in a coma could still hear, so she wanted to make sure he heard her. Heather left his room and as she walked to the OR, she passed the conference room. The room was filled to over-flowing with men in uniforms, as well as the entire Coulter family. She walked into the room and Shannon, followed closely by Helen, came over to her and hugged her tightly.

"We can't tell you how pleased we are that you are the one taking care of James."

It was the first time she had heard them use his first name.

Frank stepped up and gave her a hug, also.

"You have our full support. Just wanted to let you know the family is completely behind you." Sean stepped up and took her hand in both of his, thereby dwarfing hers. "You have our complete support. J.T. has saved the lives of everyone in the unit more than once, so we need to get him back, to lead and command." There was a tiny tear in his left eye that he quickly wiped away before anyone had noticed. Heather was so moved she too had a bit of misty eyes.

"I got this," she said and squeezed Sean's hand firmly, giving it a shake. "I will let you know what's up when I have finished with the operation. You may all go ahead and relax, cuz it's gonna be a while. Thanks for your confidence. I won't let you down."

Heather turned, her lip quivering, and strode out into the hallway. Never in her fifteen years of medicine had she seen such an outpouring of love and support from so many people for just one person. She was looking forward to actually being able to talk to J.T. *He must be an incredible man.*

Heather was caught mumbling to herself while she bent over the scrub sink in the room adjacent to the OR. The scrub nurse asked her if there was something she needed, and Heather was jerked back to reality.

"No," she replied. "I always talk to myself before I go operate."

"Ok, just checking," she answered. "You ready to proceed?"

"Yep."

"Ok then, here's your towel, let's get a move on," the scrub nurse urged.

Heather backed her way into the OR, hands held in the traditional and customary way, hands up, palms in, elbows bent so the rinse water would run down off her elbows, awaiting the drying towel from the circulating nurse. After she dried off her hands and forearms, she went through the gowning and gloving procedure before she stepped up to the table.

"Okay guys, this is Mr. Coulter 35-year-old White male, who sustained multiple significant injuries to his body during combat action thirty-six hours ago. He sustained bilateral femoral neck fractures, bilateral mid shaft femoral fractures, bilateral shoulder fractures involving multiple bones, six rib fractures confined to the right side of the chest as well as a closed head injury. Today, we will be addressing the lower extremities only and we will start on the left side. Mr. Coulter was 6'3" and 225 pounds. Let's be sure he remains 6'3" when we are done, and both legs are the same length. Let's get started. Scalpel, please."

Nine hours, twenty-seven minutes later, a fatigued Heather stepped away from the table, stripping the gloves from her hands.

"Great job everyone!!! Will be seeing you again in 24 hours to address the upper extremities. Get some rest. Tomorrow will be much longer."

She exited the OR and made a beeline for the nearest bathroom. Nine and a half hours was a long time to hold her water, and she just couldn't last another minute. As she sat down on the toilet, she let out an audible prolonged sigh of relief, as she finally could let go from holding her bladder. The last ninety minutes had been sheer torture. *Never drink anything caffeinated before surgery,* she reminded herself. As she finished washing and drying her hands, she realized she needed to go find the Coulters and bring them the good news. There was a briskness in her walk that she always felt when she was going to deliver good news to a waiting family. She strode into the conference room and was not really surprised to see that no one had left the entire time.

She stopped at the entrance to the room and announced, in a loud voice, "Listen up everyone. I'm tired and I only want to go through this once. J.T. is fine. He went through the procedure wonderfully. Both his legs work exactly the way they are supposed to, and we will be starting him on rehab after I finish fixing everything else that he managed to break and tear up."

There was a combined laugh, cheer, sigh, and a round of applause that all seemed to erupt at the same time. The family all came over to her, hugged her, and thanked her one by one. Surprisingly, she was overcome with emotion and that was something she was quite unaccustomed to, as she usually kept a tight rein on her feelings, especially where patients and their families were concerned.

So, she made an appropriate exit, citing fatigue and the need to get ready for the surgery that was planned for tomorrow. She departed to another round of applause and thank yous.

When she arrived at her townhouse, she kicked off her shoes, slipped out of all her clothes, put on her favorite robe, poured herself a glass of her favorite wine and turned on her stereo. She hadn't changed the selection of music in years and surprisingly, familiar strains of some 1960s rock and roll music filled the room. Heather had listened to that music for her entire life, and it made her feel secure and well grounded. She plopped down on her love seat, curled her legs underneath her, and finally allowed herself to relax and congratulate herself. The surgery today went perfectly, and she had to admit it was the best work she had ever done. Her mentor, Dr. Wilfred Hyde-Smithe, her 5th year residency attending physician, would be beaming with pride. She had to admit that she had always wanted to make him proud of the surgeon she had turned out to be. She knew her parents, were they both still living, would be proud, but that was just the way parents were. Wilfred knew what she had gone through, what she was responsible for and how dedicated she was. She hoped he would feel she was an excellent extension of himself. He was a precise technical surgeon and an excellent diagnostician. She had striven all her professional life to achieve the level of expertise she now had, and she was proud of herself. She allowed herself to revel in that pride, knowing how hard and long she had worked for it.

She realized she was starving because she hadn't had anything to eat all day, so she headed into the kitchen, opened the refrigerator and scanned each of the shelves, looking for something that caught her eye. Spying nothing that piqued her fancy, she retreated to the freezer and chose a frozen pizza. Popping it in the microwave, she poured herself another glass of wine and sat down to wait. As she waited, her mind started drifting to the next day's surgery. She was going to have to do a complete shoulder reconstruction on both shoulders. *Wait a minute.* She didn't know whether he was right or left-handed. She grabbed the phone and called the hospital. Speaking with the charge nurse, she asked her to search through the chart and see if she could find any mention of which hand was dominant. When the response was that there was no mention of hand dominance anywhere in the chart, she asked for the phone and dialed the Coulters' number.

"Hi, this is Heather Dunkirk," and before she could get

another word out of her mouth, Shannon yelled, "Hey everybody, it's Dr. Dunkirk."

Turning her voice back to the receiver, Shannon asked, "Is J.T. all right?"

"He's fine. I just noticed that there's something missing from the chart that is kind of important. Do you know which side is J.T.'s dominate side?"

"Do you mean is he right or lefthanded?"

"Yes, exactly."

"Sean, do you know which hand J.T. is?"

"Yeah, he's righthanded, although he has almost made himself ambidextrous, especially with weapons and martial arts."

"Ok, thanks, it was important for tomorrow's surgery," Heather replied.

"We just want you to know we really appreciate all that you are doing for J.T. No telling what things would be like if there was someone else taking care of him."

"Well, thanks for the vote of confidence. I'll try to live up to that. See y'all in the morning," Heather said as she hung up.

I must remember that they are waiting for the other shoe to drop when I call, she thought to herself. She hated the thought of causing any more worry than they were already experiencing. The bell from the microwave went off.

"I'm starved," she said to no one there.

Grabbing a TV tray, she went back to the sofa, turned up the volume and had her first bite in twelve hours.

J.T. and John

CHAPTER
FIVE

6:15 AM came quickly, but Heather woke up raring to go. It had been quite a while since had felt so invigorated, alive, and enthusiastic. She could hardly wait to get to work. She repeated her morning regimen exactly as she had done yesterday. She wasn't superstitious, but then there really wasn't any reason to screw around with success. Heather headed out to work, replaying the surgical techniques over again in her mind. She was amazed at how many things Wilfred had taught her, repeatedly pounding things into her head, and now she understood why he had spent all that time with her. It was to get her to the point that she would remember all the things he taught her when she needed to. Like now.

She entered the unit, asking for J.T.'s chart, then scanned labs and updated notes. The charge nurse came over and offered an observation that J.T. had appeared much more comfortable last night compared to the previous nights. That sent a warm flush up and down her spine. Even though he was in a medically induced coma, chemically it was next to impossible to completely control pain. Being more comfortable indicated she had corrected some things, and they were having to use less pain meds, which allowed the system to clean itself out and start to return to normal function. These thoughts gave her a renewed sense of confidence.

Dr. Sun came up and asked her where she thought she would place this set of muscle modules.

Heather said she thought on top of the scapulas, for the same reasoning as the modules in the lower back.

"Great minds think alike," Li replied. "See you in the OR. Oh, do you want to implant the electrodes today? I was thinking that it would be one less anesthesia and one less moving and transferring for tomorrow. Be a little easier on his system in general."

"Sounds like a good idea, you wanna tell the OR nurses? They will have a few things to get set up."

"Sure, I will as soon as I get there," Li replied.

Heather handed the chart back to the nurse, then headed over to J.T.'s room.

"Hey big guy, it's me, Dr. Dunkirk. Gonna finish putting you all back together. If things go as planned, tomorrow we will start to bring you up out of this coma. Hang in there, J.T, we got this. See you tomorrow."

Heather headed out and started down the hall. She was lost in thought and almost walked past the door to the conference room.

"Hey Dr. Dunkirk!" A familiar voice called out. "You were sure lost in thought you almost passed us by." It was Sean calling out.

"I am sorry. Really, I am. I was lost in thought." Heather replied. "Good morning, everyone! I'm really pleased to tell you all a couple of developments. First, we are going to complete all of the planned procedures today instead of some today and the rest tomorrow." There was a small round of applause following that announcement. "The other thing is that J.T. was much more comfortable last night. The significance of that is that we do not need to use so many pain meds and other chemicals to keep his pain level under control. That means the body can start acting like normal. If it continues, we can start to let him come out of his coma as early as tomorrow evening with visitors the next day. A few at a time."

The joy on the faces of the family told Heather all she needed to know.

"I hope you guys have all the info we are going to try to implant. We will put the electrodes in as the last procedure done today. The information transfer will begin the next morning if everything goes the way we hope."

Frank said, "We will have everything ready when you give the word."

"Okay then, I have to go to work. See you when we are all done." Heather turned and exited the room, headed for the OR.

Eleven hours, fifty-three minutes, and one bathroom break later, Heather stepped back from the operating table and pulled off her gloves and then her gown.

She announced to the OR team that she thought the last two surgical procedures had never gone better in her entire career, and she was eternally grateful for the teamwork and extremely proud of all the members of her OR crew for the work they had done. Heather headed for the locker room, relieved her bladder, put on her lab coat, and headed down to the conference room. Everyone was crowding around the door, so she was forced to address everyone from the hallway.

"J.T. did marvelously. We got everything done and there were no apparent problems or complications. If everything continues to improve over the next twelve hours, we will start lifting the coma. And if all continues to improve, and I have no reason to believe he won't, we will allow visitors in thirty-six hours."

The volume of the response was enough to throw some of the admitted patients into cardiac arrest. There was lots of hugging and backslapping, and Heather received more kisses on the cheek than she ever had in her entire life. *This is why I do what I do. It's worth more than all the money in the world,* she thought. The family came up to her one by one, hugged her and effusively thanked her for all that she had done. Even Sean had hugged her. First time she had ever been hugged by a mountain of a man.

"I, I need to get going. I will call you with an update around noon. I will try to give you a more solid timeline for the next few days. Go home, get something to eat, then get some rest. You may want to be sure all the information we are going to start implanting is ready to go so there are no holdups," Heather said as she extracted herself from the mini mob in the conference room.

She went home, fixed herself some dinner, then got ready for bed. Slipping between the silk sheets brought a smile to her face. She closed her eyes and tried to relax. An hour and forty-five minutes later, she had flipped herself around for the umpteenth time, trying to get comfortable.

Why can't I sleep? She asked herself. All the hard work was done with the Coulter case. No matter how much she thought about it, she was unable to come up with an answer. The clock said 1:54 AM, so she just said to heck with her life, got up, showered and got ready for work.

There was a strange excitement flowing through her. Unexplainable, nonetheless, it was still present. She was starting to review all the strange and different things she had been through in the last four days; the most complex case of her career, the strange bonding and affinity she felt for her patients' family. The success with her work so far. Did all of this mean something? Was there something she was missing? *Oh well*, she said to herself, dismissing the thought from her mind. *I have other more important things to address right now.* With that, she strode into the hospital, making her way to the unit where J.T. Coulter was.

The night charge nurse looked up from her charting and said, "Dr. Dunkirk! What are you doing here? It's 3:45 in the morning! Is there something wrong?"

"No, no, nothing is wrong. I just couldn't sleep, so I thought I would come in and get an early start. Can I have Colonel Coulter's chart please?" she asked.

After scanning the chart, she commented, "He seems to be doing quite well. Any signs of him being uncomfortable, having any respiratory issues?"

"No, actually he appears to be quite comfortable. That is a

notable improvement from the first day he was here," the nurse stated.

"How are all the drains I put in doing?" Heather asked.

"There is mild to moderate serosanguinous drainage from the shoulder and chest drains, scant to mild from the hip/thigh drains. All in all, I think things are going remarkably well considering everything he has done to himself over the last five days. I don't think I have ever taken care of anyone with such extensive injuries in all my days of critical care nursing. Doc, you have really done a great job on this one, some of your best work yet."

Heather blushed at the comment and replied, "thank you." Nurses did not offer compliments like that very often, and that meant this one carried a lot of weight. Heather grabbed the chart off the counter, nodded at the nurse, and then made her way down the corridor to J.T.'s room.

Using the immersion tank allowed the application of the MMJRF (multiple moveable joint rehab frame) only once instead of having to reapply it daily or, worse yet, having to sleep in it in a bed. It cut down on pressure sores and skin tears that came from frequent turning of the patient, and it would allow uninterrupted physical rehab that could be more precisely controlled.

"I'm not sure if you can hear me, but I stopped by the other day to introduce myself. I'm Dr. Heather Dunkirk. I'm the one that put you back together. Did a pretty damned good job of it, if I do say so myself. I don't usually brag, but I have never had a more complicated, extensive case to work on in my entire career. I am quite pleased with your progress and a little later this morning, I am going to start the process of reversing the coma we have had to use. This is going to allow you to come back to consciousness. The downside is that a lot of the medications we use, are also used for ancillary pain management. To put it bluntly, you will have a lot more pain than what you have experienced to this point. We will address that as soon as you are able to quantify and localize it for us. I know you may not hear or recall this conversation but rest assured, I will have this conversation again when you are awake. Just for my own information, if you have already heard this stuff from me, just tell me. I will be curious to see."

She reached for his left wrist to take his pulse. Forty-six and regular. Normally, in a post- operative patient, she would have expected a heart rate around eighty-five to ninety, but then she recalled that he ran anywhere between five and six miles six days a week. His heart was in a fabulous condition and being in such good shape, it beat far more efficiently, so it did not have to beat faster. She grabbed the skin on the back of the hand and lifted it, allowing it to snap back so she could determine turgor, then she applied her stethoscope to his chest, listening to the heart sounds. There were no murmurs; it meant all the valves were working properly. Then she moved on to the left side of the chest, listening to the breath sounds, listening for rales, possibly an early sign of fluid in the lungs or pneumonia. She heard none. She moved the stethoscope to the right side of the chest, listening very intensely, as this was the side she had operated on so extensively just twenty-four hours before. There were a few rales towards the bottom of the lung. Were he awake, she would have asked him to cough a few times to see if the sounds moved or cleared out. She would have to remember to ask him to cough when he was awake. She reached down and moved the sheet covering his abdomen. She noted the pattern and distribution of the ecchymosis around the area. She gently laid the palm of her hand on his abdomen and gently began palpating in a systematic fashion, looking for softness, rigidity, guarding, (a movement reflexively done by the body when touching an area that was injured and/or painful) and finding none. She knew she would do this exam again while he was awake and compare the two. She then exposed both legs, from the crotch to the ankles. Supporting the left leg just below the end of the thigh and above the knee, she tapped the patellar tendon and elicited the reflex that was brisk and normal. She moved to the left foot and scraped up the sole of the foot, noting the splaying of the toes, for which she was relieved. She repeated the whole regimen on the right side of the body, stepped back from the bed, very pleased with what she had just found with her examination.

"Not bad, big guy, not bad at all," she murmured. Heather repositioned the sheets, smoothing them out, picked up the chart and made her way back to the nurses' station. She made her notes, checked to see if her dictated surgical notes were in place and the current labs were present, reviewed and signed off. She then began writing orders with a timetable for decreasing the coma medication and then signed it off, then sent the chart to the charge nurse for her to get started on.

It was 4:28 a.m. *Guess I'll go get something to eat in the lounge.* As she turned the corner, she ran right into Dr. Sun and both said,

"What are you doing here this early?" This caused a simultaneous laugh and an attempt by both of them to answer the question at the same time. More laughter when Heather held up her hand and said,

"Couldn't sleep, so I thought I would get an early start."

"I was just going to say the same thing."

"Let me buy you breakfast, and we can discuss the case." Heather took Li's elbow and the two of them headed to the doctors' lounge.

Heather started first since she had already reviewed the chart and examined the patient. "Colonel Coulter is doing extremely well. Labs are all normal, his physical exam is fine, has a few rales in the right lower lobe, but that is to be expected since you did all that reconstruction on that side. Neuro is grossly intact for someone in a coma," she finished. "I have written the orders to start reversing the coma. I think he will be awake by 9 or 10 a.m. I have a few more tests I need to do post-coma before we can start III."

"So, how long should we let him have visitors?" Li asked.

"I think ten minutes for family, five for all the rest. Should be done not later than 1 p.m. We should be able to get him in the rehab frame and into the tank by 2 p.m. You can get with the family about the input data after he is hooked up and before the tank."

"Sounds like a plan," Li replied.

The tank was an immersion therapy with sterilized, filtered fluid that was recycled every ninety seconds. It was compatible with human blood and tissue, and it contained minerals, vitamins, antibiotics, proteins for wound healing and nutrients that provided total nutrition for the entire body, even in a heightened metabolic state of extensive healing. It had originally been developed for thermal, chemical and radiation burn patients, after WW3 and had unbelievable results with other patients that had sustained extensive injuries, so it was the perfect choice in this case. The downside would be a different chemical coma and positive pressure breathing introduced to his face mask, since he would be completely submerged. The need for heavy pain meds could be lessened every other day as the healing and rehabilitation progressed. Hopefully, there would be very little difference between his physical shape and stamina pre-injury and post-injury. It would make a huge difference in how hard J.T. would have to work to get back to where he was before the injuries. He would be able to pick up his workout regimen and feel almost back to normal. It would help him get past the injury and return to normal life.

By 8:45 a.m., J.T roused from the coma and by 9:25 a.m. he was awake enough to speak. Heather entered his room, walked over to the side of the bed and again reached for his hand and wrist, automatically taking his pulse. She was a little surprised to see that it was down to 40. She had expected that the removal of the coma medications and the resultant increase in pain would cause his pulse to go up. She looked at him and noticed he was staring at her.

"Hi I'm..." She never got to finish her statement.

J.T. interrupted her saying, "Dr. Heather Dunkirk, you put me back together. Bet you did a damn good job of it, I hope." His voice was a little weaker than she had expected, but then again, she had never heard his voice.

"Guess you heard me when I came in before," she commented. He raised his hand just a little off the bed and extended two fingers, "twice," he said, barely above a whisper.

"Ok, just a few questions, one finger for yes and two for no. Are you having pain?"

One finger.

"Shoulders/arms?"

Two fingers.

"Chest?"

One finger.

"Any trouble breathing, meaning do you feel like you are having to work a lot to breathe?"

Two fingers.

"Does it hurt when your chest moves?"

One finger.

"Do your hips hurt?"

Two fingers.

He was getting tired fairly quickly.

"Okay. On a scale of one to five, with five being the worst pain you have ever felt and one being like a scratch. How bad is the chest pain?"

Four fingers.

"With movement?"

One finger.

"Ok. We are going to stop for now, give you something for the pain and then in an hour I am going to come back and listen to your lungs. I am going to ask you to cough then so I can be sure you are not getting fluid or pneumonia in your lungs. After that, there are a whole truckload of people that want to see you. Your family first. Do you have a girlfriend you want to see?"

Two fingers.

"Okay. I am going to limit the time people are here. Ten minutes for family, five for everybody else. When they leave, there will be some things to discuss, like what's going to happen from here on out."

One finger.

She squeezed his hand, turned and left the room. She went back to the nursing station, sat down, and started filling out her evaluation notes. She closed the chart, thought about what she was going to say to the overflowing crowd in the conference room, that were starting to act like a party was about to break out. She sat back down and grabbed the phone, dialed '0' and then asked for Skip Johansen to come to the nursing station SFU4. When she was finished, she put the phone back in the cradle and leaned back. She felt as though she had been working for God knows how long. Skip reported to the nursing station about five minutes later.

"Skip, I'm sure there is quite a crowd gathering in the conference room," she said.

"You're tellin' me. Overflow is going down the halls," Skip returned.

"I am going into the conference room. When I tell them he is doing well and will be able to see him, I am going to let the family in for ten minutes, the troops in groups of five for five minutes. I need you to keep order and flow moving smoothly. If you notice Colonel Coulter getting fatigued, stop the flow, send the rest back to the conference room and then we will see when we can start back up to finish off the crowd. Are we clear?"

"Aye, Aye Doc."

"Okay, I am going to talk to the family now and in about a half hour, they should be able to go see him. Can you get the family into a quiet, private room so I can talk to them?"

"Sure Doc, be right back."

CHAPTER SIX

Skip returned with the Coulter family in tow and ushered them into the secretary's office, closing the door. Heather followed him in, closely behind.

"Hey everyone! Good morning, hope you are well rested and anxious to see J.T.," she said.

There was a chorus of good mornings, thank you's, yes, and well rested.

"Okay," she started, "James is awake, but tired. He is as fine as you might expect, given everything he has been through in the past week. He is very tired so do not be surprised if he nods off while you are talking to him. Please remember, don't pat his shoulder, or lean over to hug him, especially on the right side of the body. Don't grab his foot and wiggle it too much. Remember, he had both hips replaced. I have suggested he use one finger for yes, two for no. So if you can ask questions, try to make them answerable by a yes or no. I have not discussed the information implantation as of yet so, just leave that on the back burner.

"I will inform him of the role each of you played in this part of his treatment. Okay, Skip is going to take you back in about fifteen minutes. Please try not to spend more than ten minutes. As you have seen, there are a ton of people that want to see him and the last thing I want to have happen is to get J.T. overly tired. It will make his pain more difficult to handle, delay his healing and, in general make him miserable. I will speak with you again before you guys leave." With that, she walked out of the room and back to J.T.'s room.

"Okay, we're gonna get started. If you get tired, tell me and we can stop for a while. There's no rush."

"I will see everyone that has come to see me. My troops need to know I am okay. After all, I have to order these men into combat, where they can die. They deserve to be able to see me and shake my hand. Discussion is not solicited nor appreciated." There was a tone that indicated he was used to being obeyed and not questioned.

"This is my area of expertise, Colonel, and I make the rules here, not you. I am not going to entertain any discussion. I have the last word here." She stared at him, unblinking. He blinked, and that was that.

"I understand your position Colonel, and as long as I see no evidence of detriment to your condition, you may have your visitors, but I will stop things if I think otherwise." She turned and walked out.

"Tough broad," he said to no one there.

"Skip, you can bring in the family now."

Skip opened the door to the office and then led the group

down to J.T.'s room. Helen and Frank went first, followed by Shannon and Sean. Helen leaned over and kissed his forehead.

"Hey mom," he said, trying to muster some forcefulness to his voice.

"We were all so worried. How are you doing?"

"I'm ok, tired."

"Of course you are." Frank shook his hand gently. "We're so glad you are still with us."

"Me too," he said with a smile.

"Heather has been wonderful to us, keeping us informed. She's such a lovely person," Helen said.

"Yes, she is."

"She's not married either."

"I know, mom."

"I'm just saying."

"Thanks mom."

Shannon leaned in and kissed his forehead. "Your house is really nice. Could use a woman's touch, though."

"Not you too. Sean, can't you control your wife?"

"No more than you could."

"I want to thank you for getting me out of the wreck. I owe you one."

"I'll settle for a couple of beers."

"If you can get permission from your wife..."

"Cheap shot, boss."

"Those are the best kind."

"Take care of yourself and listen to your doctor," Helen admonished.

J.T. gave them his standard, "I will, I'll try to and, of course, I will."

Heather stuck her head in and asked how he was doing.

"'Bout as well as can be expected."

"Are you ready for the troops?"

"Send them in."

"By the way, do you happen to keep any kind of record of your workouts, like weight and reps, etcetera?"

"Yes, it's at home in my desk, upper right-hand drawer. Spiral notebook. Have kept it for the last fifteen years. How come?"

"Well, as you know, we are going to be putting you in a rehab frame later today. It is programmable, so we need to know where you were before the injury. We are thinking that it is going to take eight to twelve weeks in the frame, for you to be almost back to pre-injury state."

"No, it will be less than eight weeks. Arrange whatever you have to, to make it work out to eight weeks."

"J.T., I am the doctor here and I will decide what your pace is going to be."

"Either set it up to be done by eight weeks or you are fired. Are we clear on this? And, by the way, I had better not wake up from the coma after twelve weeks or you will have one seriously pissed off patient on your hands. Believe me, it would not be pretty."

"I will decide what I think is appropriate, based on what my training and experience have taught me."

"Doctor Dunkirk, have you ever met me before?"

"No."

"Have we ever talked before?"

"No."

"Then what makes you think you know me, my body, or

what motivates me?"

"Well, I am in charge of this case."

"That, at the moment, is a little debatable."

"Unfortunately, you are not a doctor, therefore, you would not be able to write or issue any orders concerning your care."

"Then, since you are bound and determined to not listen to the patient, you are officially fired as my physician. I will hire someone that will listen and agree to my wishes."

"You can't do that!" Heather said with more than a little exasperation in her voice.

J.T. reached over to his call bell button, pushed it three times, then relaxed his head backward. The charge nurse entered the room with the urgency that let everyone know she was ready to dive in and help with whatever was wrong.

"I have just discharged Dr. Dunkirk as my attending doctor. Please bring me a list of physicians that are available to take over my case." J.T. commanded. The nurse looked at Heather, and all she saw was a look of incredulity on her face.

"Don't look at her. Go get me a list!"

The nurse turned and walked out of the room, wondering what the hell was going on.

"Still think you are in charge, Doctor Dunkirk?"

Heather looked at him and said, "Perhaps we should start this conversation over."

"The outcome is not going to change, if you do not agree to my requests."

"We can discuss them." He reached for the call button again.

"Look, did you put the hardware in properly, with correct alignment?"

"Of course."

"Did you hook all the muscles back up correctly?"

"Certainly."

"Would you guess my total muscle mass loss as twenty percent or less? Does all the other hardware you installed work as it is supposed to?"

"Yes, of course."

"Then there shouldn't be any problems with the timetable I have given you."

"I think…"

"It doesn't matter what you think. The answer is either yes or no. If it is yes, then we can get on with other things. If it is no, then you will have to explain to me why your work is not up to par and not capable of dealing with my requests."

"My work is perfect."

"I will take that as a yes then. Look doc, I know me. I know what I require. I have to be challenged. Has been that way all my life. That's why I have so many degrees. Was the only way I could learn and succeed. You just program your rehab doohickey to get me back to where I was before all this, flip the switch, then get me out of the tank in eight weeks, you'll see."

"This is against my better judgement and training."

"Do we need to go through all of this again because I can absolutely guarantee that my position will be the same as it has been."

"OK, fine, have it your way. But if you manage to get yourself damaged, it's on you."

"That's right…but if it works out, it will be on me also."

"Are you ready for troops now?"

"Yes, you may send them in," J.T. said, slipping back into his commanding officer persona.

Heather moved to the door, turned and told J.T. "Do not let yourself get over tired. It will negatively impact your recovery. Of that I am 100% sure."

She then left to get the next round of well-wishers into some kind of controlled, organized madness.

As Heather turned the corner heading down the long hallway towards the conference room, she saw Skip step out of the doorway. He walked towards her, trying to get as far away from the crowd in the conference room, in case there was going to be some unpleasant information forthcoming. He looked her full in the face and said,

"You must have just met the real Star Trek, the one that is the commanding officer. Hardheaded and stubborn, ain't he?"

"He threatened to fire me as his doctor if I did not lay out his rehab the way he felt it should be done," she lamented.

"Doc, he has been commanding a unit of warriors for fourteen years, sending them into combat and being there when they got wounded and killed. I think he has lost a total of five or six men, KIA, in fourteen years. He is used to getting his way because he is the CO and he is almost always right. Hard to argue with success."

"I have never been so frustrated."

"Well, this may sound pissy… but you'll get over it."

"I'm sure. Groups of five, five minutes per group. Try to have them keep the hand shaking and pats on the back and legs to a minimum. I have told him to let me know if he gets tired."

"You should have saved your breath doc. He's the CO. He will see each and every one of the troops. They have to know and believe that he is going to overcome this, and nothing will stop him from being personal with each man. You want to see something, just stand there, and watch him with his troops. This is the kind of thing that they try to teach at the service academies, how a successful commander handles the troops. Maybe you can teach theory. This man is the real deal, a natural commander who gets it."

"Five to a group, max. Five minutes per group, Skip."

She turned on her heel and headed back towards J.T.'s room. She stopped at the nurses' station, picked up the phone, and dialed Frank Coulter.

"Frank, this is Heather. Need to have you go over to J.T.'s house. In his study, in the desk, the right upper drawer, there is a spiral notebook that I need here at the hospital. As soon as you can get here. Thanks."

The first group of five soldiers walked by her, stopping to tug on her coat and thank her before moving on into J.T.'s room. She moved over to the doorway where she could hear and see what was going on inside.

J.T. shook each man's hand, called him by name, asked each a personal question and then thanked each and everyone, as Skip ushered them out and the next group in. It was something to see, the connection J.T. had with each of his troops, the respect, admiration and, yes, the love they had for him. There was more than one misty eyed man that made their way past her, some stopping to effusively thank her for keeping Star Trek alive.

It took the better part of ninety minutes for everyone to come and go. Skip was still in the room after the last group was ushered out. He came over and handed two small flasks of Irish Whiskey to Heather.

"Took these from a couple of the senior non-coms. They

wanted to have a nip with the skipper. Before you ask the question, answer is, of course he had a nip with each and every one that asked."

"I knew I should have stayed in there."

"Doc, I saw you watching everything. Didn't you learn anything from what you saw? Each one of them would give up their lives for him, if he ordered it. Have you ever met anyone that instills that kind of devotion in his subordinates? The sips he took meant more to them than anything else in the world." Skip's tone changed to a very deep commanding tone.

"You will not go in there and say anything to him about this. This was as private as the confessional in church. It's just between a commanding officer and his troops, you understand?"

Heather just nodded. She finally realized what she had just witnessed. It was something she had never witnessed before, but she was honored to have been able to observe this, even from a distance. She had to admit to herself that there had never been anyone in her life that she would die for, and she now felt as though there was something missing in her existence.

Heather entered the room and looked at J.T. with the eye she had been taught her first day in med school. The diagnostic medicine professor had stated, you should already know what 75-80% of patients had something wrong with them just by looking at them. This, of course, was after you had been trained and had the opportunity to practice.

He looked tired, but there was a spark in his eyes that had not been there before he had a chance to see his men. This little event had given her a new appreciation for her patient, what he did and who he was down to his core. He truly was a great man on multiple levels.

"Before you say anything," J.T. said, "some of my non-coms wanted me to have a taste with them. I faked it most of the time. It was important to them that I join in. I didn't imbibe much because I am not sure what meds you have been giving me so I did not know whether or not it would cause me problems."

"I wasn't going to say anything about that. I will say this though. I have never seen a demonstration of admiration, respect, devotion, and love in my entire life, from a group of people to just one person. I am very impressed. It gives me more insight into who and what you are all about."

"These are a great bunch of men. The job they have to do is poorly compensated and usually unappreciated. Would probably be appreciated more if they had to fight, clearing street by street, so the citizenry could look out the window and actually see people die or get blown up. But if we got to that point, we, meaning myself and my men, would have failed in doing our jobs."

"So, they learn to rely on each other for kudos and me for the atta boys and the well dones, and for them, that's enough. So, taking a nip with them speaks volumes about our relationship. I'm still the CO, but I am right in there with them."

"I called your dad and asked him to bring the notebook. There are a couple of things to go over, namely the amount of initial weight and the rapidity of increases for the arms and then the legs," Heather said.

"I would like to stick to the schedule that is in the notebook. I have been living that schedule for fifteen years and since my body is used to it, I would think that it would cut down the stress to the system. I also think that I should stay on dialysis for at least two weeks before we ponder stopping it. What, with the muscles healing, then being torn down to build them back up to where they were, pre-injury? I would suggest starting at 47-60% of what I was lifting both arms and legs then increase by 5% per week, each extremity. My IV hydration feeding fluids is going to need to be increased by 50% minimum. I did the calculations in my head. Obviously, they may need to be adjusted if there are changes in the labs."

Heather had forgotten how intelligent he was. He had almost done all the work for her.

"Hope I wasn't intruding into your area of expertise."

"I was just running that through my mind. I do have one thing to discuss with you. III," she said.

"Intracranial Information Implantation," he responded.

"You've heard of that?"

"I read a paper on it a couple of years ago. Was something I was thinking of, to be used during long space flights so that the crew could be kept up to date while in hibernation. Cuts down on the time spent bringing them up to speed when it is time for them to wake up and takeover running the ship."

"Dr. Li has already implanted the data ports. I have asked your parents to figure out where you were at in your studies so we could pick it up from there. Your mother has also said she would pick a couple of subjects that she thinks you would be interested in. I have not heard what those subjects are, as of yet."

"Would you ask her to dig up a number of texts on metallurgy and space flight? Are you and Dr. Li planning on running the data input continuously or in segments?" J.T. asked.

"We have not had a chance to discuss it," Heather replied.

"May I suggest that you set the data flow to forty-five minutes per hour, with 15-minute respite before starting the next download? My body is going to be going through quite a bit and I want to give my brain the best shot at absorbing everything that is being inputted."

Heather nodded her head, as though deep in thought.

"I think that is both reasonable and appropriate. I do not foresee any problems with it, but I am going to consult with Dr. Li before making a final decision, since this is her area of expertise."

"One more thing," J.T. said, "were either of you planning on waking me up midway through this little experiment? I would like to weigh in on that. I think it is crucial to do so. We need to see if the data importation is successful before I spend a total of eight weeks, not knowing if any of it was successful or if it needs to be adjusted for the next round."

"We will discuss it. I think you have had enough for one day. You need to get some rest. Are you in any pain?"

"About a three, maybe a four," J.T. responded. There was a note of fatigue that Heather had not noticed before.

"I'll have the nurse bring you in something. Get some rest. I am going to let your parents come in and visit in the morning before we get started."

"Thanks Doc, I appreciate it. Just so we are clear, I would have fired you. Make no mistake about that," J.T. said.

"I don't doubt it a bit," was her reply.

Five minutes later, the charge nurse appeared with a syringe in her hand. She stepped over to all the IV tubing that was hanging down running from his arm to the different machines controlling the flow of fluids in to J.T.'s body. She traced down the correct tube, gripped the junction and wiped it off with an alcohol swab. She then punctured the connection and began slowly injecting the medication until she was completely done.

"This should kick-in in about ten minutes. Try to relax and let the medication work. You should sleep quite well. By the way, you still want that list of doctors that can take over your case?" she asked.

"Yes, I do. If you could just leave it on the bedside table, that would be great," he said as he stifled a yawn.

"In twenty-five years, I have never seen a patient ask to have a doctor removed from their case, certainly not Dr. Dunkirk. She's one of the finest physicians I have ever had the pleasure of working alongside."

"Well, nurse, thank you for your glowing recommendations. I do value co-workers' opinions. Dr. Dunkirk forgot the first tenet of practicing medicine. That they are an employee of the patient and if they chose to act high handed and not take the patient's wishes into consideration, then they should either be dressed down or fired. So we had a meeting of the minds. I made my positions known and also what I would do if she chose not to amend her attitude. I believe she saw the error of her ways, understood my position and we have had a meeting of the minds, so to speak."

When the charge nurse didn't speak, J.T. continued. "There are a lot of issues that are going to face ME, not her, ME. Issues that I am going to have the final say in, and, if she can't deal with it, then she will find herself replaced." Another yawn interrupted his tirade.

"Remind me not to piss you off," the nurse said.

"From the first minute you and I had any kind of interaction, you have treated me with the utmost care and respect, much as I would think you would treat a family member. I wish to thank you for that. It is what every patient deserves, and I appreciate the way you have treated me."

His words were starting to slur a little, so the nurse stepped over to the door, flipped off the light and said as she departed the room, "Good night, Colonel."

As she left, she heard him say, "You too, and it's J.T."

CHAPTER
SEVEN

I t seemed as though the time he had been asleep had passed in the blink of an eye. A hand was gently moving his left shoulder.

"Colonel, time to wake up." Heather tried to rouse him from sleep. "You awake? How do you feel? Any pain? Do you feel refreshed? Are you hungry?"

As J.T. attempted to open his crusted eyes, he was still trying to move as well as orient himself. Finally, he managed to lift his right arm and try to wipe off the mucus particles that had accumulated on his eyelids. Right side first, followed by the left. It was pretty stiff and uncomfortable. He was having a little difficulty getting his vision to focus. He had a vague sensation that he had to urinate. Perhaps he should reassess his timeline on rehab and how fast he was going to be able to muscle his way through the rehab.

"I am thirsty, stiff, achy, have to pee, and a little disoriented and uncomfortable. Did I miss anything?"

"No, you pretty much hit the high points. I am going to check you over quickly, then the nurse will be in with something for pain and then get you ready for dressing changes and a bath or shower, if you prefer. Right now, take in a deep breath, again."

Heather put a stethoscope on the lower right lung and told J.T to wrap a pillow around the right side of his chest, take a deep breath, and cough deeply.

"Good, the noises are gone, no fluid, no pneumonia." She moved the sheets and lifted the left drain first, squeezed it gently, then reached for the right one and repeated the same action. She then told J.T. to bite down on the pillow and, as he did, she yanked the drain out. "There, that wasn't so bad, was it? Only three more to go."

She avoided looking directly at J. T. until she had pulled out two more drains. Only then did she chance a look. His face was like a stone mask, unrevealing, unresponsive to the pain she had inflicted, a little red around the edges and both jugular veins were pronounced.

"Last one, here we go," and she yanked the final drain out. She heard him suck in his breath.

A few moments later, he asked, through slightly gritted teeth, "Are you going to be the one that gives me the shower, or are your Marquise De Sade talents used up for the day?"

"The charge nurse is going to do that. I have to recharge my De Sade batteries, after such a strenuous workout," was her retort.

"Least you could have told me you loved me," he responded.

"How 'bout lick my boots, you worm?" she quipped.

"I don't know you that well. Now I know why you are a surgeon."

At that moment, the charge nurse chose to enter, dressed in a surgical wet suit.

"I assumed you would prefer a shower. Was I wrong?" she asked.

"No, a shower would be just perfect."

Heather used this time to leave the room.

The Charge nurse bid Heather goodbye before turning back to J.T. "Before we do that, I need to see you stand. If you can't, then I have a harness we will put on to hold you up. So, let's try to get you up on the side of the first. You will sit there for a full five minutes before we let you slide to the edge and let your legs hang down and touch the floor. You will sit there for another full five minutes. After all, you have not used those legs for five days, had them operated on and had to be given gallons of fluids, we would not want you to pass out and fall on Dr. Dunkirk's work, now, would we?" asked the charge nurse.

"Not if it meant having to go back through everything I just went through," J.T. replied.

After the passage of the prescribed amount of time, the charge nurse stepped to his left side, slipped his arm around her neck and over her shoulder, his hand hanging down right over her left breast.

"No cheap feels don't care how big you are, I can still knock you on your ass," the charge nurse stated firmly.

"Thought never crossed my mind, ma'am."

"You should stick to the truth. You don't lie worth a damn, Colonel."

He was very tentative as he walked where the nurse was

leading. The walk was only about twenty steps, but he was sliding his feet over the floor, a little afraid to actually lift each foot up off the floor, not sure he trusted his balance and the strength of his legs.

The nurse whispered in his ear, "Everything is still all there and working just fine. Relax, have a little faith. You got this."

With that, the next step was with his left foot completely off the floor. It was a little shaky, but there was a growing confidence with each successive step.

"Good job. Now we have to turn right. I suggest that you take baby steps slowly around the corner. Turning puts unnatural stress forces on the joints so until it is well seated, and bone has started to form over it, we try not to have you stress it too much. Ok, we need to stop for a moment, while I get the door open and turn on the water. You gonna be OK, standing here for a moment?" she asked.

"I'll be fine," J.T. responded.

"Don't try to walk until I get back."

The door opened, and he could hear the water hitting the floor. The nurse returned, and they started forward, entering the shower room.

Once the door was shut, the nurse said, "First, I need to remove all your bandages. I promise that it won't be anything like what Heather did."

"She was deriving a little too much pleasure from that," J.T. said sarcastically.

"That's what you get for threatening her with being fired," the charge nurse responded.

"Hadn't thought about that," J.T. admitted.

"OK, off with the robe and let's get started."

"But I'm naked underneath," he complained.

"I've seen it all already. And I need to speak to you about that. Some men spend their whole lives trying pills, gimmicks and other things to achieve what God has given you naturally. That's one bandage."

"That didn't hurt," he noted.

"I've been doing that longer than her. That's two. That thing will ruin women and you need to understand that. You can give a woman a lot of pleasure, but you can also give them a tremendous amount of pain. You should always allow women to mount you, let them run the show. Don't get any male ego stuff going on. Tell any woman you are going to be intimate with about it. You don't have to brag, but you have to let them decide if they wish to proceed. That's three. Turn around a little. That's four. Let me start scrubbing down your back."

"My first husband, God rest his soul, was well endowed, eleven inches, I think it was. Took me four months after we got married before he was actually able to completely penetrate me. Was sore for two weeks. Finally went to my gyno and she gave me pessaries that I had to have inside me day and night for two and a half months. Slightly larger one every week. But when it was all said and done, it was worth it. He gave it to me better than any man I have ever known for thirty-five years. No one has measured up to him since, which is why I am single. Step over to the wall, put your butt against it, lean forward just a bit and bend your neck so I can wash your hair."

"You're more than welcome to try it on your own if you can get your arms up high enough to wash without a lot of pain."

She gave him some shampoo while she started to wash his legs. "Dr. Dunkirk does good work from the look of your incisions. Hold still while I rinse your hair. You want to wash yourself? I'll take the Texas catheter off, and you can wash yourself. You heed what I've told you, boy. You'll make a fine husband and father, but there are those considerations you need to have for your woman."

"Thank you, ma'am, that's very good advice. I am truly thankful for you bringing it up. It has been a vexation to me for years. Your insight and thoughts have given me plenty to ponder," J.T. said as he stepped away from the wall, raising his arms over his head, waiting for her to hose him off.

"Step over here and stand on the pad," the charge nurse commanded.

As soon as he was situated, a fine mist was sprayed all over him. An ultraviolet light came, and he basked in it for two full minutes. The nurse then moved him to the other side of the room, put him on another pad and he was bathed in warm air until he was completely dry.

"You know," J.T. said to the nurse, "I don't recall hearing your name".

"Emma Jackson," she replied.

"It is my honor to meet you and to get to know you on such an intimate level," J.T. said.

"You ready to head back? Just stop at the door so I can get you a new robe, then we will head on back. You feel steady enough to walk, or do you need to lean on me?"

"I want to try this on my own but, wouldn't hurt for you to be fairly close." He slipped the robe on and belted it up tight. He knew that a shower would feel good, but not this good. Most of the stiffness he had originally felt was gone. The trip down the hall back to his room went uneventfully. Emma helped him sit on the edge of the bed, then kind of fall back into the middle of the bed. They hitched and scootched around until he was in the middle of the bed. Emma fetched a sheet to lay across his middle, then removed his robe.

"Get comfortable and, if you are ready, I will go get your family. When you are done with the family, tell me if you are up to more visitors or if you wish to rest. Don't feel bad if you need to rest. Short rest periods will keep you from getting too rundown."

"Okay, Emma, heard you loud and clear."

As he waited for the family to show up, he began to ponder the next period of his life. As much as he loved what he was doing, this last incident had shown him that combat was a young man's game. He had also figured out he was no longer a young man, and it was time to start thinking about starting a family and working on what legacy he was going to leave the world with. His thoughts turned to space and what that held.

Man had certainly fucked up this planet and maybe it was time to think about leaving this world and going to another, where man could start over, this time, with the knowledge of how badly he'd done things the first time around and how things should be done the second time out of the gate. The concept grabbed his brain, and he became lost in a world of new possibilities, created in his own head, but still possible if he were to work hard, stay true to his convictions and try to plan for as many eventualities as he could think of. Success was always predicated on good and thorough planning, with a heaping amount of anticipation and perseverance, and just a skoosh of luck.

He heard the intentionally loud throat clearing at the doorway. There stood the family, all of them with smiles on their faces that went from ear to ear.

"Hey son," Frank said. "Wasn't sure if you were sleeping or not."

"Wouldn't have mattered with the way that you were trying to clear that hairball from your throat. Told you long ago to quit giving the cat a bath," J.T. replied with his own big smile.

"See, I told y'all he was gonna be fine," Frank remarked with his know-it-all smirk on his face.

"Hey baby." That came from Helen as she pushed Frank to the side so she could get over to him to give him one of her "mom" hugs.

"How ya feeling?" she asked, trying to read his face to see if he would lie to her like he always did, mainly so she wouldn't worry.

"Honestly?" J.T. asked, "I am a lot better than I deserve. Still have some pain, but the meds do a good job of keeping me comfortable. All in all, I'm thankful to be here, which reminds me, Sean, come here. I don't know if I have had the chance to thank you for saving my ass, but I want to thank you from the bottom of my heart. Don't know if I would still be here without you. So, thank you. I'd give you a hug, but since that would really hurt and I am not a huge fan of pain. It will have to wait until some other time."

"No problem, bro, was glad I was there to return the favor. After all, you have already done the same for me." There was a good solid handshake as they both relived the last time J.T had saved Sean's life.

"Hey, what am I, the redheaded stepchild or something?" Shannon whined. "Why am I always at the tail end here?"

"Because you are the youngest and shortest, that's why."

On reflex, Shannon's right arm flashed out and landed a solid punch on J.T.'s left shoulder. Her hand immediately withdrew to cover her mouth when she saw the flash of pain and the "ugh" that popped out of J.T.'s mouth.

"Oh my God, I am soo sorry, I didn't mean to hurt you," she cried.

"It's okay, it's okay, Shan. I'm alright. Don't worry about it." Shannon now had crocodile tears running down her face from both eyes.

"Come here, give me a hug," he said. "Everything is fine." He let her go from the hug and she stepped back.

"It's what you get when you jerk my chain all the time. Speaking of redheads, where's the doctor lady? You know, the hottie that's making all those goo-goo eyes at you."

"I don't know what you are talking about?" J.T. replied sincerely. In all honesty, he hadn't noticed any *goo-goo* eyes coming his way from Dr. Dunkirk.

"She's over here, making goo-goo eyes at the back of Frank's head," Heather said with a little chuckle. She always got a little kick out of catching people when they were unaware.

Heather walked into the room and said, "Good morning, everyone. I trust everyone had a good night's sleep and something to eat?"

Shannon mumbled an apology and turned ten shades of embarrassing red.

"Shannon, it's ok. I can tell when it is brother and sister good natured ribbing." She continued as she looked around at everyone. "OK, everyone, grab a seat, so we can go over a few things. Later today, the Colonel will be put in the rehab frame, and we will begin the tank sessions. What I need to know from y'all is, is the III stuff ready? We have to hook him up to the wiring as we put him into the tank."

"Colonel, is there anything that you would like to have added to the implantable data base, anything that you think may be of benefit sometime in the future?"

"Give me a sheet of paper, please."

It took a few minutes to get paper and a pen. J.T. spent the next couple of minutes writing down the names of books and the information he would like. He gave the slip to his mom. Helen perused the list, shook her head a little then, as if a switch had been thrown, she suddenly understood her son's thoughts.

"I will see what I can do. Doc, this is going to take at least 24 hours to research and process all this material. Is it possible to add this material on after everything has been started?" she asked Heather.

J.T. jumped in and stated, "That's possible, as long as they knew where the end of the original data files is, and when the last II data dump has been imparted to me."

"When you have that info, then you can add in all this other stuff. That's doable. I will have to check with Li, since this part is her baby, but I do not foresee any problems. So, moving on, when we start the process of immersion, J.T. will be unavailable for four weeks. We discussed interrupting the treatment at the four-week point to access how the information transfer has been going. While he is in the tank, I am going to have his professors set up a comprehensive examination to see how much info has been imparted and then, perhaps more or most importantly, how integrated that information has become.

"The testing and getting the grades and assessment will take about four days. During that time, we will assess how well his musculoskeletal rehab has been going, mainly trying to see how close to his pre-injury state he has returned. This will determine when and if his rehab is done. It goes without saying that he is not going to be available to anyone, family included. So, if there is anything you want to say, now would be the time."

There was some back and forth amongst all the family members, and then J.T. signaled to Sean to remain behind for a couple of minutes, as the family walked out.

"Yeah boss, what's up?" asked Sean.

"Coulter weekend is in two weeks. I know we have always kept this private but, take Mom, Dad, Shan and Heather with you. They deserve to know that we do more than just kill everybody."

"You sure about the doc?"

"Yeah, I got a feelin' about her," replied J.T.

"Well, Shannon was not wrong about her interest in you. Even Mom and Dad could see it."

"You know how things have gone between me and women. I am hoping this one may be different, but I'm getting tired of being alone. I mean, I am great company but people will talk if they see me constantly talking to myself. Anyway, getting back to the doc, be sure she meets Doc Horner. He may need her services sometime in the future and it is always good to have someone to call, when the need arises."

"Good luck, bro, will see you in four weeks."

"Thanks."

"What was that all about?" Helen asked Sean when he left J.T.'s room.

"Okay, everybody in the conference room, you included

Heather. I have something to tell you, but it must be in a private area. What I am going to tell all of you has been kept a secret for the last fourteen years. I will take questions in due time. J.T. has given me permission to tell all of you and only you!" Sean scanned the faces of the family and Heather.

"Are we clear on this? It is serious. This is not for dissemination to every Tom, Dick, and Harry on the street. I am not kidding. I need everyone to swear to me to keep your mouth shut, or we are done right now."

There was a chorus of 'okay' from everyone. They all head into the conference room. Sean closes the door and begins his story.

"Fourteen years ago, right after J.T was made XO of the unit, the CO had gone to some kind of meeting when we got notified that there was something going on at pumping station #3. J.T. called a unit meeting to go over the mission. We had just transferred in a new second looie, Lt. James Hanratty. Damn, he was a know-it-all. Couldn't teach him a damn thing, not anything. During the briefing, J.T. told Hanratty to take squad one and position them according to pattern A12. Overwatch squad, under Skip Johansen were sent to grid 12 to set up sniper protection for the squads while the situation was assessed.

"Hanratty, on his own, decided that he and his squad were going to be badasses and take care of this on his own. So, he ordered his men to go up around the bend, without benefit of overwatch cover fire. Fifteen shots later, Hanratty comes running back around the bend. No squad with him. J.T. ran up to Hanratty, asked him what happened and why he disobeyed direct orders, and showed cowardice in the face of the enemy. Hanratty got really pissed off, cursing and saying, 'How could he say that when he was almost killed?' J.T. ordered me to take Hanratty into custody."

"While I was doing that, Hanratty grabbed one of my pistols. He turned and shot at J.T., grazing him in the right trap. J.T dropped, rolled, pulled his pistol and fired twice, hitting Lt. Hanratty over both eyes. Finest exhibition of combat pistol shooting I have ever seen. Since Hanratty was dead, J.T. asked me to find a megaphone and a walkie talkie for him. So, I did. J.T. turned on the megaphone and said,

'You in the trees. This is Major Coulter XO of DSF unit 17, charged with protecting the people and property of Dome 17. I am sending in a walkie-talkie so that you may talk to me. I want to be crystal clear. If there is one shot fired from now on, we will enter the area and kill every single person, men, women, children, dogs, cats, cows, horses, chickens, pigs and sheep. There will be nothing left alive in the area. Are we clear? Whoever is in charge of your group, I wish to speak to you about this situation. You have ten minutes. Remember, not one shot fired, even accidentally, or the consequences will be severe, total, and permanent.'

"Then he said to me, 'Sergeant, take the walkie talkie to the center of the field. You may stop to check any bodies for signs of life and report back to me as you leave the area. Go.'

"Seven minutes later, J.T asked me for an update. I told him, we have three dead and two wounded. J.T said, 'Try to drag the wounded closer and I will send some help.'

"Then he called for the Doc. He told the Doc to take two people with him to help transport. Then we heard from someone called Charlie Harrison. He said,

'This is Charlie Harrison. I'm the spokesman for our little

group. We are sorry about your men, but we were not prepared for your men to attack. We didn't mean to damage your property, but we are dying of thirst. Our water supply has dried up and there was nothing we could do. There is no one out here to call and ask for help, so we did what we needed to do to survive. Can we meet face to face?'

"J.T responded, 'Very well. But remember the warning that I have already stated.'

'We accept your conditions,' Charlie responded."

As Sean recounted the story, he set the stage of how a group of starving survivors had ended up encroaching on their territory, leading to a violent collision with three dead. But when J.T. encountered the rag tag bunch up close - elderly, emaciated, thinly clothed, and armed only with aged hunting rifles - his hardened demeanor softened. This was no longer a hostile force, but helpless men driven by human desperation.

Sean continued, "J.T. walked with their leader Charlie into the woods, taking in the deprivation that permeated their makeshift camp - meager outdoor fires surrounded by dilapidated lean-tos and teepees, a broken-down horse, and partially dressed deer carcass which likely constituted their only food. What caught J.T.'s attention was the nearly depleted water source - a mere mud hole allowing only a swallow per person when it slightly replenished each morning. J.T. immediately dispatched the team to address water needs and bring full supplies for humanitarian support.

"When Doc Horner pointed out injuries, J.T. ensured the wounded received dedicated care. But I could see that J.T's mind had turned to a more lasting solution, as he started directing engineers to repair failing infrastructure at a nearby pumping station.

"Yet even as J.T. tackled immediate relief efforts, he talked about plans for establishing robust systems to uplift the entire community. What had minutes before been an invasion of potentially hostile forces now represented families who had faced no choice but the threat of starvation. And J.T. by nature, is a man programmed to protect and provide for those in need - a calling that comes from his heart, not just his uniform."

"J.T looked at Charlie and said, 'Charlie, we are going to help out. Right now, we will get you some water and I am sending out my sharpshooting unit to get you some more food. The rest of my troops will help with safe latrines and better shelters. After that I will see what more I can do. You keep this walkie talkie so you can call me anytime you have issues or a problem. Right now, I have a lot to do.'"

"So twice a year, every year, early spring and late fall, the unit takes off to Coulter for seven to fourteen days, depending on what they need us to do. The village has grown to over a hundred people, including children. Doc Horner has an infirmary that he goes to twice a week, more often if needed. He brings meds and vaccines. He has delivered eleven babies. And solved a major community health problem," Sean told them.

"See, there was a huge problem with both child abuse and spousal abuse. One day they brought in this 4-year-old with a broken arm. He asked him how he did it and the child wouldn't answer. However, his 6-year-old sister said, 'Paw got really upset and hit him, knocked him clean across the room and into the door. That's when it got broke.'"

"After finding out that the man does this to the wife too, Doc walked up to the child's home, knocked on the door and when the father opened the door, he hit him dead in the face, knocking him back into the house. He then proceeded to beat the man within an inch of his life. When he was done, Doc said, 'this is number one. The next time you hit your kids or your wife, it will be a month before you will be able to walk. If there is a third time, I will put a bullet between your eyes. You feel a need to discipline your child, you can spank them with an empty, open hand on a bare ass only. No belts, paddles, switches, or any other objects. Understand? Speak now, if there is anything you are not clear about, cause once I leave, you'll be on number two and remember, number three is permanent. Sarah, make sure the whole village hears about this, including anybody that moves in. I won't stand for abuse. This will happen to anyone that abuses a family member. Wives hitting husbands, parents hitting kids, no sir, I won't tolerate it.'"

Sean continued, "Since then, we have not had one case of abuse. The point of this is that next weekend is the early spring weekend so all of us are going to Coulter. You'll like Doc Horner, Heather. He's been a family practice PA for forty-five years, been in combat, worked in prisons, and can be mean as a snake, but he has a heart of gold, and everybody there loves him. He's smart and has never voiced a desire to be a doctor. Well, that we know about. What I need is for everyone to make your excuses as to why you are going to be gone for a week. Pack accordingly and get your mind wrapped around working. It is going to be an insightful week."

There were the usual grumblings about *how could he have kept this from us, and now I know why he was never available in the spring and fall.*

From Shannon, "Who'd have thought my big brother was capable of something like this?"

"And one more thing," Sean said, "keep your mouths shut about this. These people are not part of a circus, and they are not a sideshow for folks to come and gawk at. That's why we don't talk about this place. These are good, kind, hard-working folks, not a sideshow for folks to pity them."

Heather told Sean and the family she needed to get back to work but would confirm next weekend with him as soon as things were finalized. All of this new information about J.T. was swimming around in her head. *Who'd have thought a guy who kills people for a living would be capable of something like this?*

She headed back towards the unit to get everything ready for the application of the rehab frame and get everything set up for the tank. Two and a half hours later, she had finished all the paperwork and double checked the orders. She stopped by J.T.'s room to spend a couple of minutes answering any questions and trying to put him at ease.

Spending four weeks immersed in fluid was somewhat of a sensory deprivation event, and a lot of people were quite freaked out about it. Granted, he was going to be in a light coma and his mind was going to be occupied forty-five minutes of every hour with a 15-minute respite hourly. The musculoskeletal rehab was going to go on for two and a half hours, followed by four hours of rest and fluid hydration. One extremity would be worked at a time, lifting the same amount of weight as the other side. When that side was not lifting weight, it was being actively put through a complete range of motion. As she stopped by J.T.'s room, she noticed he was sleeping. *So, I have a choice to make; wake him to go over things or come in early tomorrow and do it.*

As she turned in the doorway to leave, she heard, "I'm just resting my eyes. These lights seem to bother them more than usual."

"You aren't having any difficulty with your vision, double, or blurred, are you?"

"No, they just seem to tire more easily."

"I have a few things to go over with you before we get started. I have one question for you."

"Shoot."

"What's with Coulter?"

"I'm not sure I understand the question."

"What prompted you to help out?"

"Oh, that's easy. These were folks just trying to make their way in the world, no help from anyone or anything, meaning the government, and they weren't asking for a handout, just a little help. They just wanted to live off the land, respecting it and living by their own code of behavior and conduct. They were near starved and quite dehydrated, but still really proud and unbending. There was no pity on my part, just the thought of, *what if that was me? What do I hope someone would do to help me out with my situation?*

"It was kind of like when my dad told me, give a man a fish and you will feed him for one meal, but teach him to fish and he'll never go hungry. That's all there is to that. It just kind of mushroomed into a twice a year thing. They can use the help and the troops learn that their lives are not just killing, but also helping the deserving and less fortunate. Hopefully that will keep them from getting their heads screwed up with all the killing and destruction they end up being involved in."

"I had not thought of that."

"No disrespect doc, but you fix bodies. The rest of us have the heart, mind, and soul to look after and I take the wellbeing of the men under my command very seriously. So, what do you need to go over with me?"

"Just the schedule, protocols, and time frames for the first segment of your rehab. We were planning on waking you at the 4-week point, regardless of the objective data on your performance and level of improvement. Forty-eight hours after you are awake, we will give you a battery of tests that will let us know if you are having any cognitive impairment. If not, twenty four hours later, your professors will administer your final exams for each of your PhD courses. Depending on how you do, we will make adjustments on the III for the last segment of your tank rehab. We will adjust the information input to whatever you decide you want. We will decide that after you are awake, and we see how things go."

"Sounds like a plan. When are we going to get this plan underway?"

"Later this morning, we will start the process of applying the frame and moving you to the tank room. That will take about two hours. At that point, we will reintroduce the coma. Once you are out, we will transfer you to the tank and start the various programs like joint mobilization, muscle strengthening, and the III.

"You will be monitored around the clock for any abnormal responses, indications that the programs are moving too fast, any laboratory or other changes. If any of these things manifest themselves, we will first try to correct them and if that does not resolve the issue, we will then remove you from the tank and further investigate what occurred. I will just let you know that, to date, we have never had to remove someone from the tank."

"Well, okay then, guess that clears up any questions I might have," J.T said sarcastically.

Do you have any questions?"

"Yes, in fact, I do. After the testing by my professors, will the testing reflect any information that was not retained, and will that information be put back into the III database to be reintroduced to see if it can be retained with the second application? Next, how long is the second section of the tank going to be scheduled for and what are the deciding parameters, or the mitigating factors involved in that decision? I assume I will be consulted prior to any decision being made or implemented."

"Of course, we would not proceed without your knowledge and approval."

"Excellent. Now, doc, if there is nothing else, I'm kind of tired and would like to get some sleep."

"Just one more thing. What am I supposed to wear for the outing in Coulter?"

"I would probably not call this an *outing*. This is more of a work weekend type thing. So long johns, blue jeans, warm waterproof mid-calf boots. A sweater and a waterproof insulated coat with a cap and water-proof insulated gloves. I have no idea what you will be doing, so I would check in with Sean as he has all the particulars. Doc Horner may have a patient or two for you to take a look at, but you will need to check in with either Sean or Doc for those particulars. Whatever you do, I am sure you will find it interesting, personally rewarding and maybe even life changing. The place and these folks have that effect on people. You will also come to understand me a little better. I look forward to hearing your thoughts and impressions when you wake me up. Anything else? If not, then good night, I will see you in the morning."

"Sleep well."

Heather left his room, shut off the light and headed to the nurses' station. As she approached the station, Emma noticed she was shaking her head.

"What's up? Is there a problem, Doctor?"

"No, not really," she answered. "It's just that every time I talk to the Colonel, I get more and more confused. I originally thought he was just a macho 'kill all the bad guys' type of man, but he has so many different layers to him that it is hard to stay on track with what level I am talking to. Have you heard about Coulter, the place?"

"Oh, sure," Emma replied. "Almost everybody knows about it to some extent. The word is that he, the Colonel, doesn't want a big deal made of it, so nobody does."

"Oh well, I'm supposed to go out there next weekend, for the bi-annual work weekend."

"Oh my," Emma replied. "That's a huge deal, girlfriend. I have not heard of anyone, not related to the unit, ever being invited there. He must think you are something special. Is this a budding romance by any chance?"

"I don't think so. I do think that he wants me to understand him better. We had that little confrontation you know where he pointed out that I did not know him and if I did, I would have addressed things differently. He was right about that but I don't think this is the beginning of a romance."

"Well honey, do not close the door on that room just yet. I have this feeling, and I am usually not wrong about that sort of thing. He's a good man, with a big heart, morals, principles, and values, that ain't so easy to find nowadays. You'd be hard pressed to find a man like him runnin' around these days that ain't married, engaged or spoken for."

"Well, I am not looking for love at this point in my life, thank you very much."

"Look here, you take love where you find it, when it presents itself, or you may end up old and living with a bunch of cats and no one else in your bed at night to keep you warm, because you were too blind or pigheaded to see what was right in front of you. That's all I'm gonna say. Just keep the doors open. Anything you need for me to do?"

"Yes, would you call the Coulters and have them come by tomorrow at 8:30am. please? Couple of last-minute things to address. Thanks, Emma. I'll see you in the morning. Good night."

"Good night, doc."

Heather headed on home, pulled into her driveway and parked her zippy little red electric sports car. Entering her home, she shut off the alarm system and threw her keys on the quartz countertop. She stopped at the fridge and surveyed the contents, trying to decide what she was hungry for.

"Guess I'll have some tomato soup and a grilled ham and cheese." Popping the soup into a microwave bowl and slipping it into the microwave, she set the timer for four minutes. She reached over the island to the hanging pots and pans, selected a frying pan, and set it on the burner of her gas stove, grabbed two pieces of wheat bread and smeared butter on one side of each piece. She opened the fridge and got out the sliced cheese and some shaved ham out of the meat keeper. Slapping everything together, she turned on the burner to low and walked to her bedroom, shedding her clothes as she went.

In her bathroom, she slipped into a bathrobe and walked back to the kitchen, flipped the sandwich and then took the soup from the microwave. She shut off the stove and put the sandwich on a plate and then had a seat at the island. She hadn't realized how hungry she was until she swallowed the first bite of the sandwich. The soup tasted so good she wondered why she didn't have it more often.

A bone-tired weariness settled over her as she pondered the occurrences she had just been through, over the last three days. The surgeries had gone better than she had a right to hope for. J.T was doing better than she had expected and as much as she didn't want to admit it, he had been right about most things. Not knowing him, she had a problem with, mainly because she had always maintained a professional distance with all her patients. Trying mostly to keep an objective perspective, not allowing personal feeling or interactions to get in the way with her practice of medicine. There was something about J.T that intrigued her, made her want to dig deeper. The work weekend that was coming up in a couple of days held a lot of promise, both for trying something new, getting outside her medical mind and yes, learning more about J.T. That thought actually scared her a bit.

She had walled off that portion of her life; the portion that might involve a mate or spouse, and she was not sure she was ready for it. She did not want to have to choose between having a romance and her practicing medicine and surgery.

"I am getting ahead of myself, so I can just give this a bit of a rest," she said to no one.

She cleaned up the kitchen, put the dishes in the dishwasher, turned it on and wiped down the counter. Satiated with food now, the fatigue pounced on her like a cat hiding on a perch, waiting for her to walk by, unaware she was about to be attacked. She slipped off the robe and climbed into bed nude, something she rarely did but couldn't care less right then. She wrapped herself around her favorite body pillow and in less than thirty seconds, was out.

CHAPTER
EIGHT

Heather started her day by taking time to dress up. She settled on a navy-blue suit, a pale pink collared blouse, thigh-high stockings and a set of matching two and a half inch heels. She stood in front of the full length, three-sided mirror and inspected her outfit. A smile decorated her face as her green eyes contemplated the result of her thoughtful dressing. The only jewelry she had on was a watch, earrings and a simple gold necklace that hung perfectly between her breasts. Satisfied, she took her purse and keys and set out for the hospital, taking her third cup of coffee with her. She didn't have any surgeries today, so she didn't mind being caffeinated.

By the time she arrived, she had finished her third cup of coffee and was enjoying the nice little caffeine jolt that was starting to envelop her. She put her ID badge and keyfob around her neck, swiping it at the doctor's entrance as she entered the building. She noticed a couple of turned male heads as she made her was to SFU unit. Even though she hated to admit it, it was nice to see that she could still turn men's heads. A little shiver went down her spine as she approached the nursing station and saw that Emma was there.

She raised an eyebrow and said, "What's the special occasion, girlfriend?"

"What?" Heather replied.

"All dressed up and all, like there was someone important you were seeing today."

"Why is it that, when I decide to dress professionally, everyone assigns some ulterior motive to it?" she asked.

"Cuz you don't do it that often, and besides, you have to admit, you ain't been yourself lately. And don't give me that 'I don't know what you are talking about' look on your face. You know exactly what I am talking about, don't you?"

"Well, maybe, just a little bit." Heather admitted.

"OK then, let's just cut out the BS between you and me. I am not going to say anything about it to anyone," Emma said.

"Thanks," Heather said. "I have never been in a situation like this before and I am unsure as to how to proceed or if it is even mutual or not."

"Well, I can tell you that there is interest there, but looking at it from his perspective, he's more uncertain about how to proceed than you are. After all you are his doctor. You know, it is kind of an unwritten rule that you don't hit on your doctor. So that means you will have to take the lead, at least in the beginning, until he knows it's okay for him to proceed. I don't mean walking into his room and jumping on him. Just drop a hint that his advances would be welcome. Suggesting that the two of you could get together to discuss your experiences at Coulter would be a great place to start."

"Anyone ever tell you that you missed your calling? Should have been a matchmaker."

"No, and I ain't doing that right now. You two are both good people. You have a couple of roadblocks in the way that you must figure out how to get around. Whatever happens after that is up to the two of you and God."

"Remember that in matters of the heart, men ain't all that bright and unless you are clear about things, he will not catch on and that will lead to misunderstandings and hard feelings. He won't be dating you or anyone after that," Emma, the charge nurse, concluded her little speech.

"Well, thanks anyway. By the way, have you seen Dr. Sun?"

"Did you check J.T.'s room?"

"Not yet, was on the way but got a little sidetracked."

With that, Heather strode off down the hall to number four. There, sitting on the edge of the bed was Li, absorbed in conversation with J.T.

"Hey doc," J.T. said with a huge grin taking up most of his face. "We were just discussing III and if we were going to be able to add in information once we start or if I have to wait until I have been awakened and tested before we can add in data."

Li joined in by saying, "Since the whole procedure is so relatively new, I would hesitate to add info and data in while he is in coma, receiving the download. Since he is going back under, for round two, so to speak, it is reasonable to assume that we can add data to the end of the data stream and have it absorbed the same as the initial download. To my knowledge, the ability of the brain to absorb information is limitless. We may be able to try adding in data at the end of his second download and see how it goes by testing him after he is completely done with rehab and the III download."

"Okay, so let's go with Plan B, by the way, are my parents here yet?" asked J.T.

A couple of seconds later, the in-room intercom squawked, "The Coulters are here at the nurses' station."

"Send them to room four please," said Heather.

A couple of moments later, the clan came through the door led by Frank, then Helen, and Shannon, with Sean pulling up the rear. There were 'Hi, how are you doing, 'Gee, you look so much better' along with the standard hugs from Helen and Shannon and hearty handshakes from Frank and Sean.

J.T. spoke first to his mom by asking her how she had been doing with the data accumulation he had requested her to look in to.

"I think I managed to find everything you had on your list. There were a couple of people that said they would get back to me early next week as they were not anywhere they could access what was being requested."

"Then we will have to add that to the second download. We were just discussing that very thing before you guys came in." Li said. "Heather, why don't you go over the timeline for the next couple of months."

"Sure. Okay, later today we will be putting J.T. in a rehab frame that he is going to have attached until the end of his rehab. It is designed to move the repaired joints in complete range of motion, any field or plane. Resistance will be added so that each joint is stressed until we reach the weight J.T. was routinely lifting prior to the accident. He is going to be submerged in a rehab tank. As we put him in the tank, we will attach the leads to the information data bank and start infusing the information straight into his brain. At the 4-week mark, we will remove him from the tank, then wake him up.

"After he has been judged to be free from the effects of the coma, his professors will administer his *final exam* for each of his PhD subjects. These tests will be graded and then we will see if the intracranial information implantation procedure was effective in transferring information."

Heather laid down the exact way everything would go, including testing by his professors and the second round of data importation. Everyone listened, amazed by the technology involved in the procedure.

"Oh, I almost forgot. We will be continuing the dialysis while he is in the tank for the first go around. This is mainly because of muscle breakdown that is expected to be caused by the weight resistance being added to build up the muscles back to where they were pre-event. This is purely precautionary. The last thing we want is to have to stop everything in the tank, take him out, hook him back up to the dialysis unit until his kidney function returns to normal, then re-introduce the coma and the III and start all over again. That would really overtax the system."

Shannon raised her hand and asked, "What about infection?"

"J.T. will be undergoing scans this afternoon, prior to being put in the rehab frame. That will tell us if there are any areas of concern for infection. We will maintain him on antibiotics for a full 10-day course, continuing even as he is in the tank. Currently, there is nothing that we are able to see, measure, or evaluate that would indicate J.T. has any source of infection going on anywhere. Anyone else have any questions?" Heather asked.

J.T. raised his hand. "What about my bodily functions while I am in a coma? I assume you will be feeding me intravenously, but what about defecating? There must be some type of residue either from the nutrition or from working my muscles?"

"With the nutritional fluids we are using, the residue is minimal and will be passed through a rectal tube that will be placed after you are in the coma. You have already seen what the Texas catheter is like. The rectal tube you won't know about because you will be asleep," Heather answered matter-of-factly.

"Not one joke from any of you or when I get out of there, you will have the chance to experience it without the benefit of the coma."

There was murmuring and stifled chuckles from the family, but no one thought of challenging J.T. and his promise.

"Since there are some things that need to be accomplished, I am going to have to shoo everyone out of here," Heather said.

"Sean," J.T. called, "don't forget to get the list from Charlie and to get with the people in charge of milk, cream, eggs and decide on all the things they want to talk about," J.T. lectured.

"I have this under control J.T. You can relax," Sean replied.

Heather made a shooing motion to everybody, getting them to start leaving. One by one, each family member stopped by J.T. hugging, shaking hands, expressing love and good wishes as they moved en mass, out the door.

Heather turned to J.T and asked if he had any other questions or comments and J.T. said, "You look really nice today. Excellent choice of suit. It really complements your hair."

"Well, thank you kind Sir, I would return the compliment, but you still look like you got blown up, but much, much, better than the first time I saw you." She gave him a full radiant smile, and continued, "The staff will be in to take you down to imaging. You will not be coming back to this room, instead you will go from imaging to the area where the rehab frame will be applied. Please, please do not try to be some kind of stud during this process. It is going to cause you some pain. You won't get a gold star on your chart for suffering. Say something if you hurt. Let people help you. That's why we are here."

"Will I see you before they put me out?"

"Of course, I will be sure to see you and give you the results of the scans. She reached down and squeezed his hand. "We need to get started. I will see you soon."

A few minutes later, the nursing assistant arrived with a full-length, sterile gown and a wheelchair.

"First, I want you to sit up and slide to the edge of the bed. We will put on the gown and then transfer you to the wheelchair."

He held up his hand in a STOP motion.

"No, you can't walk to imaging. I do not care if you think you can, that's not the point. You will be riding in a wheelchair, as per hospital policy. I do not expect any arguments. Just get in the chair."

The ride down the long hallway only took a couple of minutes with a right turn and then a left turn.

"Well, here we are. Just hang on for a minute while I check to see if they are ready for you. Be right back."

A few seconds later, the orderly returned and pushed J.T. through the door down a short hall to the right and then backed into a darkened room where the movement of the two of them caused the automatic lights to come up several levels. J.T. was wheeled up to a long low table, where the wheels were locked, and the orderly helped him on to the table but left him seated until the tech came out from behind a wall. The tech told him to slide down the table to his left before he moved around behind him to support J.T. As he leaned back, trying to lay down, there was a jolt of pain from the right hip down the right leg that took J.T. by surprise, causing him to suck in a breath, as a moan escaped his lips.

"Sorry, thought you had this," the tech apologized. "Just lay flat and let me move you around."

The tech stepped on a lever on the floor and the tabletop shifted around until J.T. was centered. He then draped a lead flap over J.T.'s groin.

"Try not to move until I tell you it's OK," the tech instructed him. He then disappeared around behind the wall.

J.T. could hear the sounds of the settings on the control panel being changed. Then there was the sound of the unit ramping up, getting ready for the study.

"Take in a deep breath and let part of it out, then hold and do not move."

There was a high-pitched squeal that seemed to go on forever when J.T heard the tech tell him to go ahead and breathe.

The tech then came over and said, "Just stay put, try to rest while the docs look over the study. They will let me know if anything else needs to be done."

Finally, after what seemed like an hour but was actually only about fifteen minutes, a doctor came out and stopped next to J.T.

"There were a couple of areas, one on each thigh that need a closer look, so we will repeat a portion with some different settings. Try to remain still to minimize any artifacts that will make it more difficult to interpret."

Again, the previous procedure was repeated and J.T. did his absolute best not to move. This time, it was another twenty minutes when both Heather and the radiologist came into the exam area.

The radiologist was the first to speak. He said, "Everything looks fine. The areas we noted on the first set of films were no longer there when we repeated the study, so you are good to go."

Heather came over and leaned over J.T. "How are you doing? Any pain, and don't lie to me."

"Yeah, I have had a couple of really good zingers, that kinda took my breath away. Not too awful right this moment, but I can't swear how it's going to be when I get up and head back to my room."

"Well, we'll give you something right now because you are headed to the tank room where they will put you in the rehab frame. You won't be in your room for the next month."

Emma came in a couple of minutes later and injected the analgesic into his IV tubing and in less than five minutes, he was no longer feeling any pain. A couple of attendants helped J.T. slide to the edge of the table, then helped lift him from the table to the locked wheelchair. Heather got behind the wheelchair, unlocked it and started wheeling him down to the tank room. As she pushed him, she asked if he had any questions. It was kind of a "Speak now or hold your piece" type of situation.

"I suppose you will be here when I wake up?"

"Wouldn't miss it for the world."

"Be sure to explain to the folks in Coulter why I am not there. I have never missed a Coulter weekend. Let them know I am thinking about them, and I will see them when I am released from here."

"I will be sure they understand."

"They are going to assume that we are an item since there has never been a woman attend a Coulter work weekend. I hope that it will not make you uncomfortable."

"We may not have actually dated, but you have to admit, there is an attraction between us. So, let's just see how things go. They will think what they want. I don't have a problem with us," said Heather.

"Neither do I," replied J.T.

"Okay, we are here. The staff will be over in a minute after we get the rehab frame set up."

"So, I just need to sit here and wait?"

"Being in the military, you should be used to 'hurry up and wait'. It's right up your alley." She chuckled.

"Thanks Doc, I appreciate it."

"It shouldn't take too terribly long. They knew you were coming."

J.T. just leaned back in the chair and watched everyone

scurry around like little ants, but he recognized they all had a function, and each was doing their job, everything coming together like a well-orchestrated symphony.

"Colonel, we are ready for you."

"What do I need to do?" he asked.

"We are going to help you stand, then remove the wheelchair. Then we will bring the backside of the frame around behind you and fit it to you. Then we will bring the front portion around in front and attach it to the rear portion of the frame. Once we have everything attached, we will check all the connections and the resistance mechanics to be sure everything is working. At that point, we will hook the frame to the overhead hydraulics and lift you up and recline you. And the nurse will attach the cranial electrodes and test them. The nurse will then start putting you into the coma and we will attach the catheter and rectal tube. Once all of that is done, we will put in the helmet and the breathing mouthpiece. Once the helmet has been judged to be airtight and you are getting air in, we will hook up all the other tubing for fluids, nutrition and medications.

"When we are sure everything is hooked up properly, working the way it is supposed to and you are at the level of coma you need to be at, you will be hoisted and lowered into the tank. Once you are submerged, all systems will be rechecked and, if all is working as expected, we will initiate the rehab program. The III will not be initiated until twenty four hours after submersion."

Forty-five minutes later, the staff were ready to start submersion. J.T. was unconscious, with all the wires, tubes and electrodes hooked up and functioning as expected.

J.T. was unconscious but was still able to perceive the sensation of being enveloped in warm, soothing fluid, and he felt like he was floating. There was no pain or discomfort, just a sense of calmness and relief. Meanwhile, all of the monitoring stations were manned, and all were reporting to the doctor in charge of the immersion rehab. Now all there was to do was wait for time to pass.

———

Heather checked in with the rehab specialist in charge and then walked up to the tank and gently touched it. She said a silent prayer and then left the area and headed back to the nursing station in the SFU. Emma was there, and she walked over to ask how things went with J.T.

"Well, I admitted, and so did he, that there was an attraction between us, and we agreed to just let things go where they go in the future. I think he understands my interest and I definitely understand his. He has even left it to me to tell the people of Coulter whatever I want to about our relationship. I have never had a relationship with any man I have never even dated."

"Well, girlfriend, you've never met a man like him, so I would say all the rules have been thrown out the door," Emma said.

"You are right about that," Heather replied.

Emma handed her a piece of paper.

"What's this?"

"The name and number of my GYN. You need to go see her and get started," Emma replied.

"I hadn't even thought that far in advance," Heather said.

"Given what is going to have to happen to move to the next more intimate level, you need to get started as soon as you can otherwise you will have to put him off in six or seven weeks and that is going to change the dynamic of this budding relationship. He will think that you are no different from any other women he has dated and that will pretty much guarantee that he will never date again, certainly not you. And if there was ever two people meant to be together, it is the two of you," Emma replied.

"You go do what you want, you are going to do that anyway. I just hope you really think this through thoroughly before you make any type of decision."

"Thanks Emma, I will," Heather responded. "Good night, I will see you on Monday and let you know how the work weekend went."

"You do that, I'll be here. See ya then."

Heather grabbed her purse and coat and headed down the hallway which, for some reason, now seemed longer than she recalled. The drive home was uneventful as she pondered all that Emma had said. It had been two plus years since she had last had sex, and it was not that impressive. She had always felt that she was a sexual woman and while she was aware of the issues that would present themselves should she decide to be intimate with J.T., the thought of stretching herself to accommodate a male organ of that size caused her pause.

However, what Emma had said to her was undoubtedly right on the money. What was she afraid of? Was she afraid of taking steps that would alter her physically for the rest of her life when she hadn't even gone out on a date with him? Granted, she did have to admit that there was a very strong attraction that she felt towards J.T. He had all the characteristics she had felt were paramount in any man she would consider as a mate and a father for her future children.

I just need to leave all this alone for a while, at least until after the work weekend is over and I have a chance to interact more with the family and the people of Coulter. With that, she made a conscious effort to push these thoughts out of her head.

She had to make a stop before arriving home, to get outfitted with the appropriate clothing for the work weekend. The store was basically a renovated Army-Navy store, but it had everything that she needed and surprisingly, it all fit to a T. She added a large hunting knife that had a striker fire starter with it. She had to congratulate herself on being so well planned for the weekend but realized she had forgotten to ask what the sleeping arrangements were, but decided that she did not need to buy a sleeping bag. She could always go out and get one on the way if needed.

After she got home, Heather called the Coulter residence wanting to speak to someone, either Sean or Frank, who would clarify the whole event.

Helen answered. "Hello dear, what's up?"

"I was just checking in because no one had said anything about sleeping arrangements. I have the appropriate attire, but I didn't know about a sleeping bag."

"Hang on dear, and let me ask Sean." Helen yelled to Sean, "what's the scoop on sleeping arrangements for the weekend?"

Heather could hear his response. "We will be sleepin' indoors, in beds, like regular folks."

"Okay, that answered my first question. Second question.

Do I come over there or are ya'll stopping over here to pick me up?"

"Heather wants to know, should she come over here or are we gonna pick her up at her place?" addressing Sean once again.

"We'll pick her up at her place in about an hour, if that's okay?" said Sean.

Heather heard Sean's response. "That's fine. I have a call to make prior to us heading out, so that should work out just right. I'll see ya'll soon."

She hung up, then dialed the hospital's main number, asking for the rehab tank room.

"Good morning, this is Dr. Dunkirk. May I speak to the physician in charge of the Coulter case? Thank you."

After a while, "Hi, this is Heather Dunkirk. I am calling to check on the status of my patient, James Coulter."

"Hello Heather, this is Bill Henderson. I'm covering tank rehab this weekend. Mr. Coulter is doing really well. In fact, we just started the III and the data stream seems to be going in without a hitch. Do we have your number in case we need to contact you for some reason, this weekend?"

Heather gave them her number and thanked them for the job they were doing and told them she would check-in with them on Sunday. She hung up, checked her watch, and hurried into her bedroom to get dressed. She put on a sports bra and a pair of comfortable panties, since she had no idea of what type of 'work" she was going to be doing and didn't want to be uncomfortable. Everything else went on easily except the boots, which took a few minutes to lace up. She had barely finished when the doorbell rang.

She went to the door and opened it, seeing Frank and Sean both standing there.

"You ready to go? Sean inquired.

"Just have to slip on the knife," she said as she wove the belt through the webbing sheath, holding the knife to her side.

"You planning on skinning a deer with that thing?" Sean inquired.

"Never hurts to be prepared, ya know," she remarked. "Ya'll didn't tell me what I was going to be doing this week, so I figured I would just be prepared for whatever."

"Well, let's load up and get going," Sean instructed.

Everyone headed out to the truck that Sean had borrowed from the unit. It was filled with what looked like junk, siding, a couple of freezers, 10 solar panels and a load of PVC pipe.

"Anything else we need to pick up on our way?" Heather asked with a little sarcasm in her voice.

"Need to stop by the grocery store and have a chat with the manager. That should only take fifteen minutes, then we will be off. I have to negotiate with management, so I know it will go quickly," Sean said as he headed into the store.

In thirteen minutes, he was back out, climbing up into the truck with a huge grin on his face.

"Well, we're ready to go and I negotiated a 33% increase in our contract. You see, Coulter provides eggs, milk, butter and cream during the year as well as two or three different flavors of fresh berry ice cream. In return, Coulter folks get to stock up on things like sugar, coffee, vanilla, yeast and a laundry list of other things they can't grow or make for themselves. I also got a tentative contract for homemade breads. J.T. and the villagers are going to be seriously pumped over this. J.T. is going to be so proud of me."

It was obvious how pleased Sean was with the outcome. Driving through the trees, into the entrance of a sweeping mountain valley. The valley was populated with multiple long, wood, three-story structures, with stone chimneys about 1/4 the way, all the way down the total length of the building, providing each section with its own heating device. There were numerous other wooden buildings spread out over the right side of the valley, with a couple that were obviously covering the entrances into the mountain. There was a very large building, centrally located, that appeared to be a large barn and more than a dozen large windmills strategically placed to avail themselves of the wind coming from one direction.

All the roofs had solar panels and there were a few free standing poles with solar panels that could rotate following the sun. Off to the far right at the base of the hill was an obvious pumping station with an enclosed attachment. Each building had a number of strategically placed trees, mainly to provide shade during the summer. At the far end of all the buildings was a large one-story building which could have been a church or a community center. There were several three-sided enclosures with large gates most likely garages. A few enclosed structures were attached to the garages. Heather looked out the back of the truck and was surprised to see they had been joined by four more trucks and six ATVs, all filled with men in winter camouflaged gear.

After stopping, Sean hopped down out of the truck and was busy directing traffic. Four of the ATVs headed off into the woods while the others, plus the trucks, pulled up into the center of the village. All of a sudden, the doors opened to most of the buildings and a swarm of people rushed out to the vehicles. It reminded Heather of the way ants did when you stomped on an anthill.

There seemed to be a lot of hugging and handshaking going on. It was obvious that the village folk were really happy to see their old friends. The menfolk and older boys immediately began unloading the truck. Sean came trudging back to the truck, a huge grin on his face, really quite pleased with himself.

"Everybody stay put while I park this thing, then we get to go eat. They have put out quite a feast, and believe you me, it is some really good eating. We will get to the introductions before the food. They do not stand on a lot of formality, they are just plain, regular folks, so ya'll just relax and enjoy yourselves."

Frank asked if he needed to help unpack and Sean informed him that it would be done before he could get out of the truck and besides, guests weren't expected to work, leastways not till after they had been fed. With that, he started up the truck and pulled it into the center of the village, but nearer the barns and the gates leading into the mountain than the rest of the vehicles.

"All the stuff we are carrying has to go in these buildings, so I parked closer, so folks wouldn't have as far to carry stuff," Sean explained.

All of a sudden there were eleven men and boys crowded around the truck bed with a couple more in the truck bed itself, handing things down to the rest of the work party. In less than five minutes, the bed was empty, and everybody was walking towards the church and community center. Frank hopped out, turned and extended his hand to help Helen, Shannon and finally Heather climb down from the cab. It felt good to stretch her legs and to loosen up a bit.

They walked about twenty-five yards to the front door, which was being held open by a tall, lean man, late 50s, weatherbeaten, as though he had spent his whole life outdoors.

"Ya'll come on in, kick the snow off your boots. My name's Charlie Fields. My missus is Lynn, and that's her over there near the end of the table. Lynn, come on over here so we can get on with the introductions, get the questions answered and get to eatin' this feast."

Sean said, standing on a chair, "Guys, line up in front of me so everybody can see ya. Okay, everybody, first things first. The Colonel has been badly hurt, which is why he ain't here today, but he sends his love and prayers and wishes he could be here. Ya'll know, he's never missed a weekend since the beginning, but there is a first time for everything. So, he sent his kinfolks in his stead. I would like to introduce Frank and Helen Coulter, his mom and dad."

There was a round of applause and quite a few welcomes, and *pleased to meet ya.*

Sean continued, "This beautiful young lady is his sister and who just happens to be my wife, Shannon McCann."

Again, another round of applause, along with a few groans from some of the younger unmarried women.

"Told ya'll I was spoken for. And this is Dr. Heather Dunkirk. She's the one that put the Colonel all back together."

There was a thunderous round of applause, whistling and noise made by the entire crowd, so much so that Heather had to blush. There was a warm fuzzy feeling going up and down her spine.

"Dr. Dunkirk is going to give ya'll an update on his condition and will answer any of your questions."

With that, Sean stepped down from the chair, offered his hand to Heather to help her get up on the chair.

She cleared her throat and looked out over the room. It was huge, with two twenty-five feet tables and chairs dividing the room into thirds. There was enough room for everyone with a fair amount left over. At one end of the room was a crude altar and at the other was a huge white sheet hanging down, covering the wall. The tables were all covered with all manner of food-stuffs, table clothes and cloth napkins. Reminded her of pictures she had seen of feasts in medieval England.

"The Colonel," she started, but then a voice from the back of the room shouted, "He gonna live?"

Heather continued, "was flying a drone and was shot down and crashed. Doc Horner did a great job of keeping him alive until he could get to the hospital."

She was interrupted by another round of applause interspersed with a few, *"Way to go Doc. Ain't none better".*

Heather continued, "He had extensive injuries to both legs and both shoulders, as well as a bunch of broken ribs and a partially collapsed lung."

As she looked out over the crowd, she noted that there were quite a few misty eyes, even amongst the men. "I replaced both of his hips, both of his shoulders, and repaired his ribs. Currently, he's undergoing submerged rehabilitation in a large tank at the hospital. He will be submerged for eight weeks."

"Ain't that gonna make him a mite pruny?" came a voice

from the back of the crowd. The comic relief could not have come at a better time if she had planned it.

"The liquid he is floating in doesn't penetrate the skin. The tank, lets us work his muscles and joints harder than we could if he was doing regular rehab outside the tank, against gravity. My prediction is that he will make a full and complete recovery and I promise you, I will have him come out here just as soon as it is safe and possible for him to do so."

The applause and whistling went on for a full five uninterrupted minutes. Sean helped Heather down and leaned over to whisper in her ear, "That was just what everyone wanted to know. You get ready, I'm gonna let the crowd at ya, so be prepared."

He stepped back and the rush of people wanting to hug her, kiss her cheek, her hand, pat her on the back seemed to go on for days. The older women of the group crowded in close to tell her he was the reason they all were alive and doing well.

One of the younger adult women hugged her, then looked her right in the eyes and said, "You're fixin' ta marry him, ain't ya?

Heather surprised herself by saying, "Yes, I am."

"You be sure to take real good care of him. Ain't many men around like him. Do anything for ya without 'spectin' nothin' in return. That's a rare man. Surprisingly, there are a few men here that are doin' their best to act like him. Makes us women-folk's lives a lot easier and happier. Bless you for what you did for him, and in turn for us."

"You're welcome," Heather responded with a little choked voice.

Lynn, Charlie's wife, started banging on a pot to get everyone's attention.

"Let's get this feast a goin'. Ya'll start passing round the food. Our guests will sit over here. Ya'll can get to talking to them later, but right now I'm starvin'."

The sounds of pulling back the chairs were grating but stopped quickly.

"Lem, it's your turn to say grace." There was the sound of a chair scraping the floor as it was pushed back by a big, burly, bearded man, who stood and took off his cap, a signal for all others to follow suit.

His deep baritone voice filled the room. "Heavenly Father, we thank you for getting us through another winter without loss of life. We thank you for keeping food on our tables, clothes on our backs and a roof over our heads. We especially want to thank you for sending us these good men who come to help us in our time of need just because they are good Christian men who chose to help folks because they can and it is the Christian thing to do. We thank you for allowing us to have fellowship with the colonels' kin. We thank you for giving Dr. Dunkirk the skill and ability to repair the damage done by evil men to the one great man you sent us, to help us, and show us the way to live. Bless this food for our use and us to thy service. In Jesus' name, Amen."

The rest of the attendees all said amen. Then the clanking of spoons and ladles against the side of large bowls of mashed potatoes, creamed corn, sweet potatoes as platters of pheasant, venison and antelope were all passed around. At the head table, Heather, Shannon, Frank, and Helen all marveled at the quantity of food that had been prepared. It was reminiscent of thanksgiving meals in days gone by. The volume of the conversations decreased as everyone paid more attention to eating and less to talking. This part of the festivities went on for at least forty-five minutes, until it was evident everyone was satiated. Charlie stood up and immediately thanked the women for putting on such a fine feast and then he went on to say that as per the custom, the women cooked and the men would clean up, right after Sean had had a chance to update everyone.

Sean tapped his water glass with his fork to get everyone's undivided attention.

"I had a meeting with the manager that oversees what we produce here, and he was quite pleased with the quantity, quality and the timeliness of delivery of our products, so much so, that we have been given a 33% increase in the amount we have to spend on the products we get from his store. In return, he would like an increase in the production of the different berry flavored ice creams and the amount of low-fat milk. He also wondered when we would begin offering some different cheeses, cottage, goat and maybe mozzarella, and maybe some type of cheddar or gouda. He seems to feel that the quality of our products is far better than what he has had to buy from other providers."

"Who are the dairy men here? I want to meet with you either later today or tomorrow to discuss stuff. We have brought a lot of repairing stuff and we need to set up a schedule to get things organized so we can get everything done before the weekend. Okay, Charlie, please get everyone together. Be sure they bring a list of what needs to be done. I am going to take the group on a tour. We'll schedule things when we get back."

Back at the time they first met, J.T. was initially concerned with getting the villagers, of which there were maybe twenty all told, water, until he talked to the group. At that point, he decided he was going to kill a bunch of problems in one fell swoop. He went to the people that ran the dumps for Dome 17 and 18 and got permission from both of them to take whatever he wanted or needed and they would separate everything out so all he had to do was borrow a bunch of trucks to haul it all here. He started with laying pipes to haul water from the pumping station they had originally broken in to.

What he originally started to design were three story-apartments that was powered by solar panels and chimneys, two for each apartment. One hearth was to heat water for cooking, bathing and clothes washing and one was for heating the home, run on wood. The bottom floor was for shops and family run stores like home canneries, leather working, quilt making, etcetera. The second floor had a kitchen, living room, dining room and master bedroom with a full bath. The third floor has three bedrooms and 1 ½ baths. There was storage on all floors and a large deep basement that was fifteen feet deep by twelve feet wide. The length is the whole length of the building, with wooden walls separating sections from one another.

When this all started, the original group had three cows, four pigs, twelve chickens and three horses. J.T. designed a barn that had a system of collecting mechanisms to catch all the manure, urine and straw and funnel it into huge storage tanks that can be heated and run through a huge blender. It was accumulated from May until March, at which time it heated through, killing any harmful bacteria and blended mixed so it can be sprayed.

"This weekend these tanks will be put on the back of a wagon pulled by a tractor so it can be sprayed over all or the 700 acres of farmland. In addition, all of the sawdust that comes from our sawmill will also be spread over the farmland. Once that is done, both of these things will then be plowed into the fields, thereby fertilizing the fields that will grow corn, wheat, oats and hay. We will use all natural stuff to grow food. No chemicals. Once the ground is prepared, planting will take place. Once planting is done, we have netting that will cover all of the fields so there will be no need for insecticides. The fields will be surrounded with electrified fencing to keep deer, antelopes, and buffalo from coming in to the fields and eating the crops. Currently, we have twenty milk cows, thirty-five steers, forty hogs, six thousand chickens, and twenty-five horses."

"This whole village is completely self-sufficient. The village eats deer, antelope, elk, moose, bear and buffalo. Right now, the overwatch squad is out hunting for meat. These will be brought here. Two or three of the guys here are butchers. The skins will be given to those that do leather work. The non-edible parts of these animals will be used as part of fertilizer. Most of the power used here is generated by solar panels, windmills, and hydroelectric methods. The only petroleum powered devices are tractors and the sawmill. We cut the wood needed for construction and for furniture making, otherwise the sawmill is turned off.

"The overwatch crew that is out hunting right now have battery powered locators. When they find trees that are either dead or knocked over, they mark them, then a crew goes out, and either cuts the tree down or strips off the limbs and put it on a stretch wagon pulled by a tractor. When the wagon is full, they head back here and unload the trees next to the sawmill. The sawmill will run when there is enough wood to justify running it. There are a couple of guys here that make furniture. When they have a couple of orders, then they will cut up the wood, otherwise the trees are left intact until they are needed. They get stored inside away from the bugs," Sean continued.

The problem, as J.T. saw it, was that there were things that the village needed that they could not grow themselves. Tea, coffee and sugar to start with. That meant they would have to produce something that they could sell. So, he thought about it and came up with dairy products. They managed to find all the components for milking and separating machines. J.T. improvised a large butter churn and an ice cream machine. He bought and paid for the vanilla and 50lbs of sugar himself, and the rest is history. After the unit built the two apartment complexes, it took four weekends and the unit all showed up every weekend to work without having to be asked. There were a number of hidden skills in the group. An electrician, plumbing and hydraulics and hydro-electrics techs, all kinds of stuff, and each one of them had thoughts and plans and J.T, as the Colonel, made each and every one of them happen. That was what was so special about this place and the people. If you could dream and think about things, you could make them happen. J.T. figured that out and now look at this place, over one hundred people and that number keeps growing and they all love J.T.

"We're gonna have a look at the barn and the dairy set-up. It really is an engineering marvel, clean as a whistle, and it hardly smells like a barn. Behind them was a honking coming from a line of three ATVs all piled high with animal carcasses.

"Where are they heading to?"

"The slaughterhouse where the process of skinning and hanging the meat would happen. It is located in the mountainside."

"That's where those doors go?"

"No, one is the smokehouse and the other is for aging."

The meat that went in these two places was what the village lived on year-round. It kept the herds thinned out, which meant the land could support the herds. That meant that the wolves, coyotes, and bears didn't come down and bother the cattle, pigs, and goats. If they are left alone, the land supports itself and the village does well.

About that time Doc Horner strode up and said, "Doc, if I could bother you, there are a couple of folks I would like your opinion on. They really can't take the time off to go to the hospital and sit around waiting to be seen, so if I could have you look at them while you are here."

"I would be happy to, Doc. Do you have any imaging studies?" said Heather.

"Just plain radiographs. It was all we had back in the day. You had to learn by history and physical examination. In the correctional facilities I worked in, if you wanted an x-ray, you had to take it yourself, so you had to develop it yourself, read it yourself, and type up the report yourself. If you couldn't interpret it, the film was sent out to a consultant radiologist, and it was a minimum of two weeks before you got an answer. Made you really good on the history and physical exam," Doc said.

"You must be great. What you did for the Colonel in such a short period was exactly what needed to be done in the sequence it needed to be done in. You sure you're not a doctor?" Heather asked, honestly.

"No, I'm not. I am flattered that you think my skills are worthy, but I have never been to med school. I learn fast, read a lot, I ask a lot of questions that usually require detailed answers, and I pay attention. I also know what I don't know, and I never cross the line between the two. In addition, I really do care about all of my patients. Now, can we please get on with the business?"

"Sure."

"Sarah is in my office. It's her right hip. Got thrown from a horse about four months ago. Landed on her right hip. Hip was tender to touch, mild bruise over the trochanter and some mild decreased range of motion. She sucked it up for about five weeks, then I saw her limping and leading with her left leg on the stairs. She is not shortened or externally rotated. No fractures on x-ray but I am worried about a traumatic AVN, which will put her out of my area of expertise. She's all yours."

They reached the office entered, and Doc said, "Sarah this is Dr. Dunkirk, I've asked her to take a look at you cuz you're not getting any better, and I have reached the limits of my knowledge and abilities. Besides, you deserve the very best. After all, she fixed the Colonel and if she's good enough for him, I think she's good enough for you."

"Hey Sarah, I'm Dr. Dunkirk. I understand you hurt your hip. Can you show me exactly how you landed?"

And so, the evaluation started. Heather asked additional questions about fevers, rashes, blood in her urine, stool, or weird vaginal bleeding? The answer was no to everything.

"Any problems with having sex?" Heather asked.

"I can't have sex, not that I don't have a partner, but I haven't found a position that doesn't really hurt. I mean it hurts enough to make me stop, right then and there."

Heather moved on with her exam. Doc was surprised how thorough she was. No cutting corners. When she was done, Heather sat down and looked Sarah right in the eyes.

"Sarah, what I think has happened is that when you hit the ground, you broke a part of your hip that contains the blood supply to the other part of your hip and as a result, the part with no blood supply died. I can't tell that for sure. I need to do an MRI to see the extent of the damage. Then I will need to operate and replace your hip bone. It is going to take a day and you go home after it's done. You don't stay in the hospital. After that, we will have you do a bunch of exercises and that's that."

There was a strange look on Sarah's face; apprehension, relief, and worry were all there. Heather touched her forearm and said,

"No worries, this is what I did for the Colonel. I've done it hundreds of times. Piece of cake."

Sarah visibly relaxed.

Doc said, "I will take care of all the arrangements, and I will let you know."

"Thanks Doc, Dr. Dunkirk. I don't know if I could have gone the rest of my life without sex."

Both providers had a little chuckle over that. Not because of what was said, but the fact that she said it. Sarah slid down off the exam table, grabbed her dress, dropped the exam drape, and put herself back together before limping out of the office.

"Very honest and straight-forward woman," Heather remarked.

"That she is," Doc added in. "The next case is Louis. Louis is a 59-y/o white male who is one of the dairymen here. He has been squatting and sitting on very low stools for fifty years and his knees show it. His knees are so accurate that he can predict rain within two hours every time, without fail. And he suffers each time it rains. I have injected his knees about every three months or so, but he is not getting as much relief as he used to. I managed to find some old Synvisc, and we tried that about two years ago.

"What a waste of time. It did nothing for him and he was absolutely miserable until I agreed to restart injecting him with the steroids. So, what I have left with options are total knee replacements bilaterally and stem cell injections. My training is such that you start with non-invasive stuff first and if that doesn't work, you go to total knee replacements. The only issue I have is the length of time it takes to regenerate the cartilage in the knees and his life as a dairyman here in Coulter.

"He still has to do the milking and all the other stuff that keeps the income coming in to the village, which affects every-one. On the flipside, there is the recovery period from the total knees that will impact him in pretty much exactly the same way as the stem cell injections. So, let's take a look at Louis."

Doc call to Louis. "Louis come on in here and get up on the table. Pull your pant legs up over your knees. This is Dr. Dunkirk."

"Nice to meet you. I hear you are the owner of the weather knees of Coulter," Heather teased.

"Yes'um I am. And they have never been wrong. I'm 'bout done with that part of stuff," Louis responded.

"Doc and I have been talking about you and your situation.

So, here are your choices. Total knee replacement or stem cell injections. The upside to knee replacement is that once it is done, you will never have issues with the knees. The downside is that it will take between three to five months for all the healing and therapy to be done with. The stem cell upside is there is no surgery, so there is no rehab or therapy. The downside is that it takes three to five months to regenerate the cartilage that has been worn away and during that time you can't have any steroid injections, because that will stop the stem cells from working," Heather said. "Do you have any questions?"

"Yep, just one," Louis replied. "Which one is going to interfere with my dairy work the most?"

"Good question," Doc said. "I think the knee replacement is going to keep you from doing a lot of the dairy work in the short term, with the healing period and then some rehab time, but then no more issues. The issue with the stem cell injection is that while you are waiting for the cartilage to regenerate, we will have to do something else for the discomfort and pain. But you will still be able to do your work."

"Doc, Dr. Dunkirk, I'm gonna have to think this over and discuss this with a couple of people cuz the downtime stuff will impact other people here in the village."

"Sure, no problem. Talk to whomever you need to. I will be around if you have other questions. There is no pressure here, Louis. You take as long as you need," Doc said.

"Well, those are some interesting cases. The last one was pretty complicated when you add in all the ancillary issues like work within the community, added workload for other community members, prolonged pain management. Have to say you've done quite a job here. Well done, very well done. You really do know your limits. Hope the town appreciates the work you do," Heather commented.

"You should see the office around the holidays. I was always told that you can judge how people think about what you are doing by what they give you during the holidays," Doc muttered.

"Cakes, pies, quilts, sweaters, handmade coffee cups, plates, bowls, knick-knacks. You name it. If it can be made by hand, I've been given it. Touches my heart. Just love these folks, truly do," he continued.

"They feel the same way about J.T. They would do anything for him. Anyway, it's time for supper and tonight is movie night. It's really a big deal. The whole village gets involved. They hang a huge sheet on the wall at the communal center and show the movie on it. As an honored guest, you get to pick the movie. We will take you into the movie closet and let you pick from the vast array of movies that have built up over the years. So, let's get over to the center and eat these good people's food. What do you say?" Doc said.

They strolled across the communal area to the center, where they entered and found their seats. The fare was typical picnic food: burgers, brats, potato salad, corn and baked beans. There was lots of conversation and fellowship and Heather found herself having a better time than she had thought she would and, she had to admit, felt accepted as part of this community, a feeling that she felt in her soul. In the back of her mind was the thought that this was because of J.T. He had told her she would be changed. She felt Doc tugging on her sleeve, pulling her back from her thoughts.

"It's time to go pick the movie. Just to let you know there is no right or wrong choice. Everyone is going to enjoy the movie."

They walked to the back of the room, where a large door was partially open. Doc entered first and flipped on the lights. Heather was taken aback by the sheer size of the room, hundreds of DVDs on fourteen different shelves, carefully stacked by the alphabetically arranged titles. She walked the length of the shelving, running her fingers over each one when she stopped and pulled one out, handing it to Doc and said, "This is the evening's selection."

Doc looked at it, and his eyes grew wide.

There was almost a shocked look on his face.

"This is a sign," he whispered.

Heather couldn't figure out what Doc was referring to. He left the storage room and walked over to where Helen, Frank, Sean, and Shannon were sitting.

He showed the choice to the group, raising his hand to the sky, said, "I had nothing to do with it. I didn't give any hint, direct her or give any gestures' or anything."

Helen said, "This is J.T.'s all-time favorite movie."

Heather was standing behind Doc and heard everything he said. She was struck by the unbelievable coincidence.

Helen said, "J.T. used to say the final aria, Nessun Dorma, defined his character and motivated him through everything he ever did or faced. Vincero. This was never sung by anyone better than Pavarotti."

Helen turned to Heather and said, "You will see what I mean at the end of the movie."

The chairs were re-arranged, and the DVD player was set up

and connected to the speakers that were scattered around the entire room.

Doc stepped to the front of the room and said, "The movie for tonight was picked out by Dr. Dunkirk. It's Yes Giorgio. And no, she had no help from anyone, I swear."

The room broke into spontaneous whooping, hollering, and clapping. They all knew it was the Colonel's most favorite movie. A lot of them had to admit that the movie made them laugh and tear up a little bit.

Lights, camera, action! And with that, the movie started.

Heather had never seen the movie, and she laughed, cried, and was completely moved. The Nessun Dorma aria stunned her with its power, beauty, gut, and soul wrenching intensity. *Now I get what J.T. meant when he told me I would understand him better after this weekend. I like how this is going, and there is still tomorrow to experience,* she thought.

After the movie, there was more socializing to do. Helen, Frank and Heather all kind of hit a brick wall and needed to find a place to sleep. They were directed to a cabin set back off the town's central square area. It was very nicely appointed and quite comfortable. Helen and Frank got the bedroom with the king-sized bed, Heather got the room with the bunk bed, and Sean and Shannon got the room with the twin beds. Afterwards, there was a quick orientation walk-through to find out where the bathroom was, where the kitchen was and where the linens were. Heather was surprisingly more tired than she had thought she would be.

After making the bed, she went into the bathroom. Only had a shower, so as she pulled the shower curtain back, she could see, clear as day, the instructions on showering. She turned on the water and pushed the start button. A flashing timer lit up, starting at thirty seconds, and started counting down. She jumped in and got herself wet down. The water flow stopped and the timer rest itself for ninety seconds. She lathered herself thoroughly and then decided against washing her hair. At the end of ninety seconds, the timer reset itself for seventy-five seconds and the rinse water began to flow. She had completely rinsed and still had twenty seconds left on the timer, so she just let the warm water run down her back, trying to let some of the muscle tension relax.

She marveled at all the complex planning, the progressive thinking and at J.T.'s ability to get everyone to accept and follow all the things he had set up and laid out, thereby getting this community to be a successful undertaking, providing a living for all these people. Why had he never become involved in governmental management? How much better would people' lives be if he were able to orchestrate cities and provinces with the same success?

The water shut off automatically, so she stepped out of the shower and grabbed a towel. As she dried off, there was a knock at the door, followed by Shannon's voice asking her if she was done.

"Be out in two seconds," was her reply.

"No hurry, just didn't want to barge in."

Heather wrapped the towel around herself and opened the door.

"Wasn't sure if you had figured out the timer and everything. Takes a little getting used to," Shannon said.

"Yeah, but it sure did feel good. I was surprised I could get everything washed in a short time. Had to skip the hair though," Heather lamented.

"Should have asked. There is a code you can enter that adds more time for those that want to wash their hair," Shannon said.

"You're right, I would have liked to wash my hair, but I can go for two days without washing it every now and then."

"You have beautiful hair, seriously," Shannon said. "It always looks like you just got out of a beauty parlor chair."

"Well, I'm off to bed. Ya'll sleep tight. See ya in the morning." With that Heather retreated to her room, finished drying, slipped into a T-shirt and was out within sixty seconds of her head hitting the pillow.

CHAPTER
NINE

There was a gentle knock on the door and Heather awoke from the best night's sleep she had had in ages.

"I'm up and getting ready. Be done in ten minutes."

"Okay," was the return. "Breakfast is at 7 a.m. We are going to head out at 6:45."

"Got cha," was Heather's response.

Wish I knew what they had planned for me for today. Guess I'll have to play along and find out when they let me know, she thought. She dressed in a clean pair of long Johns and jeans, thermal undershirt and the same shirt she had on yesterday, since she felt she hadn't done anything to get dirty. On with the boots and winter jacket, knit cap and gloves and out the door she went.

The trek to the community center took all of ten minutes. She could smell the bacon, fresh biscuits, bread and sausage cooking as she made her way through the door. There were quite a few *mornin Doc* from the handful of people that were

139

there already. It was set up cafeteria style, except you served yourself, so she grabbed a tray, got a plate, knife and fork as she surveyed the fare. There were steam table pans of bacon, sausages, scrambled eggs, biscuits, and redeye gravy, hashbrown potatoes, country fried ham and chicken fried steak. The smells were intoxicating. She found herself almost drooling as she made her way down the line. There was a large urn with a black liquid that smelled like coffee. As she poured herself a steaming mug, one of the cooks said,

"It's coffee with chicory. What with the cost of coffee? We have just gotten used to makin' coffee with our own chicory. So, we mix half and half."

"This food is absolutely amazing."

"Well, ya know, most of these folks are farm folks. They eat huge breakfasts, medium sized lunches and small dinners. Gives 'em enuf energy ta get through the day."

Heather took her tray and cup of coffee and sat down next to Sean.

"This is so cool, all this food, the comradery. Why would anybody want to live in a big city?" Heather questioned.

Sean jumped in, "It's a hard life. They don't have a lot of 'niceties and conveniences' most people are accustomed to. It's great for a weekend or a two-week vacation, but life gets hard in the dead of winter. You have to learn to rely mostly on yourself and sometimes others. It is not easy. That's why J.T devoted so much of his off hours to developing all the stuff that they have here. He wanted them to have a better life based on what they could do for themselves, not living off the government but by the sweat equity they have built up here. Most of these folks would have a very hard time inside the Dome in the city. They really would not do very well. They know it and accept that things may be tougher out here, but it is what they know and want."

"This is our living legacy. It makes up for all the destruction we are forced to inflict on those that would do us harm. Hey, look at me, I'm starting to sound like J.T."

Shannon elbowed him in the ribs lovingly and said, "Glad you noticed that, and I did not have to remind you."

"Yes, dear," was the chagrined response.

"What time is the service this morning?"

"Usually, 9 a.m.," Sean replied. "Louise, who is speaking this morning?"

"Ralph, I think," she replied.

"Thanks."

After the meal was finished, everyone helped clean up and re-arranged the chairs into rows that resembled the inside of a church. Everyone went outside to await the time of the service. They all milled around, chatting with each other.

At 8:50 a.m., Ralph strode up the stairs and into the center. One by one, the attending villagers followed him and took their seats. When everyone was seated, Ralph asked Josh to close the doors. When they were shut, Ralph walked to the front of the pews and took out a bible.

He opened it to one passage and read, "Spare the rod and spoil thy child."

He continued, "I used to hear that line from my mother and my father, just before I received my daily beating. I grew up living like that and after I married and my wife had given me children, I practiced what I had been taught. I hurt my children badly, but I justified it by saying it was how I was raised, and if it was good enough for me, it was good enough for my family. Then we, came to Coulter where we were accepted and we tried to fit in. I continued to beat my children as I had been doing. One day I hurt my eldest boy badly, and he was taken to see Doc Horner."

"Well, Doc fixed him up, put his arm in a cast, then he came over to the house. He knocked on the door and I opened it and he commenced to beating my ass up one side and down the other. He hurt me really bad."

"What he told me was that child abuse was handed from parents down to their kids and then later, the kids passed it down to their kids. The only way to stop it was what he had done. He had hurt me worse than I had ever been hurt before and promised to make it worse the next time I hurt my kids or my wife, and by God Almighty, I believed him.

"He told me that as a parent there was gonna be times that I would have to discipline my kids and that was okay, they could be spanked, bare butt, open hand. No objects like spoons, paddles, switches, or belts. The idea was to impress on them what they did was wrong and that after the spanking, I needed to talk to them about what and why it was wrong and how they should act differently in the future. Then they need to be given a chance to change their ways. That was how you taught people to change their behavior. It took me three weeks to get back on my feet. I had to rely on other members of the community to help me out while I was healing up. Every day they got to see what happened to me, what caused it, and how I was going to do things differently in the future.

"They also saw that Doc continued to treat me just the same as everyone else. He held no grudges or ill will towards me or my family. I will be forever grateful to the community, the folks that had to pick up the slack, and to Doc for teaching me how to be a better man and a better parent to my kids. Let us pray."

He prayed the Lord's Prayer, but at the end he added a request to the Lord to grant patience to all parents and to realize hurting kids doesn't improve them. There was a chorus of *Amens*, then everyone got up and went and hugged Ralph. Ralph wiped the tears from his eyes and thanked everyone for allowing him to share his story.

After the service was concluded, Sean, Shannon, and Heather met outside. Doc walked up and said that he had two projects that needed doing that day and that they were not the kind that could be put off. One was skinning and preparing all the deer, elk, antelope, and moose that the overwatch group had bagged and brought in late last night. The other project was getting the dairy barn, chicken coop, hog, and horse stables cleaned out and hosed down. There would be four other people, three men and one teenaged boy, in addition, to help with that huge job. This had to be completed about a week before the fields and gardens all needed to be fertilized. Sean volunteered for the barn project and like a good wife, Shannon joined in.

"Guess that leaves the skinning to you, Doc," Doc said. "Sean, you know where the barn is. You can get your boots and apron in there; the guys will show you." He looked over at Heather. "Heather, come with me and I will show you where the processing plant and smoke house are. There will be two other guys in there helping you. They will show you where everything is that you will need."

They walked almost the entire length of the "square" to one of the two doors that looked like they were set into the side of the hill. The odor of a smoke house permeated the workspace. Surprisingly, the work area was about forty by twenty with an overhead metal rail and dozens of hanging hooks, many of them holding freshly killed game, hanging head down. There were four very large metal tables with wood butcher-block cutting boards at each end. Doc introduced Heather first to Jerry, a broad shouldered, well-muscled man in his late thirties and Lucien, a short, squat man in his late forties. Jerry spoke first.

"Have you ever skinned a deer?"

Heather shook her head no and replied, "I work on people."

Jerry pulled the first deer in front of himself, then he started to lecture and demonstrate.

"Oh, then this should be a breeze. One incision around each leg and down the inside portion of each leg. A similar incision goes circumferentially around the neck then down the center of the chest and belly, connecting with the incisions inside the legs. Then you separate the skin from the underlying tissue and pull the hide off. After that, you remove the entrails and put them in the large metal container at the end of the table. Change knives and put the knife you just used in the tray with the blue solution.

"With a fresh knife, you will need to remove the head. Feel the back of the neck and upper spine. You will find a lump under the skin. Cut through there on the side that is nearer the head. Just cut on down through everything. The head should come right off. Change out the knife again. Find the knee joints and remove the lower legs with the hooves attached, and put those and the head in the large plastic tub next to the wall. Then tell us you have finished, and we will take it from there. You can then start on the next carcass. One good thing about this, eh Doc, you don't have to sew them back up and they don't sue."

Jerry slapped his thigh and Lucien slapped him on the back. Both of them were really tickled at the joke they had on Heather.

She smiled, allowing them their little bit of fun. In less than ten minutes, she told them she was ready for the next carcass. They were both surprised that the city lady was not grossed out and was quick dissecting the animals. They slid the next carcass, a 275-pound elk, shot perfectly with a quick, killing heart shot. This animal did not suffer. Again, in less than eleven minutes, she was done and was scrubbing the knives in the soaking tray.

"I have been a surgeon for almost ten years, this is just like cadaver lab except I don't have to label the parts," she said with a huge grin on her face.

The next two hours went by in a blur. When they were done, a total of twenty-four animals had been skinned and twelve of the largest ones were being transferred to the smoke-house right next door. By the end of the next day, they would be ready to package for freezing for next winter's food. One half of the meat left would be packaged and sold at a premium price at the grocery store inside the dome city. All of the money would be put into an account that would be used to pay for the items the village was not able to hunt, fish or grow on their own. J.T. would renegotiate the cost of those items.

The food products, including all the milk and eggs, were in high demand and brought a very good price. With J.T.'s negotiating ability, the items the village needed only costing 30% of what the rest of the people were paying. As the carcasses were moved into the smokehouse, two women came in and began applying the seasoning rub. Janice looked at Heather and told her the recipe had been handed down in her family for over four generations. It was a mix of coarse salt, black pepper, garlic powder, and onion powder. This was rubbed into every nook, cranny and surface of each animal. The carcasses were then cut in half and put on a revolving rack so that in the end, there were twenty-four sides of meat hanging individually in a fashion that nothing dripped from one carcass to another.

Lucien and Jerry exited the house, went outside, and opened another door to a small basement where the actual wood that was going to be burned was located. Lucien turned to Heather and told her that every year they went out and found a hickory tree, cut it down, then hauled it back to their sawmill. It was then cut into sections and further split into manageable pieces and stacked down in the basement of the smokehouse to age for three to six months. This was wood they had processed the previous fall, still a little wet, but ready to burn and produce a lot of smoke. Jerry ushered Heather back upstairs so Lucien could get the fire going. This fire was going to burn for about thirty hours.

When that was done, the meat would be moved to the butcher shop where it was cut into steaks, ground up for hamburger and some was made into sausage. The village sold two or sometimes three types of sausage, depending on the availability of certain spices. There was smoked sausage, kielbasa and a summer sausage that was actually seasonal. They had the know-how to make salami, but getting the seasoning was difficult sometimes, so they were never able to consistently provide a hard salami to the store in the city. After Jerry had finished explaining everything to Heather, he went back inside the smokehouse and brought the tub of entrails out, set it down by the meat shop, went back in and got the tub of legs and heads, set it down outside then went in and got the soaking tray and all of the knives that had been used and brought them outside and set them on the ground.

He went back in and looked the whole place over, then made sure the motor that would run the rotisserie was properly hooked up, then went outside, opened the door to the basement and summoned Lucien. Lucien came up the stone stairs and promptly walked into the smokehouse, checked every corner and rechecked the hookup of the rotisserie. When all that was done, he came out and said, "Clear," to Jerry, who then closed the door to the smokehouse and locked three different locks.

Lucien went back downstairs and started the fire. After it was going to his satisfaction, Lucien exited the basement and closed the door, locking it with three locks.

Jerry looked at Heather and said, "We prett' near killed one of the kids about twelve years ago by locking them in the smokehouse when we didn't know they was in there. Now we just automatically check behind one another to be extra careful."

Heather hadn't thought about kids sneaking into some place like the smoke house but when you are trying to win at Hide and Seek this would be a perfect place to hide.

"That's a really good system," she replied.

"All these knives have to be washed, sharpened, then rewashed and sterilized before we can put them into storage until the next time. We have one machine that does the washing, and that is the only machine we use for this whole thing.

Nothing else gets washed in it, ever. Don't want folks getting sick, ya know," Jerry explained.

As Heather walked out of the door, she inquired where she could find Sean and Shannon.

"Most likely, they are over around the barn. Just go to the far corner of that building and turn right. It will be straight in front of ya. Can't miss it," Jerry pointed out.

So, Heather started out on her little journey. She noted that most of the snow around had melted or was in the process of doing so. As she got to the barn door, it opened out towards her and Shannon stepped out, taking in a deep breath.

"Hey Heather," she called out, "how's it goin'?" With that, she took another deep breath. "I can only stand it just so long in there, what with the smell, till I have to get out and get a few deep breaths."

" You guys about done?" Heather asked.

"'Bout an hour or so. Sean says that the next step is the hose down part, which is the second to the last part, but in the overall scheme of things, it is one of the faster parts."

"Can I take a look?" Heather asked.

"Sure but beware the odor and be sure to get a pair of rubber boots. This is a barn after all, and there are droppings all over the place," Shannon cautioned.

Heather slipped on a pair of rubber boots and walked inside the barn. The typical barn odor slapped her in the face two seconds after she came through the door.

"I can see what you mean," Heather commented.

At that moment, Sean strode up and said, "I see that Shannon has mentioned the smell."

"It was only fair that I mention something beforehand," Shannon said defensively.

"Well, come on in and I will give you the nickel tour and ten-dollar explanation for the place," Sean said and began narrating how the system worked.

"First off, J.T knew that if the village was going to survive and even thrive, they were going to have to grow a lot of stuff in the fields for their own consumption, to sell or barter and to feed livestock. That meant the land was going to need fertilizer that was not chemical, cuz they did not have the money to buy large amounts of fertilizer, nor the equipment to apply it to the fields. The first thing that came to his mind was manure and urine from all the livestock, chickens included. So, he set about designing a barn that would catch all the animal waste and urine, as well as the hay and straw that was put on the floors for animals to eat and lay on during the winter.

"He designed a collection system with holding tanks for liquids and solids. The solid holding tanks were kind of like huge blenders or food processors. In the mid-spring the barns were cleaned out, like now, all the straw was stuffed into the solid holding tanks, the blades were lowered into the tanks, lids applied and then attached to a motor that turned the blades. The blades chopped up all the hay and straw into a very fine mulch. The tank would then be emptied into a larger tank and the liquid waste tank that was chopped up the same as the solids and then the two tanks are mixed. This tank would then be mixed with a much larger blade system until it was all liquid. The tank would then be set off to the side to sit and ferment.

"A gas release valve was attached and pipping run to a tank that would store the methane that was produced. The methane produced was used to run different things around the village like stoves, heating systems for the home and hot water tanks. Some of it was even used to run generators that produced some of the electricity used daily.

"Right now, we have gotten all the straw and hay out of the entire barn and I am going to hose down the inside of the barn. All of this is going into tanks that will collect everything that is washed down the drain. Then the floor will be brought back to normal. We will re-apply a layer of hay and be done for now."

"Oh, I forgot something. Everyone who lives here gets a ½ acre garden of their very own to grow whatever they want, usually sweet corn, tomatoes, beans, potatoes, onions, squash, herbs, lettuce, carrots, celery. Remember, they have to eat what they grow. Now almost everyone grows more than they need. They can some and sell the rest for a little extra cash. Then the ground is plowed and re-tilled then a third application of fertilizer and a final plowing."

"Before actual planting, it's Jesse's job to see how much corn, oats, wheat, hay bales are left after the winter and then it is decided how many acres of each are going to be planted."

"Since we do not use pesticides, after a field is planted, we put up the irrigation piping and then hang the netting. We use that netting to keep the bugs out, so we don't have to use pesticides. We use irrigation piping to keep the field enclosed, keeping the deer, antelope, elks, bear and moose out of the fields. We have a battery system that is charged by solar panels during the day and is turned on automatically at early dusk.

"The charge is enough to hurt whatever animal brushes up against it. It also triggers a trail camera so we can see what animal is trying to get into the fields. Then we send out a hunting party to either drive the animals a good long distance from the fields or to kill them. Then, if we kill them, we use the meat the same as we do in the fall and spring. This way we live in harmony with the land and nature, with the benefit of some modern technology, to make things easier and possible. J.T. wanted to prove that man could be sustained, living off the land, without using chemicals, that in the long run, could be toxic to people," Sean finished his description of the farm and food production.

They reached the end of the residence building on the right, turned the corner. At the far end of the building was a door. Jerry opened the door and turned and instructed the women to watch their heads and their steps. He started down a wood and cement staircase to a small landing, where he flipped a light switch and continued around the corner and down the last four stairs. When he reached the bottom of the stairs, he reached around to the left and flipped a bank of light switches. There before them was a large area with multiple hallways branching off the central hallway.

"Over here, to the left, is the storage area for grains and next to that is our grist mill for grinding the corn, wheat, and oats. Next door on the left is a huge room that has plastic bins stacked from floor to ceiling all labeled either corn, wheat or oats. They had all been ground to flour consistency." Jerry turned off the light inside the storage area and closed the door tightly.

Heather noted that all the floors, walls, and ceilings were concrete with perfect joints and corners. Twenty feet further down the central hallway was another door on the left. This room was about the same size as the last room but had sacks of corn, wheat, and oats, also from floor to ceiling. After both women had a look inside, Jerry closed the door tightly. There was a cross hallway that led to the other side.

"What we have on this side is the tanning area. It is specially vented to the outside and while the guys that do the tanning of the hides of all the animals, no one is allowed down here and that includes for the next three days after they are done with all the tanning chemicals. So, they announce when they are going to be tanning, everyone comes down here and goes through the storage rooms getting everything they will need for almost a week, then the tanning guys get started. Since we just got all that meat in, they will be tanning in three to four days. These next three doors are the actual area where the tanning will take place. On this side of the hall is the storage area for all the canned goods made here." With that, he opened one of the doors and there seemed to be miles of shelves all stacked with glass jars of different foodstuffs.

Heather entered and looked in both directions, struck with awe by the amount of food stored.

"Moving on," Jerry continued. "The doors at the end of the hallway are the entrance to the freezers."

He opened one of the freezer doors, allowing both of the women to look inside and see the same amount of metal shelves loaded with wrapped frozen meats, floor to ceiling.

"Some of this is meat that will be taken to the grocery store for sale, and some will be for local consumption. This whole area is accessible by each individual residence with separate entrances in each residence. With everything being cement and metal, we also empty out each and every storage area every three to four months to check for things, not only mice and rodent infestations but also fungal and bacterial issues," Jerry said, sounding like a tour guide at Walt Disney World.

"To date, we have never had an issue with any of the things I mentioned." His voice was full of pride, and rightly so.

Heather had to admit that J.T. had thought and addressed everything that could cause any type of issue to or for the residents of Coulter. She was amazed as to how deep her developing admiration for James Tiberius Coulter was becoming. He definitely was an incredible, accomplished, far thinking man. She was looking forward to seeing what he was like when he was no longer a patient.

Shannon and Heather climbed back up the stairs to the outside. Jerry took one last tour of the area to be sure none of the kids or creatures had managed to find their way inside the storage area. Locking the door, Jerry turned to the women and told them there was an escape hallway that led to a spot inside the area 17, protected by the dome force field. This was to be used should the need arise to activate the force field for protection from an impending attack.

Heather looked at Shannon and told her she was a lucky woman to have a husband like Sean. Shannon acknowledged the compliment and responded that J.T. was still available and that he was a pretty great guy. Heather responded that she was just saying that because he was her big brother.

"You wouldn't say that if you had to grow up with him," Shannon responded. They both chuckled.

"Any idea what time Sean is going to be ready to go? I have a few things to catch up on and I need to check-in on J.T.," Heather said.

"I'll go ask Sean," she replied. "Meet ya back here."

Shannon was gone for about 10 minutes and when she got back, she said that Sean said they could go now or after supper and Heather pondered that for about five seconds.

"After supper would be fine," Heather answered.

Helen and Frank came strolling up, asking how her days had gone.

"I am incredibly impressed with the amount of thought, planning and leadership that had gone into getting Coulter from a bunch of ramshackle shacks to a fully self-sustained, fully functioning community that really could now take care of itself and thrive," Heather replied.

That caused a smile to break out on both of their faces.

Heather asked what they had been up to, and Frank replied that he was working on making the hydroelectric system work more effectively and efficiently. He went on to explain that J.T. had set up seven hydroelectric pumps on the water supply and they needed tweaking so they could produce more electricity. He also had to figure out how to keep the water flow going year round regardless of the outside temperature.

"I managed to increase electrical output by 23% and leave a spot to add in another pump that would add another 42% to the total output of the system," he said with a little hint of bragging.

"Yes, honey, you can walk on water and only occasionally get your ankles wet," Helen said patronizingly.

Frank feigned a hurt look. "Where is my loving wife's support when it is needed?"

Helen said, "Well, I had to tweak the solar panel system for each of the residential buildings and the community center. They were not as efficient as they are supposed to be and now they are. So, energy production and hot water production are up by 32%. Guess I didn't do too bad, did I, honey?"

Frank leaned in and gave her a big kiss and said, "Babe, I am always proud of everything you do."

"Nice recovery, dear, very nice," Helen smirked.

"It's all true, babe," Frank said with his most sincere look.

"You always were a silver-tongued devil."

Shannon tossed in, "Do I have to get you two a room?"

Everyone started laughing.

Heather remarked, "It still is nice to see two people who have been married, as long as you two have, still flirting with each other."

"Thank you for the compliment," Helen said with a gentle, motherly look.

"Let's go eat. I'm starving," Frank announced.

They entered the community center and were joined by Sean after he had cleaned up. Shannon sniffed all around him before passing judgement that he was fit to be around other decent smelling humans. The fare was a light supper of sandwiches, potato salad, bean salad and iced tea. When they were through eating, Heather went around and personally thanked everyone that she had interacted with, including the cooks who had provided such wonderful fare.

When they had entered the vehicle for the ride home, Heather remarked that other than her first day in a cadaver lab in med school, she had never been more impressed than she had with the village of Coulter. The amount of thought, planning, construction, and overall leadership that had been invested in Coulter was awe-inspiring.

She looked at Sean and said, "The two of you have done

something spectacular, and not for praise or profit. Thank you for allowing me to see it and contribute to it in some small fashion. I hope this won't be the only time I am invited out here to help out."

"Thank you for the compliment, but you need to tell that to J.T., since most of this was his idea, his baby," Sean remarked.

"When he wakes up, I will be sure to tell him what I think," Heather said. "I also want to thank all of you. You did not have to include me this weekend, and this has been one of the best weekends I have had in many years. So, again, thank you all." Shen then exited the vehicle, gave everyone a hug, kissed Sean, Helen and Frank on the cheek, turned and walked in to her condo.

Helen said, "I hope that boy is smart enough to marry her."

"You never know, dear," Frank murmured.

Heather entered her condo, put the keys on the island in the kitchen, opened the fridge and took out an opened bottle of Moscato. She poured herself a full glass and took a big swallow. She headed into the bedroom, where she set the glass on the dresser and began shucking out of her clothes. She threw all the smelly, dirty clothes in the hamper, grabbed the glass of wine, and took a smaller swallow this time before heading into the bathroom.

CHAPTER TEN

The next morning, as Heather got ready for the day, she found herself comparing her life to the one at Coulter. Drinking her cup of coffee, she remembered the one she had at Coulter and made a mental note to get some chicory from the store. Stepping out of her condo, she set the automatic controls for the hospital and hit the engage button, all the while appreciating the difference technology made to living.

As she drove down to the hospital, she went through the to-do list in her head. First thing on her list was to coordinate the MRI for Sara, the woman she had evaluated for Doc Horner in Coulter. She pushed a dashboard button and said, "Doc Horner," and the phone automatically dialed the number. She got voice mail so she left a message basically telling him that she was going to make an appointment for Sara's MRI on Wednesday, late afternoon and that she would let him know exactly what time, later on that day.

Heather arrived at the hospital a few minutes later,

entering the same door, walking down the same hallway that still had the same smells of cleaners and disinfectants. This time she just briefly stopped by the nursing station at SFU and didn't see anyone, so she continued on, down the hallway, around the corner and in to the doctors' Lounge. She swiped her card and stuck her head in trying to see if Dr. Li was in and there she was at her usual table, books and charts spread all over.

"Hey Li, how was your weekend? Any excitement with Colonel Coulter?" she asked.

Li looked up, a smile forming on her face. "Hey Heather! I should be asking you that. How was Coulter?"

"It was absolutely amazing. The people were wonderful, truly the salt of the earth. The sophistication that has gone into Coulter is actually unbelievable. J.T. has taken a couple of ramshackle cabins and a handful of hillbilly survivalists and built a functioning, self-sufficient village that is, for the most part, completely green and it has been done with junk from the dumps of two different domes. They produce enough food to feed everyone, live off wild game, killed by the sniper team under J.T.'s command. It is amazing how coordinated every-thing is, from commerce to food production and even waste management."

"Sounds interesting," Li responded.

"So, how's the Colonel doing?" Heather asked.

"I just finished looking in on his paperwork and he is above the curve on all parameters."

"What about the III?"

"That is the most amazing part. It should be done by this evening. It's like his brain is a huge sponge. He just sucks the info in, and he has almost completed all the information compiled."

"Well, I need to get in touch with his mother and see if she has another file to download, and some insight as to what he is looking into, so that we could prepare another file for importation as soon as she can," Heather said.

She reached into her pocket and pulled out a phone and said, "Helen Coulter."

The phone rang for a full minute before Heather heard Helen's voice.

"Helen? Heather here. No, J.T. is fine. Can you put me on speakerphone? OK. Hey guys! OK, here is an update. Currently, J.T. is doing great. His progress is above predicted values. The reason I am calling is that as far as the III is concerned, his brain has completely sucked in all the other information we had for impartation, which leads to the reason for my call. He still has a while in the tank, so we need to get another tape full of info that we can start on an impartation. Do you recall what his interests are and where his thought processes are heading to? If so, can the family get on the stick and produce another information tape for impartation? Get as much info, ancillary or directly, related to his fields of study. His brain is sucking up information faster than we can input it. We would like to take advantage of this phenomenon. This has huge implications, but I will tell you this, we had no idea that the human brain would respond in the fashion that J.T.'s brain has reacted."

"It opens up a whole new area of knowledge concerning education. And raises questions about education that will take years to figure out and exploit. So, the quicker ya'll can get me the info to implant, the sooner we can hook it up to J.T. The rate of absorption has been well beyond anything we could have imagined. This also means that the estimated tank rehab schedule has been scrapped and we will be adjusting our expectations downward and I can say right now that if things continue at the pace and rate they are currently moving, J.T. will be out of the tank at the end of the second week or the beginning of the third week."

"Yes, I am pleased with this. I did have a wonderful time this weekend. It was great to spend it with your family and I want to thank you again for including me. I can't tell you how much I appreciate being included. I have to go, I'm going to be looking in on J.T. in a couple of minutes. Yes, I will keep ya'll informed. Talk to ya'll later. Bye." With that she hung up and looked at Li.

"Wanna come with me to the tank room?" Heather asked.

"I've already been, so you go ahead," Li replied.

"OK then, I will see you Wednesday morning right here," Heather replied and walked out of the lounge and down the hall to the tank room.

She entered, staring at the tank and J.T. in the rehab frame, floating in the liquid. It was a moving experience. All in all, things looked good. She watched the frame moving and being able to see his muscles contracting and relaxing as the frame moved. Heather made her way over to the monitoring station. She asked the staff for J.T.'s chart. After she received the chart, she had a seat and began perusing it. Every parameter had exceeded norms in a positive fashion. In all her years in medicine, she had never seen a chart with such positive parameters this shortly after such a major injury and with such extensive surgical intervention and correction. Heather had a fleeting thought. *Are we creating some kind of super-brained intellectual monstrosity here? Are there any limits to the amount of information this man can absorb? Are we obligated to see how far we can take this? What do we do if we take it too far?*

"I will stop back tomorrow," she told the attendant as she handed back his chart.

She opened her purse, looking for the note the nurse had given her. When she found it, as she stopped at the first phone available and dialed the number.

"This is Dr. Dunkirk. I would like to see Dr. McKnight for a consultation. No, it is not an emergency. 3:30 this afternoon would be fine. Thank you."

The rest of the day went by with blinding speed, although, truth be told, she could remember very little of it at the end of the day.

Later that afternoon, she went for her consultation.

"Heather Dunkirk," the clinical assistant called from the doorway of the entrance back in to the office area.

She was shown to Dr. McKnight's office where she took a seat across a very ornate walnut desk. Moments later, Dr. McKnight walked through the door. She was a short, somewhat overweight woman in her early 50s, radiating a "you can tell me anything" air of confidence and knowledge. She took a long-practiced glance at Heather, extended her hand, and warmly shook it.

"It is very nice to meet you. Your reputation precedes you," she said.

"Excuse me?" Heather responded.

"You just completed a most astounding surgery, probably the greatest surgery ever done at this facility. And on the

Dome's most eligible male, I might add. It is the talk of the entire facility," she continued.

"I had no idea it was that well known," Heather replied.

"Oh yes, and the fact that there were six members of the Council on that train that the DSF unit protected was even more noteworthy. The talk is that there will be a promotion and a number of medals due him for his actions. Like I said, he is very high on the desirable list, but let's get down to business. What brings you in to see me?" she questioned.

"The charge nurse of SFU and I were talking, and she told me about coming to you for assistance concerning her love life," Heather said.

"Yes, I remember Emma. Her vagina was too small for the size of her husband's penis, and we did a course of pessary introductions to enlarge and stretch her to accommodate his size."

"That is correct," Heather replied.

"And, am I to assume you find yourself in the same situation?" she asked.

"Yes, I am," Heather replied.

"How big is your partner's member?"

"A little over twelve inches by seven inches around."

"Oh my, I can understand your situation. Have you had sex before?"

"Certainly."

"When was the last time?"

"Two years ago."

"And what size was the largest partner you have ever been with?"

"A little over 7 inches, probably closer to eight."

"How long ago?"

"Eight or nine years ago."

"Okay, let's head into the exam room to take a look."

After the exam was done, Dr. McKnight told Heather to get dressed and she would be right back. Ten minutes later, she returned, pushing a cart in front of her.

"Here are the pessaries you will use. Start with number one and if there is no discomfort in three days, move to number two. Use discomfort as a guide to increase to the next size every three days. Do not go without having a pessary in place all the time. If you start your period, use a pad and not tampon, but do not stop using the pessaries. If you have discomfort, at the three-day point, go another two days before increasing to the next size. I will see you in six weeks. The fact that you are not particularly sexually active is going to make this take a little longer than you would like, but I can't make it go any faster. Good luck with the Colonel."

"I don't know what you are referring to," Heather replied, somewhat indignantly.

"It's okay dear, I can keep a secret," the doctor replied.

Heather could feel the blush come over her face.

"Let me know if you need anything. You know where to find me," said the doctor as she moved to the next exam room.

I hope that everyone in the world doesn't know about this. I would be so embarrassed, she thought. Heather pushed the thought from her mind and headed back down to the tank room. She decided that she should talk to Helen about the III and see where she was in acquiring the information to be imputed.

As she entered the tank room, she stared at the body, suspended in the solution, wondering what he was thinking about, if anything. She made a mental note to herself to remember to ask. She walked over to the monitoring desk, pulled his chart, and scanned the notes and other data. Things were going like a fine Swiss watch, so she picked up the phone and called Helen. Helen answered on the fourth ring, a little out of breath.

"Hi Heather," she said, slightly out of breath. "I was just down in the basement looking at all the books he has stored. I think J.T. is really studying either how to design a spacecraft or to go into space himself. He has the strangest assortment of books down there. Things I never knew he had any interest in, Ancient Aliens and the like. Lost civilizations like Atlantis, cultures like the ancient Sumerians and Indians, not the American kind, the eastern ones."

"Are you ready for us to add to his download schedule yet?" Heather asked.

"I have an appointment at the archeology section of the university tomorrow. I want to see if there is anything new that J.T. has not had the time or opportunity to go over. I should have something for you late tomorrow," Helen speculated.

Heather then asked, "Do you think that perhaps the complete medical school curriculum, including genetics and genetic engineering, and maybe even some of the latest literature on nanotechnology might interest him?"

"That is a splendid idea!" Helen exclaimed. "He could have all the knowledge of a physician without having to go through all the rotations and residencies. I'm sure he would appreciate having that knowledge base to draw on. Besides, he's not going to practice medicine. It's just a knowledge base."

"The more I think about it, the more he would make a pretty good doctor," Heather offered.

"Let's face it dear, J.T. will be great at anything he takes a shine to," Helen said.

"You're probably right about that. I just finished checking on him and, as per his usual, he is ahead of the curve in everything we checked. Why don't you stop by tomorrow afternoon, between three and four and I will buy you a cup of coffee. I'd like to pick your brain a bit."

"I'd love to, dear, 3:30pm tomorrow. I'll be there, not with bells on, but I will show up. Do you want me to bring along the old guy or is this just a girls' thing?" she asked.

"Why don't we keep it a girls' thing," Heather said.

"Sounds lovely, dear. See you then. Bye," and then she left.

Heather closed his chart and made her way out of the hospital to the educational building, looking for one of her favorite professors, Dr. Samuel T. Kendricks, Professor Emeritus of the medical school. After a rather extensive search, she found him coming out of the cadaver lab.

"Dr. Dunkirk, how wonderful to see my favorite student," he said effusively. "I heard about the surgeries on Colonel Coulter. From all accounts, it was a brilliant piece of surgery, although, knowing you, I would have expected nothing less."

"Thank you for the praise, but I have to admit it was a group effort."

"With you at the helm, my dear girl. But enough of all that, what can I do for you?"

"If you can spare a few minutes, I have something I would like to get your opinion on, as I do value it more than most of the other instructors."

"Flattery, my dear, will get you anywhere you want to go, so shall we adjourn to my office where we can speak in private as well as be comfortable? When you reach my age, comfort is a paramount consideration," he waxed philosophical.

"You are not that old, Dr. Kendrick."

"Sam, please. We have known each other long enough to not stand on formality. I will be ninety-three in three weeks. Never thought I would live to be this old, but it has been a grand and wondrous journey. Now, what can I do for you?"

"I do not know if you are aware, but when we were operating on the Colonel, we asked and were granted permission to enroll him in a study for Intracranial Information Implantation. He, the Colonel, was currently working on three different PhDs at the same time. So, we went to his professors and asked them to give us all of the projected course work necessary for him to take the final exams in all three areas. They complied and provided us with all the coursework. This has been completely input and absorbed by the subject. This was supposed to be done over a four-week period, but the subject has absorbed all of this information in four days, not weeks. Since it is obvious that this is a unique individual, I have discussed with his parents as next of kin about adding more information in subjects he has not previously studied. Specifically, medical school and all of its areas of instruction and, to change intellectual gears, nanotechnology. Any thoughts?" she asked.

"Well, the most obvious one is, what about the rights of the subject? You are going to be implanting information that personally he may not want in his brain. How would you remove it if he wakes up and finds out this information has been added without his consent?"

He continued, "Secondly, what is he going to do with that information? If he learns how to do a physical exam, he would be qualified to take the boards and become a Physician? This would be without the benefit of the instruction and guidance of members of the medical profession. I am sure there are other points. At my age they do not spring to the fore with the rapidity of my younger years."

"To take a different tack, you, through no ideas of your own, have been given a chance to expand our knowledge of how we learn and how we can improve the use of a larger portion of our brains. My advice to you is to be sure that you have as many parameters documented so that they can be reproduced by many other scientists; expanded on by even more innovative scientists. So that others may take your work, and run with it, to who knows where the end point may or will reside.

"You are at the entrance to one of the most inspiring times of mankind and science. God bless you for opening the door. Try to make the road a little easier for those that will follow. I am so proud of you," he said with a quaver in his voice.

Heather noted that he had a tiny tear in his left eye. *What is with all these men crying?* she wondered. *Never have I seen so many men tear up. Hope they are not all going emotional on me, don't know as I could take that.*

She walked around his desk and gave him a daughterly kiss on his cheek and a hug. "We need to have dinner soon. Perhaps you would be up going out to Coulter in the fall. This is a fascinating village of people living by themselves, living off the land with minimal technology. They have this older PA that has taken it upon himself to provide all of them the healthcare that they need. He has been doing this for fifteen years, actually practicing for forty-five years total and surprisingly, they all are healthy."

"Really?"

"Yes. Those that need more sophisticated healthcare, he arranges it through the appropriate physician here in the hospital. In fact, he just presented two cases to me, both well thought out and managed. I would love to have you meet him. Currently, he is the chief medic for the DSF unit 17 and was responsible for keeping my patient alive until he could get medevac'd out. I am sure he would love to meet you and show you what he has done in Coulter."

"Maybe so, my dear. Perhaps when you are done with your current situation, something could be arranged," he said noncommittally.

"I will hold you to that, Sam," Heather said in response to his lack of commitment. "You have given me some things to think about and I would appreciate it, if in the next four weeks, you think of anything that I should be made aware of or need to do, something with or to the current situation, you would contact me ASAP."

"Of course, my dear. I shall contact you straight off if I think of anything significant. You, of course, will contact me about a dinner date. I shouldn't say this, but try not to wait too long. One never knows how long people my age will remain upright, if you catch my meaning."

There was a lightheartedness to his tone at the last comment.

"I understand perfectly," she replied, leaning over to bestow another daughterly kiss on his cheek. "Be well, Sam, I still need to pick that incredible brain of yours."

"I shall do my very best, my dear, but we both know I really have no say in the matter, now do I?"

"Well then, watch yourself crossing the street and try not to play in the middle of the highway," she joked. Both had a little chuckle over the thought as Heather left his office. She did wonder if she was ever going to see him in any spot other than a coffin.

She headed back to the tank room for one last check of J.T.'s status, then out to the car to head home.

While she was on the road, she decided to contact Sean and see if there was anything he had to contribute. She touched a button on the dashboard and said,

"Call Sean McCann."

Three rings later, she heard, "Command Sergeant Major McCann, how may I help you?"

"Sean, this is Heather Dunkirk. I have a couple of questions I need to discuss with you, if you have a minute."

"Certainly Doc, Is J.T. ok?"

"He's fine. What I would like to know is if the two of you ever discussed what you would be doing if you were not in DSF or after you leave the DSF? You know, shooting the breeze over a couple of beers type conversation," she asked.

Sean took a couple of seconds to answer, then said, "I just had to move to a more private area to talk. The only thing I can recall that he talked about was designing a spacecraft and going to a different planet in it. He got really pumped up over it. I mean, he rarely gets all worked up over any subject, but this one really got him going," Sean said.

"Anything in particular that he said that makes you think he had done any research or studying on?" Heather asked.

"Suspended animation/hibernation were the biggies, I guess. He always said that until we could travel at light speed or faster, we would have to take two or three crews along and change them off every couple of years, using suspended animation or hibernation. That way everyone would age at the same rate," he said.

"Anything else?" Heather asked.

"We never really spent that much time talking about stuff like that. I may be his brother-in-law, but I was still subordinate to him in the other areas of our lives. Guess he didn't want me thinking that he was a little off upstairs. That would really have gotten in the way of DSF stuff, ya know?"

"Well, I can understand that, especially when you have to believe everything he tells you, for missions that are being planned, or you could end up dead and if not you, then some or all of your men," Heather said. "Anyway, thanks, that has been a great help and it just may allow him to follow his dream if things go as planned. I'll talk to you later when I have something more concrete to tell you." With that, she hung up.

Heather spent the rest of the day and well into the evening adding volumes of information into the III Database that was running into J.T.'s brain. She also decided to add quite a few different language bases, including Aztec, Inca, Mayan, Sumerian, three different ancient forms of Arabic, ancient and modern Egyptian, Latin, ancient Greek, Indian both ancient and modern, Japanese, both ancient and modern as well as Thai, and both ancient and modern Chinese.

Heather added a number of advanced archeological texts on hieroglyphics of Egypt, South American ancient Indian, Central American ancient Indian cultures, as well as middle Eastern cultures. She was quite proud of her work and knew that with this knowledge base, he could read and interpret texts as well as tomb writings where there were references to ancient space travel. Tomorrow, she would make arrangements with all the professors that would be involved, to come to the hospital and give J.T. tests after he was removed from the tank and brought out of his coma. The amount of absorbed information could be empirically tested, and another round of implantation could be accomplished before he was allowed to be discharged from the hospital.

Tomorrow, Doc Horner was supposed to be bringing Sarah for her MRI and she had some reading she needed to accomplish before any of that took place. So as soon as she got home, she fixed herself a light supper, ate, then slipped into her favorite jammies. She got comfortably propped up on her bed and began reading. Three and a half hours later, she shut off her computer, set the alarm and went to sleep, glad she had done her research. She had found an orthopedic surgeon in the U.K. that was addressing AVN of the femoral head, with stem cell injections. In the morning, she would see if she could actually speak with him and obtain a consultation when the MRI films were available. All in all, this week was turning out quite positively.

CHAPTER
ELEVEN

The next day, as soon as she arrived at the hospital, she made her way to the tank room, reviewed J.T.'s chart, made a couple of notes, and added in the data files for implantation. By the time she took a breath, it was 1115 and there was a page from radiology. Sarah and Doc were waiting.

Sarah had already had her MRI done, and they were waiting to go over the results. Heather stopped at the Radiology information desk, picked up the copy of the study and headed to conference room nine, where Sara was anxiously awaiting the results.

"Good morning, Sarah, Doc, I trust I haven't kept you waiting too long, have I?" she asked, not really expecting an answer.

Doc was the first to speak and offered that they had only been waiting maybe ten minutes at the most.

"We had been told that we were going to have to wait to be worked into the schedule, but apparently, when the check-in person saw that Sarah was your patient, she was moved to the head of the line. You must have some kind of clout here, Doctor," he opined.

"Well, I don't know about all of that." Heather blushed. She put the first film up on the view box and the second on the next and so on until all five films were hanging. That made the room a lot darker, so she had to wait for her eyes to adjust.

"Sarah, come over here where you can see real closely, and I will explain what's on these films."

Thirty-five minutes later, Heather asked Sarah and Doc if either of them had any questions. They both replied that she had gone over everything very thoroughly. Heather then sprang the news on them.

"There is an orthopedic surgeon in the U.K. that has started treating this condition without surgery. I have a called him to discuss this case, but it won't be until much later today due to the time difference. Doc, I will call you personally and tell you what's up and you can give Sara the news yourself. We can then make plans to fix this issue one way or another. I hope that this is satisfactory," she said.

Sarah got up out of her chair and limped over to Heather and gave her a very intense hug and a soft-spoken *thank you* in her ear. "I absolutely dreaded walking funny, hurting and not bein' able to satisfy my man for the rest of my life."

"You are very welcome. This is why I got into medicine, to help people like you," Heather whispered back.

They all got up together and exited the conference room.

The rest of the day went by like a blur. The call to the U.K. could not have gone better. Dr. Wilfred Pennington IV said that, from her MRI films, she should be able to have a full recovery without a lot of rehabilitation. He was quite profuse in thanking Heather, because the treatment had not gained wide acceptance in the U.K. or the continent. He also asked permission if she could forward the patient's chart so he could use the info in his next publication, due out in eight months. Heather said she would be happy to as long as she got mentioned and sent an autographed copy of the paper, to which he immediately agreed. He said he would fax her the formula for calculating the amount of stem cells to be injected and other guidelines about repeated injections, dos and don'ts and a list of things to watch for. Heather thanked him profusely, gave him a fax number, and then signed off.

She then called Doc with the good news and told him to ask Sarah when she would like to get it done. Doc thanked again for her help and asked if she had any suggestions for a procedural date and Heather thought about it for a minute and suggested a Tuesday, two weeks down the road. That was the scheduled date for the Colonel's removal from the tank. Then she could be here to say hey and then be able to tell everybody in the village that she had seen and personally spoken with him. Doc said he thought that was a great idea and would let her know Sarah's answer in the next day or two.

—————

The rest of the day was pretty uneventful right up until there was a knock, on Heather's office door and before she was able to get up, come around and open the door, in walked a man she was unfamiliar with.

"Can I help you?" she questioned.

"David Blake, with the Dome Informer. Is it true that Lt. Colonel Coulter is a patient of yours?" The tone was inappropriate and offensive to Heather.

"Who is or is not my patient, is no business of yours. You may leave or I will call security. Get out now!!!" She had raised her voice more than she had intended, but in her mind, he was invading her privacy and trying to get her to betray her doctor-patient confidentiality oath. Blake made no move to leave. She reached over and grabbed the phone.

"Security, I have an unwanted intruder in my office. White male mid 30s, about 5'10' 165, plaid shirt, white and blue, and a black windbreaker. I have told him to leave but he refuses. Please send Mr. Johansen ASAP."

"Hey lady, you can't stop the press. People have a right to know," he pontificated.

"No, they do not have a right to know about anyone's personal health. I have received no authorization to make public anyone's private health information." She turned towards the door and was immediately relieved to see Skip standing there, listening to her tirade.

Skip entered and immediately got in Blake's face. "Sir, do you want to leave of your own volition, or after the emergency room doctor treats your injuries and releases you?"

The tone of Skip's voice was more menacing than Heather had ever witnessed.

"You can't stop my investigation. I am a member of the press and I have a right to search out the truth," he shouted.

"Sir, you are trespassing on hospital property and have been requested to leave. I have given you two choices; I am fine with either one. If you should choose the second option by default, I will personally put you through the wall on the way to fix your broken bones and I will enjoy every moment of your pain." Skip was 6" from Blake's face as he said this.

"You wouldn't dare. I'll sue," he threatened. Before he could finish the next part of his statement, Skip had grabbed his right hand, twisted and bent it into a classic Aikido pain compliance hold, designed to get a perpetrator do exactly what he is commanded to do. If they did not comply bones could end up broken.

Skip kept applying more pressure. He took his left hand and grabbed the collar of Blake's jacket and shirt and started shoving him out the door, which he managed to hit his head on the door frame twice in quick succession. The final impact split his eyebrow open, and the blood flowed freely down the side of his face and into his eye.

"The more you resist, the worse things are going to get," Skip whispered. "Just keep walking down the hall and stop resisting. If you don't, this hold will break your wrist and hand, I guarantee you." Skip stated and reinforced with a little added force, applied to the wrist. This elicited a loud yelp of pain, immediately followed by a series of *"OK, OK, OK."*

Skip continued to direct him down the hall, turning as needed, pausing to release his collar so he could open the door to the treatment area of the ER. He maintained control of Blake until he got to a treatment table. He then sat Blake down on the table and told him he was going let him loose but if he acted out, all bets were off about him getting hurt further.

"If you think I am kidding, please feel free to try something. I have been pretty reasonable and far gentler with you than I am predisposed to. I like and respect Dr. Dunkirk and I would take it really personally if she gets harassed by you. Do you understand? Because I would be happy to repeat myself, explain my position so you are crystal clear on how things are going to go! I expect an answer."

"I understand," Blake replied. "Oh, just so you know, I used to be with DSF 17, and I still have a lot of comrades on active duty, so if you think you can harass her off the hospital property, you do so at your own risk because I can guarantee you, they will never find your body. Understand me?"

"I hear you," Blake replied.

"You can claim I threatened you, but again, you will never make it to any kind of court date, and I will deny that I ever said this until the day I die, which will be long after you are gone, dirtball."

"Skip, what's up?" the ER doc asked.

"This individual was trespassing and when given a choice to leave on his own or be removed, he chose to be removed. Unfortunately, he was injured during the process, something he was warned of but obviously didn't really think would happen," Skip replied.

The doctor looked at Blake and said, "You obviously did not know who you were dealing with. Although I do have to say, Skip took it easy on you. Usually, others that have chosen poorly leave with one or two casts, and a new found appreciation of choosing better."

"You can wait outside; I think Mr. Blake has a keen understanding of what will happen if he acts out. Don't you?"

"Yes, I understand."

"Good, then we can get started. Are you allergic to anything?"

The ER Doctor called Skip when he was done and Skip walked into the treatment bay, ready to escort Mr. Blake off the property.

As they arrived at Blake's car, Skip said, "Remember what I told you. Some of you journalistic assholes think we are just blowing smoke when we make the comments I did. Almost every member of DSF17 detachment feels the same way I do about Dr., Dunkirk. There would be an all-out fight to be your executioner, believe me. None of the members of the detachment make promises they can't or won't carry out. Neither do I. Remember that. Now get off our property. Next time I hear about you being here without having need for our services, you will."

Skip made his way back to Heather's office, where he found her going through a stack of papers.

"You were a little hard on him, weren't you?" Heather asked as Skip entered.

"Have to. Most people like that don't learn when you ask nicely. You just saw that, didn't you?" Skip asked. "Speaking about that, if you have any issues with Mr. Blake, I need to have you contact me immediately. Do you understand? I'm serious. This guy is weird, and that makes him dangerous."

"Okay, I promise to let you know if anything happens," Heather promised.

"I hope you are not trying to placate me. You could end up badly hurt, even to the point that you would not be able to continue practicing as a doctor, should you choose not to take me seriously," Skip warned.

"I believe everything you say and will be extra careful in looking out for my wellbeing," she replied.

Internally, Skip was not convinced of her honesty. Mentally, he began to make plans to ensure her safety and wellbeing.

The next ten days went by rapidly, with nothing out of the ordinary occurring. Heather had seriously pondered her next move with reference to III and decided to rerun all the data tapes already implanted, just to make sure that J.T. absorbed as much of the information as he could. She went to the tank room and logged on, typed in the instructions to the computer, hit enter and then signed out. She returned to her office and found a message from Doc Horner confirming that Sarah had agreed to delaying the procedure until the day before J.T. was brought out of the coma and rehab frame.

He's finally getting out of the tank, and we will be able to see how much progress he has made with healing and III, she thought. She noticed that those thoughts caused her to flush and become a little aroused. She had managed to put those thoughts to the back of her mind, so they would not interfere with her care, but now they were encroaching more and more into her thoughts. A moment later, she picked up the phone and started calling all the professors she would need for the testing that would start two days after removal from the tank. She knew J.T. would fight her on the starting point of the testing, sure that he had recovered from any residuals of the coma, but she had prepared her arguments supporting her decision, and, well, if he didn't like it, he could fire her.

She made a mental note to check with Li about continued III and whether it could be accomplished without being in the tank. It might be a good idea to get him out of the hospital to have him go through three days of his daily workout to see if he had lost anything; stamina, coordination, both body and hand-eye. If he needed any further implantation, Heather wondered if it would still work if he was not immersed or in a coma. *Better ask her now so we know one way or the other*. Besides, it would add a new variable to the study by changing some of the parameters. That would make for a better all-around study and if the environment was not a factor, then the procedure would be available for a larger number of people that needed it. She could have J.T. stay at her place so she could monitor things and be available if something went wrong. With that thought, she picked up the phone and called Li.

Li answered on the fourth ring, and they immediately dove into the conversation.

"I didn't realize that it had been two and a half weeks already," Li commented. "To tell you the truth, I got so busy that I never went to check on him. I just figured that you would be on top of things, what with the goo-goo eyes you were making around him." Li commented.

"Why does everyone say that?" Heather asked.

"Because it is true, Heather, it is obvious to everyone watching that you find him attractive. There's nothing wrong with that. I find him quite attractive, he's a very desirable man, but, sad to say, I am already committed, spoken for and very happy, so I can appreciate his qualities without jeopardizing my objectivity or relationship with my husband. So, what did you want to discuss?" she asked.

Heather went over all her thoughts and finished by saying, "So, what do you think?"

"Very interesting ideas. You may be on to something about changing the environment. As of right now, there is no data, and I mean no data about the effects of a medically induced coma on brain function or information learning, retention or application. It would be great to be able to prove, one way or the other, immersion and the use of an induced coma. I will re-read all the available info on III and see if there is anything that I missed the last time I went through the papers," Li said.

"Oh, I forgot to tell you I added a bunch of stuff to the data flow when I noticed that his brain was literally sucking up every bit of data at a phenomenal rate. I have also restarted the data stream and it should be done about thirty hours before we bring him up and out of the coma."

"What type of data did you introduce?" Li asked.

"Nine languages, reading, and interpreting hieroglyphics and a number of archeological textbooks on ancient cultures and civilizations," Heather replied.

"That's amazing! And you said his brain just sucked it up as fast as it could be transmitted?" Li said incredulously.

"It was like watching a thirsty horse sucking up water. I have never seen anything like it," Heather said.

"Like I just said, this is one impressive hunk. You have great taste, girlfriend!"

With that, Heather blushed a very bright shade of red.

"So, next Thursday is the big day, right?" Li asked.

"Yes, next Thursday is the day. I have a procedure on a patient Doc Horner referred to. She's got a traumatic AVN of the hip. I consulted an ortho guy in the U.K and I am looking forward to trying it. If it works, it will revolutionize treatment for AVNs. We'll do J.T. after that procedure, which is scheduled for 9 a.m. So, I would guess somewhere around 10:00-10:30a.m.," Heather said.

"Ok, let me make a scheduling note so I won't miss it," Li replied. "I gotta run, so I'll see you then.'

The rest of the week and the weekend seemed to zip by, and the next time Heather had a moment to think was in the car, Monday morning, on her way to work. She scheduled a meeting with the nursing staff on the unit and then walked down the corridor to the tank room, where she checked the chart, then asked the charge nurse to round up the rest of the staff on the day shift for an impromptu meeting.

Heather started by informing the staff about plans to wake J.T. She went over the procedure and how it was going to go, what problems might be encountered, and how they were going to be handled. She went over the medications they needed to have on hand and when they may or may not be needed. She made sure that they had a gurney on hand that could handle J.T.'s size. She made sure they understood that the connection to the data port for the III was to remain intact and in place until he was on the gurney, then they would uncouple the leads, and after that, the whole head helmet. She thanked everyone for a fine job and told them that she would be present after the scheduled procedure that should be over between 10:00 and 10:30 a.m.

She left the tank area and headed back to her office. When she arrived, she got herself a cup of coffee, sat down at her desk, put her feet up and rested for a few minutes, surprised about how tired but somehow excited she was. Maybe because she was close to finding out how all her hard work had turned out and how J.T. was doing. Heather decided she needed to talk to the family to update them and bring them in on the plan.

"Hello."

"Hey Helen, it's Heather. I have decided to bring J.T. out of the tank on Thursday morning. Around 10:30 is when we would start. It is going to be four hours before he is going to be awake enough to talk. So maybe it would be best to come around 2 p.m. I just checked in on him about an hour and a half ago and everything was great. I forgot to tell you guys, I added about fourteen total new programs to his data stream. A bunch of languages, archeology, hieroglyphic interpretation. I also ran his data input stream a second time from start to finish. I am really excited to see how things turn out."

"Languages?" Helen queried.

"Yes, languages and archeology," Heather said. "You got him ancient aliens because they had information about space flight and other planets. They happen to be in a number of different languages, both ancient and current, hieroglyphics and that falls under the archeological umbrella and ancient cultures, again under archeological auspices. Now he will be able to delve in to these areas without having to use anyone else, to come up with his own thoughts. You know, Sean told me that J.T. wants to build a spaceship and go to another planet and that this was something he intended to pursue when he retired from the unit," Heather explained. "Since he was absorbing the information at an unbelievable rate, I thought I would give him more tools to accomplish his dream. Look what he did with Coulter. He did all that because he read things and knew how to implement his ideas into something that worked and benefited people."

"Number one, neither of us knew anything about designing a spaceship. Two, flying to another planet, Three, that he was actually going to do this when he retired from the Unit and four, that you are in love with him, without ever going out a date with him," Helen said. "Don't tell me you aren't in love. Women know these things."

"Is it that obvious?" Heather asked.

"I've known it since Coulter and, speaking for the entire family, we couldn't be happier. You are the first woman that is worthy of a man like him. You are intelligent, talented, caring, observant, sensitive, dedicated, as well as being very attractive. I am sure that he will return the feelings," Helen finished her discussion.

"I think we will be there around noon. You know how he is with following the norms for other people."

"You are right about that," Heather replied. "I'll look forward to seeing you at noon on Thursday. Bye."

She hung up, sat back and pondered Helen's point about falling in love without ever being on a date. She had always thought that "Love at first sight" was cliché but she couldn't argue the point honestly. *Well in two and a half days, we will see how things pan out,* she thought.

Heather made a couple of phone calls to answer a couple of messages, went over some reports, finished dictating a discharge summary from her last surgery, closed up her desk and left the office.

When she got home, she did not even remember walking down the hall, getting in her car and driving home. *Where was my head at?* She sat down at the desk in her den and reviewed her day planner, noting that she had nothing to do at the hospital on either Tuesday or Wednesday, so she made a decision right then and called the hospital and told them she would not be in for a couple of days.

She then called the Coulters and asked Helen if she would like to go to lunch the next day setting the time for 11:30 at Sabatini's on Main St. Helen was a little surprised, but quite eager for a girls' get together. She asked if Shannon could come with and was genuinely happy when Heather enthusiastically agreed and begged her to be sure she came. Heather found herself floating through the rest of the day. Done with that, she whipped up some spaghetti and meatballs and even made a small amount of garlic bread. She pulled the cork on a bottle of a dry, red wine, poured herself a tall glass, went in to the living room and had a seat. She flipped on the video unit, picked something mindless, leaned back and began eating, all the while her mind was going 200mph.

Racing thoughts jumped from what she was going to wear tomorrow to how she was going to handle waking J.T., up and what was going to become of that. Had she found the one man that was her soulmate? He was principled, intelligent, unwavering, very attractive, not easily intimidated, opinionated, thoughtful, thorough, sensitive and honest. Plus, he could cook and he had a vision of what and where he wanted to be in the future. The question was, where was Heather's place in this scheme? Would she be an active partner or was she just going to be window dressing, along for the ride? Heather vowed, within herself, that there was no way in hell she was going to be window dressing. She was a prize, not a trophy, being his wife not withstanding should have no bearing. She was intelligent, educated, and talented. Regardless, she was going to be an integral, active partner, finding ways to contribute to J.T's dreams. *Now, what do I wear tomorrow?* She had a brand new pair of jeans that would go great with the cashmere sweater she had gotten from her mother a couple of Christmases ago. She loved the feel of cashmere against her bare skin. Heather had long denied herself little feel-good things during med school and residency. Now that she was out in the real world, she had begun allowing herself some of "life's little pleasures", such as her hair products, satin underthings and cashmere sweaters.

The rest of her stuff was good quality but not the high-end stuff. Worked fine for her and was not nearly as expensive. She was so looking forward to lunchtime tomorrow. She had not had a chance to actually bond with the Coulter womenfolk when they were out at Coulter. Tomorrow was going to be a huge, glorious day and she could hardly wait. With that she cleaned up the kitchen and headed to bed. She slipped beneath the covers and was out within forty-five seconds.

She had set the alarm for the usual time. She would get up and cursed out loud for forgetting to reset it for her day off. There was a good point to this. She could hit the off button and go back to sleep. She rolled and immediately returned to sleep. She loved her sleep like she loved a great medium rare filet or a rich, gooey dessert. She woke precisely at 9:30 am, enough time to take a luxurious bubble bath, spend a little extra time on her hair and make-up. She slipped into the cashmere sweater, relishing the texture on her skin. The jeans she had decided on was pretty tight and it did take a little extra time to wiggle into them, but when they were on, boy did they feel great! A bit on the sexy side, too.

She slid in to her high calf leather boots, grabbed her waist length brown calfskin leather jacket and was out the door. She arrived at the restaurant a few minutes early, giving her time to find a parking space. She checked in and was given a front window table, which worked out perfectly, because she had a great view of the city street and all the passing traffic. She could not remember the last time she had had a chance to people watch. Must have been twelve years ago. She remembered the day her med school professor had given out the assignment.

"You will take a video camera, go to the airport and video passengers. You will pick different subjects, observe them, dictate what you observe and then ask them questions about what you have observed. A superb diagnostician should be able to figure out what a patient's medical state is just by observation. We will then contact the patient and verify your observations," he had said.

"There she is. Heather dear! Don't you look fabulous!" Helen said, with a great deal of sincere enthusiasm.

"My God, you are so hot!" Shannon exclaimed.

"I am not just brains and intelligence, you know. I can clean up pretty good when I need to," Heather said jokingly.

They all had a good chuckle about that. The waiter came and took their order, as the ladies sat down and got comfortable.

Heather started the conversation with, "We never had a chance to talk and get to know each other last weekend out at Coulter and I wanted to get to know you guys. Let me get this out of the way right up front. Helen, you and Frank have created the most amazing man I have ever met. Yes, I am attracted to him and would not be opposed to things going further, but I am not sure of J.T.'s position concerning me."

She went on to go through the whole firing threat and the head butting that they had done before being put in the tank. Helen and Shannon were sitting across the table, sipping wine occasionally, with huge smiles on their faces, nodding their heads occasionally.

Helen was the first to respond. "Heather, all of that was a test and I think you aced it," she said.

"Definitely," Shannon tossed in. "First," Helen continued, "he was trying to see if you had the guts to stand up for yourself. Second, he wanted to see how you think, because how one thinks has always been huge to him. Third, were you kind and sensitive because he was incredibly kind and sensitive? When he comes out of the tank, it will be a big deal. He has opened himself up to you and he wants to see your reaction and whether or not you accept him for who he is because he definitely is not one of those guys you can plan on changing after you get married. What you see is what you get."

Shannon jumped in with, "You are the first woman he has ever introduced us to much less invited out to Coulter."

Helen cut in and said, "Even Frank and I have never been there and, frankly, had never even heard about it, much less talked to J.T. about the project. It is highly significant that he asked us, you and Shannon, all out to Coulter at the same time. I think this was J.T.'s way of telling us that he had finally found a woman that he could share his life with, and he wanted us to meet and get to know each other without him being there, so there was no interference, influence or pressure from him. Hence, we could make up our own minds about you and that would be all on you. You were perfect, and it wasn't forced or fake and we are all so thrilled. We were beginning to think J.T. set his standards so high no one could ever meet them. Then you walked through the door, and viola there she was. Live right there in front of us. We could not be happier!! Amazing how he had to almost get killed to find a mate."

Heather injected, "The only thing that worries me or should I say is a concern, is what my role would be in his life, window dressing or an integral, active partner, because I don't think I can do the window dressing thing."

Shannon responded. "I know my big brother, you are definitely going to be an active integral part of whatever he has planned and believe me, he has something planned. My brother doesn't go to the bathroom without having a plan."

They all broke out in a good-sized laugh, fueled by a couple of large glasses of wine.

"That makes me feel a little more secure," Heather remarked. "Were either of you aware of his other issue with women?"

Both women responded, "No, what are you talking about?"

"Well, I don't want you to say anything to J.T., and I need you to swear to keep this to yourself, do you swear?" Heather asked.

"Of course," was the immediate reaction from both women.

"J.T. is a virgin."

"You are kidding me, for real?" They both responded incredulously.

"Yep. Apparently, he has tried a number of times, but when the women see him undressed, they leave. He is really, really well-endowed like a foot long and big around also."

"That explains a lot of things. It all makes sense now why none of the women he has dated has ever stayed very long. Poor baby, that must be horrible to have that much rejection and no one to talk to about it," Helen said.

"I always thought the girls he dated just didn't measure up, and he ran them off. I feel so bad for him," Shannon said. "Well, Heather, are you going to repeat the same thing with him?"

"No, I have already started treatment so I would be able to accommodate him, if we ever get to that point," she replied.

"Wonder where he got that from, certainly not from Frank," Helen mumbled. That brought a bunch of guffaws from all the women at the table.

They suddenly realized how loud they had become, signaled the waiter to take their order, so things could tone down a bit, but they still had frequent outbursts of stifled laughing.

"I didn't mean to imply that Frank was lacking in that department, because he certainly isn't. He's just not as massive as what you're gonna get." Helen smirked.

"Well, I am more than satisfied with Sean. He is such a bull. Three times Saturday night. Guess he took all that "grandkids" hints you guys were dropping, seriously. It has been almost five years and we ain't getting any younger! I guess I am ready. Sean surely is. He wants to be a dad so bad," Shannon said.

"I wonder how J.T. feels about kids?" Heather remarked.

"You know, I haven't the faintest idea," Helen said.

"Surprisingly, neither do I," Shannon chimed in. "Now don't run right out and ask him the first time you go out with him. Tends to scare guys away."

"No kidding," Heather replied.

The conversation drifted to fashion and travel as they each consumed their meal. Helen had the lobster ravioli; Shannon had the Fettuccini Alfredo with scampi, and Heather had the mushroom risotto. They also managed to polish off two bottles of white wine and had a small buzz on.

"All this talk about making babies. Sean is gonna get lucky when I get home," Shannon said.

"I think I will go home, take a bubble bath, slip into a sensual dressing gown and maybe let Frank have his way with me," opined Helen.

"I'm going home, check-in with the hospital and see how J.T. is, then sit back and relax. Maybe put in a movie, because unlike two women I happen to know, I have no male stud muffin available to service me," Heather lamented.

"Hey, we don't want to hear you moanin' and groanin' over what you don't have, when what you will have is gonna be available soon enough," Shannon remarked.

"That doesn't help me right now, girlfriend," Heather said.

The ladies all got up from their chairs, hugged one another for what seemed like a long time. Helen kissed Heather on her cheek and told her how happy she was that they had had this time to get together, to get to know one another and that this was only the first of many lunches the three of them were going to share. They parted ways at the parking lot and said they would see Heather at noon or so, on Thursday, in the conference room where they had waited on the day of J.T.'s surgery. Heather acknowledged the comment, turned and headed for her car, all the

while thinking how lucky she was that the women of the family had so completely accepted her and she had not even had the first date with their son and brother Amazing, absolutely amazing.

———

Heather dozed as she watched some borderline monotonous daytime movie until she decided she needed to get a good night's sleep. After all, tomorrow was going to be the big day. There was Sarah and her stem cell hip injection and then getting J.T. out of the tank and back into real life. She fluffed the pillow, rolled over, and got comfortable. In a little while, she had drifted to sleep.

CHAPTER
TWELVE

Once she got settled, she went looking for Sarah and found her sitting with Doc. She grabbed a seat and asked if there were any questions. Sara wanted to know if it was going to hurt and when she should expect to see some improvement.

Heather replied, "It won't hurt because you would be unconscious, and it would take three months for the stem cells to regenerate the hip.".

These answers seemed to satisfy her, so Heather had her sign all the necessary forms and told her she would see her in the procedure room, just before she was put to sleep. Doc asked when J.T was coming out of the rehab tank and Heather replied that the process would begin about thirty minutes after Sara was awake, after her procedure. He was welcomed to observe the whole thing firsthand. She also told him that there was a professor of medicine she would like to introduce him to later, maybe even today..

Heather went into the scrub area, changed into her surgical scrubs, slipped on a mask, and began the process of scrubbing in. After she had finished scrubbing and was wiping her arms and hands, she went over to the operating table and spoke to Sara, explaining the procedure and trying to relax her and allay her fears.

The nurse anesthetist stepped up and inserted the anesthetic syringe needle into the IV Tubing and pushed down on the plunger.

"Sarah, please count back from 100."

Sarah got to 97 before she fell asleep. Heather had finished gowning and stepped up to the table to address the team, giving them positioning instructions. These were carried out efficiently, and she was held in position with sandbags. The fluoroscopy unit was wheeled in and positioned. Heather stepped up to the table and began the prep of the area. After the prep was done, the hip was draped, the fluoro unit was positioned so Heather could see the joint.

"This looks horrible," Heather muttered under her breath. The more she looked at it, the more she started considering a total hip reconstruction. She could always come back and redo a hip procedure and besides, she had not discussed a THR with Sarah, so ethically and legally she did not have permission to do anything other than the stem cell injection. She called for the injectable material, inserted the needle into the joint, checked positioning via fluoro and then injected the stem cell solution. She withdrew the needle, cleaned up the injection site, then asked her assistant to help her move the leg through a complete range-of-motion to move the injected solution around so it was evenly distributed.

"Okay, we can wake her up now." Heather removed her gown and exited the OR. She went looking for Doc to give him the news. After she found him, she explained how the joint actually looked and asked him to keep a close eye on her over the next three months. She said would look in on Sara when she had been awake for an hour so she was not foggy-headed and could understand what was going on. She asked Doc if he wanted to accompany her to the tank room and watch J.T. being removed from the tank and woken up. Doc was quite excited to be allowed to observe this aspect of his CO's care.

As they walked down the corridor, Heather took the opportunity to discuss with Doc, about him furthering his education and becoming a physician.

"Doc, I can help grease the skids, so to speak, and the doctor I want to introduce you to is a legend and has considerable weight with the medical school admissions board. Just a warning. Don't be surprised if he doesn't pimp you while he is talking to you."

Doc asked, "Guess he's like a second father as well as a mentor?"

"He's brilliant and very old school. You will like him a lot. He's a lot like you, no bullshit, straightforward, black and white, with very little gray areas in life," Heather said.

"Let me think about it. It would be difficult with my duties at Coulter as well as missions with the Unit," Doc replied.

"Well, his name is Dr. Sam Kendrick, should you want to research him."

"You sound a lot like J.T., researching upcoming contacts with the enemy. Anyway, let's get to the tank room so we can get J.T. back among the land of the living."

Meanwhile, back in the tank room, the staff were getting all the equipment together to get J.T. out of the tank. They would start when Dr. Dunkirk arrived and started the reversal of the medically induced coma. In preparation, the cables were attached to the frame, and the valves were opened to start draining the fluid from the tank. Heather walked through the door, wrote some orders in J.T.'s chart, then she and the guy following her walked over to the stairs leading up to the top of the tank. They were talking between themselves when they got to the top and stepped on to the platform.

"In 10 minutes," Heather said. "You can start winching the frame out."

"Yes ma'am," was the reply.

They watched as the blue tinted clear fluid level slowly dropped. It seemed like it was taking forever.

"Okay, guys. Haul him out of there."

Slowly, the winch turned with an occasional twang as the chain links snapped into alignment. As the second third of the frame rose above the edge of the tank, the left-hand hook broke, causing the frame to settle back into the tank and then bang against the side of the tank. Unfortunately, it also trapped the air supply line between the tank wall edge and the frame, almost completely severing the line. Doc leaned to his right and hit the emergency drain button that in less than fifteen seconds emptied the tank.

Heather yelled at the team responsible for lifting the rehab frame out of the tank, urging them to get the frame out as soon as possible.

"His pulse has dropped to 82, 76… continuing to fall," the technician monitoring J.T. called out.

Heather and Doc climbed up on the tank frame. Doc was trying to get the helmet off when Heather told him about the release latch under his chin. Doc found the latch, flipped it open, and yanked it off. J.T. was unconscious and not breathing. Heather leaned over and started mouth to mouth. After two minutes, there was only a little response from J.T. They stopped for twenty seconds as the frame cleared the border of the tank and was laid down on a support table while the rest of the team set to the task of disconnecting J.T. from the frame. Heather restarted mouth to mouth until finally there was a response from J.T. He opened his eyes. He was a little startled at seeing Heather's face so close to his.

"Wondered how long it would take before you kissed me," he said.

"Would have been a lot longer if you didn't try that grandstand play of almost dying," she replied.

"What can I say? I was waiting for you to make the first move."

"Why was that?"

"If you wait for the woman to make a move, you can be sure she is interested. There aren't any mistaken signals."

"Oh."

"I was just kidding. That happens every single day, across civilization. Causes lots of bad feelings and embarrassment."

"Oh, what do you think now?" Heather asked.

"Pretty sure that you are interested," J.T. said, lowering his voice. "Besides, you kiss really well."

"Thanks, although I would have preferred that you not come so close to dying, not after all the work I put into repairing you."

"Yeah, well, a guy's gotta make an entrance when the opportunity presents itself," J.T. remarked.

"Next time I could just let you die to prove a point," Heather responded with a little attitude.

"Doc would have saved me," was J.T.'s comeback.

"So now you'd rather kiss Doc? Boy, did I have you wrong, I'm outta here. You have got family and a Coulter resident that wants to say Hey! I may see you later, maybe I won't. I had expected more from a man like you. Sometimes women just have standards they won't trade away. Sometimes you must just walk away. Tell me what orders you need written so you can run your own show. One day you will realize what you let get away." She turned on her heel and headed for the door.

"Heather, I was just kidding. Wait. Come on, wait a minute. Look, may I please have two minutes of your time, please?" J.T. was sitting on the table, two towels wrapped around him, drying off.

Heather stopped.

"Please come over here. I don't want to yell at you across the room."

Heather turned and slowly walked back to him.

He reached out and took both of her hands in his and said, "I'm sorry. I'm not very good at being in love. In fact, the more I think about it, this is the first time I have ever actually been in love. Oh, there have been times where I thought I might have, but they never worked out. So, this is completely new territory for me. Please be patient with me. I don't want to screw this up," he pleaded.

"Glad to hear you say that. How'd you like getting your chain jerked? Until you and I have been together for a while, let's not do this to each other. Right now, as we are starting out, getting to know each other, it's hard to know if you are joking or not. So, let's not jerk each other around, at least until we know each other better. FYI you need a lot of practice kissing and I intend to see that you get plenty of practice." With that she kissed him again for real and he now understood.

"I just finished work on Sarah's hip. She wanted to say hello and to see how you are doing so she could report back to the rest of the village. I just love all of them. Helen, Frank, Shannon, and Sean will be here at noon. Then, I would imagine, the unit will most likely be waiting and now that you are all healed up, try to keep the nips to a minimum. I must go get Sara." And off she went.

When she found her, she reminded her that he had been immersed for the last month and maybe a little mentally foggy when talking to her.

J.T. was deep in conversation with Doc as she approached.

"Colonel, I am so glad you are still with us. The Village will be waiting for my report," Sarah said.

"I hope you will give them a glowing one and tell them I will be out to visit in two weeks, and we can have a wild boar roast," J.T. replied.

"You will be sure to bring Dr. Dunkirk? She is such a kind and wonderful person. You fixin ta marry her? We've all talked and think the two of you would be perfect together. After all she picked 'YES, Georgio, on movie night!" Sarah exclaimed.

"She did, did she?" J.T. said.

"Martha said it was a powerful sign, almost like a foretellin!" Sarah went on.

"Doc, I'm tired, and we have a journey. Let me say goodbye

to Heather, then we need to head out." She gave J.T. a kiss on the cheek and gave one also to Heather.

"OK Doc, let's go," Sarah said.

Doc turned to Heather and said, "Thanks for everything."

She gave him a cheek kiss. He walked over to J.T. "Colonel, will see you soon, Sir,"

"Yep Doc, you will." With that, Sarah and Doc departed.

Five minutes later, the entire Coulter family entered the area. Helen, as usual, was the first one to hug J.T.

"Oh James, let me see you. We were all so worried. Heather helped us through it all, including us where we could be helpful, keeping us informed, helping us understand where you are headed in life. She's so lovely and kind. Don't let her get away, son, you hear me!" Helen lectured.

"Yes mom, I hear ya. I have already had a talk with her."

"Oh, good son, we all just love her to death. Did she tell you all the things she did for you?" Helen asked.

Sean butted in. "She came to me and asked me about semi-private conversations we have had over beers."

"Concerning what?" J.T. questioned.

"What you had said or mentioned you were interested in doing after you left the Unit".

"What did you tell her?" J.T. asked.

"I told her about your fascination with spacecraft, space travel and visiting other worlds," Sean responded.

"Did you mention anything else?"

"Nothing I can think of."

"Well, she has loaded up my brain with tons of ancient languages, archeology stuff, medical school, hieroglyphic interpretation. South American Indian tribal history, India

Indian history. Guess I should probably ask her," was J.T.'s answer.

Frank stepped up and said, "I can help with that. She and I discussed most of this. The med school stuff was so you could understand medicine and physiology. She thought that it would help with your entertainment of the hibernation concept for long space flights. The rest of the stuff was because she thought, now follow my logic with this, you'll love it. To accomplish your dream of interstellar travel, you will need to either build a spaceship, requiring you to collaborate with multiple people where you would not necessarily be in charge, or you would have to go find one.

"With all the ancient Aliens stuff you had implanted, she figured you could take the info currently available, look at all the ancient civilizations, look at the hieroglyphics yourself and see if there was something they missed, and maybe, you just might have a breakthrough, possibly leading you to finding an alien spaceship that you can study, fix and use. How's that for reasoning? I forget if it is inductive or deductive reasoning. The point is, she thought this out, acted on the things she could to achieve a goal and did it on her own, because she believes in you and wanted you to have the best shot at achieving your life's dream."

"She loves you, really, truly loves you. Like married for forever type of love. Didn't think I could get that all out without yelling at you."

"Where's Heather?" J.T. asked, looking around and not seeing her.

Shannon piped up with the obvious answer, "She's a doctor, she has patients. She doesn't have the luxury of sitting around in the middle of the day, shooting the breeze, like we do. Well, Big Brother, I think you look fabulous. Heather did a fantastic job of putting you back together. I hope you gave her a sincere, heartfelt thank you."

"I said thanks…more than once," J.T. said defensively.

"You asshole! If it were not for her, you wouldn't be here and if you had someone else do the work, you might not be able to walk or use your arms, and all you can tell her is thanks a couple of times. You should be on your knees groveling at her feet for her working so hard to give you back your life and allowing you to have your dreams. You can be such a jerk sometimes." Shannon stamped off, bordering on crying.

Helen turned and followed her out, but not before saying, "I thought I had raised you better than that." Sean leaned over and whispered, "You really stepped in it this time bro,"

"Don't I know it," he replied.

"Well, what are you gonna do about it?"

"I guess make some type of a grand gesture that would let her know how I feel," J.T. said.

"That's a start," Sean said.

"Maybe tell her how I feel about her," J.T. said.

"There's hope for you yet, bro," Sean commented.

Frank chimed in, "Why are you still standing here? Being here is not getting it done, son."

"Thanks, Dad, Sean. Please tell Shannon and Mom that I'm sorry and I am going to rectify the oversight right now," J.T. said as he exited the room. He found her just as she was leaving to see if the Unit had showed up.

"Hold on for a minute." Pulling her off to the side out of most everyone's sight, he pulled her close, looked into her eyes and said, "I'm sorry that I haven't done a better job saying thank you for all you have done for me. I didn't know the extent of what was done, cuz you never told me. What you have done is incredible. No one has ever done more for me on so many levels. I am going to spend the rest of my life trying to show you how thankful I am that you came into my life. I love you." He then gave her a deep long kiss that received a round of applause from all the Unit members that had stopped by to see him.

"At ease, gentleman," he said, the commander part coming out of him.

For the next hour and a half, the last of the Unit clapped him on the back and headed out of the door.

"I am kinda tired. Might be time for me to go."

Heather said, "Well, you can stay here, or you can come home with me. Either way, someone needs to be keeping an eye on you for the next forty-eight hours. My place is a lot more comfortable than the hospital."

"Make a deal with you. Why don't you come and spend the night at my house? It has been more than a month since I was home, and I am so looking forward to sleeping in my own bed," J.T. whispered.

"We can do that. I will bring the equipment out to my car, and we can leave," Heather said.

While Heather retrieved two separate bags, J.T. got dressed in some hospital clothes and was waiting for her to help her in carrying the bags out to her car. But then a man ran up to them. He shoved a recorder in her face and wanted all the details of Lt. Colonel Coulter's injuries.

"Didn't you get enough the last time we went through this?"

She opened her phone and called security.

"Skip, this is Heather. He's back, outside the back door near the doctors' parking lot. Thanks."

Heather hung up the phone and walked over to the door, swiped her ID badge, and opened the door just as Skip arrived. J.T. was close behind.

"Apparently, you like pain and you don't learn very well. Or maybe you thought I was kidding when I said I had friends left in the unit and your body will never be found," Skip said with a mixture of anger and amazement at how dense some people were.

"Skip, what's going on?"

"J.T. this gentleman is a reporter, and he's been pestering Dr. Dunkirk. Barged into her office demanding information on Lt. Colonel Coulter and whether he was a patient here and what his injuries were. Dr. Dunkirk refused to answer his questions, and he became belligerent. That's when she called me, and I had to forcibly remove him from the premises. Unfortunately, he was injured during the removal.

"He chose to be removed when he was offered the choice of leaving or being helped. He declined to exit under his own power. I even informed the man of my friendships with members of the Unit and the possibility of his body never being found, but apparently, he must have thought I was kidding when I was being deadly serious. So, I guess he leaves me with no choice. I'm gonna call a couple of the guys from the unit then take him out into the boonies and thoroughly get his attention, making sure he never, ever forgets what I have impressed on him."

"OK, but Skip, it's better if he dies from the wilds rather than human hands, understand?" J.T. said.

"Wilco, sir," was the response.

Heather was surprised at her reaction to hearing Skip's response. Even when he was no longer part of the unit, there was still the respect and obedience in his voice, respect and obedience for the man she loved.

After Skip had removed the reporter, J.T. exited the building.

"So, you had to deal with pushy, overbearing newspaper reporters too, huh?" J.T. asked.

Heather's response was, "All in a day's work."

"You have some pretty exciting days," he replied.

"Some more than others, but then some others. Well, ya never know how things are going to turn out," she said with a wink and a smile that was just radiant.

"I understand. Though it is not something they teach in medical school, is it?" he asked.

"Is what taught at medical school?" she said.

"How to deal with pushy reporters?" J.T. responded.

"Oh, I thought you were referencing falling for patients," she remarked.

"Well, that too," J.T. answered.

"The answer is yes and yes. They taught us about patient confidentiality and how to address the issue and about falling for patients. It was very simple. Don't ever or you will be kicked out of med school or worse, lose your license. Guess that was enough said," was her straightforward answer.

"Get in the car. We'll start by stopping at my place. There's no food at yours, so we will stock up on what I have, so nothing must be thrown out because of spoilage. Then, after I get some clothes packed up, we can go to your place, where you can cook for me." There was a subtle note of command in her voice.

"You got a deal," J.T. wisely agreed.

"Well then, let's get a move on." Heather hit the automatic address button for her car's navigation unit, then settled back and enjoyed the trip. J.T. offered his hand to her and they held hands for the rest of the trip. It felt good and right, and somehow long overdue.

CHAPTER
THIRTEEN

Upon arrival at her condo, J.T. was impressed with the whole layout. "You are a perfectionist. Everything in its place and a place for everything," he noted.

"That's the way I was trained. All your parts work just the way they are supposed to, hooked back up the way they are supposed, everything in its place. Just like my training," Heather explained.

"Well, gotta thank you for following your training," he said, hyper flexing his arms like a weightlifting pose, with a wide grin.

"Nice physique for an older guy," she said with a wink and a smirk.

"Cut me to the quick with that older guy comment. You know how much work I put into looking like this. Served me well recently, don't you agree?" he questioned.

"That is true. If you weren't in that great of shape, you probably would not have survived," Heather opined.

"OK, got my clothes. How are we set on the food and drinks?"

"Very good selection of whites and I already have a great selection range of reds, so we are set to go. All my herbs are fresh. And I got an aero UV/ grow lamp chamber for fresh salad makings. I am sure there is some meat from Coulter in the freezer, shouldn't take very long to thaw. We can have a couple of glasses of wine and start to get to know one another, like we would have done in the regular world, our jobs notwithstanding. Just a guy and a girl who met and decided to take a chance and get to know one another before deciding to progress with getting more involved," J.T. said softly.

"I'd like that. This has all been moving at a fast pace and if we are going to go forward, we need to take our time. We have the rest of our lives and the knowledge that we are connected, soulmates, if you will, so hurrying everything is unnecessary, as we already know we were meant to be together," Heather explained.

"Ya know, you make complete sense. No worries, that if, you know, I don't do everything correctly, you will interpret that as us not being appropriate for being together. And if you don't do everything completely and correctly, I can say that you are not right for me. This is very freeing. Well done, doc!" he said.

"I have never been in a situation like this, and I find it to be extremely freeing and unsettling at the same time."

"Sure, I'm glad that I already know and believe that we were meant to be together. Cuts down on the anxiety and worry part of building a long-lasting, forever relationship," J.T. philos-ophized.

Heather tried getting things back on track.

"I love your mom. What kind of a mom was she? I mean, she has all those degrees, and you can't get them online, at home, with a snot-nosed, crying baby, demanding all of your attention. How was she?"

"She was a wonderful mother. She and my father divided up the childcare time, got jobs that were flexible with the work hours, and they worked like a well-oiled machine. I always knew I was loved and cared for equally by both of them. I found out that learning fascinated me more than anything else. Constantly challenging myself caused me to be an overachiever. With brilliant parents, they were supportive and acted as though this was expected given the genetic material I was created with."

"No resentment or questioning when you chose to study over extra-curricular activities?" she questioned.

"Still played cross-country, basketball and baseball and I ran a little track, mostly long-distance stuff. I was pretty exceptional, even went to state as a senior," he mused.

"You had no troubles?" she asked.

"Only in the locker room. Why only there?"

"The showers and the non-stop kidding about my male anatomy."

"Like?" she questioned.

"Like "Hey man, how many girls you gonna ruin for the rest of us? Did you have to pray for that thing, or was God just having a good day when you were born? Years of that gets really old. Then the girls got to talking amongst themselves. The next girl I went to the movies with asked me if it was true and could she see it. I had been out with her nine times before and she wouldn't even let me kiss her and here she was asking to see my male anatomy. I didn't show her, but I did let her feel it. It was all around the school in less than twenty-four hours. I was humiliated and that was the end of my dating in school. Since I went to college in the same town, there was no college dating. When I joined DSF, I got to move to Dome 17."

"Nobody there knew anything about me, so I could kinda start over, almost. I have had a couple of women that I dated but they left as soon as we tried to get intimate, actually when they saw me without any clothes, so I thought that part of my sex life was just not going to happen. Then you came along. I knew you had seen the *goods* and you were still interested. Then I had a talk, actually, I was lectured by Emma, the day she gave me my shower. It was an honest, straightforward conversation about my condition, and how I needed to proceed forward with any woman, in order to make any type of intimacy successful."

"She had the same conversation with me, so I took her advice, and I am under treatment that, if successful, will allow you and I to enjoy a wonderfully intimate sex life. You know that there are other sexual activities that do not require penetration, and as things move along, I will be happy to introduce you to them and I will ensure that you are able to meet all challenges, until there are none left to conquer," she said confidently. "If that is OK with you?"

"Yes, Ma'am. Think I can go start dinner now. Should take about an hour. You can sit at the island while I cook."

"It sounds like a plan." Heather grabbed the wine glasses and made her way to the very large island, where she plopped down on a rather comfortable bar stool chair.

"Do you want to eat as I go or fix everything at once and eat it like a regular meal?"

"Let's eat as we go, cuz I'm starved," Heather whined.

"So be it. Salad first." J.T. grabbed some scissors and walked into an adjoining room and returned with a handful of lettuce, some herbs, parsley, chives, and basil. Stepping up to a Teak and Maple checkered cutting board, he slid a large French knife out of the butcher block and started chopping up the lettuce and chives, tossed them into a bowl and put it in the fridge. Then he chopped up all the herbs and divided them in half. He put half in a mixing bowl, grabbed some balsamic vinegar, olive oil, ground salt and freshly ground pepper and whisked it all together in a simple balsamic vinaigrette, that he then drizzled over the salad and put it in two portions on salad plates. He gave Heather a fork and one of the plates while he moved on to the meat. Five minutes later, the sound of meat hitting a hot cast-iron skillet filled the air, while a couple of minutes later the smell of sizzling meat and seasonings filled the air. J.T. added in a small amount of beef stock, a copious amount of red wine, some sliced baby Bella mushrooms and finely diced shallots were added as the stock reduced volume.

"Is medium rare, OK?" he asked.

"Perfect. How did you know?" she asked.

"You don't look like a rare chick, nor do you look like a medium well or well-done chick. Sorry about the reference to you about being a chick. It has been a long time since I have had the opportunity to cook for a beautiful woman. Sometimes I forget how to act properly," he explained.

"Well, I am, but I just have not been referred to that way since high school and college," she remarked.

"I haven't cooked for a woman here since just after my college days, so sorry, no offense intended," he apologized.

"None taken. I love being your chick. Let's just keep that between us as something intimate and personal, okay?" she said.

"Okay."

Four minutes later he made the initial cut on a bias, through the meat, placed it on the plates, then ladled the shallot-mushroom reduction over the meat and handed Heather her plate.

"Smells divine," she said.

"Elk always tastes best with a red wine reduction. Brings out the undertones of the meat. Add a merlot to it and you have a heavenly dish. Shall we eat? I am starving. It has been more than a month since I have actually eaten real food using my mouth and I can hardly wait to taste this meal," J.T. said.

With that, they dove in.

Twenty minutes later, Heather pushed back, "I have to stop before I lick the plate!!! That was absolutely the best piece of meat I have eaten in years, restaurant meals included."

"You have no idea, how you saying that makes me feel," J.T. confessed. "I so wanted to show off for you, cuz it was really important for me to impress you."

"There's not much left for you to show off to me about. You've already done all the most important ones." Heather said.

"Like what?" he asked.

"Well, let's start off with the admiration, loyalty and obedience you inspire in your men. Every one of them would obey you even if they knew they were going to die by following your orders. In my life, I have never seen that anywhere, in anyone, ever before. It is incredibly impressive. Next was Coulter, and the way you selflessly put that place together, keep it going and still allowing people to live by their own rules and talents. That's as impressive as the Unit. Third, you have not let your role as commanding officer of DSF Unit 17 turn you in to a man with no regard for human life. Yes. You kill the enemy because you must or he will kill everyone in Dome 17, yet you try to make sure your men see that this is not who they are, but simply what they do, that they are capable of great kindness and humanity, helping people, as much as they are keeping people safe and living well.

"That is just as impressive as anything that you do. These are the qualities that I have spent my life looking for in a man, and you are the first man to show me all of them. That's why I know that I love you. The other things are going to be a lot of fun figuring out together," Heather said, then falling silent.

"How do you feel about helping with the dishes?" was the question.

"You wash and I will dry," was the answer.

After everything was cleaned up and put away, both of them agreed they were tired and ready for bed.

"Would you like to try together or separate beds?" J.T. asked.

"Do you have a preference?" Heather asked.

"Yes, I do," he replied.

"Well, I would like to have you decide," she said softly and submissively.

"I think together would be wonderful," he said.

"You know I am still in therapy, so intercourse is out of the question," she reminded him.

"I understand completely, and I will wait until you tell me things are okay, before we try to progress to that level, and more than that, I am completely fine with it as you know that I have less experience than would normally be expected of a man my age. I so want to do this right. I want to please my lover, give her what she deserves and wants. So, to that end, my love, you are going to be running the show. Teach me what you need?"

"Yes, my love, it is perfectly fine with me, and I am up to the task. That is another thing I find attractive in you. You are not afraid to admit you don't know everything and neither are you afraid to ask for help," she commented.

"Let me show you the rest of the house. Where's your bag?"

"By the front door."

J.T. walked, still with a slight limp, into the front room, grabbed her bag and headed down the hall.

Pointing out the second and third bedrooms, bathrooms, his den and then the spacious master bedroom and ensuite, complete with huge 2-person walk-in shower, jacuzzi tub and a clawfoot soaking tub. A flip of the switch started the process of warming the bath sheet sized towels and bathrobes, hanging on the walls. The décor had a feminine feel with a large make-up mirror with a circle of adjustable intensity bulbs for different lighting scenarios.

The master bed was an extra-large, custom-made bed. J.T. was a large, muscular, and tall man, and he liked to move around in bed while he slept because, in the words of an old, historic comedian, Bill Cosby, "I like my sleep like a good steak."

Heather had never been in this house and was still walking around the master bath in awe of the layout of the room. It was like someone had come over to her house and written down everything she had ever said about what she wanted in her master bathroom.

"Would you like to shower before bed?" he asked.

"Would I like to shower in this shower?" She said, pointing

to the largest shower she had ever seen outside a locker room at the local gym. "Oh yeah, but it may take me a couple of days to finish. This place is amazing!" she gushed effusively.

J.T. turned toward the room and said, "Towels on, bathrobes on, shower, all nozzles 94 degrees on." With that, he began taking off his T-shirt, then slipping off his pants and putting both in the dirty clothes hamper.

Heather watched as her man got naked, unashamedly, before her. It was one thing to see a man naked during a medical exam. There was a certain amount of professional decorum and detachment. However, when it was someone built like J.T. there was much more to see and seeing it in a different mindset than when you are staring at a man that you have an emotional attachment to.

She felt an internal stirring in her loins, a slight hardening of her nipples and a flushing of her chest and neck; feelings she had not had for a very long time. She began removing her clothing and putting them in the same dirty clothes hamper. She pulled her hair back and J.T. looked out of the shower and pointed to the second drawer. She opened the drawer and found a large hair rubber hair band for her hair, which she then wrapped around her thick, luxurious mane of red hair and stepped into the shower. There were eight shower nozzles. The first two hit her from the right and left sides, shoulders to ankles, the second two were at an angle from the front and back, the fourth and fifth were the face and hair. After she was soaked, she stepped into an area designed for soap and shampoo application.

"May I? he asked.

"Of course," she replied.

"I have a confession to make. The day I first met you after surgery, I had the team investigate you. They entered your home, took notes and made observations which were reported to me by members of the unit. No, Sean had no knowledge of the order and did not participate. I have stocked your shampoo and crème rinse as well as soap, in case you haven't noticed. The investigation was standard protocol for anyone that is going to be in a position to impact the health of any senior member of DSF Unit command personnel. I hope you understand and can forgive the invasion of your privacy. I couldn't have stopped it even if I wanted to. Its protocol approved by people way above my paygrade," he explained.

Initially, Heather was miffed by the admission of violating her privacy, but she understood the concern and need for the protection of certain people. Secretly, she was thrilled and pleased that he had told her about this at the first real opportunity and had apologized for it even though he had no control over it and couldn't have stopped it even if he wanted to. More so, he had been thoughtful enough to have her personal products made available for her use should she ever decide to spend the night. Very considerate and thoughtful on his part. Score two more points for him.

She felt a slight shiver as the soapy loofa moved across her shoulders and down her arms, then back up and across her upper and mid back. There was no attempt to wash her buttocks, breasts or pelvic region, just a slow deliberate motion designed to address her posterior thorax, quite sensually actually.

"You may wash lower if you wish," she whispered.

"I didn't wish to be too forward or aggressive," he responded.

"You are doing just fine. Do not change anything," as she shifted her feet farther apart allowing him more access to her intimate parts. He was doing a very good job for someone who had such limited experience. He proceeded to wash down the back of her legs to the ankles then back up the outside of her legs to the sexy flare of her feminine hips, across the upper part of her buttocks then curling down he washed the inside of her legs, avoiding the more intimate parts of her anatomy, around to her flat, soft, womanly, belly, lingering, as though he was memorizing every inch of her, having it forever burned in to his memory, becoming part of his persona.

"You missed quite a few places," she said.

"You said you were getting treatment; I didn't want to ruin things by being too heavy-handed in a sensitive, irritated area," he replied.

Pays attention and is thoughtful and considerate, two more points for him.

"Thanks for the consideration. Now what?" she questioned.

"I'm gonna wash your hair," he announced. He turned and flipped a switch and a shower chair lowered out of the side wall of the shower,

"Have a seat." Behind the seat on the wall was a hand-held shower head. He pulled the nozzle out, turned it on, and let it run until it warmed up to the same temp as the shower. He gently removed her hair band before he ran it over her head, thoroughly soaking her scalp. He then pulled out a small hose with squirt nozzle attached from the tiny portico, then squirted a copious amount of shampoo onto that glorious mane.

"Been looking forward to this for a very long time," he whispered softly in her ear.

Heather turned in her chair, looked him right in the eye and said questioningly, "Really?"

"Oh yes, since the first day, right out of surgery. I knew I wanted to wash your hair. It is so beautiful," he whispered in her ear. His warm breath sent shivers down her spine.

"Well, get on with it, and you do not need to hurry, and if you do an excellent job, I may let you do it again sometime in the future," Heather said in her most commanding voice.

"Of course, Ma'am, I will surely try my best, of course. You will tell me if I am not living up to your standards, won't you?" he said playfully.

"You can count on it mister, I am waiting," she said with mock sternness.

Forty-five minutes later, he finished with the final rinse and squeezed the water out of her hair, then ran his hands slowly down her chest, over her ample breasts, squeezing the water off her glowing, supple skin, briefly pausing over her turgid nipples before continuing down her belly.

"Shower off," he said, and all the nozzles stopped and retracted into the ceiling, walls, and floor. He reached around the door and grabbed a warm bath sheet and began drying her off, avoiding the intimate areas, then wrapped the towel around her and got another for her hair. She chose to dry her own hair, still trembling from one of the most sensual, non-intercourse experiences she had ever had. The boy wasn't going to need a lot of education, just some refinement and exploration.

J.T. dried himself off and announced he was going to bed.

"You coming? he asked.

"Almost," she replied with a smoldering look in her eye.

"Right or left?" he asked. She looked at him with an unspoken question in her eyes.

"You mean side of the bed?"

"I like sleeping on the right, if that is OK with you?" he replied. "By the way, I sleep nude, just an FYI."

"You expect me to sleep nude?"

"That's up to you. Not like I haven't seen everything," he replied.

"Guess that was kinda stupid, wasn't it?" she said with a bit of chagrin in her voice.

"Just reverting to old responses and behaviors," he responded. "Coffee in the morning?"

"Yes, I would like it."

"Excellent answer." Off he went. She watched his muscular buns wiggle as he walked out of the bath. *God, he is incredibly gorgeous, from any angle.*

They slipped under the covers and J.T. leaned over to kiss her goodnight.

"That was the finest hair wash and shower I have ever had. Thanks."

Her return kiss was quite passionate. "What did I do for you?"

"You allowed me to see that I can be naked with a woman, and she is not killing herself trying to get away. You allowed me to touch you without reeling from fear that I am going to shove this monster up inside you. That's what you have given me, and there is no way I can thank you enough."

"I was referring to sexual pleasure," she said.

"So, this was going to be the only time we will ever be

together until when? When is all this instructional intimacy time supposed to occur?"

"No, you misunderstand. You have just given me one of the most intense sexual, non-intercourse, sessions I have ever had in my entire adult sexual life, and I was feeling bad that I had not reciprocated to you, given you one of your best, non-intercourse sexual experiences of your life. It certainly wasn't a complaint by any stretch of the imagination," she explained.

She then gave him one of the gentlest, prolonged kisses he had ever felt. It told him volumes about her and where she was coming from. He felt a little stupid at that point and when the kiss broke, he immediately apologized.

"Now do you see why I said we need to take things slow? You have just given me something that I didn't know was possible and we ended up miscommunicating over the giving of intense personal pleasure. Now curl around me, hold me close and let's go to sleep because you, my adorable lover, have worn me out.

She rolled on her left side, lifted her leg and arm, and whispered, "Put that thing between my legs and be sure to hold my boobs. I love you and we are gonna be great. I know it."

He, being incredibly intelligent, did exactly as he was told, responding, "Yes, we are."

When Heather woke the next morning, she was surprised at how good the male log between her thighs had felt there. She, in all her sexual years, had never slept with a lover in such an intimate posture. J.T. had already slipped out of bed and started the coffee. *What are we gonna do today? I think I will start off by giving him a massage and then let things go where they may.*

"Hey," came his voice from the kitchen, "you want some Eggs Benedict for breakfast?"

"That's a stupid question. Of course, I would love some Eggs Benedict. Do I have time for a shower?" she asked as he walked through the door with some unbelievable smelling coffee and a full service on a tray. "Hope you are not allergic to anything?" he asked.

"Nope."

"This is one of my all-time favorites, Coconut Crème. How do you take it?"

"Small crème, small sugar."

"Perfect choice. Smooths out the bitterness and accentuates the sweetness. You have about twenty minutes before breakfast is ready. How was the temp on the shower last night?"

"Perfect."

"In order to get things started, you have to say, shower on, temp 94 all nozzles. Before you enter, you have to say towels on, robes on. Then stand at the door and say shower on, temp 94 or it won't work. I may have to reprogram the voice recognition software because there has never been a woman in here, that includes my mom and Shannon, to use the system so it may not recognize anyone else's voice. Just let me know if it doesn't work," he explained.

"Okay." She leaned over and kissed him, with a kiss that promised more later.

J.T. returned to the kitchen to continue making their breakfast. He heard Heather's voice, following his instructions, and heard the water come on. He was glad that the system had accepted her voice... always a good sign. Twenty-two minutes later, she walked out with a towel wrapped around her head and another wrapped around her trunk, breasts bared and jutting out proudly, nipples erect and pointy.

"You trying to draw my attention away from my cooking?"

"Just letting you know what the next course of instruction was going to focus on."

"Glad I am done with the knife work on this dish. Don't think you fancy fresh man-meat in the hollandaise sauce."

"I do fancy man meat, but you are right, not in my Hollandaise."

"Well, here's your plate, utensils are in the left top drawer in the island. Need a refill on your coffee or a glass of orange juice?"

"Yes, and a glass of OJ would be great." J.T. poured her a large glass of OJ and refreshed her coffee. They ate in silence, if you could call moans of gustatory delight interspersed with the sound of sloppy wet kissing silence. They did not hear the front door open, nor did they hear Shannon and Helen chuckling in the doorway as they watched the lovers enjoying life.

"Mom, Shannon, what are you guys doing here?" J.T. exclaimed.

Shannon replied, "Obviously not having as much fun as the two of you! She was staring at Heather's bare, magnificent set of breasts, just proudly sticking out for all to see.

Helen remarked, "Mine used to do that thirty years ago."

Heather finally noticed what they were all looking at, as she hurried to cover them up.

Shannon said, "Nice rack, all natural, I assume? My brother has excellent taste in women and personally, Mom and I are really happy for both of you."

She leaned in and whispered, "I always wanted a sister, and

it looks like I may get my dream fulfilled. Have you sampled the wares yet?"

"No, I am still in treatment, so it will be four weeks before I am done."

"Promise me that I will be the first one you tell all about it when it happens, just like sisters would do."

"Okay, okay, I'll call you before anyone, including my priest."

Shannon squealed and wiggled and jumped up and down as though she had just got the bike for Christmas she had always wanted back when she was twelve. Her dream was going to be realized. She had wanted this since she realized that she was going to be stuck with an overachieving, perfect older brother. Not that she didn't idolize him, love, and trust him to death, he just wasn't a sister and she felt she really, really, needed and wanted one.

Helen came over after she had gotten herself a cup of coffee. "Ummm, what kind is this?"

"J.T.'s favorite, coconut crème," Heather answered.

"I want you to know how happy I am that the two of you have gotten together. I managed to get a look at that appendage my son has between his legs. It is an impressive tool. Sampled it yet?" she asked.

"No, it will be four weeks before the treatments are completed. I have been concentrating on teaching him how to please a woman. Most men get some experience when they are much younger. J.T. never had the opportunity to learn by chance or to be taught by an older woman, so the task, fortunately, falls to me his first and last lover. And, I must say he is a natural."

"How so?"

"His touch is so gentle, and he doesn't go after the fun parts first. He takes his time and demonstrates no rush to get somewhere, and he is considerate. He knew I was having treatment, and he avoided that area. Didn't even ask if he could touch it. Sure, is nice not to have to undo bad habits and beliefs before you can start teaching new things. That is what I mean by being a natural. He almost made me cum from a 40-minute hair washing. Head hair, not pubic. It was the most amazing thing I had ever experienced," Heather breathlessly gushed.

"I'm so glad. We all are so happy that you and James have found each other and are working to overcome any issues that may keep you apart. We all hope that you end up a member of our family. We would all be so thrilled for both of you. Sorry about barging in on you, but curiosity pushed us to see for ourselves. It won't happen again now that we know. The men are so dense, they would never consider coming over here to verify things on their own," Helen pontificated. "Shannon, it's time to go."

Shannon came out of the other room, ran over and hugged Heather, whispering in her ear, "don't forget to call me about you know what."

"I won't forget. Helen, thanks for stopping by. I have a huge urge to call you mom, may I?"

"Of course, my dear. Nothing would make me prouder. We shall see you soon and talk to you later." Over her shoulder, she yelled,

"James, we are leaving now. Love you both. Bye, Bye". And out the door they went.

J.T. immediately went over and locked the door. He returned to the kitchen and said, "Now, where were we?"

Two hours later, they both headed into the master bath. Heather's nipples were almost half a size larger, almost a fiery red. There were multiple small hickeys on both breasts, testifying to the intense attention that had been paid to both breasts. They were both fatigued looking. Heather had obviously had multiple orgasms, and they both needed a shower and a nap. They bathed each other, dried each other off, then, they adjourned to the master bed, curled around each other, the same as they did in their recent first night together. They were both out quickly.

When they were both awake, Heather pushed J.T. on to his back and said, "Now is time for you to learn to accept oral love. Put your hands under your head and relax. You are not to use your hands for anything, period."

With that, Heather began using her lips and tongue on J.T.'s body, neck, ears, lips, throat, chest, arms, belly, buttocks, groin, male anatomy, legs and toes, stopping only to return his hands to their original position. When she finally stopped, he remarked that he had never had anything like that and was completely unaware of some of the new erogenous zones she had found. They curled around one another as per their usual configuration and slipped into an exhausted deep sleep.

The next morning, Heather woke around 8:30, to the smell of the coffee permeating the air.

"Want an omelet for breakfast?"

"Would love one."

"What do you want in it?"

"Mushrooms, onions, bacon and cheese."

"No green peppers?"

"Okay, you twisted my wrist, green peppers too."

"Salsa or Pico de Gallo?"

"Salsa."

"Twenty-five minutes."

"Then I'm gonna shower."

"OK."

"Don't forget you have all your testing, at least for the PhDs starting at 11:30 a.m."

"Okay, I had forgotten. I know, no prepping, or it will screw up the experiment."

J.T. went back to prepping for the omelets, chopping up the veggies, cooking the bacon, and making the salsa. He decided to make souffle type omelets; splitting up the egg whites and egg yolks, whipping them both up separately, then folding them together and adding the ingredients, putting them under a broiler for cooking). The omelets were perfect, as was the freshly made salsa, coffee and cran-apple juice.

After cleaning up from breakfast, J.T. took a shower and then had a seat in his den, trying to clear his mind and begin the process of focusing on the task at hand. He wasn't worried about nuclear engineering or the Astro-metrics courses, basically it was all math and physics. The aeronautical engineering one was a mixture of math, physics and design and that was time consuming, as well as very precise. After all, if the design were to actually be constructed, it would have to fly, not crash, and allow the people inside it to survive.

The medical school exam was a series of six different exams in the sciences plus the complete primer on the medical and diagnostics part of the curriculum, something he had only read about and never actually done. He felt that put him at a distinct disadvantage. Just reading all the literature and texts gave him a knowledge base to refer to, but he had never actually examined a patient, made any kind of medical life or death decisions, and he certainly would not equate himself on the same level as Heather.

He would have to discuss this *degree* with her so he could understand better why she had included this download in his regimen. On some level, he wondered if she felt that doing this would put him on a more even keel with her, make them more equals, so that there would be this common ground to help with the long-term relationship. It would allow one to understand what motivated the other, and make them each understand when one had to leave to go to the hospital to attend a patient.

As the calm and focus settled over him, he felt an inner peace that was mixed with the intense self-challenge he always experienced, before any type of task, one that he had come to rely on, one that gave him the confidence to strive and to succeed, one that gave him that added extra that had always kept him safe and successful.

There was a ding on the computer, telling him that instructions for the upcoming exam were en route. Heather was standing in the door, watching him like a hawk, as he went through some of his rituals, helping him to focus.

"You ready for this?" she asked.

"Yep, I am," was his reply.

"You will do fine. If you can think of it, while this is going on, try to see if you can notice any defects in the information flow, where things may not have been implanted quite right."

"I will see if anything 'sort of' pops out at me," he replied.

Heather walked over and gave him a big, lingering kiss and a "you'll be fine."

Instructions showed up on the screen and the testing began. The nuclear engineering and Astro-metric testing took a total of 5.3 hours. The screen informed him that his test results would be ready in thirty-eight minutes. It also asked if he wished to continue today or would prefer to start fresh in the morning at 8:30 a.m. He opted for the better part of valor, choosing resumption in the morning. Having heard the ding of the computer, Heather stuck her head in the den and asked him how he thought it went. Unwilling to jinx things, he replied to the grades would be back in thirty-eight minutes and that would answer the first part of the question as to how things went. He also informed her that he would complete the testing in the morning.

"By the way, sweetheart, could you explain to me why I am being given the medical school final exam? You trying to tell me something this male brain is having a hard time understanding?" he queried.

"I did it because I love you," she said matter-of-factly.

"I sort of thought it would be something like that," he replied.

"To tell the truth, I did it because I thought you would need a base from which to work when you are trying to figure out hibernation for prolonged space flight," again matter-of-factly.

"I was wondering if that was the reason. It was really great thinking. That was a huge factor that needed to be thought out and resolved before there could be any type of intergalactic or interstellar flight. Thanks. I would not have thought of that at that time," he admitted.

"Well, your brain was half gorked at that time. I wouldn't have expected you to be able to do that type of critical thinking while you were focused on trying to survive," she said.

"Oh yes, where was my head at? And I always thought that I could think and chew gum at the same time. Silly me!!!" he said sarcastically.

"It's okay dear, after all, you are working with a handicap, being a male and all!" she said just as sarcastically.

"Woman, comments like that will get you turned over my knee!!!" J.T. said, quite sternly.

"You wouldn't dare!" Heather said defiantly.

"Oh look, your first major screw up of our budding romance," J.T. stated. With that, he was out of his chair and across the room before Heather realized what was about to happen. He grabbed her arm and before it registered, she was over his shoulder, her head towards his rear end, and he was pulling her panties down. He plopped down on the bed, rolled her down into his lap, trapped her legs in a scissor move and was pushing down on her posterior mid thorax. She was completely restrained and helpless.

"In the future, my love, you will show a lot more respect or you will find spankings are likely to become the norm in your life. Now count each one out loud, do you understand?" he forcefully commanded. With that, he began spanking her bare, delectable ass.

"I don't hear you!" he announced. Then he started over again! Her ass was turning a bright pink, which he found somewhat erotic. "Count!" he commanded.

"One, two, three, four, five.,"

J.T. stopped after five, since he had already given her six or seven before she started counting. With that, he released her legs and gave her butt a gentle rub, trying to alleviate some of the stinging.

"Never, ever tell me what I won't dare to do." He pulled her around, so she was straddling his lap, pulled her close and kissed her very deeply. "Do you understand me?" he asked.

"Yes, Sir."

He was just about to carry her to bed when the computer dinged again.

"You may take me to bed sir, but I would like to see how things went since I also have a vested interest in seeing the fruits of my labors, if you do not mind, Sir," she said submissively.

"I'm just as curious, so let's go have a look. By the way, how's your ass?"

"Warm and tanned, Sir."

He took her hand and gently helped her up, put his arm around her and together they walked back into the den.

J.T. plopped in his chair and then helped Heather sit down on his lap. He could still feel the heat radiating from her butt. He logged in and navigated to the results page and there for everybody to see was his score. Nuclear Engineering, 98%, Astro-metrics, 97%. He pushed the printout tab so he could see what he had missed, glanced at the questions he had gotten wrong, grabbed a piece of paper, wrote down calculations and then redid the calculations. He then typed a message to the certifying educator, scanned in his calculations and requested that his grade be amended because the professor had made an error in his calculations. Ten minutes later, the bell dinged again and there was his amended grade reflecting a 99%.

He moved on to the Astro-metric exam. As he perused the

answers, he thought another one was incorrectly marked wrong. He sent a request for reconsideration and cited his reasons. Fifteen minutes later, there was an apology letter returned; it was as if a light had gone off in his head. He typed a message to that professor, asking a question, pointing out that a certain parameter had not been specified in the question and since it had not been specified, the standard norms were used and using standard norms, his answer was correct. Fifteen minutes later there was a reply acknowledging that J.T. was in fact correct, and that his corrected grade was 100%. There was also an acknowledgement that there had been only one other perfect paper in the whole time the class had been offered and that was fifteen years prior.

He turned to Heather, took her into his arms and kissed her deeply, telling her thank you. Now I have just two more exams tomorrow.

"By the way dear, If I pass the medical school exams, will I be considered a MD?"

"Technically, you will have passed the same exams as MDs, so I would assume that you could, in fact, call yourself a physician, although I would strongly urge you to refrain from actually trying to treat someone since you have never actually examined anyone."

"Oh, ye of little faith," he said mockingly. "I am really surprised at you, thinking I would actually try to treat someone without knowing what I am doing. I am not that egotistical to think that a degree confers absolute knowledge, thereby allowing me to take someone's life in my hands," he said indignantly.

"I know that you were not that kind of person, but you are

incredibly brilliant, and you do have a penchant for thinking you can fix lots of things. It is not a large step to thinking you can help every sick human. It is in your nature to help alleviate suffering and misery. Look at Coulter. You helped hundreds of people have a better life and if you weren't bound for the cosmos, being a doctor would be a perfect choice for you. You have the intelligence, attitude, mindset and drive necessary for being a superb physician. I am definitely not trying to insult you, or denigrate you, but being an MD is more than book-learning," she lectured.

"Thanks babe, didn't mean to sound like you thought I was some type of a megalomaniac. But I do want to go on record. I am willing to help whomever I can, but, one thing about me, my love, I know my limitations and I never exceed them nor do I exceed my abilities," he said.

"I know that, my love, and that is one of the endearing things I adore about you. Take me to bed my love, tomorrow is a huge day and I want you rested and refreshed, ready for what faces you," she said.

"What do you want for breakfast?" he asked.

"Look stud, if you keep cooking like this, I am going to weigh 200 pounds in nothing flat," she said with a bit of chastisement in her voice.

"Then you will have to start working out with me every day, same workout I do. That way, I will be able to cook for you and keep that magnificent figure you have."

"You are a silver-tongued devil."

"Always aim to please."

"Let's get to bed."

J.T. was up at 4:45 a.m., as was his custom. He always knew he was a morning person, and his work productivity studies proved it. He had always felt he was able to accomplish far more than other members of the Unit when he got up early, plus it did allow him to work on his schoolwork while it was still daylight. Coffee was on and everything was ready for him to make breakfast, but the sleepyhead was still crashed out, so he decided to take a long hot shower. He walked into the shower, "Shower on normal temp, continuous flow for 11 minutes, high pressure rinse, same temp."

He dropped his robe and strode into the shower. He stood there for thirty seconds and then said, "Increase temp by four degrees, continue with all other parameters."

The warmer water felt great as the residual stiffness slowly drained from his body. He knew he was not completely healed from his ordeal, but he also knew that he had a few priorities before he could completely concentrate on his recuperation. The upcoming testing was at the top of the list, so he needed to focus on that. He felt rather than heard her enter the shower, but was pleased by her kiss on the back of his neck and over the scar on the left shoulder as she groped his manhood.

"Good morning, my love, nice to see I can still get a rise out of you."

"Good morning sweetheart, did you sleep well?"

"Like the dead. Are you ready for the testing?"

"As ready as I will ever be. By the way, I do not recall any gaps in information transference right off the top of my head."

"That's great news. How long do you think this round of testing is going to take?"

"Since I have never before taken this type of test, I figure nine hours or maybe a little longer. I have too many things that are going unattended, and I can't spend any more time on testing other than what I have committed to today. I have my duties to the unit that need my attention as well as training schedules, threat assessments, personnel transfers, discipline dispensation, and a slew of other things, so I will continue testing non-stop until I have completely finished and can get back to my other duties. I want you to understand that I take the testing seriously and I'm willing to help out science in any way I can, but I have a responsibility to the security of the Dome and Coulter and I can't spend a lot more time on all this testing to the exclusion of my sworn duties. I hope you understand," he said.

"Yes, I do, and I do agree that in the bigger picture, your responsibilities to the security of the Dome and Coulter take precedence. But we have an experiment that will impact a lot of people in the future, and I think you should finish it as best you can so that you can get on with your duties. That's all I am going to say about it." She held her hands up, signifying this part of the conversation was over.

J.T. sat back down at the computer desk, hitched himself around in the chair to get comfortable. His wait time to start the medical school examination was only a couple of minutes when the computer dinged, and the initial examination instructions popped up on the screen. He hit enter, and the exam was started. The exam was long and tedious, and the two 10-minute breaks did little to make him more comfortable. Six and a half hours later, J.T. hit enter, and the exam was over. He pushed himself back, reached up and rubbed both eyes, then stretched his arms, followed by his lower legs.

"I didn't realize that I would get this stiff from sitting on my ass," he lamented.

"Well, how do you think you did?" Heather asked.

"I answered all the questions, so I guess I did okay," was his response.

Just as J.T. was about to walk out of the room, the computer made a strange series of bells and chimes along with the screen flashing red and white. J.T. said, "Oh, oh. and retook his seat.

"What?" Heather asked. "High priority alert," he said.

"About what?" Heather asked.

J.T. typed in a pass code and five seconds later, the message formulated on the screen.

DSF17: set condition two for surrounding area, Dome 17. This is not a drill. More to follow. The printer began zipping back and forth, printing out three quarters of a page of info. J.T. rolled his chair over to the printer and tore off the recently printed page. He speed-read it once, then laid the paper on the desktop and started reading every line from start to finish. After he had completed the third read through, he leaned over and pushed a red button on the far end of the computer console.

"Attention DSF Unit 17. This is not a drill; this is not a drill. Alert status 1, condition 2. Unit meeting at 0830. Camo uniform. This will be a planning meeting. Coulter out."

"We need to get to bed. It is going to be a tough few days, and besides, I need to get back into my routine. I may have been rehabilitated by that tank, but I am a long way from being in the shape I was before the injury. So, it is back to the grind, starting at 4:15 a.m. You want to join me?" J.T. asked.

"I'd like to give it a go. Which part do you start with?" she asked.

"Five-mile run, followed by the gun range, then the weight room. Still want to join me?" J.T. asked.

"In for a penny, in for a pound," was her reply.

With that, they headed into the bedroom for a short night's sleep. Both of them were out within a minute of their heads hitting their respective pillows.

4:15 came early. J.T. had an internal alarm clock that came from years of getting himself up for his self-imposed workout regimen. He dressed in workout togs, noticing that they felt looser than the last time he had put them on, confirming his feeling that he had lost a lot over the last three months.

"I have a lot of work to do," J.T. thought to himself.

"Come on sleepyhead, time to get up and get going." He said to Heather lying in the bed.

"J.T., what is this all about?" Heather asked with more than a little concern invading her voice.

"There is a report of a band of marauders that attacked an outlying community of Dome 18, with significant property damage and considerable loss of life about seven or so days ago then six days ago the same thing happened at an outlying community of Dome 19, again with notable loss of life and property damage. The warning is they should arrive in the area in four days at most. The target most likely is Coulter," J.T. commented.

"What are you going to do?" Heather asked.

"Defend Coulter and completely wipe out this band of brigands. Wipe them out so completely that the world will know that Dome 17, Coulter included, is an area that should be left alone, or you will not survive the attempt, period," he said forcefully mixed in with a portion of commitment. "Any idea what you want for breakfast? Will you be joining me for this workout?"

"Of course, wouldn't miss trying it on for size, for the world," she responded.

"You do know this is going to involve pistol and rifle shooting, as well as self-defense, right?"

"If that is part of your workout regimen, then of course, bring it on," she said with a little of a challenge thrown in.

"You also know I am not toning anything down, just because you are a woman?" he said.

"You had better not. I would be seriously pissed if you did," she responded. "Omelet would be nice."

"With what?"

"Onions, bacon, mushrooms and cheese. Do you have any smoked gouda?"

"Of course."

"That will do nicely."

He headed to the kitchen to fix breakfast. He slipped into his workout clothes and put on his favorite running shoes. Heather came out of the bedroom, dressed in her workout clothes, and kissed him good morning before plopping down in a chair to have breakfast. J.T. asked if she was going to participate in the shooting part of his workout. Heather's answer was immediate and affirmative. That brought a smile to his face even more than the look he got with the first mouthful of breakfast as she ate breakfast.

"Let's head out and get started. Keep up if you can. I'll wait for you at the finish line."

"You just worry about your own performance, and I will worry about mine, smarty pants."

"So, it's smarty pants now, is it? We will see what your attitude is when we are finished."

"Race you to the car. Get set, go." They raced through the kitchen and out to the garage.

"I win," Heather said, giggling.

"You want to drive, or you want me to?"

"You can drive. After all I am the winner and winners get to pick."

Twenty minutes later, they arrived at the compound. Ten minutes later, he was going over the course with Heather, being sure to point out all the chuckholes and slippery places. He did not want to be on the receiving end of her displeasure should she slip and fall or twist an ankle. Thirty-six and a half minutes later, he stopped running, bent over at the waist, huffing and puffing as he worked to catch his breath. *I knew I wasn't going to be in the same shape as I was before everything*, he thought to himself.

Four minutes later, Heather trotted up to him, went through the same things as J.T. before her breathing returned to normal.

"Five miles in 36 1/2 minutes. I have nine minutes to pick up in training. Used to run five miles in twenty-five minutes," J.T. said.

"Well," Heather replied after catching her breath, "I don't have anything to pick up since this is the first time I have ever run five miles."

"Not bad for a rookie," J.T. replied.

"Rookie, my ass," Heather retorted.

"Just wait until I have had a chance to get in shape, then we will see."

"Weapons range is next. You will shoot 50 rounds right-handed, then 50 rounds left -handed. You have twelve minutes to complete the course."

Heather walked over to the first shooting lane, picked up the pistol, pulled the slide back to make sure the weapon was empty. She slipped a clip into the handle, made sure it was locked in place and racked in a round. She put on the hearing protection and eye protecting glasses, then stepped up to the firing table, took aim at the target twenty-five yards down range and began firing.

She was not fully ready for the kick of the weapon but after six shots, settled into a comfortable rhythm. Each clip held ten shots, so Heather even managed to get into a smooth rhythm, ejecting and changing out the clips. When the last shot had been fired and the slide locked in its rearward position, Heather laid the weapon down on the table, muzzle pointing down range.

She stepped to the left to the next range and began the same routine as she had just done, only with the left hand. Things moved a little slower because she was right-handed. When she was done, she cleared and secured the gun, then stepped over to the console and pushed the RETRIEVE button, waiting for the targets to come up to where she stood. When the paper silhouettes arrived, the automatic counter above the line registered the count. 41/50 right hand, 33/50 left hand.

J.T. stepped in behind her and put his hand on her shoulder, giving her a little squeeze. "Not bad for someone that doesn't shoot much, be it for pleasure or professionally," he said.

"Gives me room for improvement," she responded.

J.T. took her elbow and moved her over a few lanes and said, this is the 150-yard rifle range. 100 rounds right-handed and 100 rounds left-handed. Each clip has 30 rounds in it." He then lifted a rifle, showed Heather how to change out the clip and how to rack in a round, as well as where the safety, shot regulator, clip ejector button and slide release buttons were located. "Be sure to keep the butt of the rifle tight against your shoulder. If you don't, you are likely to bruise your shoulder, and that will take a couple of weeks to heal up," J.T. lectured.

Heather hefted the weapon to get a sense of its weight, then stepped up to the line, rested her elbows on the ledge, sighted in on the target and began squeezing off shot after shot. She readjusted the stock in her shoulder after the third shot, mentally noting that J.T. had been correct. She had a little trouble seating the second clip, but returned to her smooth shooting routine. The next clip change went smoother. The final clip change did cause the rifle to jam, which she cleared quickly and finished out this segment of shooting smoothly.

"Very nicely done," he praised.

Moving to the left, she went through the same regimen as she just had without the jamming issue. The rapidly moving retrieved silhouette targets came to a sudden stop after the 150-yard trip. The counters registered 86/100 right, 72/100 left. "Guess you are going to need to work on your marksmanship. How does your shoulders feel?" J.T. asked.

"Just a little sore, but I can see what you were talking about," she responded.

"Next we will practice some Tae Kwon Do for about forty-five minutes, then we will be done for today." J.T. showed

Heather some basic practice routines, then watched her to be sure she had the techniques down pat before he stepped back to practice his routine. The time passed quicker than Heather thought it would and before she knew it, J.T. called time and she was done.

She was surprised as to how tired yet so completely invigorated she felt. As she sat on a bench and caught her breath, she noticed that J.T. had disappeared. She started to wander around the facility, calling his name. She could hear him respond, but it was muffled. As she turned the corner, a door opened and there he stood, a bath towel wrapped around his waist. He was dripping wet from his shower.

"Sorry, thought you heard me say I was going to shower. You have two choices; you can shower here or head home and shower there. The unit will be here in about forty-five minutes, so you need to decide."

"I didn't bring a fresh set of clothes, so I guess I will head home." She moved over to him and kissed him goodbye, grabbed a little feel of his butt, then headed out to the car for her trip home.

J.T. returned to the locker room to finish shaving, getting dressed and ready for what was going to be a very long and important day. J.T. finished shaving, combing his hair and brushing his teeth before putting on one of his starched fatigue uniforms with polished combat boots. As he headed to his office, he stopped by the auditorium and turned on the four coffee maker urns so the coffee would be ready before the troops arrived. His destination was his office, where his coffee maker had already turned on automatically. He poured himself a large mug of coffee and turned on his computer. While he waited for it to boot up, he picked up the phone and dialed a number from memory.

The call was answered, "Aviation DSF17, Staff Sergeant Furness speaking. How may I help you sir?"

"Frank, it's J.T. I need to speak to the boss."

"Yes, sir, and may I say that I am glad to hear you are back at the helm, Sir. I hope you are all mended."

"Yes, I am and thanks, it feels good to be back."

"Hold one for the Colonel, sir." There was a short pause before the connecting click was heard.

"Jim, great to hear your voice. Wasn't sure I was gonna hear your voice again."

"Me too for a while, but I am back, and I have a situation brewing."

"You referring to the alert, I assume?"

"Correct. I am going to require at least three drones, two armed and one with offensive countermeasures. The others are going to need an infrared, heat seeking capabilities and configured to broadcast to multiple night-vision units."

"I have a number of drones that can be configured to meet your needs. What were you referring to when you said offensive countermeasures?"

"One of the drones is going to do long range scanning of the opposing force and I do not know if they have any anti-air capabilities. I am assuming they do, and I want a drone that can protect itself and be able to put the anti-air weapon out of business permanently. This is going to be 25 to 35 miles from Coulter, so they are not aware we are going to be setting up an ambush. Obviously, I need strength of force info, any armor or mobile high-tech weaponry, etcetera so I get no surprises when we engage."

"From the other two drones, I want them to be able to identify each and every combatant so that all of my troops will be able to see what they are dealing with. What I am planning is to put my guys in the trees, 10-15 feet off the ground and allow the opposing force to walk right by them. I am setting up three skirmish lines, 12, 9 and 6 miles from Coulter. The troops are going to be armed with dart rifles with rapid acting poison darts that will kill within thirty seconds, so that there should not be any type of alarm about the attack. I want the drones to be configured so that when the enemy dies, the indicator on the night-vision screen goes out. That way, everyone will know if there are enemy combatants still alive. I do have some plans for the village, in case some of the opposing force manage to slip through."

"I am trying to avoid any kind of impact on the village. The towns people will be sent under the dome and allowed back when things are done."

"Well Jim, I have just the configurations you have described on two drones and a third drone that can be ready in four hours."

"Okay, Bill, let's make it happen. I will be back in contact to let you know when to launch."

"We'll be ready, Jim, just let me know."

"Roger that. Talk to you later."

By now, the troops had started to arrive. Sean stuck his head in the door and said, "Good Morning, Sir, need a refill?"

"That would be nice. Come on in, there are a few things I need to go over before I address the troops. See if you can round up the XO too."

"Yes, Sir."

Ten minutes later, the two of them strode into J.T.'s office, pulled up a seat and sat down facing J.T.'s desk.

J.T. started in. "You have seen the alert message. I have already contacted aviation and made arrangements for drone support." He went on to explain the plan to his XO, Major Maxwell Stein and Sean, the units' sergeant major.

Questions were asked and discussed until J.T. got to the part about protecting the village. His suggestion was pretty simple, roof top fortified automatic machine gun squad and draping the buildings with the units' bullet proof material. Each of the troops would be given a 10 by 10 section that they would take up into the tree and double it over and surround themselves to protect and hide their body-heat signature. The buildings in the village will have an erected frame three feet from the actual building, then hang the bullet proof sheets over the frame at a 2-or 3-fold thickness. Hopefully, this would stop any type of RPG that may be aimed at the building. The theory that the tree hidden troopers would kill off all the attacking forces before they even got within five miles of the village, but in case a few managed to sneak through the village would not sustain any significant damage.

Sean wanted to discuss the actual role of the troops in the trees and had a few points to make, all of which were valid and well thought out. The main one being that there was no way of knowing if the opposing force was going to be using any type of body armor, therefore using the poison darts was going to be hard to be effective unless you were aiming for the lower body. J.T. offered to discuss with aviation if it was possible for the drones to be able to discern whether or not the troops were wearing any type of body armor. J.T. terminated the meeting, giving both men instructions to get started on and a suggestion that the three of them would meet again at lunchtime to update each other.

J.T. got back on the phone to the aviation CO, Lt. Colonel Derek Stills, and put the question to him. "Was the technology sophisticated enough to be able to tell if the ground troops were wearing body armor or not?"

"Well, I am glad you called when you did. I was just about to call you. The drones are almost completely configured, and I needed to see if there was anything else I could offer you. To answer your question, to discern that, would require two drones, scanning the troops from different angles and heights. We would be looking for the differences in the torso heat radiation, understanding that body armor would suppress heat radiation and give a difference in thermal readings that could be obtained. We would be able to obtain that information in two or three passes overhead and above 10,000 feet with the second drone making an oblique or perpendicular pass from say 12,500 feet. That info would be transmitted back here for integration and interpretation. We could have that info inside of 10 hours."

"Derek, you have no idea how many questions that have answered and how that impacts my battle plan. A couple of other questions. How long can each of the drones stay aloft? Can they be refueled while in the air and what is the minimum altitude needed for optimum performance?"

"That's easy, ten hours, yes, they can complete mid-air refueling and 1200-1500 feet."

"Then let's get the birds in the air and once you have the information, I will decide how many birds we will need to have on station. Oh, and I have changed my mind, I want all birds with full ordinance loadout."

"I will give the order and get back to you ASAP after I get your info compiled." J.T. hung up and allowed himself to relax.

He decided to call Heather during a free moment. "Hey, babe, what do you want to do for dinner? I should be finished here by 8-8:30pm at the latest?"

Heather perused her desk and replied, "That sounds about right for me. How about Sabatini's, the new Italian place downtown?"

"Sounds great. You want to call for reservations or do you want me to?"

"I'll do it. I have the number in my phone already."

"You mean you have been there with someone else? I'm crushed."

"Yeah, I have. Your mom, sister and I went there for lunch when you were in the tank. Had a wonderful time getting to know them. They are great people."

"I thought my ears were burning while I was in the tank."

"Nobody said anything bad. They were quite pleased that you and I were attracted to each other. There were a few snide comments about your previous female interludes, none of them were felt to be correct for you. I however, am an excellent choice and that comes from both, so there."

"Who am I, to dispute the knowledge of my two favorite women in the world, present company excepted?"

"Thanks. Glad to know where I stand."

"Hey look, I have to address the unit in three minutes, so I have to run. Love you."

"See ya later, love you too."

"Ten-hut," was sounded upon J.T.'s entrance into the auditorium, followed by the entire DSF17 unit members jumping out of their chairs to stand at attention. J.T. stepped up on the stage and strode to the podium.

"As you were," he commanded. This was immediately followed by Sean commanding, "Take seats" and the subsequent rustling of the troop getting comfortable.

J.T. looked out over the crowd and started his comments, saying, "I want to thank all of you that came by the hospital to see me, and the few of you that offered me a little taste. I am deeply touched and can't think of anything to say but to tell you, with a heartfelt thank you, how touched I was and to let you know that it helped me to return sooner than expected, so I could stand before you and say thanks. I shall never forget the kindness and love I received from all you."

A voice came up from the back, "We're glad you're here, Sir, so can we get on with business. We all got the alert, sir, so what are we gonna do?"

J.T. looked out over the crowd and said, "Right, so let's get on with it. Five days ago, an outside the dome village from Dome 18 was attacked by a band of marauders. The village was completely leveled and there were no survivors, that includes women and children. The response from DSF18 unit was four hours too late. There was very little info gleaned from the site other than there was very little evidence of explosives and shell casings ranging from 22 cal to 50 cal. The buildings were ransacked and then torched. Some farm animals were missing, and the rest were run off into the countryside. Thirty-six hours later, an outlying village from Dome 19 succumbed to the same fate as the previous village. The findings were not very different from 18. The upper-level commanders think they went from 18 to 19 instead of 18 to 17, so that there would be some confusion and less time to prepare a response. They obviously do not know who they are fucking with."

That comment drew a loud, vigorous response of OOH-rah, followed by the usual "fuckin 'ay rights."

J.T. raised his hand and waited for the murmurings to die down. "The plan of battle is going to be a little different from what we are used to. Currently, I have dispatched three armed drones to locate the enemy force and when I receive the info we will plan further." J.T. clicked his remote and a topographic map of the area appeared on the screen. "Currently, from my anticipated guess, they will be approaching from the upper right area and as you can see there is only one road, and this is a firebreak line, not an actual road. I think this is going to let them think that we will not be paying attention to this avenue of approach, so as soon as I get info from the drones, I can determine if they have vehicles and whether they are armored. Once I can say with certainty, they will be using this firebreak, we will dispatch two squads to line both sides of the firebreak with claymore type explosives on both sides of the road and about one mile or so in, we will bring a large dead tree and drop it on the road. Then we will put explosive devices around the area so that no matter what they decide, they are not going to be able to to get by alive and still mobile. The other aspect of our plan is going to be three skirmish lines manned by two augmented squads. You all will be in the trees, 12-15 feet off the ground."

"You will be cocooned inside a Kevlar type blanket covering you from head to toe and underneath you. This should make you invisible and it will block any heat signatures if they are more sophisticated than I give them credit for. You will be outfitted with service rifles, outfitted with darts that will have poison loads. This poison should cause death in 30 seconds. The first skirmish line will be 12 miles from Coulter. The second line will be nine miles from Coulter and the final line will be six miles from the Coulter village limits. All the farm field fences will be attached to a generator that will be putting out 10k volts at 150 amps. This is going to fry anyone that touches the fence, so remember that. The squads assigned to Coulter will erect Kevlar and plywood walls around the sides that will be facing the assumed approach routes. There will be two machine guns on the roof of the barn and the largest apartment building. These will be protected by Kevlar draping. Everyone will be outfitted with night vision equipment with a heads-up display that will be connected to the overhead drones. The HUD will show everyone, every enemy combatant in the area. You will attack the enemy after, I say again, after they have passed your location. I hope to be able to tell you if they are wearing body armor."

"So, it goes without saying you will be aiming from the waist to the feet. That way, the dart will hit meat and not armor. When each opponent dies, they will disappear from your HUD. This way, you will always know who is left alive. Skirmish line one and two will not pursue anyone that gets by. Using darts will not allow any of you to get wounded. I do not want to have to call your families to tell them you were killed by friendly fire. Skirmish line 3 will pick up anyone that gets through."

"So, until I get further info from the drones, everybody needs to get their gear together, check it all out, then get with your squad leaders who will explain the portions of the plan that apply to you. We will go over things as soon as we have more definitive info. Questions should be directed to squad leaders, squad leaders to Sergeant Major, or the XO, if Sean does not have an answer. Dismissed!"

J.T. headed off the side of the stage and then made his way back to his office. The phone on his desk was blinking, indicating a priority message was awaiting his attention. He got himself another cup of coffee, sat down in his chair, and made himself comfortable before addressing the phone message. He picked up the headset, punched the blinking button on the phone. A few seconds later, the call was answered.

"Lt Colonel Stills, flight ops."

"Derek, J.T. What you got for me? "J.T. asked.

"First, the size of the enemy force is between 65 and 80. There are two jeep type vehicles and four trucks, probably 6x6's, in a column that is one jeep followed by two trucks, one of which is towards the front of the column that appears to be carrying fuel and probably foodstuffs, followed by one truck that appears to be carrying tents and other equipment. This is followed by two columns of foot mounted troops with two trucks and a jeep pulling up the tail end of the column. The force appears to be about 26 miles from Coulter. They appear to be using fire-break roads, rather than clearing a path or using larger established roads. Time estimates for them entering the contact area is twenty-four hours. The data is still coming in, but it suggests that they do not have a full complement of weapons and body armor. They appear to be wearing only front chest armor. This is based on body heat determinations. Specifically, they are only covering the front and not both sides of the torso."

"How fast is the enemy moving?" J.T. asked.

"About 1-2 miles per hour on average," was the reply.

"Okay, so let's get the fully armed drones in the air and keep them there until this situation is resolved. Please double check the ability of transmitting the info to individual troops. I need to be sure the troops can tell who is alive and who is dead and where they are located."

"Wilco, flight ops out."

"17 out." J.T. sat back, then reached for the intercom button and requested the XO and Sargent Major to come into his office.

Both men entered the office within seconds of each other. J.T. indicated that he wanted them to take a seat. He started by bringing them up to speed on the drone info. He then began by telling Sean that he wanted two signs placed along the firebreak road that they were going to be using. The signs would state, 'Warning entering live fire zone effective first of April through 30 June and 15 October through 15 Feb. Contact DSF 17 for planned dates. Remain on the road. Unexploded artillery shells are located throughout the live fire zone. DSF 17.

"Have these placed at intervals along the projected route. Also, I want CLAYMORE type anti-personnel mines every 30 feet on both sides of the road, offset placement. Two miles in, I want a dead tree dropped across 75% of the road with contact mines put underneath and alongside the area where the vehicles may drive to get around the tree. This should thin the ranks and supplies out quite a bit. Now let's talk about Coulter. I want all the fields that are surrounded by wire fencing to be attached to generators that have the setting adjusted to 10,000 volts at 150 amps. I want anyone that touches the fence to be fried on the spot."

"Next, I want two sides of the biggest buildings covered by layered Kevlar sheets, plywood, and sheet metal, at least four layers thick and five feet away from the actual physical building. I want these to be able to stop an RPG round without any damage to the building. On the roof of the two biggest buildings around the chimney, there are two sniper areas for squad machine guns and three personnel assigned to each spot. Plenty of Kevlar protection for both. If things go as planned, there should be no bad guys that get through the skirmish lines. For the troops in the skirmish lines, everyone should have 10 of the poison darts. As you recall, the heads-up displays will show white dots indicating live targets, blue dots will indicate dead ones and green dots will indicate friendlies.

The troops are going to have to hold their fire until the enemy has passed them and aim for the back. The enemy will have frontal armor that the darts won't penetrate, so they can't waste shots. I want the enemy dead before he realizes he has been ambushed. I want all the troops going home alive and unscathed. Sean, pick a six-man squad. They are going to plant signs, claymores and set up the tree and the surrounding area. Try to make the tree look like it has been laying there for more than a year.

"I want the dirtballs lulled in to not paying that close of attention to this area, so we can thin the ranks out, as much as possible. Technically, very few of the walking ground troops should survive the mines. That means the troops in the trees have only a few of the enemy to deal with. The vehicles should be damaged and basically unusable. What's left will be addressed by the drones and no, I will not be in the air. I'm getting too old for that shit."

"Now, about the day after. We are going to need to round up all the bodies, their weapons and ammo, any explosives and any usable equipment, clothing, shoes, backpacks, tents, cooking gear, blankets and sleeping bags. The bodies will be gathered, taken up into the mountains and dumped in a gorge. We will cover them with rocks and gravel dynamite from the sides of the mountains. What remains will be food for the wildlife. I think the rifles and pistols will be given to the people of Coulter after they are checked out, by the armorer. They can use them for hunting or self-protection.

"It would be nice to be able to call on the villagers in times where we need extra personnel, and have them, with basic training, available to be called upon. Could make a difference, sometime in the future. Oh, and before I forget, try to make the signs look like they have been there for a while and the claymores are well concealed. I don't want anything given away. If things go really well, all the enemy troops will be dead and or wounded to a level that they are not able to resist." J.T. finished his brief.

"I would really like to have all of them dead and none of our guys even slightly injured. I am expecting an update from flight ops, letting me know the enemies' progress. Hopefully, they will set up camp and spend the night and then set up an attack to come after dusk tomorrow evening. I will brief you as soon as I have more information." The XO and Sergeant Major stood and exited J.T.'s office.

J.T. finished a couple of minor items, stood and walked out to Sean's desk.

"Sean, please come with me. I want to make rounds of the troops and answer any of their questions before stuff hits the fan." They made their rounds and observed all the troops were busy getting their gear together, inspecting it or repairing or replacing it if needed. All their weapons were disassembled and the smell of cleaning solvent, gun oil, and sweat permeated the area. A couple of the men stopped J.T. and asked point-blank if he was kidding about them being up in a tree and shooting the enemy in the back.

"I was as serious as a heart attack. There are no rules in combat, especially when the enemy kills women, children and unarmed combatants. I have no intention of having any of my men in harm's way fighting these animals. I am sorry if this approach to the battle offends anyone, but just remember that there are no rules in combat, and you never give the enemy a break or a chance. Is that clear?"

"Aye, Aye sir!" was the universal response from all those listening. J.T. raised his voice so everyone in the squad ready area.

"Those of you that are new to the unit, there are only a couple things that we adhere to in combat. One, all the enemies die, period. No prisoners, no wounded. Two, everyone from DSF17 goes home in one piece, preferably with no injuries. Is everyone clear? Are there any questions? Each of you be sure to pack an extra piss container or 2. I do not want you climbing down from your perches to pee, and I don't want some sharp-eyed enemy dirtball stepping in a puddle of piss then wondering where it came from and spreading the alarm. Does everyone understand?"

"Yes Sir."

"Carry on, good luck and good hunting!" J.T and Sean turned and left the squad bay. They made a little chitchat on the way back to the office. Sean asked him how things were going with Heather.

J.T. responded, "Things are wonderful, and I am glad I had waited for the right one to come along and, in fact, she had."

Sean got this stupid look on his face and replied, "Your sister has been telling me that for the last month. I hate it when she is right."

"I know what you mean. She gets so smug that I just want to bitch slap her into next week," J.T. replied.

"You have no idea how many times that idea has crossed my mind," Sean lamented.

"You're a better man than me. She always had Mom or Dad to protect her from that, or she would tattle-tale on me. After a while, I just gave up. Seemed to be a little easier to just give in. Guess that's why I do not give in with the troops and standing combat orders," J.T. said.

"Well, the troops appreciate being able to count on the command to back them up, I know I do," Sean replied.

J.T. patted Sean on the back and then said, "I must be doing something right." J.T. looked at his desk and saw the blinking red light.

"Have a seat after you get the XO back in here."

When both men were present and seated J.T. picked up the

phone and pressed the blinking red light. He then pushed the speaker button.

"Flight ops, Lt. Colonel Stills here."

"Derek, J.T, here, you are on speakerphone. What's the scoop?"

"Well, J.T. it looks like they have settled in for the night. They are about thirteen miles from the firebreak road. I am not able to see any change in the number of combatants. Heat signatures still indicate they are just using the front body armor plate. I'm only able to make out one jeep with a brace of rear-mounted 50-caliber machine guns. We have not been able to pick up any anti-air countermeasures or mounted rockets."

"Are you able to discern any such posturing that would indicate they have advanced knowledge of what they should expect when they assault Coulter?" J.T. asked.

"From the pictures of their camp, there seems to be a relaxed state of security based on the number and positioning of guards and patrols. This is a very relaxed camp. I would think that they think, their strategy of appearing to attack in an entirely different direction has succeeded in catching us unprepared and with "our drawers down". I don't think that we should change the current battle plan or lower the level of vigilance currently in place."

"Comments, gentleman?" J.T. asked.

"I assume the drones will be up continuously?" the XO asked.

"That is the current plan," J.T. replied.

"I suggest we get the troops out accomplishing the signs and claymore placement early in the morning, then we will get the village prepared, and the troops disbursed," Sean suggested.

"Questions, comments, thoughts?" None were forthcoming, so J.T. dismissed both with an admonishment to get everything done soonest.

"Derek, great work so far. Please keep me posted at any hour if there appears to be a significant change in the current status."

"Thanks, Jim will do. Flight ops out."

J.T. checked his watch and noted that it was 4:45 p.m. and with that, he got back to the business of running DSF17. There was always going to be paperwork, and as his mentor had said, it won't do itself. He looked at the stack of papers on the side of his polished mahogany desk, let out a sigh, and reached for the top file and settled into the least thankful aspect of his job.

When he finally looked at his watch, when he grabbed the last file, he realized he had been at it for three hours non-stop. He reached over and hit the intercom button and when Sean answered, he requested both his and the XO's presence in his office. He finished the last file of paperwork when both men entered his office.

"Ok, bring me up to speed. Where are we at?"

The XO spoke first. "The signs have been done and I must say they look like they are ten years old, and they have been placed along the firebreak road. The claymores have been laid out every 15 yards and that distance split on the other side of the road. The tree was brought in and laid as per your request and the area has been mined and boobytrapped."

"Excellent, that should stop this group in their tracks," J.T. said.

Sean began, "All the troops have been issued the darts, Kevlar drapes. The other forms and Kevlar steel is up against the side of buildings, ready to be assembled first thing at daylight. Almost all the children and female residents are already inside the dome. The force field will be turned on at 0800 tomorrow and will remain on until you order it lifted. All the night vision equipment and HUDs are disseminated amongst all the troops.

"They have been synced with the drones and everyone has been personally instructed as to what to do and what each blip means, and they are all set to go. I anticipate the troops hitting the trees as soon as we find out when the enemy is moving. Hopefully, it will be dark before they get to the road and we have plenty of time to get into the trees, get the Kevlar disguise up, so that they become invisible. I have estimated that everyone will be in position ready to fight not later than 11:00 a.m."

"Excellent. I suggest we meet here at 0700 and update everything before we move out. Please beware that the enemy may decide to move out early in the morning, so before you head home, ensure that the troops are ready to hit it with ten minutes notice. Great job guys. Don't know what I would do without both of you. Thanks. Now let's get everybody situated and relaxed. See you in the morning. Dismissed," J.T. stated.

J.T. finished clearing his desk, called flight ops for an update and, after being assured everything was unchanged, he donned his uniform cap and left the building. When he reached his vehicle, he took out his phone and sent a message to Heather telling her that he was headed home to change clothes and that he would meet her at the restaurant. He received a confirmatory message back just as he entered the house. Shedding all of his clothes as he entered the bathroom, he was able to walk right into the shower.

Exactly eight minutes later, he was dressed in a pressed pair of khaki pants, a blue button-down shirt, tasseled loafers and a dark blue sports jacket.

He paused briefly in front of the mirror, then sauntered out of the house to his vehicle. Fifteen minutes later, he was parked within fifty yards of the front door. Walking down the street, checking out the windows of the different shops, he stopped in front of the jewelry store and glanced at all the diamond rings on display, then moved on to the entrance to the restaurant.

As he entered, he scanned the room, wondering where the most beautiful woman he had ever known would be sitting. He spotted her sitting at the end of the bar, alone.

He strode over and touched her shoulder saying, "Hey lady, can I buy you a drink?"

Her response was, "Sure GI, looking for a good time?"

"Yes, I am. How much?"

"Me love you long time, $5?"

"Too much, $3?"

"GI, you too cheap, $5?"

"You drive hard bargain $5 but you sucky and fucky, OK?" J.T. bartered.

"GI. You number one. How are you doing?" Heather asked.

"As well as can be expected." was the reply. "We are all set, just waiting for the bad guys to commit to a plan of attack so we can deploy. Have I told you how beautiful I think you look tonight?"

"No, you just propositioned me, that was all."

"Well, you look stunning and are the most beautiful woman in the place by far."

"Bet you say that to all the girls," Heather chided.

"Course I do. I'm trying to get laid."

"No doubt. So how has that been working out?" she questioned.

"Not really well, but I never give up hope," J.T. responded.

"You hungry?" she asked.

"Haven't had anything to eat all day," J.T. lamented.

"Me neither."

J.T. walked over to the check-in podium, gave his name and signaled Heather to follow him. The greeter pointed to their table and J.T. held Heather's seat. After she was seated, he went to the other side of the table and had a seat. While they were perusing the menu, the waiter arrived and asked them for their drink order.

Heather popped up and said, "Since I have already eaten here once I will order the drinks."

She turned to the waiter and ordered a bottle of Pinot Grigio. They both went back to the menu when Heather remarked that her previous visit was for lunch, with his mother and sister, and it was a different menu, so she really couldn't offer any suggestions on what to order.

J.T. commented on the menu by saying how diverse it was, especially with the different types of homemade pasta. He then ordered a Caesar salad, seafood fettuccini Alfredo with scallops, shrimp, lobster and porcini mushrooms with tiramisu for dessert.

Having put the orders in, the conversation turned to Heather's work. She related some of the difficult cases she had been asked to consult on.

J.T. said," Do you remember Sara, the Coulter resident you worked on her hip a few months ago?"

"Of course, I remember her," Heather responded.

"Well, all the Coulter residents will be inside the dome tomorrow when I order the force field turned on so perhaps you will get a chance to see her."

They continued with the conversation, stopping only when the waiter served the salad and then the entrée. Both were very impressed with the meal, so much so that J.T. asked the Chef for his Alfredo sauce recipe and impressed the chef when he mentioned he could taste some cream sherry in the sauce. The chef whispered in his ear his appreciation if J.T. and Heather would keep that information to themselves as the restaurant business was very competitive and any edge that he could keep would help to keep the business open. J.T. mentioned the products that were available in Coulter and suggested that perhaps a visit could be arranged, and the chef could taste products to see if he would be interested in an exclusive arrangement for those products. J.T. went so far as to suggest that perhaps the farm section of Coulter could grow some specific things that may be difficult to obtain but might add some variety to the menu that would make his restaurant unique, thereby ensuring the restaurant stayed open. The chef was truly appreciative and promised to contact J.T. next week.

J.T. paid the check, then held Heather's seat as she arose from the table. Heather took his offered elbow, and they exited the location of their first actual date.

As they left the restaurant, J.T. turned to Heather and whispered, "This has been the finest first date I have ever had. I shall remember it for the rest of my life. It was perfect, just like you, my love."

Heather kissed his lips gently, but with obvious love. "I could not have said it better, my love."

They walked on until they reached Heather's car. They again kissed, this time with more passion.

"Coming to my place or going home?" he asked.

"Your place," was the answer.

"Good choice," he said as he opened the car door.

"See you at home." J.T made his way to his car, again stopping in front of the jewelry store, where he paused for a couple of minutes. He walked on to his car, got in and set the nav system to return home. He pulled in nine minutes after Heather had, and parked behind her because he had a feeling that he would be leaving earlier than she would. As he entered the house, he turned and locked the door then threw the keys on the counter in the kitchen and hung his jacket up.

He could hear Heather in the shower, so he went in to the kitchen and fixed coffee for the morning. Then he retired to the bedroom, removing his clothes the whole way, throwing them in the hamper before stretching out on the bed. Heather came out of the bathroom, still toweling herself dry. She had not washed her hair; it would have to wait until the morning.

"Things are going to start happening sometime today, but I don't know when. Might be a good idea if you bring some clothes and stay here. I don't expect to be involved in the battle. I do not know when I will be home or when I will be able to contact you, but I will call you with updates when I can. Might be a good idea if you were to go to work, it will be a good idea to keep you occupied. This whole thing should not last more than a day at most. I will give you the address of the building where all the Coulter people will be housed and might be a good idea to stop in and see how they are doing. Maybe even have a chance to see how Sara is doing," J.T. said.

"Are you sure you are not going to be in danger?" Heather asked.

"Only if I fall out of my chair or slip on a banana peel," he replied.

"You'll call when you can, right?" she questioned.

"I promise," was the reply. "We need to get to sleep. Tomorrow is going to be a long day."

CHAPTER
FOURTEEN

J.T.'s internal alarm went off at 4 a.m. As he was getting out of bed, his phone vibrated.

"Lt. Colonel Coulter here,"

"Sir, this is the Drone Duty officer Lt. Simkins. I was told to contact you with any change in the area you have under surveillance."

"OK, let's have it," J.T. stated.

"Sir, the camp appears to be waking up. Readings indicate that they have a kitchen that is now active and there is a lot of movement throughout the camp, but no evidence of anyone leaving the encampment or the general area," Simkins replied.

"Very well. Keep an eye on things and let me know when they appear to be packing up the vehicles," J.T. ordered.

"Aye, Aye, Sir," and then Simkins hung up.

Heather was sitting up in bed. *She is the only woman I know of that can still be incredibly beautiful even getting right out of bed,* he thought.

"It's starting. I must leave now." J.T. leaned over and kissed Heather, told her he loved her, then went straight into the bathroom to shower, shave, and get dressed. He stopped in the kitchen to grab a cup of coffee, snatched up his car keys, and he was out the door.

On the way to the office, he called Major Stein, the XO, and updated him. He then did the same thing with Sean, so the whole command structure was up to speed before J.T. walked in the door.

Sean was there and handed him a cup of fresh coffee as they entered J.T.'s office. Max Stein came in a couple of minutes later. Everyone got comfortable as J.T. began to go over his thoughts about the upcoming battle. Placement of the troops was laid out but J.T. was quick to say that he did not want the men up in the trees until the enemy was about an hour's walk away. That way, the men would still be limber and relaxed and able to be moved to a different location if the situation mandated it.

He also decided that Major Stein would command a 12-man squad that would be able to watch the "back door" so to speak. There was discussion back and forth about rules of engagement, strategic placement of assets, use of firepower and a few other issues pertinent to the current situation. About an hour and a half later, there was a phone call from Lt. Simkins with an update on the drones.

"Sir, it appears that they are moving right along with breaking down camp. The heat signatures we assumed were the kitchen stoves and steam tables have all gone cold. The areas that had tents are now showing bare ground, so I would venture a guess that they will be ready to move out within the next ninety minutes. I expect to be able to predict movement direction and speed within thirty minutes after they move out," Simkins reported.

"Lt. Simkins, are you able to give me a body and vehicle count at that time?" J.T. asked.

"Yes Sir, I will also be able to describe the layout of the column, as well as mounted and dismounted troops," Simkins replied.

"Excellent Simkins. We need that info soonest," J.T. said.

"Aye, Aye, Sir," Simkins replied.

"Well, gentlemen, we have things to do. We will meet back here in one hour forty-five minutes. Make sure your troops are ready to move out after that. Sean, I want all electronics rechecked and weapons sighted in at fifty yards. Remember, the darts are going to have to be aimed at the lower thighs, front, back, sides, it doesn't matter. Center mass front and back will not be available due to body armor in front and backpacks and web gear in the back and around the waist. I really want to stay away from using bullets because they will give away our positions and tactics, increasing the risk the troops will have to face. Remember, no enemy survivors and no troop injuries or deaths. That is the goal. Won't be easy, but this is the type of thing we train for year-round. With hundreds of thousands of rounds fired at the range by every member of this command, that should improve and increase our likelihood of success. Dismissed."

Both men stood, popped to attention, pivoted, and exited the room. J.T. shut off all the electronics in his office. He left his office, striding with a purpose, turning right at the third inter-section before stopping in front of a large metal door without a window. He flashed his ID Badge in front of the reader along-side the steel door. There was a loud clacking, and the door swung open inward, allowing J.T. to enter the combat control center, the nerve center of the day's operation. He picked up a headset and put it on, adjusting it for comfort. He stepped over to a console on his left and typed in his passcode number. There was an immediate acknowledgement of him coming online.

"Drone command," he said into the attached microphone, and was rewarded with a, "LT. Simkins, drone commander here."

"Coulter here. I need a current update."

"Yes, Sir. The enemy has broken camp and has formed two columns. Main column is about two miles from entering the firebreak road. The second column consists of 26 to 30 ground troops, one jeep with a single machine gun in the back. No evidence of armor. There is one other vehicle, a 6x6 truck with covered material in the truck bed, no mounted troops seen. They are about 2.5 miles away from the main column headed in a northeast direction, over rugged terrain with no road being seen. They are moving at about two miles per hour and are about seven miles from the northern border of the village of Coulter."

"Can you give me an estimate of enemy strength in the main column?"

"Yes Sir, there are two vehicles at the front of the column, a jeep with a brace of machine guns in the bed and no evidence of armor and one 6x6 truck appears to be carrying the camp equipment, stoves, tents, storage boxes. There are between forty and fifty-five dismounted troops in two columns, walking along the edge of the road, standard placement. The rear of the column is two 6x6 trucks carrying the rest of the encampment gear and the second truck is carrying what looks like a pair of large bladders. Most likely, one is gas and one is water. The second Jeep is pulling up the rear. It has one machine gun in the bed, also with no armor. Their speed is about two miles per hour, and they have just started on the firebreak road. I am switching cameras to your console split-screen, left side is main column and right side was the second column."

"Very good Simkins. Now arm all the drones. Attack patterns will be at the rear of the main column, from the rear to the front of the column. After confirmation that all the vehicles have been destroyed, you will dispatch one of the drones to join up with the drone surveying the second column. When it arrives, the second columns vehicles will be attacked in the same manner as was used for the main column vehicles. Are you clear on this?"

"Yes, Sir," and he read back the orders exactly as they were given.

"Excellent Simkins, carry on. Coulter out." J.T. readjusted his rolling desk chair and returned to watch the monitoring console screen.

He then heard, "Star Trek, Beer Mug".

"Star Trek go."

"Star Trek, we have an issue that has popped up. All the residents of Coulter have left except for about twenty male residents who refuse to leave and wish to help defend the village. Over," the XO stated.

J.T. thought to himself, *I should have expected this. They feel a need to defend their home and property. I really should have them removed, but that would be an insult to the citizens if I refused to let them defend their own homes.*

"Roger beer mug, get them armed and find places at the northern entrance to the village where they can back up your squad, but have a low probability of actually being involved in the shooting. Be sure to give them communication equipment so they can stay under your control. Over," J.T. ordered.

"Wilco, out."

At this point, J.T. had notified Dome Control to activate the force field, and that there were about seventy-five residents entering the city from the Coulter escape tunnel. They would be met by the city's security services and escorted to a secure facility where they would remain until J.T. had decided that everything was over, and it was safe to return.

J.T. returned to looking at the console, carefully watching the progression of the main column.

"Kilt man, Star Trek," J.T. said into the microphone.

"Kilt Man here, go."

"Can you send me the code for controlling the firebreak mines over?"

"Sending text now."

There was a ding on J.T.'s phone. He retrieved the message, turned to the keyboard and typed in 1161151. The screen dissolved into a schematic that laid out the placement of the mines along the firebreak road. He entered his own pass code and hit enter. Alongside the schematic, a column of numbers appeared. J.T. moved the cursor to the top number and clicked on it. On the screen, the top line of mines lit up. Moving the cursor to the next number, he clicked, and the lower line of mines lit up. Moving to the next number, he clicked and every other mine on the top line lit up. Moving on down through the numbers, he developed a clear picture of how he could use the mines to his best advantage. Moving back to the monitor, he took note of how far the main column had moved in the road and guessed he had about an hour before the column was in position for him to use the mines.

————————

Major Stein, aka Beer Mug, was standing in front of the group of Coulter male citizens, attempting to put this ragtag group of passionate men into some sort of controlled armed group that would be of help and not cause other issues. Boy, the group of men were really pissed off and determined to be involved. Major Stein began to speak.

"Men, I am Major Stein, XO of the unit and I am in charge of this sector of the upcoming battle. I understand how all of you feel, as does Colonel Coulter, with whom I have already been in contact. He has decided to allow all of you to participate in the defense of Coulter, under the proviso that you adhere to my orders and directions. Now, is there anyone here that honestly feels he can't or won't follow my directions?"

Seeing no hands, he moved on, "I have been instructed to issue you weapons and ammunition and to point out where you are to be placed and when you are to engage the enemy. The first thing you must understand and accept is that you are not professional warriors, but you will be supplementing them. They have been given their instructions and deployed in a manner that will ensure successful contact with the enemy. Your function is to back up their work and to kill any of the enemy that happen to slip past the deployed Unit members. Understand, the Unit does not take prisoners, nor do we help enemy wounded.

"They have chosen to attack a peaceful village and will pay for that decision with their lives. Am I clear about this? There is no room for debate about this. If you are not able to kill the enemy, then you should leave now and head to the escape tunnel. There will be no recriminations. Some men are simply not able to take another's life. There is no shame in not being able to kill, but having you here, where it may be necessary to kill, to save another's life, may jeopardize other members of the team. We can't have that, period. It has always been a goal of this unit to never have any KIA troops ever. The last time we had a KIA was two years before I arrived here, which was ten years ago. We will not have that record broken because someone refuses to, or is not able to function on our battlefield. Now I ask again, is there anyone here that doesn't think they can take a life?"

After what seemed like eons, there were no hands raised. "OK, then let's move on. Each of you will be given a weapon and 100 rounds. Gunnery Sergeant Johanson will place each of you where he wants you to be stationed. Do not leave that spot until one of the Unit comes by and tells you that you can move. There should not be anyone from the Unit wandering around the area. Each of you will be issued a comm link and the unit will let you know if they are in or going to be in your area of protection. If there is someone in your area, you will shoot first and ask questions later, so to speak." With that, Major Stein turned the men over to Skip, who immediately took charge and moved the men out.

Ten more minutes, J.T. thought to himself. *Ten more minutes and they will be ready for the surprise.*

"Kilt man, Star Trek."

"Kilt man go".

"About to activate mines. You alternated the direction of the mines, as instructed."

"Aye, Aye. Sir, every other one starting with number two north side of the road."

"Excellent. Once the rubble settles, I will notify you which way to move the men if necessary. Get them saddled up and ready to move," J.T. ordered.

"Aye, Aye, Sir. Wilco. Out." Sean answered.

"Star Trek out."

J.T. returned to the monitor and updated his estimation of the columns' situation. After a couple of minutes of study, he turned to the screen that had the mine schematics displayed and clicked on two of the three numbers. He then called Lt. Simkins at Drone command.

"Simkins, this is Colonel Coulter. Be prepared to execute the attack in 05 minutes on the main column only. Are we clear?"

"Aye, Aye, Sir. 05 minutes, Main column only, aye."

"Coulter out." J.T. returned to the monitor and congratulated himself on being correct on the estimation of time before shit hit the fan. He programmed the computer to set off the mines on time, on the south side of the road and every other mine on the north side of the road. With luck, when this was over, there should be no ground troops left alive.

Mentally, he began a countdown as the timer itself counted down at the same time. He flipped a switch, and the drone nose camera began showing real-time images of the enemy column, jeeps and trucks included. The timer on the monitor reached 0 and everything on the screen exploded at the same time. The drone shuddered and jiggled the camera, while three rockets left their attachments on both wings. The camera caught the trails of all three rockets as they each headed towards their assigned target. Downward into the smoke and dust, followed by multiple explosions.

There was a buzzing in his ear followed by Lt. Simkins voice saying, "Birds away, on track and all targets destroyed, Sir."

"Well done, Simkins. Coulter out."

The smoke and dust finally cleared, and the battlefield finally came into focus. J.T. flipped a switch on the monitor and infrared and heat seeking functions were activated. J.T. looked over the battlefield, looking for evidence of life. He was unable to find any evidence of anyone living.

"Kilt man, Star Trek."

"Kilt man, go."

"Fire break road attack complete. Unable to tell how thorough. Take five men and sweep the area for signs of life. Watch your back. Used all the mines on the south side of the road and every other one on the north side. Contact me soonest with your answer about enemy combatants. Star Trek out."

"Kilt man, wilco. Out."

"Drone control, Coulter."

"Simpkins here Sir.

"See if you can clear up the sensors over the attack area. Compensate for the burning vehicles. We need to be able to see who survived the attack. Send the updated info to Kilt man and his cleanup squad."

"Working on that right now… they should be able to see the scanned area with the heat and infrared scans adjusted to remove any intense heat source. That should allow them to see who is still alive and where they are located and moving to."

"Excellent, also turn the aerial firefighting unit loose so we do not have a forest fire getting started. They should have a few armed guards in case there are enemy troops left alive and they are hiding. Switch to the second column. I need a location, movement and direction update and an estimated speed of movement. Make sure that one of the drones from the first attack has joined up and is prepared for a second attack."

"Aye, Aye sir. The second column has advanced 2.7 miles from the last scan. Speed of advance appears to be unchanged. It does not look like they are even aware of the attack on column one. Spacing and vehicle location remains unchanged."

"Which of the drones is armed with anti-personnel armament?"

"The drone that has just joined up with the one currently on station," was the reply.

"Set the detonation parameters for the anti-personnel round to explode 10 feet off the ground. Have the drone attack the vehicles in the same manner as column one. Launch in 10 minutes. Coulter out."

"Beer Mug, Star Trek."

"Beer Mug, go."

"Vehicle attack and one air burst anti-personnel missiles will be launched in nine minutes, so get your men ready. Are the armed citizens in position and counseled?"

"Beer Mug here, Skip Johansen has the civvies in hand and the rest of the troops are awaiting directions on final placement."

"Remember that the heat from the explosions is going to interfere with infrared and heat seeking scans. Before you send in any recons, wait until I tell you to. I will have drone control adjust the sensors to remove the scan effects of the explosion and until we get that done, I do not want anybody exposed to things they can't see."

"Beer Mug, roger. Wilco. Out."

"Star Trek, Kilt Man."

"Star Trek, go."

"We have at least six to eight personnel indicators of the attack still showing signs of movement. They are moving through the forest. They are west of the troops, waiting for position orders. The troops will need to be moved about ½ mile to the west of their current location.

"Kilt man, Star trek. Go ahead and move the troops ½ mile west, then up in the trees. No need to use darts. There aren't that many survivors that we need to conceal ourselves from. I will notify you if we need to move the troops to a different location."

"Kilt Man wilco, out."

"Drone control to Coulter. Missiles away, targets destroyed."

"Coulter, roger. See if you can clear up the scanners from

the heat signatures from the explosions. Notify Beer Mug when you have the scanners cleared up."

"Drone control, roger, wilco. Out."

"Star Trek, Kilt Man."

"Star Trek go."

"Skirmish line has been moved and are established. Estimate there is 1.5 miles until enemy contacts skirmish line one. We have heat signatures for eight hostiles current direction of movement indicates they will contact the middle of the newly established skirmish line. The current attack was extremely successful. I have dispatched part of the squad to retrieve the unexploded mines, 10 of them. The estimated casualty count was 65 KIA no WIA. This count is approximate due to the condition of a number of the bodies due to the mines. Couldn't tell about the vehicles. They were totally destroyed and then burned up. Staff sergeant Kenney is in command of skirmish line one. He will check in with me when he has completed the mission. Kilt man out."

"Excellent Kilt man, Star Trek out."

Meanwhile, in the northern part of the forest, the second platoon was lying in wait as the 12 remaining enemy troops made their way through the dense undergrowth, toward the coordinates originally laid out during the briefing that had been conducted earlier before breaking camp. They were unaware that the main column had been wiped out and that they were all that was left of the grand plan that was supposed to make them all secure and well taken care of for a long time. They were still noticeably shaken after seeing the devastation that had rained down on their friends and comrades-in-arms. All dead and gone in just a few seconds. So bloody and gory. It had taken them the better part of an hour to get oriented, rehash the original plans and decide which direction to go, and what they were going to do.

It was obvious that the community they were going to take over was prepared for them and had some serious firepower supporting them. Basically, they were unsure of where to go and what was waiting for them. He knew that they could not stay where they were. Someone was going to come and search the area for survivors, which meant they needed to get a move on. Hanging around would surely get them killed. This whole thing sounded so simple and easy; the way Jeb explained it. The first two towns were simple. The townspeople did not fight back. Only took a couple of hours. There wasn't much to load into the trucks. He still did not know what happened to the people, but he had a sneaking suspicion that they had all been killed. Didn't matter to him, he wasn't the one that pulled the trigger. More than likely, those members of the group were now dead or in the other column anyway.

"Regardless, Saddle up" he called out, "Move out. Single file. On me, try to keep the noise level down. Be alert." And with that, they moved out slowly, following their new leader.

Major Stein had arranged his men along the predicted path they were felt to take. So far, they had not seen nor heard anything from the leftover stragglers. The men were all under cover, locked and loaded, and eager to finish off the last of the brigands.

"Skip, Beer mug".

"Skip, go."

"Are your troops in position, loaded, locked, and safeties off?"

"Aye, aye, sir."

"Maintain area silence and no excessive movement."

"Aye, Aye sir. Wilco, Skip out." Skip stood, stretched out his legs, grabbed his weapon, making sure the was a round chambered and the safety was off, and he moved out, going to each of the hidden villagers, stopping by to speak to each, reiterating the silence and no movement orders. He personally checked each man's weapon for a chambered round and safety off. He was pleased with the level of calmness and focus each of these men displayed. He just hoped that they would hang tough when the shooting started.

Meanwhile, the survivors were making good progress towards the rendezvous point previously agreed to at the original briefing. So far, they had not seen nor heard anything other than regular sounds of a vibrant forest. Made for an unnerving walk. He had to work at putting the sounds out of his mind, making him focus his mind on his surroundings. Not much further, he thought, until we meet up with the rest of the force. Then we can get on with the mission.

He suddenly stopped, raised his fist to signal halt to the rest of the men. He stood there listening for five long minutes and hearing nothing, signaled to the men to move out. About 500 yards ahead, the DSF troops sat quietly in hiding. Their sensing equipment alerted them to the approaching group of men. Since the unit was aware that there were no other authorized people supposed to be in the area. Major Stein indicated the advancing troops to his hidden force, intending to get them sharper and more on alert. A few minutes later, the first two enemy troops stepped out into a clearing 75 yards from the hidden DSF Unit members.

They were immediately cut down as everyone that could see them unleased four or five shots per rifle. There were a few shots returned from the enemy, but none of them connected because Major Stein and the seasoned troops of the unit were well hidden, having done this type of activity dozens of times before. Didn't seem fair, but this was combat and there is no such thing as fair. This was not like a duel in the 1700s where you stood 10 paces from your enemy, then both of you shot at each other. There is no *"fair"* in combat. The whole idea is to go home alive and leave your opponent dead on the field of battle, period.

Unfortunately, opening fire on the enemy when only two of them were visible allowed the other 10 to scatter and find a different path towards the objective. Major Stein ordered his men to drop back, in a southernly direction, 50 yards and reset their positions. He told Skip what had happened and told him to have his men stand fast. Skip passed the orders on to his men but was unable to answer how many bad guys were headed his way, mainly because the unit had opened fire before they had all become visible, so there was no count made. Skip did his best to lead these non-military troops, keeping them under control and supported and informed while they waited for the time to act.

The enemy group was again suddenly rudderless, as the first man taken out was the one that had taken charge, made decisions and issued orders. The only thing missing from this group right now was that there was no one yelling at everybody else, trying to shout orders. The retreat was only 25 yards and then, as if by telepathic communication, they all regrouped. After a hushed discussion of options, Billy Williamson was elected the default leader because he had been in the military for two months before being kicked out for disobedience and unmilitary behavior.

His decision was to skirt the clearing that had already cost them two men and continue in the same general direction as before. He broke them up into two columns instead of single file. They started back on the same heading, the right column moving 10-15 yards, then the left catching up and alternating this movement pattern as they attempted to advance to the rallying point set out earlier that day down south. They still were unaware that the main force along with the supply lines had been completely decimated and wiped out. Not coming in contact with opposing forces, they continued to push forward.

They stopped after moving almost two miles before stopping to rest. The last few hundred yards, they had not maintained the silent movement practice and Skip was the first to hear their approach. He signaled to the rest of his detachment the fact he could hear people approaching and to hold their fire until he gave the word. When the enemy was within the 25-35yard range, Skip adjusted his position, extended the muzzle of his weapon, and waited until he could clearly see leaves moving. Then he fired, and another invader dropped. He switched to full-automatic and sprayed the area in front and behind. Another three invaders fell. There was return fire and one of Skips' men was hit. Wayne Franklin was hit in the arm but was still able to shoot. All of a sudden Sam Hansen jumped up and charged the enemy position, emptying his clip. He then ducked behind a boulder as the area around him was peppered with enemy bullets. He changed out his clip, moved to the opposite side of the boulder, and started charging the enemy again.

Meanwhile, the rest of the citizen troops laid down a steady flow of rounds, keeping the invaders' heads down as Sam advanced on their position. Sam cut to the right and stopped dead in his tracks. He flipped the switch to full auto and sprayed the area directly ahead of him. As soon as the clip was empty, Sam dropped prone and switched out the clip and crawled forward as his comrades also charged forward spraying the enemy and that allowed Sam to again stand and move to where he had a better line of fire, and he opened up and emptied his fourth clip. He dropped to his knee and changed out to his fifth and final clip. The shooting stopped for five minutes, so Skip and two other citizen soldiers ran to the area where enemy firing had come from. One enemy soldier raised his hands and dropped his weapon. As soon as he stood up, Skip put a round through the center of his forehead. The rest of the unit advanced to the area where all the enemy dead and badly wounded were laying and followed Skip's lead of shooting each body in the head.

"Beer Mug, Skip."

"Beer Mug go."

"Sir, all enemy combatants are dead. Please request drone control to scan infrared and heat sensing to confirm the same. We have one wounded. Not seriously, could you send Doc Horner up? Over. We are where we were originally placed. Over."

"Beer Mug, wilco, out."

Skip walked over to Sam and said, "You have a problem following orders, don't you?"

"Well Skip, you fired, but you never said, 'open fire' and when Wayne was hit, I just couldn't sit there and do nothing. It was like waiting for everybody to get shot," Sam responded.

"Didn't I say, "Open fire"? The rest of the group all shook their heads no.

"My bad. Ya'll did wonderfully. Obviously, we had some concerns about your ability to keep your shit together when being shot at and your ability to follow instructions and not shoot our own people. But you guys defended your home as well, actually better than we could have hoped for. Holding your placement conceivably impacted the Unit regulars, because they had dropped back, and you prevented them from pulling an end around and getting behind us. Thank you for your service," Skip said and then went around and personally shook each man's hand.

At that moment, Doc Horner showed up and was directed to the wounded man. He had Wayne bandaged, splinted, an antibiotic injection, pain shot, and tetanus shot. Wayne was showing some signs of shock, so Doc started an IV and threw together a litter. Four of the civilian troops hoisted him and headed off to the village. Take him to the clinic." Doc then called J.T.

"Star Trek, Doc."

"Star Trek, go."

"You can tell the dome they can turn off the force field and dispatch a medevac to the village center. We have one civilian WIA forearm and hand injury. Is going to need surgery. But will survive. Doc out."

"Star Trek, roger, wilco, out,"

"Beer Mug, Star Trek."

"Beer Mug go."

"I need AAR soonest with explanation. Out."

"Aye, Aye Sir".

"Skip, Beer Mug."

"Skip go."

"AAR soonest with WIA explanation."

"Aye, Aye, Sir, out."

J.T. picked up his phone and called the force field control and gave them the all clear. He then called a medevac and ordered them to pick up the wounded man in the center of the village. His third call was to Heather.

"Hi honey. We are sending you a wounded man, one of the civilians. Doc has him stabilized. The wound is to the hand and forearm. Doc says he will need surgery. The situation has been resolved. No survivors or other wounded for you to treat. The guys did a wonderful job. I should be home around 10. Want me to whip something up? Any preferences? OK, call if you are going to be later. Love you," J.T. said and then hung up.

He got up and got himself a cup of coffee. The pride he felt for his troops welled up in his chest as he sipped the first cup he had had since the whole thing began that morning. He was curious about what happened to cause the civilian soldier to get wounded. He thought he had given the Major clear instructions to keep the civilians out of harm's way. The AAR, after action report, should explain it, but those didn't always contain all the nuances needed to fully understand the occurrence. J.T. called the XO and Sean instructing them to meet him in the office.

J.T. got himself a cup of coffee and made himself comfortable at his desk when the XO and Sean entered.

"Get yourself a cup of coffee and grab a seat," he said. As they got comfortable, J.T. started in.

"Sean, bring me up to date about your end of things."

"Well," Sean began, "After we surveyed the road, the men did a great job. There was almost complete decimation. The placement of the mines was perfect. We counted 63 bodies, which, by the way, was difficult because some were almost totally destroyed. The vehicles were also destroyed, two jeeps and three trucks. We made sure the fires were under control before we went after the ones that got away. I moved skirmish lines two and 3, 1/2 of a mile to the west, dispatched to their direction of travel, according to drone command. We caught up with them. There were nine of them, just before they would have engaged with skirmish line two. They were destroyed. Rechecking all the bodies did not show any to still be alive. Drone command found no scanning evidence of life among any of the enemy. The air mobile fire fighters arrived and extinguished the fire, and I regrouped the assigned group and we then proceeded to the southern section of the village. We could hear gunfire coming from the north of the village, but it stopped before we arrived. End of my story."

"Guess this will be where I come in," Major Stein said.

"Yes, it would," J.T. remarked.

"OK then, I turned over the village volunteers to Gunnery Sergeant Skip Johanson with specific instructions to place them where there would be very little chance for their actual involvement in combat when the shooting starts. He assured me that he would be able to place all the men where the risk of involvement was minimal. Moving along, the drones took out both vehicles and the majority of the ground troops. There were eight or nine survivors, and according to the info from the drones' scanning. They, the survivors, headed off in an easterly direction. I positioned the squad directly in front of their predicted path. Skip took the volunteers and went south, forming a dome over the northern approach to the village. We were expecting to engage the enemy in about 20 minutes after we got set but, they decided to turn south. Skip had set up an ambush and when they arrived, he told the volunteers to hold their fire until he told them to shoot. When he had a shot, he took it. He thought that when he opened fire, the volunteers would start shooting. Since he did not verbally say commence firing, they did not. The enemy started shooting at the volunteers and actually wounded one. This pissed a couple of the volunteers off, and they went a little hog crazy. They started charging the enemy, shooting on fully auto, changing clips like they had been combat dozens of times before. They killed all the enemy troops they faced and other than the one that sort of kicked off the whole thing, there was only one casualty. Doc has seen to him, and he should be in surgery right now. The hospital or its designee will contact us when he gets out of surgery."

Stein continued, "I think that a couple of things need to happen. One is that there needs to be a permanent village militia, trained and controlled by us, and second, there needs to be a few medals and commendations handed out. "

J.T. scratched his chin thoughtfully, then nodded his agreement.

"You write it up, I'll sign it," J.T. replied.

"There are a couple of things I need to get done in the next 48 hours. First, I want all the destroyed enemy vehicles moved into the area above the firebreak road where they were hit. Clear the area 30 yards in all directions. I do not want any live fire rounds to start a forest fire. Second, take a backhoe out alongside the road and make a trench five feet deep and five feet wide. Then use a bulldozer to push all the bodies into the ditch, then cover them up. Take three 6x6 ATVs along and collect all the weapons on the scene and return all of them from both sites to the armory. Get the company gunsmiths to tear all the weapons apart and repair any that are damaged. Damaged wooden stocks will be taken to the cabinetmakers in the village. Have them repair, refurbish or replace any stocks that need it.

"Have the armors reassemble all the weapons, pistols, rifles and SAWs and give me a complete list of everything. Have the training sergeant compile a training list and schedule. Have it on my desk in 48 hours. XO, prepare a speech to be delivered to the residents of Coulter and the appropriate enlistment forms, training schedules and handbooks for DSF members. A town meeting will be held in ten days on a Saturday night just before the movie starts. Sean, you and Skip, the XO and myself will be in attendance. Questions?"

There was a chorus of "No Sirs" from the two men.

"Very well. Dismissed. And by the way, outstanding job today. Simply outstanding. I'm so proud of you and the troops. Difficult operation and we got by with one non-life-threatening injury. I could not be more pleased. Carry on."

With that, they both stood, came to attention, pivoted and left the office. It had been a while since he had had an operation come off so smoothly, with so many enemy combatants killed, and vehicles destroyed. Reminded him that he needed to sit down and formulate future plans to be ready for other scenarios that may need to be dealt with in the future. He also realized that some structural changes need to be made to the buildings of the village. Ones that would be ready and not put together at the last minute like this time. Still, he had to smile with deep felt pride at how the troops had done. He couldn't be prouder.

As he sat at his desk pondering future scenarios, the phone rang.

"Lt. Colonel Coulter speaking," he said.

"Of course it is, silly." Heather replied.

"Hi sweetheart, how's things there?"

"Things are great. Your guy is out of surgery. Things went splendidly. Not a bad wound at all. Ten weeks and he should be back to his old self. How did things go on your end?" she asked.

"Complete success, all enemy troops destroyed. Coulter is safe and unaffected. You fixed the only casualty we had, so I couldn't ask for anything better. We still on for dinner?"

"Yes, I am famished. Have a couple of things to finish, then I am out of here. Meet you at the restaurant so we can celebrate. Love you."

"Love you too," With that, he hung up and smiled to himself. He reached over and shut off his computer, switched off the desk light, slid the chair back and made his way out of the building to his car, got in and headed off to the restaurant to meet his love.

———

J.T. entered the restaurant and strode over to the table where Heather was seated. He leaned down and gently kissed, communicating his love and happiness on seeing her, and his need to spend more time with her.

"Hey babe. How was your day, other than my guy?"

Heather smiled up at him and replied, "Not bad actually. Kinda reminds me of when I worked on you. Reminded me that I always wanted to be a hand surgeon. Life gave me a funny turn, and I ended up being an excellent general orthopedic surgeon that is great on all types of problems, not just hands and forearms. So, it was nice to work on a forearm injury. Tell me about your day."

"Where do you want me to start and don't say at the beginning."

"I'll let you choose."

"Okay, you know that there was an armed group of men that had attacked a couple of outlying dome villages and killed everyone there, children included. They moved in a manner intended to keep us from figuring out where they were going to strike next. I felt that we were the next target and since I was part of putting Coulter together, I decided to be prepared for them, enough in advance that we would put an end to their plans once and for all. I devised a plan, assigned men to put it into action, and directed them as they carried out the plan.

"There were 96 bodies tallied up when all was said and done. 7 vehicles, three of which were armed with heavy automatic weapons. There were no survivors, as per my orders. Digressing from that point, when I first took command of DSF 17, 18 years ago, we averaged about one assault every 10 to 12 days. The reason we had so many is that when the battle was over, half of the enemy force was still alive. This allowed them to regroup and try it again. That is why, after the 4th or 5th attack, I realized that we could not keep allowing the enemy to regroup and attack again or one day they would succeed and that would mean Dome 17 would cease to exist.

"That was why I set down rules of engagement that mandated no survivors, no wounded. The opposing force was not going to allow survivors, so neither was I. Besides, I think, the amount of resources, needed to incarcerate or provide medical care, food, clothing and shelter is more than we need to expend. Why should we house, feed, clothe and provide medical care to people that chose to attack us and try to take what is ours?"

"The word gets around that if you try to attack Dome 17, you will be buried there without exception. That has caused a significant drop in attacks down to maybe one every 6-7 weeks. Sorry to sound like I am on a soapbox, but I am passionate about the security of the Dome, and it is my job to protect it, so that is what I am doing and will continue to do. We had a significant display of bravery and courage today by men who were village citizens and not members of my unit. In fact, I established a Coulter militia today to be available for DSF17 to call upon. 25 men who will train, be outfitted by and work closely with the DSF unit so that there will be more reserve troops available to call up should the need arise. Surprisingly, this is not going to cost the Dome anything. I am outfitting them with the weapons, ammunition and other supplies confis-cated from defeated enemies. So that, my dear is how my day went," he finished.

"Well then, tell me about this heroic deed," Heather requested.

J.T. spent the next few minutes describing the deeds that occurred on the north side of the village. She was quite impressed with what had happened and did admit that J.T.'s reasoning for the militia was quite brilliant and well thought out.

"Thank you, my dear," he said with a dramatic bow. "So, how was your day?"

"It was interesting. I had a man with a mass on his right femur. Was pretty sure it was bone cancer, but after I biopsied it, it turned out to be benign, so I didn't have to amputate his leg. Just had to do a few things that would keep his femur from snapping in half. So, all in all, it turned out to be a good day."

The dinner arrived as they continued to discuss several things, and J.T. was again struck by how much he relished and enjoyed her company. They finished dinner and headed to his house. He did ask her if she would rather go to her home. She became almost indignant.

"Don't you want me around anymore?" she asked.

"That's not it, just thought perhaps you would like to go to your place, so you could pack and move in with me," he said.

Heather's jaw dropped a bit as she was caught completely off guard. "You want me to move in with you, like a real couple?"

"That would be why I asked you," he replied.

"Then I guess you should probably take me home, so I may pack," she purred.

"Your request is my command," he replied. And with that, he started the car and pulled out into the sparse late-night traffic, a smug look on his face and a jolt of pleasure coursing through his body. *I love it when a plan comes together*, he thought to himself. They held hands the whole way. It felt even more right,

The stop at her home was very short. She came out with a

large suitcase and nothing else. He helped her put the suitcase in the trunk and then headed off home.

"Guess I can pick up the other stuff later," she said.

"This weekend," was his reply.

Her smile took up her whole face and contentment filled her being. After they got to J.T.'s house, they entered and put all of her things away. Then off to bed and the start of the next phase of their relationship, and both were happy and satisfied as well as being in love with their soulmate.

CHAPTER
FIFTEEN

Life continued along as normal. Heather and J.T. went through the same things every couple did when they first started living together. The adjustment period was a lot smoother than most because each of them was committed to making things work and accomplished this by open and frequent communication, good old-fashioned consideration and paying attention to the other's needs.

Tuesday, June 2, a message came to J.T.'s computer from the Office of the Chief Elder of The Council. J.T. saw it when he got home and logged on to do a few work things from home. He clicked on the message icon and read;

Lt. Colonel Coulter, Greetings from the Council. The purpose of this letter is to inform you that the Council has decided to hold an awards ceremony for Unit 17, all members, including the recently formed militia. It will be held at the Dome 17 Auditorium on July 4th. Full dress uniforms without weapons required. Each attendee may invite family (up to three members) wives, significant others. Children under the age of five are excluded. This will be televised and pertinent information concerning the same will be transmitted once all details have been finalized. Please notify all involved parties to ensure their compliance. Acknowledgement to this letter is requested and expected. Looking forward to speaking with you privately the morning of the event. Best wishes, Frank Easton, Chief Elder.

J.T. called Heather and asked her to come into the den because he had something to show her. When she arrived, he pointed to the computer and indicated she should read the message.

"I didn't know you were getting a medal or an award!" she exclaimed.

"I don't know that I am," was his reply. "Just make sure you schedule that time off the whole day. You will need a very nice dress too."

"This sounds like a really big deal. Probably ought to let your parents know too."

"Yeah, they would really be pissed if they found out there was an awards ceremony, and they were not invited."

J.T. sent himself a memo about disseminating the invitation. He would have to go to Coulter to invite the members of the newly formed militia. He would do that at the weekend when most of the town would be available to hear the news. He then typed a reply to the office of the Chief Elder, also asking for clarification on whom would be receiving an award and if there were any other things going on that he, as the commanding officer, should be made aware. He ended the letter with a note of appreciation to the Council for noting the good job his unit had continually done.

Next day, at the Unit, J.T. called the XO and Sean into his office to inform them about the ceremony and to ask them if either one of them had instigated it by communication with the Council. Both men were quite pleased with the fact that there was going to be an awards ceremony, and both adamantly denied instigating it. J.T. felt unspoken relief at that answer. He would have hated to find out that his most trusted subordinates had gone behind his back. He then instructed Sean to assemble all the men in the unit so he could inform them and make a few comments to them.

An hour later, Sean informed him that the men would be assembled at 15:30 hours in the squad bay, all would be present.

As he entered the squad bay, the ever familiar "Attention on Deck" was sounded, and all present snapped to attention. "At ease" followed by "Take seats."

Over the next twenty minutes, J.T. informed the unit of the awards ceremony and of the fact that he knew nothing about it. Who got it started? Who was being awarded what, for what, or anything else pertinent to the ceremony. He made it crystal clear that he expected shined shoes, perfect creases on the uniforms and regulation haircuts. Normally he was a little on the lax side about hair and grooming, as none of these had anything to do with the units' ability to follow orders and to kill the enemy.

He went on to say that he was as proud as he could be of the work the unit did, both on the battlefield and elsewhere. He also informed them that he had put commendation letters in everyone's personnel file, and he was glad that they were going to be recognized by the Council.

"Oh, and by the way, save the drinking until after you are

dismissed." This drew an obligatory groan from the men and the expected, "can't we even have a little nip?"

J.T.'s response was, "Normally, I wouldn't care, but some you consider half a bottle to be a nip so no, we are gonna play this one straight. Drinks will be on me at the community building in Coulter after the ceremony. That will be all, dismissed".

All the men automatically popped to attention until J.T. walked out of the squad bay. The next couple of days kind of zipped by. Wednesday morning another e-mail came in to J.T.'s office computer setting the date as July 4th, 0900 at the Dome auditorium. There was also a request for the number of attendees and guests. J.T. forwarded a message to the XO asking him to obtain the numbers requested by the end of the week. J.T. left early, having something important to do.

He returned home in the early evening quite proud of himself for all the things he had accomplished. He kissed Heather, asked her what she would like for dinner, then retired to the bedroom. He took his dress uniform out of the closet, checked his jewelry case for all the miniature medals intended to be worn at ceremonies. He then searched through the closet looking for his service issued sword to make sure the scabbard was appropriately polished, which it was not. He had not worn it in five or more years. He sighed, knowing the job of polishing was going to take three solid hours. Add to that the time it is going to take polishing the brass on his uniform and his dress shoes. He laid all of these things out on his bed and went back to the kitchen to start dinner. An hour and a half later, dinner was on the table. A nice garden salad with homemade green goddess dressing and Fettuccini Alfredo with shrimp and scallops. He had Heather pick out the wine as they sat down at the table to eat and share the day's events. J.T. brought her up to speed on the developments concerning the ceremony.

Fortunately, there was nothing she was aware of that would clash with the ceremony. She mentioned that she still did not have an appropriate dress for the event and J.T. suggested she call Shannon and ask her, since Shannon had attended a number of these events in the past.

Heather remarked, "That's a great idea. It will give us an opportunity to go shopping."

"Am I going to regret this?" J.T. asked.

Heather playfully punched him in the arm and said, "I could just skip the whole thing."

J.T. realized that this was a no-win situation and remained silent. Heather, realizing she had won this round, changed the topic and complimented him on dinner.

J.T.'s response was, "I cooked, so you clean."

Heather wisely said that was fair. J.T. scooted his chair back, took his plate and silverware over to the sink, and told her that he had a number of hours of labor ahead and he needed to get started. He gave her a kiss and headed to the den.

Four hours later, he emerged from the den smelling of shoe polish and Brasso. He spent the next ten minutes scrubbing his hands, trying to get both substances off. He finally decided to stop before his hands started to bleed. Heather was in the bedroom eyeing the uniform and all the accouterments. She was impressed with all the medals and ribbons, and wanted to know what they meant and how he got them.

Rather than go into a lengthy discussion about all 21 awards, he decided to hit a couple of the easy ones.

Pointing to the purple one, he said, "This is the purple heart. You are awarded this if you are wounded."

"What are those things on it? she asked.

"Those are there to signify how many times you have been wounded. I will probably get a few more of those. The wounds I got that ended up with me meeting you could be counted as one event or five separate wounds. I have no input on that. This one over here is for flying a certain number of air missions. This one is for combat actions. This one is for valor and this one is for bravery. Before you ask, I really don't remember what actually happened. It is all written out in my personnel file."

"Can I see it?" Heather asked.

"Maybe one day," J.T. said, trying to dodge the question.

"What are you afraid of?" she pressed.

"I am not afraid of anything. It is just that it maybe upsetting to someone who was not there when things happened," he explained.

"Well, I want to see it. Please bring your file home so I can see what I am looking at being a part of, ok?" she conceded.

"Okay, but I have no desire to rehash everything you read, understand?" His tone indicated that this was not open to a lot of discussion.

"Fair enough," Heather replied in a tone that indicated she understood his position. With that, he kissed her, and they both went to sleep.

The next couple of weeks were filled with making plans and helping out where needed in Coulter. The community house was large enough for 110 people, but there were 250 on the list, counting guests and all the locals that would naturally be there to support and congratulate the newly formed Free Coulter militia. There were going to be two pigs roasted as well as half a cow. The pass plates would be provided by the citizenry of Coulter. J.T. would have to arrange chairs, tables, silverware, plates, napkins, glasses, and tablecloths to be delivered and he would have Sean get volunteers to come out and help set things up. He also had to make arrangements for beer, keg would be best, wine and liquor.

Have to stick to Bourbon, Scotch, gin and vodka. Can't forget mixers, condiments and a couple of bartenders. J.T thought. He would check with a couple of the local restaurants and see if he could borrow some bar help for four hours. It would be self-serve, almost cafeteria style, so servers would not be needed. The ladies of Coulter had a number of great bakers. They would handle the breads, rolls and dessert pastries. Any of the men in Coulter could handle the roasting and J.T. was going to provide the rubs and sauces for the meat. He reminded himself to contact the commissary manager for ice; he figured 150 pounds would be enough for everything. I would rather run the Unit than plan functions, he thought to himself. J.T. said his goodbyes to the Coulter residents, telling them to contact him if there were any questions or concerns.

He reminded himself to make arrangements for transportation out to Coulter because there was no way he was going to try to park all the cars that would be present. J.T. hopped back into the vehicle he had come in. There were a thousand details running through his mind on the trip back to the Dome.

Before heading back to the Unit, he stopped by the store to pick up the ingredients he would need for the rubs and sauces. He would make those that evening when he got home.

His trip to the Unit tied up the last loose ends, and he was glad the day was done, and he could head home.

Heather was not home from shopping yet, so he would be uninterrupted while he was working in the kitchen. Upon arriving at home, he immediately went into the kitchen where he set down all the ingredients he had purchased, donned an apron, dug out a mixing bowl and started mixing his secret recipe BBQ rub. He decided to have a glass of wine when he started to get supper ready. Orange almond salad, Scallop Risotto, and bacon wrapped asparagus were on the evening's menu. Cooking always transported him elsewhere, letting him clear his mind yet allowed him to focus on a task that if done correctly, was going to bring someone pleasure, memories and nutrition. And, truth being told, he did like to show off in this one little area. He loved showing off for Heather. He wanted her to be proud of him, on many levels.

———————

Heather had finished her shopping, and she was really pleased with the dress she had picked out. This was going to be their first *out in public, where everyone could see them together formally for the first time.* She wanted this to be perfect and memorable. The smell of dinner assailed her nostrils the moment she entered the house, reminding her of how hungry she was, not having eaten since a coffee and bagel brunch just before noon. She got so wrapped up in shopping that she just ignored the hunger pangs she felt all afternoon. She hung the dress in the laundry room, set her purse on the counter and wrapped her arms around J.T., giving him a very passionate kiss. Heather was very glad to see him, on another level, quite surprised and amazed as to how quickly these feelings had developed. J.T. poured her a glass of wine and proceeded to set her dinner plate in front of her on the island.

"I am sooo hungry, and this food smells so divine," she said.

"Well, we need to eat because the food will get cold and not taste as fantastic as I had planned. Besides, I need to run out to Coulter after supper. I have the BBQ rub to drop off since they will start cooking the wild boar around 2 a.m."

Heather had already eaten half of her salad and was cutting into the asparagus.

"Babe, this is fabulous, and I am so starved. Thank you for cooking this. You are spoiling me, you know that."

"It really is my pleasure. You deserve to be spoiled. How was your day?" he asked.

"It was pretty much routine. I talked to the Dean of the med school and came up with a plan for Doc Horner. Since you did so well with the med school part of the III, I thought that, with Doc's medical background, we could hook him up to III and impart the med school data tape in say, a day or two. He could take the test a couple of days later and if he passes, he gets to be an MD. He has already had clinical training and experience and would be a great asset to the Unit and Coulter. So, what do you think? You could order him to accept the education, right? What do you think?" she asked.

"Not sure that would be a valid order. I will have to think about this. You want to come along with me to Coulter?" J.T. asked.

"Normally I would, but I am beat from walking all afternoon. Will you be gone long?" was her response.

"Only as long as it takes. Depends on how many people want to talk to me. I'll call when I am on my way home. By the way, I cooked, you get to do the dishes," he said.

"And here I was feeling all romantic because my lover had just served me a meal fit for a queen, then treats me like a scullery maid," she lamented.

"Just keep the first thought in mind and get over the other. Love ya, babe. Gotta go," he said on the way out of the door.

"I love you too," was her response.

J.T. headed out to the garage, threw the rub mixture in the other seat, and set the drive computer for Coulter. He headed out on his trip. Twenty minutes later, he came to a stop at the edge of Coulter. He had wondered whether he was ever going to see Coulter again when he was wounded and he had a sense of coming home as he got out of the car. Lucien and Jerry were just coming out of the community house when they happened to notice the car and J.T. exiting the vehicle. They both broke into a trot over to J.T., shaking his hand and patting him on the back.

Jerry ran back to the community house to let everyone know J.T. was outside. The house emptied faster than calling fire in a movie theater. Folks were crowding around trying to get a chance to shake his hand, give him a hug or a pat on the back, and everybody thanked him and blessed him. The subject of Heather came up along with how beautiful she was and how kind, polite, and down-to-earth she was. Of course, they had to mention her choice of the movie, and then Sara came up to him and asked J.T. if he was planning on marrying her. J.T. replied that he had not had a chance to ask her yet, but he was going to ask pretty soon. There was a huge cheer and a prolonged round of applause after that announcement. It warmed his heart and soul to be the receiver of such an outpouring of love and good wishes. He raised his hands to silence the crowd.

"Folks, I am here to drop off the wild boar rub for the cookout tomorrow. Also, for all the men that were in the Coulter Militia, the ceremony is tomorrow starting at 9a.m. You are allowed to bring family members, not little children, and you need to be at the Unit no later than 0730 to get you into your uniforms and to explain what is going to go on.

"Please be on time. Take the tram into the city and I will have a couple of unit members there to greet you and take you where you need to go. I would love to talk to each and every-one, but unfortunately, I need to get back to the city. There are a million details I need to attend to. I want to thank all of you for this spontaneous gathering and to assure you that I will be here tomorrow after the ceremony to talk with anyone that wishes to speak to me but I have to get back to work. I am looking forward to seeing you all tomorrow."

He waved his hand and made his way through the crowd to the car. Inputting the return to home info into the navigation computer, he thought, *who would have ever thought this was where things were going to end up, fifteen years after he decided to help a few folks in need?* The ride home allowed him to put together some kind of speech, even though he had not been informed that he would be expected to speak formally. He was a little concerned that there had been no contact or conversation about this ceremony. There had been no correspondence about any of the awards. Usually, it was the commanding officers' purview and decisions about which member of the Unit was being recommended for what medal. There was documentation that had to be acquired, reviewed and verified before the proposed medal was approved. He had not been consulted concerning any of this. He wondered what was actually going on.

It was late when he got home. Heather was already in bed. He smiled as he went through the kitchen, noting the dishes had been done and that the coffee was made and set up for the morning. He made his way to the master bathroom, where he got undressed and headed into the bedroom. He slipped into bed, curled around Heather, kissed her neck and went to sleep.

The next morning, after his morning ritual, J.T. got talking with Heather.

"I need to tell you a few things about these ceremonies. I, along with the unit and the militia from Coulter, will all be on stage. Due to my rank, you, Mom and Dad will be seated in the front row. Shannon will also be sitting next to you. On the other side will be Major Stein's family. Seating for everyone else will be catch as catch can. The Council members will be on the stage across from the unit. There will be a podium slightly off to the side, in front of the Council.

"Usually, the Chief Elder of the Council will make some remarks and then begin handing out the medals. Usually, I will be standing alongside the Chief Elder holding each medal. The Chief Elder may or may not read a short note about why the medal is being awarded. I have not been contacted about any of the medals or awards, so I have no idea about how things are going to be done. Usually, all medal and award recommendations come to me and I have them investigated and determined if they meet the criteria and if they do, then I recommend awarding the medal. No one has said anything or presented me with any documentation supporting the awarding of a medal to members of my unit. Very Strange."

"Guess you'll just have to wing it, improvise, adapt and overcome," she said.

"Right," was his reply.

J.T. dried himself and began the process of getting ready. Putting on a full-dress uniform took time. Fortunately, he had addressed all the medals and awards that had to be displayed in a very precise, proscribed fashion. It would not do for the Commanding Officer to be attired inappropriately, after all, officers, specifically the Commanding and Executive Officers set the standard for the command. Everything needed to be perfect. Brass polished, shoes shined to a mirror finish, pants creased, coat wrinkle free, scabbard polished, sword polished, the bill of the cap polished. Haircut perfect. Shaved clean and smooth. He was pleased that the Council had mandated a change of dress uniform back to the dress uniform of the United States Marines circa 2000.

As he stepped out of the second bedroom, Heather was in front of him, dressed in a thong and matching bra set and thigh-high stockings wiggling her shapely tight butt to get into the emerald green, knee length, V neck dress. Her hair and makeup were perfect. She was absolutely the most beautiful woman he had ever laid eyes on, and she loved only him. Could things get any better?

Yeah, his family absolutely loved her, too. She was going to be blown away when he proposed, in front of everyone, at the end of the ceremony. Another memory that many would wish for themselves. She smoothed the dress and turned around to see him staring at her. She looked him over from head to toe and they both, at the same time, said "You are stunning!!" That gave both of them a chuckle.

J.T. stepped over to her, took her hand, and kissed it lovingly.

"I have never seen you or anyone else looking so beautiful. I am so proud to have you by my side," J.T. heartily said.

"Babe, I can't tell you how amazing you look in your uniform. I have never seen a man so handsome, commanding and confident as you look right this moment. I am honored to be on your arm. I love you." she said.

"Are you ready to go? It's almost time and I can't be late."

"Yep, I am ready."

Heather grabbed her clutch purse. He put his cap on and then went out to the car, got in and headed off to the auditorium. Pulling up to the parking lot, Heather picked out the Coulter family along with Sean, standing off to the side. J.T. got out and opened Heather's door, taking the opportunity to stare at her legs as she got out of the vehicle.

"Like the view?" she asked as she took his offered right elbow and they strode up to the rest of the family members.

Surprisingly, neither Helen, Shannon nor Frank had ever seen J.T. in full dress regalia. They were struck with awe at how commanding and how confident he appeared. For a few moments, they all just stared at one another.

Helen broke the spell by saying, "Both of you look perfect together, just like Sean and Shannon."

"Thanks Mom, I forgot you have never seen me all dressed up," J.T. noted.

"Heather, you are absolutely stunning. I love the dress. It is absolutely perfect," Helen offered.

"Thank you, Mom," she said tentatively, trying the term Mom on for size and found it a very comfortable fit.

"I hate to breakup this mutual admiration society meeting, but you all need to get inside and into your seats, we," pointing to himself and Sean, "have to be with the Unit for the entrance."

J.T. and Sean each kissed their ladies and smooched Helen on the cheek, shook Frank's hand, and headed to the rear entrance of the auditorium to meet up with the unit. As Sean and J.T. turned the corner, the call "Attention on Deck" and the resultant sounds of men snapping to attention was heard.

"At ease," J.T snapped.

Sean stepped forward and said, "Fall in. Form two lines, Militia form one line". We will be marching in two abreast, militia. You will be coming in last. This is not a slight or punishment. There are only two rows of seats, so we can't enter in a column of 3's. When you have filled up two rows, Militia you will alternate filling in each row. Try not to fall over one another. There is some decorum to be maintained. Attention. Colonel, you first, Major, you are second and I will lead the troops in. They could hear the first strains of the National Anthem. Forward march, left, right, left," and the troops marched out on to the stage.

As they filled in the rows of seats, each man snapped into a salute and held it throughout the music. J.T. and Max Stein both saluted with their swords. At the end of the hymn, Sean barked out "Ready Too".

Both men and officers dropped their salutes.

"Troops, take seats," J.T. barked. The entire troop sat down at the same moment. The attending members of the Council, complete with official robes, solemnly strode in and took seats arranged in a crescent moon shape. The Chief Elder, dressed in full council regalia, strode to the podium.

"Please be seated. I am Frank Easton, Chief Elder of the Council of Elders that rule the United Dome Cities of America. This is the first awards ceremony I have ever officiated, and it is my honor to do so. In preparing for this event, I was given a quite extensive dossier on DSF Unit 17. After reading this dossier, I was inclined to believe it was augmented. 58 missions in 15 years. Three men killed in action, nine men wounded, all of which have returned to duty and no captured enemy combatants.

"I questioned why there were no prisoners taken and was told that was a standing order from one LT. Colonel Coulter, CO of the unit. I questioned why such an order was given. I was informed that the CO refused to feed, clothe, quarter and provide medical care for marauders and criminals intent on taking away things from Dome 17. It would take unit members away from their responsibilities of protecting the city, to guard them, not to mention the fact that they would have to build a prison and since they decided to attack the city, they could die for their actions. He felt that the word would get around certain circles that if you mess with Unit 17, you die. That way, there would be no one who had tried to attack us and had failed, available to be able to give information to the next group that wanted to attack us. I was unable to find a flaw in the logic. From other Domes, I learned that they had been attacked by the same people over and over again, until I issued the order to take no prisoners and to show no mercy."

"Overall attacks on Dome Cities had dropped by 63% and the soldiers had less fatalities and wounded. Today we are here to honor the men of Unit 17 and the newly formed Coulter Militia. A few of these men have earned medals for valor, distinguished service crosses and purple hearts."

He began listing the names of every single man in the unit and militia. He finished about an hour later and there was thunderous applause when he was done. Raising his hands, trying to get everyone to sit and quiet down, he said, "Now it is time to honor the men that are in charge. Sergeant Major Sean McCann front and center. For consistent leadership, bravery and professionalism you are hereby awarded the Silver Star, for wounds sustained in combat action you are awarded a Purple Heart with gold oak cluster. You are also promoted to the rank of Major and are hereby assigned to Unit 17 as the new Executive officer. Congratulations."

"Major Maxwell Stein, for leadership, courage, bravery while in combat, you are awarded the Bronze Star, The Distinguished service cross, and the Meritorious Unit Commendation medal. You are also promoted to the rank of Lt. Colonel and given command of Unit 17. Congratulations."

"Last, we come to Lt. Colonel J.T. Coulter. I must admit that as I read your dossier, I was sure that some of what I was reading was made up, so I did my own checking. Many of you are not aware that while Colonel Coulter commanded the 17th, he accumulated a total of 7 Batchelor degrees, eight master's degrees and four PhD degrees, including an MD degree. He also has been wounded four or eight times depending on how you count the events. One group of these injuries was when he crash-landed the drone he was flying, over the combat area where a train carrying six members of the Council was protected, resulting in three members of his unit sustaining minor injuries while he himself nearly died after breaking both legs and hips as well as both arms and shoulders, six rib fractures, a collapsed lung and a concussion.

"He underwent extensive reconstructive surgeries requiring 6-8 weeks of immersion rehabilitation therapy, along with a new procedure called Intracranial Information implantation. I can honestly say I have never met a man like him. In addition to his duties as commanding officer, he has designed and helped to build a self-sustaining village called Coulter, appropriately enough, and has engaged the services of the men of Unit 17 to help out twice a year, thereby teaching them that their job is to kill the enemy but that is not who they are as people. The men of the Militia come from this Village and recently have participated in protecting their homes with the help of Unit 17.

"Colonel, by unanimous consent you are hereby awarded eight purple hearts for wounds sustained in combat, A Distinguished Flying cross, Distinguished service cross and the Council Medal of Honor. You are hereby promoted to the rank of Brigadier General and appointed as regional Commander of units 16 through 22. By unanimous consent, the Council of Elders has, in their infinite wisdom, decided that you are worthy of being offered a Quest. Should you decide to accept this offer, there will be a private meeting held tomorrow at 10am in council chambers. Congratulations General. Is there anything you would like to say?"

"Yes sir, there is. First to the men of the 17th, you are the finest bunch of men, and it has been my great honor and pleasure to have served with. You truly are the best. I shall never forget you and all we have shared and been through. Congrats to Colonel Stein, you have been a superb XO and I could not leave these men in better hands. Major, I am so proud of you. You truly deserve the rank and the job, and the men will be well served in your capable hands. Next, I would like to invite Dr. Heather Dunkirk to the stage."

J.T. walked over to the stairs and extended his hand to Heather to help her climb up to the stage. They walked back to the podium, where J.T. took his place behind the lectern and continued to speak.

"This is Dr. Heather Dunkirk, the finest orthopedic surgeon in the Dome system. She is responsible for putting me back together after my little mishap. Without her skill and expertise, I would not be standing here today, listening to all the nice things being said about me. I would like to thank her in public for giving me back my life, in a shape that I am still able to do all that I used to do."

"Also," he said as he stepped from behind the podium, then getting down on one knee, he reached under his jacket and brought out a little box, "I would like to ask her if she would be my wife."

He opened the box and there was a five carat, blue, white, marquis cut, diamond that he removed from the box and offered it to her.

"So, will you marry me?"

Heather stood there with her mouth open and a dumb-founded look on her face. This had caught her completely unawares.

"Of course, I will be your wife," she said confidently, as if there was no other possible answer.

The two of them embraced and held a long, passionate kiss while the auditorium erupted in applause and cheers. Helen, Frank and Shannon all came on stage and hugged and kissed each other. Sean came over and started to shake his hand, but instead gave him a big hug. The Chief Elder and all the other Elders lined up to shake his hand and whispered that they expected to get a positive answer to the Quest offer. The entire Unit lined up to shake his hand, hug Heather and give her a kiss on the cheek.

"My friends, as you can see, she said yes. There is a celebration to be held in Coulter today, starting at 2 p.m. and all of you are invited. We, Heather and I, would love it if you all stopped by."

J.T. turned to the Council members and told them the invite applied to them as well. J.T. took Heather's hand, walked over to his mom and dad and indicated to them that it was time to go. They all headed out to the vehicles and headed back to J.T.'s place.

J.T. was sure that people wanted to see him in his dress uniform but there was no way he could attend a wild boar roast, in a full-dress uniform, and not ruin it, so the better part of everything was to go home and change clothes. He dropped Sean, Shannon, his mom and dad off at Sean's house so they could change into something more comfortable, then he headed off to his house. Upon arriving, he took Heather by the hand and led her inside and as soon as the door was closed; he swept her up in his arms and kissed her long and passionately.

After they broke the kiss, Heather said, "You caught me by surprise, with your proposal, in front of God and everybody."

"I wanted to make sure it was hard for you to say no," he replied.

"There was no way in hell I was going to refuse you. By the way, this ring is exquisite and huge."

"Nothing but the best for the love of my life," was his reply.

"You know, you caught everyone by surprise, including the Unit, your mom and dad, as well as Sean and Shannon, not to mention the Chief Elder and the whole Council. How long had you been planning it?"

"The asking you to marry me? About a month or so, the ceremony just provided the perfect venue. I wanted the proposal to be a memory you would remember and cherish forever."

"Well buster, you have surely succeeded in that area. Undo my zipper please," she said as she turned her back to him.

He did so slowly as he gently kissed the back of her neck and shoulders. The shivers he felt told him he had just done something right. She did a sensual yet sexy wiggle to get the dress to fall off her shoulders, landing on the floor at her feet. She stepped out of the dress and J.T. watched as she strode away with a little swish of her hips. The three-inch heels added an allure that took J.T.'s breath away as he watched her walk into the bedroom.

"You coming, big boy, or are you just gonna stand there and stare at my legs and ass?" she cooed.

"I kinda like the view if you don't mind. But to answer your question, I'll be right there," J.T. ventured into the second bedroom where he stored all his uniforms and proceeded to get undressed, carefully hanging up each item, smoothing each article out before putting it on the appropriate hanger then buttoning it to make sure it hung properly. After he was undressed, he walked into the master bedroom to find Heather stretched out on the bed in the most seductive pose he had ever seen by a real live woman. He felt himself starting to get aroused.

"I just wanted you to get an idea of what was going to happen later when we get home. Any questions?" she purred.

"Just one. Are you done with treatment?" he asked.

"Yep," was her response.

"Then I think I understand," he replied.

"I'll bet you do," she said seductively.

"We need to get moving. If we don't, we may never make it there," he said.

"Would that be so bad?" she cooed.

"No, it wouldn't, but it would be pretty rude since this is a bit of an engagement party," J.T. reminded her.

"Well stud, you are right, so you'll just have to wait for your gift. That is until we get home."

She said as she got off the bed and slipped into a tight pair of jeans and a pullover light cotton polo shirt. She stepped over to the mirror to check her makeup. Satisfied that everything was perfect. Slipped into some comfortable shoes, then stood there letting J.T. roam his gaze over her from head to toe. He gave her a nod of approval and then proceeded to slip on some jeans, which took a bit of doing due to his state of arousal. He also chose a cotton polo shirt and loafers, added a belt then gave her a chance to look him over, same as he had done to her.

"That thing gonna go down before we have to meet other folks?" she asked.

"Sure, hope so but, you looking as good as you do is not helping," he responded.

"If your mind wasn't in the gutter all the time, you could control yourself better," was her retort.

He kissed her and guided her towards the door. They locked up the house and got in the car, programming Sean's address, then took off, headed out to pick up the family and get to the party.

The only conversation that occurred during the trip was the initial discussion about the upcoming nuptials. Both Helen and Shannon, having been through one or more weddings each, had tons of suggestions. Heather dutifully listened, asked the correct questions, and nodded when appropriate. Frank and Sean just looked at J.T. with that 'you have no idea what you have gotten yourself into' look. J.T. just plastered a smile on his lips, nodded and only asked one question that he thought pertinent and germane to the conversation. This drew approving looks from the other two men present, along with the "uh huh" and "of course, dears," directed to no one in particular.

Thankfully, the trip was over before the conversation could lead into a realm where nothing that was said was either correct, appropriate, or sensitive enough. The three men exited the vehicle feeling relieved that they had managed to avoid a trap, the consequences of which would have lasted for days and never have been completely forgotten.

It was a perfect day for the roast. 81 degrees, low humidity, 15 mph steady, northeast breeze and literally 175 people, three-fourths of which had an awestruck look on their face, mainly because they had rarely, if ever, heard about Coulter, and now they were walking around with wide-eyed wonderment. J.T. was afraid that this knowledge that was now being shared was going to change the village, not necessarily for the better.

Oh well, what was done was done and all he could do was try to keep that information from ruining the village. There was a non-stop line of well-wishers all feeling the need to stop by and speak with J.T., to wish him well and to thank him for all that he had done for the dome and the village.

Heather had her own line, congratulating her on the proposal and thanking her for the work she did on J.T. and Sara. Sara herself was in line, holding the hand of her husband Vernon. "I just want to tell you how much you have done for me... us. I was afraid I was never going to be able to tolerate having sex again and I must tell you that is not the case anymore. I do have to tell you that my hip is a little sore, but that is because we have been screwing like newlyweds two or three times a day. Vernon stepped up and pumped Heather's hand vigorously while profusely thanking Heather for giving back his wife whole. He was afraid that he was going to have to go through married life settling for self-gratification, and Heather had given back his marital sex life.

Other villagers lined up to thank her and welcome her into the village family. They were quite serious in their enthusiasm. They had already had the opportunity to evaluate her when she was there for the work weekend. They had all decided that she was going to marry J.T. after the movie selection that Saturday night. The older women had said it was a foretellin' and that was that. These same ladies were standing in line to remind Heather that they had told her she was going to marry J.T.

Heather had enough good sense to realize that she needed to stay on the good side of these ladies, thanking them for taking such good care of J.T.

Both of them were standing side by side, turned away from each other, answering questions from people in the line when the Chief Elder, followed by seven or eight Elders, took their turn in line. The Chief Elder stepped up to J.T. and asked what had possessed him to create Coulter.

"Well Sir, the men that I initially interacted with asked for one thing, water. They simply wanted some water to drink, cook with, wash themselves and their clothes, and take care of their animals. Nothing else. They didn't want food, electricity, gas, coal, nothing that the residents of Dome 17 have and take for granted. They wanted to fend for themselves, live off the land, and live their lives in peace according to their own personal value systems. I felt I had an opportunity to help them achieve their desires without taking anything away from the Dome. I had read some old-time books on living off the grid in the mid 2000s, there were suggestions on organic non-chemical fertilizers, self-made hydroelectric plants, solar panels. I sat down one night and jotted out a plan, made an equipment list and the next day asked for volunteers. Every single man in the unit volunteered. They made a list of skills within the Unit and things took off from there," he said.

"This is one of the reasons the Council decided to offer you a Quest. The Quest is going to involve interplanetary space travel and inhabiting another planet. We will get a lot more technical tomorrow morning at the meeting. Regardless of your answer right now, your attendance at this meeting is mandatory. If you wish to bring your fiancé along, please feel free.

After all, if you choose to accept the Quest it will have a definite impact on her as well. Be that as it may, I wanted to personally tell you that the work you have done on multiple levels, including Coulter, has thoroughly impressed me, more so than any other person I have met in a very long time," the Chief Elder said.

Some of the other Elders crowded forward to lavish all kinds of praise on J.T. who had to struggle a little to show some class and not become a little annoyed at the intensity of the praise. It did give him a little ego boost, but there was such a thing as laying it on a bit too thick. Besides, he had not worn his hip waders and the amount of BS being handed out was going to ruin his shoes.

Finally, the line thinned, and it was time to eat. As usual, the food was superb and J.T. made his way to the area where the ladies that did all the cooking were hanging out. His thanks and compliments were effusive, honest and sincere. He did manage to give each and every one of them a hug and a kiss on the cheek. Heather, who was never one to miss a clue, followed diligently behind her betrothed, repeating what her man was saying and adding a little of her own personal touch to it. This did not go unnoticed by most of the populace of Coulter.

Around 8 p.m., J.T. pulled Heather aside and told her he was getting a little tired and was ready to wrap things up. He suggested that they split up and find Mom, Dad, Sean and Shannon and let them know that they were ready to call it a day. They agreed to meet near the smokehouse in 15 minutes and off each of them went in search of the rest of their party. They finally managed to get together 20 minutes later. J.T. stepped up on the stage and on behalf of Heather and himself, thanked everyone that came and especially the citizens of Coulter for the fine food, fun, and fellowship. He closed his remarks by saying that it had been a long and very event filled day and that they were taking their leave but would be back to the village in the very near future. There was a prolonged and genuine round of applause and cheering that J.T. acknowledged with a wave and exited the stage.

"You should have been a politician. You are a natural in front of a crowd," Heather whispered in his ear as they made their way to the car.

As soon as the doors were shut, the questions about the Quest offer started in. J.T. tried to answer them without violating the implied confidential nature of the offer. He promised that when the meeting was over, he would fill them in with everything he was allowed to divulge. That silenced the group for the time being, but he knew that tomorrow would be a day of reckoning when he got back from the meeting. He did inform Heather that the Council had given their permission for her to attend. That info caught her off guard a little, as she thought the meeting was private and restricted. She was pleased that she was going to be included in this meeting. They would talk about this later at home, well maybe not until tomorrow morning. She had something planned at home for tonight.

J.T. dropped everyone off at Sean's house and breathed a sigh of relief as he made his way home. On their way home, Heather asked about the quest and J.T. explained as much as he could.

"That is so up your alley and in keeping with your education and desires. I am so happy for you and proud of you too," Heather said effusively.

"Thank you, sweetheart. I hope I can live up to everyone's expectation," he remarked with some uncertainty.

"I have some expectations I fully expect you to measure up to, and I can think of no better time than right now." She purred as soon as they got in the door. "Come with me stud, I have some needs that need tending to and you are just the man to handle the job." She took him by the hand and guided him into the bedroom and shut the door.

CHAPTER
SIXTEEN

One of the few times in J.T.'s life that his internal alarm clock failed him was today. At 7:45am, Heather reached over and slapped his bare butt with an admonishment to get up. There was only one hour and 15 minutes before they had to be present for the meeting with the Council. He looked at her and all her nudity, remembering the last night when he gave her his virginity. Given to the woman he wanted to spend his life with. He now knew, firsthand, what all the fuss was about. It was everything he thought it would be, and more.

"Are you OK?" he questioned.

"Well stud, I could tell you I was fine, but that would be a lie," she paused. "I am fabulous and if last night was any clue as to what I am going to have for the rest of my life, I could die right now and be the most satisfied and fulfilled woman on the planet."

"No pain or anything?" he asked.

"Just a very pleasurable sensation of being well serviced." A smile of pride and an internal knowledge that he had pleased and not hurt his lover. This relieved him of a huge load he had carried for a long time.

"Guess we better get a move on, huh?" he said.

"I've showered so you can get started. What were you planning on wearing?" she asked.

"A regular uniform. I will need to get Stars for my collar and a new hat," he replied.

"I've already called Sean and he should be here in 15 minutes with the necessary articles reflecting your new rank," she explained.

"Thank you, babe."

Not surprisingly, 10 minutes later, Sean knocked on the back door, handed Heather a large bag and told her he hoped he had everything that was needed. Heather gave him a hug and a kiss on the cheek.

"Congrats on the promotion. Long overdue. J.T. knows you will be a great XO," she said as she congratulated him.

"I had a great teacher and role model," was his reply.

"Gotta run; it's going to be tight on time since the big guy overslept," Heather said.

"Did he really?" Sean replied with a small but obvious smirk growing on his face. He turned and headed out the door with a parting comment, "You are gonna be perfect for him and I couldn't be happier."

Heather closed the door, and the same smile grew on her face too. J.T came around the corner asking if that was Sean.

"Yep, and he was really proud of being made the new XO," she said.

"I'll have to stop by the unit after the meeting and talk to both of them. I'll be ready to go in less than 10 minutes."

"Me too." And the two of them proceeded to finish dressing.

J.T. fixed both of them a to-go cup of coffee as Heather entered the kitchen in a very attractive business suit, looking for all the world, like a general's lady.

"You ready? Thanks for the coffee."

"Yep, let's go."

They arrived at the entrance to the offices and were met by a valet who greeted them with a, "Good Morning General, Dr. Dunkirk. The offices are down the first hallway to the right. Just follow the signs and it will lead you right to the door. There is a couple of security things to go through to get in. The guard will take care of you."

"Thank you." He took Heather's arm and leaned down to whisper in her ear, "Seems so strange to be called General." J.T. whispered.

"Get used to it General. It is your new reality, and it fits you perfectly," was her reply.

They made their way down the hall to wear the guard, in full dress uniform, armed, perfectly at attention.

The guard snapped a crisp, perfect salute, sounding off, "Good Morning General, Dr. Dunkirk. Please step up the scanner and look into the center of the retinal scan and place your right hand flat on the scanner pad on the right. Thank you General, Dr. Dunkirk. You may both enter. The Charge-de-Affairs will escort you to the conference room."

J.T returned the salute, held the door, and followed Heather into the office. They were met by an officious looking, bald, slightly overweight, pale, mid-50's man wearing spectacles that could have been made a century earlier, making his eyes appear larger than they were, who started fawning all over them the moment he noticed their presence.

"General, Dr. Dunkirk, this is truly an honor meeting you. Gratulations on the promotion, sir. Very well deserved and, from what I have heard, long overdue, I am Charles Adams."

J.T. swallowed hard and said, "thank you". Heather could tell it really was hard for him to be polite to someone obviously sucking up. She tugged on his arm and generally tried to lead him away from the sycophant. Charles moved ahead of them, leading them to the door of the Council's conference room. He opened the door, stepped in and announced, "Members of the Council, General Coulter and Dr. Dunkirk." He stepped out of the way, allowing them to pass into the room. The members present all stood and gave them a round of applause.

The First Chief Elder stepped up to him and said, "John Holmes, would you like some coffee, Dr. Dunkirk, General?"

"I would," Heather replied.

"So would I," said J.T.

"Charles, please bring in the coffee service cart. Then we will need to be left alone. I will summon you if we need anything," the First Chief Elder said.

"Yes Sir," was the response.

"May we get a little less formal? I am John and the other members of the Council will introduce themselves when it is their turn to speak. How would you both prefer to be addressed?"

"Heather."

"J.T."

"Good, now that is out of the way. You and I have discussed

some aspects of the Quest, but I would like to start this meeting off with Francis Downing. He is the science person. He will explain the situation facing us."

"J.T., the long and short of it is, this planet will no longer be able to support life if things remain unchanged and none of us in the scientific community have any reason to believe that there is going to be any kind of change that will make a difference. Estimation is between 13 years worst case, and 20 years best case. So, the only option left is to leave and colonize some other planet."

"J.T., that is where you come in. Your Quest is to build a spacecraft that can find another world, take a group of colonists, drop them off and come back. We will see how many trips you can make. Those that don't make it will die. That is something we have to try to minimize, but we can't save everyone. We have a plan in place that we will implement as soon as you have a ship to head out on. That was my part of this briefing."

"Which leads to my part. Joseph Samuels. I am in charge of the info you will be able to use in constructing the spaceship. J.T. are you familiar with the late 21st century?" he asked.

"Kind of, depends on what aspect you are asking about," replied J.T.

"Ever hear of Area 51?" he asked.

"Yeah, it was a special weapons and research facility. Highly secretive. Lots of advanced weapons, mechanics, and technology," J.T. replied.

"It was also a repository of alien technology," he said solemnly.

"Really? I was not aware that legend was actually accurate,"

J.T. stated. "More of a myth that was consistently denied by the leadership even after the end of WW4."

"Well, they lied. There were 11 alien spacecraft interred there, along with eight aliens. two of the aliens lived for 25 years after they were found in a wrecked spacecraft. They were interrogated but, as you can imagine, there was a communication barrier. It took 22 years for someone to figure they were speaking an ancient language. A mixture of ancient Sumerian and Aztec/Mayan. The aliens were able to give some technical information but not enough to answer all the questions put to them. Area 51 was closed, but Area 43 was opened five years after WW3 was over. A tunnel was drilled 20 miles into the mountain range southeast of Area 51.

"The entrance to Area 43 is through an ancillary hanger off the main hangar at Area 51. There is still a security detail attached to the installation, along with some engineering and maintenance crews. There are records and video/audio tapes available that document all interactions with the aliens and every test/experiment ever conducted. With your knowledge and education, we believe that you should be able to construct a spacecraft capable of carrying a colony to the aliens' home world. Upon arrival, you will see what it takes to return to Earth for the next load. The design of the ship is completely up to you. You will have command over every decision and any personnel assigned to this ship."

"Hopefully, what you can glean from the stuff in Area 43 will allow you to construct a vehicle that can exceed light speed. You will also have to develop weapons systems for self-protection and intimidation. I think that the same technology we use for dome protection could be adapted to protect a moving spacecraft. Without saying, you will need to figure out how you will be able to take livestock, cows, horses, pigs, sheep, chickens and so forth with you both for food during the trip and to have breeding stock. There is no guarantee that you would be able to eat native animals. Also, you will need seeds for growing as well as an agriculture area to grow food during the journey, as well as an area for the colonists to be housed. That brings up the issue of suspended animation and hibernation. There is no way to build a spacecraft that would basically be an ark, having an area to grow food, raise livestock and have berthing space for 1500 to 2000 people. Hibernation solves a lot of issues."

"Currently, there is a man named Jacques LeClerc in Belgium, that has managed to get test animals to sleep for 18 months consistently without issues. He has not yet tried it on humans," he said.

"I have read his work and there aren't any glaring flaws that I have found, so having him on the team is a must. Am I allowed to have non-citizens to be part of the project?" J.T. asked.

"As stipulated when we offered you the Quest, you are running the project. You can have or use anyone you choose on the job. At this point we are not concerned with foreign interference. After all with the earth being uninhabitable, there is not any reason to sabotage this project," was the answer.

"When do I need to start?" J.T. asked.

"Yesterday," The First Chief Elder replied.

"OK, then I accept the Quest," J.T. said.

"Thank you," the members of the Council said.

"You have no idea how relieved we, the Council are having the weight of this issue lifted from our shoulders. We could not have found a better man to take charge of this project," said John.

"There is a file that Charles will give you as you leave. You may get started as soon as you wish."

Heather smiled at her man. "Never thought my man would be the man that saved the human race," she said.

"Thanks for the confidence. Don't think you are getting off lightly, my dear. Since we are moving the human race somewhere else to start over, the people we move have to be the healthiest, physically in the best shape and free of carrying genetic diseases. That is going to be where you come in. You will be overseeing physician recruitment and genetic therapy. After all, makes no sense to transfer humans to a new planet where they bring all the diseases there are here on Earth. Think you can handle that?" he asked.

"Sounds like a challenge, but it is doable," she replied.

They rose, leaned over the table, thanked the members of the Council, assured them of his promise to do his very best and promised to keep them regularly informed. He also requested that the Office of the Council notify any institution within the system of his position and require them to give him whatever assistance he requests, including access to any facility, institution, or storage depot he may need access to.

The First Chief Elder promised to make sure that was accomplished and handed J.T. a card, with a number on it, saying, "This is my personal contact number. Use it any time you feel you need to. My phone is with me 24/7/365."

"Thank you, John, for your assistance and support."

With that, J.T. and Heather headed for the door, which was

being held open by Charles, who was standing there holding a very large file, which he handed to J.T. as he passed by.

"Good day, General Coulter, Dr. Dunkirk. Good luck."

The guard outside the door snapped to attention, saluted, and said, "If you need volunteers, sir, please call me."

J.T. returned the salute and replied, "I certainly will, son."

They strode out the front door into the relatively warm midday sun and both of them almost simultaneously took in a deep breath and sighed.

"Shall we have lunch somewhere? I would like Mom and Dad to join us," J.T. said.

"Where shall we eat?" Heather asked.

"The Wine Cellar is close by. They always have excellent food," J.T. remarked.

"Works for me." J.T. took his phone out of his inside coat pocket, pushed two on the autodial screen and within 10 seconds, his mother answered.

"Hey Mom, finished our meeting and Heather and I were going to grab lunch at the Wine Cellar and wondered if you and dad would like to join us."

"Why yes dear, we would love to. Shannon is here so, if you don't mind, we will drag her along. About 30 minutes, is that OK?"

"Perfect, see you then." And then he hung up, searched the phone's memory for the phone number to the restaurant.

He dialed the number and when they answered, he said, "This is General Coulter. I would like a table for 6. Do you have anything available in 30 minutes?"

There was a short pause, and he replied, "That will be fine, thank you."

He looked at Heather and said, "I always wanted to be able to do that."

Heather responded, "Do what?"

"Call a restaurant, give them my rank, and be able to get whatever I want."

"Don't let it go to your head, General," was her response.

"You mean if I were to say, this is the General and in 20 minutes I want you naked and in bed, it wouldn't work?" he kidded.

"Well, maybe, in that case, it just might work. Depends," Heather answered.

"Depends on what? I am a General and should be obeyed!" he replied with mock indignation.

"If I am in the OR operating on someone, you are gonna have to stick that order in your ear, bud," Heather replied. That remark caused them both to break out in a good chuckle.

J.T. pulled her to him, hugged her close, kissed her, and told her he loved her.

Then he swatted her on the ass and said, "disobedience has consequences."

"Are you always gonna be such a bully?" she said with annoyance.

"Of course. I am a General!" was his pompous response.

They walked around the corner and started down the street in time to see dad's car pull up and everyone pile out, including Sean. Not surprisingly, Sean snapped to attention and offered a crisp salute, to which J.T. returned the salute and automatically said, "As you were."

J.T.'s parents and sister had never seen military courtesy displayed between the two men. After all, they were as close as brothers, yet the family had never seen the public professional side of their relationship. Deep down, all of them were moved and impressed.

"Shall we go in? I'm starved," remarked J.T.

Sean immediately opened the door. J.T. indicated to the rest of the party that they were to enter first. J.T. stopped in front of Sean and whispered,

"You can relax Sean. You and I both know our status and I have no need for public displays unless we're among other members of the military, where decorum needs to be maintained. Okay?"

"Okay."

"Let's go inside. I'm starving." J.T. entered and made their way to the table where everyone was already seated.

Shannon asked J.T., "Did you have to make him salute you out where everyone could see?"

"First off, Sean and I are both still in the military. There are certain rules that apply to our conduct with other members of the military. They generally indicate an acknowledgement of the junior member present to his superior officer. It is a greeting and an acknowledgement of the junior members' status in the military hierarchy. It is also considered good manners. Those of us that have made the military our life's work accept this, and it becomes a second nature behavior. I am his superior officer, and he was rendering appropriate military honors. It was a sign of respect," J.T. lectured.

The hostess came over to the group and indicated for them to follow her. They filed through the dining room, J.T. occasionally stopping to shake hands with well-wishers. The group each took a seat and got comfortable. Before anyone could say anything, J.T. said the meeting went as expected and that it would be discussed at his home after lunch and would not entertain any further questions here in the restaurant.

Helen was the first to speak up and comment on how much pageantry there had been at the ceremony and how much it had moved her. Frank chimed in that he was just bursting with pride for both Sean and J.T. Shannon said she wondered why the reasons for the medals were not being given. She thought it was standard practice for the reason for the medal to be described, so the attendees would know why the award was being given. J.T. responded that it was the usual custom to describe the event that caused the award to be given, but since there were so many being handed out, the readings were omitted, otherwise they would have been there all day. Helen responded that taking all day would have delayed his proposal and ruined the effect. J.T. just had to smile and blush a little.

Heather said that she thought that it was the perfect proposal and had caught her completely by surprise, but it was the most romantic thing that had ever happened to her. Shannon then recounted the proposal from Sean and asked Helen to relate hers. The conversation was interrupted when the waiter arrived to take the orders. When he had finished, there was a lull in the conversation. Helen picked up the conversation and brought it around to talking about the wedding. Unfortunately, the men were effectively excluded from the conversation. The women were still chatting amongst themselves when the food was delivered and then picked up where they had left off while they were eating. The men managed to pick up tidbits here and there, not enough to have the whole picture, but enough to be feeling glad they were not included.

The women were still discussing color patterns for dresses. J.T. told them the bill had been paid and they should all meet back at his home.

When the family was all gathered in the living room, J.T. addressed them.

"I've gathered all of you here for a few reasons. Firstly, everything I tell you has to remain confidential until otherwise told by me alone. Are we clear on this? This is as serious as it can get. I need to hear from each and every one of you that you understand and agree."

One by one, they all verbalized their understanding.

"Two. All of you are going to have significant roles in what I am about to tell you. You will need to involve others, but you will not share anything with any of them without my consent. Also, we are on a timeline, so you can't put things "on the back burner". Does everyone understand?" he asked.

There was a generalized "yes" from the group, so he took a sip of coffee, savored the taste before starting in.

"What I am about to tell you, Heather already knows the majority of but not all. The Quest offered to me involves creating and building an interstellar spacecraft whose purpose is to help colonize a new planet because the current science indicates that the planet Earth will no longer be able to support human life in the next 13 to 20 years. Now, do you understand why we couldn't discuss this in the restaurant and the need for secrecy you all just swore to?"

There was a general murmuring amongst the group.

"Moving right along, Sean. Over the next few months I will

need you to hand pick 75 troops. You may check records from any DSF command. If questions are asked, refer them to me.

"Shannon, I am going to need an executive assistant, someone to keep files, correspondence, and appointments. Do you think you can handle it?"

"Sure, I can," was the reply.

"Dad, you are going to have to design the computer system for the spaceship, starting with a computer program that has a universal language translator."

"Mom, you and I are going to design the propulsion system for the craft."

"Heather, you are going to be working on a couple of projects, putting together a comprehensive medical staff, and designing a program to test colonists for genetic diseases and then a program for correcting any and all genetic defects that are present with the chosen colonists. We are going to take only those colonists that are as near genetically perfect, and by that, I mean least likely to be carrying a genetic disease that would be passed on to successive generations of colonists."

"Now for the really big news. In four weeks, we will be taking a trip to Area 51. In case you are not familiar, Area 51 was formerly known as Groom Lake. It is in the Southwest US. It was a research area for weapons and other new technology. It was also the study and storage facility for *alien spacecraft*".

There was a stunned look on everyone's face with that information.

J.T. continued, "Area 51 was one of the first areas protected when Henry Jackson perfected the Dome force field just before WW4. It was done even before the major cities were protected. They were just lucky to have finished the force field system before the nuclear missile attack that started WW4. Unfortunately, as you know, not all the major cities were protected, only the ones with military bases close at hand. The enemy never knew of the Dome system and that is why the retaliation completely wiped out most of eastern Europe and Asia. That was the end of the war. Apparently prior to that, all the alien craft were transferred to area 43."

"The government had undertaken a project to move them to more secure facilities by drilling a double wide tunnel 20 miles long, southeast of Area 51, through solid rock and mountains, to another area that had been hollowed out of a mountain range. There is even a launch tube for vehicles that are manufactured inside the mountain."

"Dad, we are going there. You are going to look over the different craft's computer systems, see what you can make of it, and what you can get out of it, that can help you construct a universal translator. I must visit the other domes, under my new command, to check out the security forces at each one before I can take the time for an in-depth road trip".

"Mom, can you start researching unpublished papers on different forms of energy sources, Ion propulsion, magnetic field manipulation, crystal use, cold fusion reactors and the state of miniaturized nuclear reactors etcetera? In order to move things along, we need to be more focused on the leading forms of energy use, so as not to waste time on things that are probably not going to pan out."

"Anyone want more coffee or a drink of something stronger?" J.T. finally asked.

Frank and Sean piped up with, "A Tullamore Dew straight up would hit the spot."

Helen, Shannon, and Heather all opted for large glasses of wine, red for Helen and Shannon, and white for Heather. Everyone took a bit of a break from the conversation to enjoy the drink. After all, the information and instructions that were just given out and discussed were quite astonishing and, for that matter a little overwhelming. Each was lost in their own thoughts and there was a heavy period of silence. J.T. finally broke that silence.

"That was an awful lot to drop on you guys all at once, but given the circumstances, I can't think of people more equipped to succeed, and succeeding means the continuance of the human race. I think that is worth the effort, so right now, I want to thank you for the effort. I know you are already thinking about things. What would everyone like for supper, or would you prefer I whip something up of my own choosing?"

It was a thunderous "you choose" in response to J.T.'s question.

"Okay," was his answer.

J.T. headed out to the kitchen and started looking through the fridge and pantry to see what he had to work with. Heather came out to lend a hand.

"What can I do to help, sweetheart?" She asked.

"Why don't you cut up some lettuce, green onions, shave a carrot and slice up a cucumber. Toss all of it in a bowl. Then sauté some slivered almonds in butter until brown. Must watch them closely, cause they brown up really fast. Dump them on a paper towel to cool. Open a small can of mandarin oranges and drain the juice into a small bowl. Then add some olive oil, vinegar, salt and freshly ground black pepper. Stick everything in the fridge. I must cook up some chicken tenderloins and cut up some broccoli."

He quickly made up some crepe batter while cutting up the broccoli, quickly moving to the chicken he was cooking on the stove. He blanched the broccoli and allowed it to drain while finishing the chicken. He put the cooked chicken and broccoli in a warm oven to hold while he started making crepes. He turned up the heat a little to move the process along a little quicker.

After making 14 crepes, he put them in the warm oven. Next on the list was cutting the baby Bella mushrooms, which were then tossed in another skillet, with some clarified butter and olive oil mix. While the mushrooms were cooking, he started making a bechamel sauce with some prepared roux, half and half, nutmeg, salt and white pepper and a white wine/ tarragon reduction. Heather had finished the salad and dressing, so he told her to get the table set but not the dinner plates.

He asked Sean to refresh everyone's drink and get a couple bottles of white wine open to breathe. As the sauce thickened, he removed all the components from the warm oven and began rolling up crepes with chicken and broccoli inside, two to a plate, mushrooms on top of the crepes, and the sauce was ladled over each crepe. The plates were put back in the warming oven so he could get to plating the salad. Each plate had the greens placed in the center of the plate sprinkled with toasted almonds, mandarin orange segments and vinaigrette drizzled over the salad. J.T. called everyone into the kitchen to get their salads.

Heather whispered to Shannon, "He's so damn sexy in that

apron. He's even cooked naked, and I have to tell you, it was so hot."

They both giggled over that, then tried to stifle the giggle when J.T. looked quizzically at them. Everybody made their way into the dining room. The men held the ladies' chairs, then sat down. J.T. stepped up to the head of the table and proposed a toast to the group, their mission, and the success that he knew they would achieve.

Everyone took a sip of wine as he continued, "Tonight's fare is an orange almond salad with a vinaigrette and Chicken Divan crepe with Bechamel/Tarragon reduction sauce with baby Bella mushrooms. Bon Appetite."

He took his seat, and the typical sounds of dining filled the room along with moans and positive compliments about the salad. When all was done eating, J.T. stood up and cleared all the salad plates, then headed to the kitchen. Acting as a seasoned waiter fresh from a French café, J.T. returned from the kitchen balancing three plates on both arms.

Setting a plate in front of each person until his arms were empty, he went back into the kitchen, got the rest as well as his plate and a sauce bowl of the leftover seasoned bechamel sauce. Finally getting a chance to sit down and eat, he was frequently interrupted by compliments. He told everyone that there were two leftover crepes in the warm oven in the kitchen, but if they wanted to eat them, they would have to fetch them themselves. Sean got up and asked if there was anybody that wanted to share the last crepe. Getting no answer, he smiled and went to the kitchen to help himself to the remaining crepes. J.T. got up from the table and walked over to the sideboard where his carafe of Tawny port sat with eight crystal port stemware.

"Port anyone? I have a very nice 40-year-old Tawny port here that finishes a meal off quite nicely," he said.

Sean and Frank immediately said yes. Helen thought she would try some, so Shannon and Heather said they would try some of Helen's drink.

J.T. poured four glasses and passed them around.

"To our health, long life and mission success," he toasted.

"Here. Here," was the response from the group.

After taking a sip Helen said, "oh my, this is marvelous. I can taste the caramel. This is truly superb. I never would have guessed."

Similar sentiments were expressed by everyone. J.T. cleared the dishes off the table and then set about filling the dishwasher and getting it set to run after he went to bed.

Heather came out to the kitchen and gently kissed him saying, "I would have helped…"

"I got this. You fit in so well with the rest of the family, it's just wonderful to see."

"They are such wonderful people, and I am really blessed that they seem to have accepted me completely."

"They have marvelous taste and incredibly good judgement," J.T. remarked.

She playfully slapped him on the shoulder and kissed him again. When the kiss broke, he took her by the hand and walked back into the dining room. Everybody was getting ready to leave. Helen came over to J.T. and gave him a hug and a kiss on the cheek and told him that dining here was the same as going out to eat at some of the best restaurants in town. Frank followed right behind and said that he totally agreed with Helen but, whispered in his ear that he was low on Tullamore Dew, then clapped him on the back and shook his hand. Shannon gave him a hug and a smooch on the cheek, then stood in line to hug Heather. Sean gave him a hug and a pat on the back and shook his hand, then got in line for his turn at hugging Heather, too. J.T. could hear the comments that Heather was receiving from, "So glad you are joining the family," from Helen to, "Am glad I have another daughter in the family", from Frank.

"I am finally gonna have a sister and I am so glad it's you," from Shannon.

"J.T. is truly lucky to have you and we can't wait to have you as a sister-in-law," from Sean.

Everybody turned and waved and said goodbye as they filed out the door to the car to leave.

Heather closed and locked the door.

She turned and sensually strode over to J.T. and said, "Dinner was wonderful. Now it is time to pay the chef. Wanna get naked in bed and wait for your payment?" she said seductively.

"Yes ma'am," was the expected and desired response.

CHAPTER
SEVENTEEN

The next four weeks seemed to drag along as each base was a repetition of what was done at the previous base. All in all, he found most of the units were fairly well organized and well run. Several of the command staff balked a little at J.T.'s strongly worded suggestion that all the troops be involved in the planning of a battle.

Most of those commanders were holdovers from War College and Command and Control school age. The thought patterns and theories taught there had not been updated in 100 years and were woefully behind the times. The enemy they had to deal with currently were not the Russians, Chinese, Koreans or the Iranians. They were run of the mill criminals, with an occasional disgraced military professional, that never seemed to be higher rank than a Captain or a Major. Most of those types were never good enough to be thought of for higher rank and, therefore, were never sent for advanced education or training. J.T. made a note of those commanders that needed to retire, and which XOs' needed to be given their own command. When his jet landed, he was really glad to be home.

Meanwhile, while he was gone, Heather had been operating at a hectic pace, two or three cases a day. The pace had kept her mind off the fact that J.T. was gone and the worst part was not sleeping next to him at night. The only good part was that she had uninterrupted weekends to move almost all her stuff into J.T.'s house. The only things left at her home were the furniture and she was not able to move it by herself.

Besides, she wanted to discuss adding her furniture to J.T.'s house with J.T. God, she really missed him and was so glad he was going to be coming home in a day or two. She was ready for the road trip that J.T. had mentioned to Area 51, then to head on to Area 43. It stimulated her imagination. She had always wondered about whether there really were such things as aliens and now, because of her fiancée, she was going to be able to see for herself. An actual revelation that would not be manipulated, modified or covered up by government bureaucrats. The idea was consuming her waking hours at home. All because of J.T...

J.T. was quite glad to get home. The trip had its good points, but he really missed being with Heather. Before he headed home, he stopped by the airfield to check on the plane Shannon had laid on for the flight to Area 51 called Groom Lake. The crew chief pointed out that the plane was outfitted with six multipurpose missiles, three under each wing and that the nose had three-gun ports on each side.

"There is also a complete array of defensive pods throughout the plane, General. All controlled from the pilots' side of the cockpit. There is no RIO/ co-pilot in this plane.

There are six seats, three seats to a side. Normally this baby will do Mach 2.9, but with passengers, it will only do 2.4. Extra weight, don't you know?" said the plane captain.

"She will be fueled and checked out by me and my crew before the close of business today. There is a duty crew that will have the plane ready to go by 0600, earlier if you want it General."

"0700 will be fine. How much luggage can it carry?"

"Maximum, 40lbs per passenger, sir."

"Very well. Thank you."

"Aye, aye, Sir". J.T. pulled out his phone and called Sean.

"Sean, call Mom, Dad and Shannon and tell them that the max weight for their baggage is 35 pounds, no exceptions. Necessities only."

"Wilco," and with that, Sean hung up.

J.T finally got home almost two hours after he landed. Heather got home 20 minutes after he did. They kissed rather passionately before starting the "how was your day/week conversation. Heather went over all the surgeries she had done, how they went and how, surprisingly, no one had any post-op problems. When it was J.T.'s turn to talk, he summed up everything in about three minutes. After that, he broke the bad news to her, about the 35-pound luggage restriction. For a minute she was a little flustered, then asked if that was a firm number, meaning how much leeway she was going to get, and was a little taken aback when J.T. said, "One-half pound max."

"But I already have two bags packed full, and that doesn't include makeup and shoes." She lamented.

"One pair of shoes plus the ones you have on your feet. It will be highly unlikely that you will be walking around outdoors in the desert-like conditions of the southwest," he replied.

"We are going to be deep inside a mountain. You will need a couple pair of jeans, a couple of tee shirts, a couple of sweaters, underwear and socks. You can carry your makeup in your purse along with a brush. I am sure they have hair dryers as well as washing machines and dryers. In certain areas, I am sure they will provide you with appropriate uniforms. You can take a computer. That's about it," he finished.

"Well, I guess I'd better get to work downsizing my suitcase, so you'll have to pack yourself," she said.

J.T. knew the evening was not going to go well. Maybe he should have waited until later to tell her, no, if he did that, then she would be even more pissed because he did not tell her when she had the time to make decisions about what she was going to take with her, in addition to having to completely unpack and repack a much smaller bag. Guess the evening was going to be a bust, so he headed off to the room where he kept his uniforms. He packed one set of fatigues and one class A dress uniform, dress shoes; he was going to fly in his combat boots, his dop kit and his dress hat and fatigue cap. He was back in the den, sipping on a drink when she came into the room.

"You gonna tell me you are completely ready to go, packed and everything?"

"Well, yeah, I don't have a lot of choice. I must wear a uniform, so that pretty much makes up my mind as to what I must take. I take a fatigue uniform I will be wearing when I fly the plane down there. I have a second fatigue uniform and a second class A dress uniform in case they want to have a management /command dinner. One change of shoes. Of course, don't forget my dop kit. That's all I need.

"Shit, I didn't think of a formal type of dinner. That throws a wrench into my packing plan. You could have told me about the dinner a while ago," she ranted.

J.T. responded, "I didn't say there was going to be a formal dinner. I said I was taking the appropriate uniform IF they decided they wanted to throw one. I was just being prepared. You can take a nice pants suit with you in addition to one change of clothing. You will have one set you are going to be wearing, and one set to change into the next day, while you get the first one washed. What is so hard about all of this?"

"I have a role to fill. I am the General's lady and certain things are expected of me because of that status. I have to look good and perfectly put together. It is a reflection on you," she lectured. J.T. knew he had no comeback to her comment, so wisely, he shut up and took another sip of his drink. One-half hour later, Heather called J.T. into the bedroom and asked him to help her close the suitcase.

"Sorry about all that. This is all so new to me and there are different rules and expectations of me in this new role. It has me a little un-nerved. This pant suit I chose. Hope it's Okay."

J.T. looked over her choice and all honesty told her that her choice was perfect. She wrapped her arms around his neck and gave him a slow sensual kiss and whispered in his ear, "take me to bed, General."

He obliged her.

The next morning, J.T. got up at the usual time, kissed Heather, and headed out for at least part of his daily morning workout routine. He had finally arrived in the same physical state he was before the devastating injury and he felt marvelous. He called Sean from the car on the way home and made sure he understood that everyone needed to be at the plane by 0630. After being assured everyone would be there on time, he managed to relax for a couple of minutes before undressing and joining Heather in the shower. They played around under the shower for a few minutes before realizing that time was getting away from them. They had to hurry getting dressed because of the fooling around in the shower.

They each grabbed a cup of coffee and a donut as they headed out the door, trying to carry their luggage at the same time. Getting everything in the vehicle, they got in, got their seatbelts fastened and went out into the street, finally on their way. They pulled up to the hangar and parked the car next to Sean's vehicle, grabbed their bags and headed into the hangar.

Everybody greeted everyone with hugs and smooches before J.T. started his pre-flight checklist and instructions. He spent 15 minutes explaining the ejection seat to everyone. These were ejected down instead of up and out, so everyone needed to be sure they were properly strapped in. The plane was actually a medium range bomber so there were no facilities aboard, so J.T. made sure everyone went to the bathroom before starting to get strapped in. Sean would be in the seat directly behind the pilot.

Everyone else would be seated on each side of the plane's cabin to balance the weight. The plane captain was there to assist everyone getting strapped in and going over what happens with ejection. He hooked up the flight suits, then the helmet and the com system. The face mask would be snapped on after the plane took off. J.T. sat in the pilot's seat finishing the pre-flight checklist. He turned to everyone and checked with all of them to be sure everyone was appropriately strapped in before he started the planes' engines.

After all the engines were running smoothly, J.T. called the tower. "Dome 17 tower, this is Alpha 229 Lima, ready for taxi. There is a 07 and 04 aboard. Destination: Groom Lake."

"Roger A229L Winds are from the southeast at 9 miles/hour, minimal gusts to 15mph. Weather report is clear to your destination. Radio frequency for Groom Lake is 217.83. Will you be flying the computer or not?

"Tower, I will be flying. Please send a computer link for Groom Lake as a precaution."

"Roger A229L wilco. Enroute. You are cleared to taxi to runway one Right from taxiway two Left."

"Roger, A229L rolling." J.T. advanced the throttle and drove to the appropriate taxiway then followed it to the end of the runway, turning to point down the straight long runway. "Tower A229L ready for takeoff."

"Roger A229L you are cleared for takeoff. Have a good flight. Tower out."

"A229L thanks, rolling". J.T. advanced the throttle, set the flaps while holding the break. "Everyone ready?"

"Yes Sir," was the communal response.

"Here we go." With that, he slipped the brake and the plane lurched ahead, rapidly picking up speed. At 130mph, J.T. pulled back on the stick as the jet lifted off. The speed was increasing as he retracted the landing gear and trimmed the flaps. He banked to the right until he reached a heading of 190. He set the altimeter to 50,000 feet and advanced the throttles to almost full military power. Then he took a minute to tell the passengers they had to put the oxygen masks on, and that the flight time would be about two hours and 15 minutes.

The flight was uneventful. J.T. really enjoyed flying the plane as he rarely ever had a chance to pleasure fly. Most of his flying was done for combat purposes. The radio came on.

"This is Groom Lake control, A229L. Is your computer on and functioning, over?"

"This is A229L, am flying on VFR, over."

"A229L, this is control Groom Lake. We have you on radar 250 miles out. You must switch on your computer to approach and landing. I say again, you must switch to computer for approach and landing. Over!"

"Groom Lake, this is A229L, am capable and aircraft is without problems to land. Over."

"A229L, the air defense system will activate when you enter 200 miles out and will continue until you are destroyed unless you switch to computer. Over."

"Roger, wilco." J.T. leaned to the left and flipped the power switch for the computer.

"Groom Lake, A229L computer on."

"Roger A229L. establishing connection with computer. Done. We have the aircraft. State business at Groom Lake, over."

"A229L on Council business 07 aboard. Honors not requested nor desired. Have base CO meet us upon deplaning. Over."

"Groom Lake roger, wilco." The plane began to slow and descend as J.T. watched the instruments, watching for signs that the air defense system was activating. 10 minutes later, the runway appeared directly in front of him. Groom Lake contacted J.T. again and informed him the computer would disengage as soon as the wheels touched down. They requested immediate confirmation of the message which J.T. provided. He put his hands on the throttle, yoke and pedals, not applying any pressure, awaiting the sensation of the wheels touching the ground. When he felt the touchdown, he immediately took control of the aircraft, throwing the engines into reverse and began applying the brakes. As the plane slowed down, the tower called and informed him to turn right on to taxiway one right. There would be a vehicle there with a 'FOLLOW ME'.

There at the bottom of the stairs stood Col. William Farmouth, CO of the Groom Lake facility. As J.T. stepped down off the stairs, Col. Farmouth snapped to attention and rendered a smart, snappy salute which J.T. returned just as smartly.

"General, welcome to Groom Lake. It's a pleasure to meet you and I will do my best to provide you with everything you require during your stay. Which is going to be about how long, if I may ask?" the CO asked.

"Not sure how long we will be here. We have a number of things that we need to look into. There is no way to tell how long that will take." I appreciate your offer though."

"If you follow me, I will take you to your quarters. Are you or any of your group hungry? We can stop by the Officers Mess for lunch. They should still be serving."

"That would be wonderful. Thank you, Colonel."

J.T. turned to the group and told them to grab their luggage and follow him. He picked up his bag and Heather's suitcase and followed Col. Farmouth as he led the way to the officers' Mess. The others followed suit, mumbling to each other as they wormed their way through the corridors of the underground building housing quarters and mess facilities for those stationed at the Groom Lake military facility. When they arrived at the door to the officers' Mess, J.T. took the opportunity to introduce everyone to Col. Farmouth.

"Colonel This is my mother, Dr. Helen Coulter PhD, my father, Dr. Frank Coulter, PhD. Major Sean McCann XO of DSF 17, Shannon McCann, my executive assistant and Dr. Heather Dunkirk, M.D., my medical consultant and fiancée."

"To all of you. Welcome to Groom Lake. After lunch, I will show you to your quarters."

Sean popped up with, "When will we be going to Area 43?"

The question caught Col. Farmouth by surprise.

"Area 43 is restricted. Off limits to all but a very select few. I have received no notification from anyone granting you access to Area 43."

J.T. stepped up and said that he should probably check the notification letter sent from the Office of the Chief Elder of The Council. That should clear everything up. The Colonel excused himself to return to the office while everyone else went through the cafeteria style service food line, getting their choice of offerings for lunch.

Minutes later, after everyone had finished eating, J.T. got up and wandered off in search of Colonel Farmouth. He managed to find him coming out of the office of the Commander with a paper in his hand.

"Did you find the message with the authorization on it?" he asked.

"Yes, it was on the second page of the message, the one my yeoman failed to give me. I apologize for the error. You and your group are to be given unlimited access to Area 43 and any information, testing, papers published and unpublished, related to that area."

"Thank you for clearing up this matter, Colonel. My group and I have a lot of work to do, so if you could get someone to get us to Area 43 so we can get settled in."

"My chief master at arms will help you."

"Where are our quarters?" J.T. asked.

"They are in this building. We have visitors' quarters in area 43 if you would like to have me change you to them."

"That would be excellent, Colonel," was the reply.

"Will take me a few minutes, so why don't you wait in the mess, and I will send the Chief to get you when things are all set."

"Very well, your assistance is truly appreciated Colonel," J.T. said as he walked out into the corridor headed for the Officers Mess.

J.T. gathered his crew together at the door as the Chief MAA arrived. After saluting J.T. and Sean, he indicated that the group should follow him. They all felt like they had been walking for hours when, in all reality, they had only walked about 100 yards. The Chief indicated they should stop by a door on the left side of the corridor. He walked a little further, opened a tiny metal door on the wall, and inserted a key. He then put his thumb on a scanner next to the metal door and the door in front of them slid silently open.

"Everybody, please step to the rear of the elevator," The CMAA requested.

They all crowded in and sat their luggage down, trying to make room for everything. The door slid silently closed, and the Chief asked Shannon to push the SL3 button.

There was a sensation of movement, but it was not fast. There was a ding, and the door slid open, revealing a large landing with glass on two sides and a painted metal railing along the walkway. There was a set of stairs on the right going down. The Chief led them across the walkway, which traversed over two separate sets of railway tracks. On the further track, there was what appeared to be a railway car. Once crossing the walkway, the Chief cautioned them to watch their step as they descended to the railway platform. A few minutes later, they were all standing on the platform.

The Chief stepped up and said, "As soon as you get on the train, please stow your gear right down here. Put your head back against the seat and relax. You will be going 31.35 miles in nine minutes. Do not try to stand or move around during the trip. I guarantee you will get hurt quite badly. Find a seat. Strap yourself into the seat quite snuggly, like you did for the plane, an announcement when the train has stopped that will tell you it is safe to get out of your seats. There will be another Chief MAA who will take over at that point. Welcome to area 43. Relax and enjoy the trip." He stepped off the train after checking everyone's harnesses.

The door closed. The train took off pulling about three G's and in what seemed like the blink of an eye, the train slowed and came to a stop. The voice announcing the arrival was clear and sounded like a radio announcer.

"The car has come to a complete stop. It is safe to undo your seat harnesses. Gather your luggage and personal belongings and exit using the door on the left. Personnel will meet you at that point to take you to the indoctrination area to begin your instruction on rules, regulations and protocols of Area 43. Have a nice day."

"Well, that was interesting," Heather remarked as she took J.T.'s arm.

"I don't think I have ever gone that fast on land," remarked Helen.

"Welcome to Area 43. I am Chief MAA Franklin. I will be taking you through the initial phase of indoctrination. The first thing is to get your identity verified and get your pass cards issued. Then we will proceed with the tour, showing you to your quarters, the mess area, and the entertainment area. We will then proceed to the different restricted areas such as propulsion, computers, weapons, defense, scanning and naviga-tion. We will also take a moment to stop by the area containing our visitors, none of which are still alive. There will be certain coveralls you will have to wear in certain areas.

"These will be issued before you are allowed to enter the area. Each area has decontamination procedures that are to be adhered to, regardless of the situation. No exceptions. Is everyone clear on this?" he asked.

There was a group affirmation and J.T. stepped forward and was met with a crisp salute, which was returned just as crisply.

"Everyone here understands the rules, Chief. Can we get to our quarters now?" J.T. asked.

"We'd like to change and get cleaned up before too much longer," J.T. asked.

"Certainly General, right this way." With that, he turned and started off down an adjacent corridor.

"This room has two beds and a shower. This room," he said, pointing across the hallway, "has one bed with a shower, as does the room next to it. No keys. Just open the door. We would prefer it if you do not take long hot showers. We are under a bit of a water restriction until the rainy season hits, and it is not due for another four to six weeks, okay?"

J.T. turned to the rest of the group and asked if everyone understood. The answer, with a few groans, was yes. Everyone chose a room and put their luggage away and changed into jeans and T-shirts, then met back out in the hallway, ready to go on the tour.

The Chief said, "Is everyone ready to go? First stop, identification badges, follow me," and off he walked, down the corridor.

They finally came to a frosted pane glass door with engraved lettering "Identification office."

"Please have a valid ID available for the clerk. Read the sign underneath."

The Chief held the door, informing everyone to get into a single line and have their IDs in hand. One by one they each stepped up to the window, were greeted professionally, turned over their ID's and stepped to the left, to the next window, for fingerprints as the process began. Forty-five minutes later, everyone was finished with fingerprints, photos, and the issuance of the magnetic imprinted swipe cards with photos and thumb prints of both thumbs. Finally, was the record of the retinal scans.

"OK, follow me. I am going to show you where the different sections are and here is a generalized map that you should always keep with you". He turned and started walking and talking like a Disney tour guide.

"Area 43 takes up 25,000 acres, and it is pretty easy to get lost. If you should be unable to find the way to where you want to go, there are red phones on the walls every 50 yards or so. There is a number on the wall right above the phone. Just lift the phone handle, someone will answer you, just give them the number on the wall, tell them who you are and where you want to go. They will give you directions. It's as easy as that," the Chief said as he pointed to the red phone on the wall to the left of the group as they made their way down the hallway.

"The first section is propulsion. In here, the scientists are working on new forms of propulsion of air and spacecraft. The majority is based on some reverse engineering obtained from alien spaceships we have acquired. Some of these are from crashes, some were shot down and some were captured when they landed in secure areas. Currently, there are five crafts in this section. Obviously, the difficulty comes from not being able to translate the markings on the craft.

"The section of Area 43 that deals with language and translation are two sections further on, past the next one, which covers computers and universal translation. After that is weapons, and yes, all of these vehicles have had some type of defensive weapons. We are still trying to figure out how they work, how they are powered and if these types of weapons pose a threat to Earth, as well as how we defend against them. The next section has to do with scanning. Apparently, these craft are capable of scanning space for a multitude of things, from different types of elements to life forms and other things, asteroids and their elemental makeup, radiation. The list is quite endless.

"The next section has to do with navigation. This includes black holes, wormholes and other space anomalies, things it would be necessary to know to be able to navigate through the galaxy to other star systems. Clearly understanding the language and markings is key to the whole thing. If we can understand that, then we will be able to figure out how things work, and what else these space vehicles can do. The final section is for life forms that were found in and or around these craft. We gleaned a lot of information from them while the specimens were living. It was unfortunate we could not get them to help us with the language."

"Well guys, it's time for us to regroup, discuss and layout duties," J.T. said as they turned and walked back down the corridor to where they started.

They all went into the mess area and were directed to the section that was reserved for officers. After seating, the Chief steward stepped to the head of the table and recited the menu for the evening's fare as if he was the Head Waiter at a fine French restaurant in New York or L.A.

"This evening we offer a locally grown green garden salad with a southwestern dressing, slightly on the spicy side. There is also balsamic vinaigrette, blue cheese or ranch dressings. For the main course we have lamb rack, cooked medium rare to medium. Pork schnitzel served with a Hunters sauce, a bone-in Ribeye steak cooked to order. Vegetables being offered include steamed asparagus or Haricot Verts almandine. Starches include a baked potato or Au gratin potatoes. Desert is either Bananas Foster or Strawberry Shortcake with brandy flavored whipped crème. I shall start, as protocol dictates, with the General, followed by the Major then around the table starting with the person on the General's right."

As J.T. ordered, he asked if there was wine available, and the steward produced a small wine list that was quite well laid out. He questioned the rest of the table about their choices, then ordered a Merlot. The rest of the table ordered and after the steward left to put in the order, J.T. started in.

"Mom, Dad, I need to get copies of all markings inside any of the alien spacecraft. I wonder if anyone has ever thought about all the ancient aliens and the different civilizations that have artistic renderings of spacemen and spacecrafts on walls. If you stop to think about these civilizations and their growth and development, it is not inconceivable that extraterrestrials helped with language and writing, whether it was from pictograms or hieroglyphics to alphabets. To take that a step further, if aliens were teaching this, it seems logical that they would teach their own language.

"Heather, do you still have access to the III tapes that are about archeology, languages from the Incas, Mayans, Aztecs, Sumerians, Indian (eastern) and ancient Chinese? What I need from you is a program that scans all ancient languages including hieroglyphics, pictograms and drawings and the writings from inside these crafts. I have a feeling that there may be an answer to the language barrier that has plagued the different investigations that have gone on for the last 100 + years. With what I have been tasked with, I do not have another 50 years to work all this out."

"Mom, what I must work on is an ark. 1500 people plus everything needed to feed, clothe, and house them for up to twenty years. I really need to know what the power source for these craft is and are we going to be able to recreate or effectively mimic these power sources with what is available here on earth. We also must look at the materials that were used to build the spacecraft and see if we have those things here on earth. For instance, we have never sent any kind of spacecraft out to where it approaches the speed of light. So, we can see if going that fast will cause the craft to fall apart or burn up. We also need to see if we can modify the force field, the one we use around cities, to encapsulate the ark and protect it from asteroids and space debris and even help keep the ship safe, at near to trans light speeds.

"Sean, I need you to look into the weapons systems they have and see where we can improve them, targeting, the type of torpedoes, perhaps anti-matter explosives that can destroy an enemy with one or two units. We have no idea what awaits us out there. Since we know there are other beings in the universe, we have physical proof, there are, most likely, other species that act as pirates and who are belligerent and warlike. We must be able to protect ourselves when we are in space. I would also like to know if the spacecraft we have here to study have any other type of defensive capabilities, like some sort of cloaking ability or something that makes them look smaller than they are."

"Mom, are the current state of nuclear reactors as small as they can be made, or can we make them even more efficient and smaller than they currently are? I was thinking of having 12 to 14 reactors aboard, four or five running at any given time. They would be dispersed throughout the ship and be slaved to one or two sections per reactor. One to run scanning and navigation, one to run the electrical system for half the ship and another for the hibernation system, one for the engines and one for weapons and force fields. The rest on standby. One for livestock and agriculture, more if the power was needed for the engines. Can you look into that?"

"Heather, your section is going to be the medical staff. You will need general surgeons, ortho surgeons, neurosurgeons, pediatricians, OBGYN's, family physicians, Psychiatrist, dermatologist, pathologists, ENT's and endocrinologist. We will need three of each except family practice, pediatrics and OBGYN's, where we need six of each. I also want you to set up a program for screening for genetic diseases and a genetic treatment specialist.

"I want to have 1500 colonists that do not have any genes for diseases that can be passed to the next couple of generations. I don't want half of the population to be unwell and on medications or have a shorter life span. I can tell you, we will not be taking any type of tobacco products with us, period. Alcohol and cannabis are going to be tightly controlled. We are going to be building a new world and we can't have people that are always unwell. There will be no children aboard or pregnancies occurring until two years after we have arrived and gotten civilization started. I would prefer that the age group be in their early twenties, as we do not know how long we will be underway. And I do not want a lot of children born to women at the end of their reproductive life span," J.T. finished his little speech as the steward served the salads.

Questions were asked and discussed as the dinner progressed.

"I suggest we see what the entertainment section has to offer," Sean suggested.

Everyone agreed that was a good idea and after getting directions from the steward, they all set off for an evening of relaxation, as they all knew that finding a lot of playtime was going to be awhile into the future. Once they arrived at the entertainment section, they looked over the menu and decided on bowling. Two hours later, Helen, Shannon, and Heather took their victory bow and gave the losers their drink order. They spent another hour enjoying the others' company before making arrangements to meet for breakfast. J.T. got directions to the exercise area so he could work out in the morning.

Everyone headed off to their rooms, as did J.T. and Heather.

As they got ready for bed, Heather posed a question about her assignment and an ethical dilemma.

"Do you feel as though you are playing God, by choosing only those people that are near perfect specimens of the human species? We have proven that we are flawed and imperfect, but you have set very high standards for the colonists," she posed.

"I have thought about that issue for quite a while and the conclusion I have come to is this. I have been chosen to lead a group of colonists to a new world, where we will attempt to start our civilization over. Part of leading is setting a standard that will get us as close as possible to succeeding. One of the first things we will not have a lot of is the ability to manufacture medications. The supplies we bring with us will be all there is for quite a long time, if ever. We have no idea, when we land on a new world, whether there will be raw materials available for us to manufacture medications. It may be twenty years before that ability is available. So, the only thing I can do is make sure the people we take with us are in the best possible health, have no genetic predispositions to serious diseases that will determine who they are going to be able to procreate with.

"For example, there is still a segment of our population that has, let's use a common issue, sickle cell trait or disease. If the man and the woman are both carrying the trait, one out of four children will have sickle cell disease, two of them will have the trait and one will be free and clear. That means 75% of that pairing will pass along with this disease. That can spread through a civilization for generations to come. By excluding those with genetic issues, we give the whole mission a much better chance to succeed. I know that this sounds like I am trying to create some type of superhuman. I am not adding anything to these people that they don't already have. I am going to make it a little more difficult for them to cause problems like smoking and alcohol restrictions.

"We will not be taking tobacco along with us so if someone wants to smoke something, they are free to try. However, the colony is not going to waste what resources we have for health preservation, on someone that is not going to take care of themselves, and in fact, indulge in things that put them at risk for disease or detrimental/ self-injurious behaviors. Things that would make it harder on the rest of the colony to survive," he said.

"But what about personal freedom? Don't people have the right to do what they want to?"

"If we were talking about life on earth, I believe that they do have that right. The problem is that there will be no more life on earth as we know it. We will be the only living proof that Homo Sapiens were ever a species in the universe. If we die out, there will be no living proof that we ever existed. I will not let that happen just because someone wants to smoke something or use alcohol to excess because he feels it is his right."

"We will discuss this later," Heather said.

"We can discuss it but I will not be changing my mind. The mission I have been given requires some hard decisions and I am the one that has been chosen to make them and be responsible for the success or failure of that mission," J.T. pronounced.

Heather had learned a long time ago that he was usually right and that maybe this issue was best left for a much later date, for further discussion.

The next morning, J.T. showed up a few minutes late to breakfast. He went through the cafeteria line, loading up on breakfast. He sat down, took a swig of coffee, followed by a swig of orange juice, and looked at his plate. Then he spoke to Sean.

"Sean, when I plan a mission, what happens?" J.T. asked.

"Well sir, you usually call a meeting, invite those personnel that will be intimately involved in that mission, and you discuss, question and listen to the involved players, then decide, form a plan and then issue orders," Sean replied.

"That is what we are going to do this morning. Heather brought up an issue she has with one aspect of my plan. She will tell you about it. Heather," he said, turning over the discussion.

Heather started in, laying out her concerns.

When she had finished, J.T. asked, "Would anyone else care to weigh in on this issue?"

Frank kind of raised his hand and asked J.T. what his position was.

J.T. started off the discussion by stating what he felt he had been tasked to do, and specifically that was to find a new home world for the human race and to safely get them there and then do the best he could to make sure that the new colony would have the best possible chance to survive and thrive. He pointed out that it was going to take a long time before significant manufacturing was going to be available and also that there was no way of guaranteeing that the planet they chose as a home world would have materials needed to make things like medications. Taking all that into account, he wanted his colonist list to be full of healthy, fertile, intelligent, regular people that would be productive and able to work, think and procreate.

Helen commented that she felt that J.T. had a pretty good grip on his mission and she agreed with his reasoning, and she was unable to find any fault with it. Shannon wanted to know if there were going to be any therapies forced on the selectees.

J.T. spoke up and said, "Any person considered for inclusion in the colonist list would be informed of their issue and offered therapy. If they declined, they will be immediately removed from the list. If they changed their minds, they would be informed that their services were no longer needed."

He continued, "That may seem harsh, but those people were more worried about themselves, and the mission was not their top priority, so I don't want them. People like that do not give their all, and can't be trusted in an emergency, nor do they give 100% in what they are assigned to do. So, the long and short answer is, no, they are not forced to have treatment. This whole mission is voluntary. We can't have anyone in it that is not focused and committed. Meeting adjourned."

They finished their coffee and food, and each set out to get started on their assignment.

CHAPTER
EIGHTEEN

Frank and J.T. headed off to the section that housed the spacecraft. Upon arrival, J.T. sought out the section chief. After finding him, he asked if it was possible to get inside any of the spacecraft.

The chief said, "Certainly, we were just opening one of the newer units for the first time. Like to come along, and see? Just came in nine weeks ago and we finished the disinfection procedure only last night. Isolation for six weeks, one week of ultraviolet bombardment, disinfectant submersion for 72 hours, then baking at 300 degrees for 24 hours, then freezing for 36 hours, then we allow the craft to thaw at room temp for 72 hours. Have no idea what kind of bugs could be in or on the craft, so we don't take any chances. General, if you and your partner follow me, we will get you and your friend properly attired in a jumpsuit and gloves. Standard protocol. There's also a release that you will have to sign. All standard stuff. Uncle Sam does not want to be responsible for anything more than he already has to." He handed them both a clip board then pointed to the line at the bottom.

"This just says that you understand that you are boarding an alien vessel of your own accord and that you are not under orders from anyone that is your superior. It also states that you have been informed of all the sterilization procedures, but you understand that there is no guarantee that there are no infectious agents still alive. You also understand that it is your duty and responsibility to notify this command that you are feeling unwell, running a temperature or display any symptoms that you are not currently having, and the names of any personnel you have been in contact with. If you both understand what I have just told you and you agree, sign on the line at the bottom, print your full name, rank and service number, legibly, underneath the signature line. If you are not a member of the armed forces, print your full name, the word *Civilian*, and your ID number, legibly, underneath the signature line." After completely reading the entire form, they both signed and filled in the requested information.

"Gentleman, now please follow me to the staging area." With that, the section chief turned and walked to a steel door guarded by a large, muscular, armed security officer.

The chief turned and said, "We have protocols in place for the initial entry into an alien spacecraft. You will have to wait outside the craft until it is searched and cleared, understood?"

"Can you ask them not to move anything until I can look over the scene?" J.T. asked.

"I can ask, but I can't guarantee they will comply," was the answer. They entered the area where the craft was parked.

"We learned how to open the craft by accident. One of the

technicians was going over the outside of a previously crashed craft and he noticed an irregularity on the surface. He scrubbed the area clean when he noticed a marking. It was an infinity sign lying at an angle. He took off his plastic gloves and traced the outline of the marking. Somehow, he slipped and touched the center of the loops in the marking. He said he felt an electrical surge, and he jumped back, but there was a line that appeared next to the marking. A slight space indicated a door. The tech went back and put his fingers where they had been, but this time, he did not lift them off when the electricity surge came and when he did that the door continued to open. At that point, he called for a section chief, not me at the time, and they proceeded to enter the craft. Armed with this information, techs went to all the other craft and viola. The same thing happened. That was the day we started to learn more about our visitors."

The entry group moved over to the side of the craft. It really looked like a huge saucer with another saucer inverted and placed on top of the bottom saucer, the center of the top saucer had what resembled an upside-down coffee cup the only difference was the finger hole was filled in and had several small pencil-like projections. The dull, dark gray covering the outside of the craft was flawless and seemed to absorb the light that was shining on it. All the light.

There were absolutely no reflections anywhere, off any surface, straight or curved. The entry crew stood off to the side of the craft while another tech stood to the side where the markings were. He pressed the marking with a bare hand and the entryway slid silently open. There was a small rush of air coming out of the craft without any type of smell. The entry crew, clothed with hazmat suits and rebreather air supply equipment, slowly entered using probes and checking the air quality and looking for any type of pathogen they had the technology to detect. 15 minutes later, they emerged from the craft, took off their helmets and indicated to the section chief that he was cleared to enter.

"Okay General, you may enter." They had to step out of the way, as part of the entry crew was walking out with a litter, on which was the form of a dead alien. J.T. stopped the litter for a second, staring at the alien form. It was wearing a gray silver suit, large head, no ears, very large teardrop shaped eyes, small mouth and a one and one-half inch wide headband with red, green, blue, yellow, colored stones, highly polished. J.T. pulled the headband off, then motioned to the crew to continue. He looked at the headband and noticed a green liquid, alien blood, he surmised. He wiped it off on his jumpsuit, then turned it over, inspecting it closely. When he was through, he placed it in his pocket, ducked his head and entered the craft. Frank was right on his heels.

"What are you thinking?" he asked.

"Did you notice the headband the alien had on his head? Look at the one sitting in the elevated chair in the center of the craft? He has one on that is different than the one in my pocket. Looking at the configuration of the command center, I would say the chair in the middle is for the commander on this craft. There are two other chairs in the area, one at 9 o'clock and one at 3 o'clock.

"One is for the navigator and the other one is for the engineer/ scanning/weapons officer. Both are equally close to the commander. I wonder where the body of the third alien is?" J.T.

questioned. Let's look around and see if we can find evidence of a third alien. I'd like to see if we can find a third headband."

They made their way back through all the tiny compartments. In the last compartment, obviously a residence, there was one alien, semi-reclined, strapped into a contoured bed, its head set at an awkward angle. Must have broken its neck on impact. J.T. thought. This alien had a headband like the others, with different colored baubles than the other two.

"Dad does anything in here look like something you recognize?" he asked.

Frank answered, "Well, there are two workstations with their own dedicated screens and much larger screens for the commander."

"Yes, but do you see any keyboards, switches, buttons, or anything that would be involved with using a computer? So how do they make it work?"

"Well, there is voice activated computers, computers run by AI, that's about the extent of it." replied Frank.

"What about a thought-controlled computer?" J.T. threw out.

It was clearly evident that Frank just had a light bulb go off in his brain and he finally caught what J.T. was thinking.

"The different headbands either connect to a different computer or to a section of the main computer, only used by that one wearer, navigation, communication, engineering, defense, scanning. The headband worn by the commander could use any part of the computer needed to complete its job, as commander of the vessel."

"We need to obtain all the headbands from all the spacecraft. And then we need to study them to see how it works. In two weeks, I am going to put one on my head and see if I can get anything in one of these craft to work. I want you to keep this to yourself, especially talking to any of the others until we have thoroughly checked out our rooms for recording or listening devices, clear?"

Frank's reply was simple. "Clear." With that, they called the section chief and pointed out the corpse of the third crew member, then got out of the way when the crew arrived to remove it. J.T. could hardly suppress his joy and excitement.

He had hoped that he would have something like this happen that would make the rest of the task far easier. Once he tried out the headband, perhaps he could access the engines, power sources, language and communications, protective shields and weapons, history, scanning, navigation through the computer. The people he had picked to help could run a long distance if he gave them the keys to these different areas and he could concentrate on the actual construction of an interstellar ark type spacecraft. One that could carry 1500 colonists to a new home planet, before planet Earth ceased to be life supporting.

J.T. whispered to Sean that he wanted him to search his sleeping quarters for listening devices, recorders, or video devices. Frank had already been instructed to do the same thing.

J.T. pulled Heather aside and kissed her passionately, holding the hug while he whispered in her ear the plan to search their room and he would explain more later.

All through dinner, Heather was literally squirming in her seat, as were the other women. Sean passed a note to J.T. indicating he had found a bug in their bedroom and removed it.

Further searching was negative. J.T. suggested they all adjourn to Sean and Shannon's room. When everyone was in the room, seated and giving their undivided attention to J.T.

J.T. started by showing everyone the two headbands he had found in the spacecraft. They were amazed by the story he was telling. Heather was already studying them. She pointed out the fact that they were different, surmising that they have some type of differentiation that may indicate some form of rank. J.T. smiled to himself. His fiancé had come up with that association. He knew she was smart, and this just reinforced that belief. He searched their room and found both a microphone and a video recording device in his room and Frank, when he came in, showed J.T. a listening device he had found. Out in the hallway with his back to the ceiling mounted camera monitoring device, he suggested to the rest of the group that they each search for a different room, just to be sure they hadn't overlooked or missed anything. They would all meet back outside in the hall before heading over to the Officer's club for an evening cocktail and further discussion. J.T. had already decided to talk to the base commander and register a formal complaint about the surveillance in their rooms. After all, he was here on The Council's business, which if the Council wanted him to be involved, they would have briefed him.

When they all regrouped, one more video camera and two more listening devices had been found. J.T. took all these devices and put them in his briefcase, sealed it and put them in the closet and closed the door. With that completed, he gathered everyone together and herded them towards the O club. When they got into the club, they picked a secluded area and pulled two tables together and distributed six chairs around it.

In a lowered voice, J.T. informed the group of his findings and gave them the gist of what he had planned to do about the headbands. He requested that they see if they could find any more headbands, or on the QT, see if anyone was doing anything with the headbands. He also needed to get the headbands analyzed, tested, and diagrammed. He then told the group that in ten days he was going inside the newest alien spacecraft and put the headband on and see if he could get it to work.

Heather spoke up and said that he would need to practice controlling his thoughts and meditating. She felt that the brain waves would be the key, and the testing needed to be focused on trying to find out which brainwaves elicited a response with the headband.

"This was critical," she said. She also said there were certain meditation techniques that seem to cause certain brainwaves to be more intense and certain medications that can suppress certain brain waves and enhance others. Heather also postulated that the headbands had to have the ability to be adaptable, citing a situation where the navigator suddenly was unable to do his job, assuming the headband was slaved to one section of the computer, that whichever of the remaining crew members took over the job, that headband would have to be able to adapt to the new user very rapidly. This was a capability that left room for outside manipulation. The main issue was whether the alien brain waves and human brain waves were similar and/or compatible.

J.T. responded that was what he was hoping would happen, and he wanted suggestions on what system he should spend the most energy on, computer, propulsion, navigation. For the next hour there was debate and discussion and the final consensus was he should focus on the computer, then power/energy, then engines, followed by navigation. If he was able to use the head-band with any efficiency, he would try to figure out how to get plans, schematics and instructions out of the alien computer and into either a human computer or on paper.

J.T. tasked Frank to figure out how to connect the two computers. Helen was tasked to review all current information that has been gleaned over the last 100 years of study.

She also was tasked to see what questions had not been answered or were about to be answered. Sean was tasked with investigating the defensive and offensive capabilities and what 100 years of study has revealed. Heather would work with T.J. to get him ready to use the headband. The discussion around the table shifted to what each person had seen and experienced with their first day seeing and touching an alien spacecraft, Frank commented that the craft he was in looked very efficient in its layout and was designed by beings that wanted to keep the number of crewmembers to a minimum, thereby reducing the likelihood of alien/human confrontation/interaction.

Helen said she had an opportunity to see the power plant for area 43 and was a little surprised to see that it was a standard mid-sized nuclear reactor. There were no upgrades either to control, size of the reactor or incorporation of any new tech-nology. Most of the new large output nuclear reactors were about one half the size of this reactor. She implied that there was no new engineering technology that had been found or created by reverse engineering. Newly created technology had not been applied to the power plant of Area 43.

J.T. stood and looked at the group and said, "Meeting

adjourned. We will reconvene at 0800 for breakfast and a discussion of what we will try to accomplish tomorrow. Good night. Keep your eyes open for other devices. If you find any, give them to me at breakfast. I will be talking with the base commander tomorrow. Be aware, they may have replaced them as soon as they realized we had removed them."

The next morning, after finishing his daily routine, J.T. met everyone at the officers' Mess for breakfast. Sean privately handed him three more devices. J.T. stuffed them in his pocket with the two he had found in their room last night. With a nod, he ordered breakfast, drank some coffee, and rehashed what he needed everyone to get to work on. When breakfast was done, he turned to Heather, kissed her, and got up from the table.

"See you all at lunch," he said and then exited the Mess.

CHAPTER
NINETEEN

He returned to their room and put on a more formal uniform than the fatigues he had been wearing. He made sure his ribbons were in order, especially the two Council Medals of Honor he had been awarded. He then set off for the CO's office. He found the office and entered.

An obviously bored secretary raised her head from the magazine she was reading and asked, "Can I help you, Sir?"

J.T. responded in his most commanding voice, "General Coulter wants to speak with the Colonel immediately."

"The Colonel is quite busy at the moment."

"Is he having a meeting with someone more superior than a General," he spat out with quite a bit of venom.

"Well, no sir,"

"Then he will see me now." And with that, he walked over to the office door, knocked twice, then entered without waiting for a response.

"General Coulter," was the greeting.

"Colonel, do you need a refresher course in military courtesy? Is it not customary for a junior officer to rise, come to attention, and render a hand salute when meeting a senior officer?"

The colonel immediately jumped to his feet, snapped to attention, and rendered a half ass salute that J.T. did not return for a full minute. He returned the salute, then reached into his pocket and pulled all the surveillance equipment he had removed from the three rooms.

"Care to explain why me and my staff's rooms were bugged and put under video monitoring? It was unwarranted, unappreciated, unwanted, and unnecessary. We are here on a mission from the Council of Elders, your bosses, and I would think that they would know whether me and my group were trustworthy, don't you Colonel?"

The Colonel had been caught red-handed and could only turn beet red in the face and bluster a half-assed apology.

"General, those devices have been in place for years. I am not sure they are even being monitored," He replied.

"Well, Colonel, that can't be right, because half of these were removed before we went to dinner last night. The other half were removed after we got back from dinner, so someone was monitoring things, noted that all of these went offline, then replaced them before we returned to retire for the night. I want you to get the officer in charge of this, here in this office in the next 10 minutes. Have I made myself clear?"

"Yes. Sir." He picked up the phone and said, "Linda, please get Major Tesch here in my office immediately."

Eight minutes later, the door opened, and a major entered the room stating, "Major Tesch, reporting to the Commanding

Officer as ordered, Sir!" He held his salute until the Colonel returned it.

"Major, there is a problem with the visitor's quarters being bugged and video monitored. Are you aware of this?

"Yes Sir, we have standing orders that have been in place since before I was transferred here four years ago. I have merely continued to follow written orders that were given before I was stationed here. Those orders have not been rescinded, Sir."

J.T. stood, and looked at both men, and said, "There will be no monitoring of me or my staff, and any recordings already made will be given to me personally with no copies. This will be done in the next thirty minutes. Are we clear? Is there any part of the language I just used that either of you do not understand or need clarification on?"

"Sir, no Sir," was the immediate answer.

J.T. turned on his heel but stopped just short of the door.

"I trust this will be the last conversation of this kind that will be necessary, Colonel."

"That is correct, Sir."

"As you were," he said as he exited the door, closing it behind himself. Sometimes, it was a pleasure to chew someone's ass good. It had been a while since he had to unload on a subordinate. The troops at DSF 17 would never have made this type of mistake. They would have dealt with it before the visitors ever got to the rooms. It was nearing lunchtime so he called Heather and asked her if she would like to have lunch with him. He missed her and besides he wanted to gloat a little. It was the first time he had been able to throw his weight around since he had been promoted to Brigadier. It felt good. And right…

There was a knock on the door and when he opened the

door, there stood Major Tesch, standing at attention, rendering a salute. J.T. returned the crisp salute just as crisply.

"Major Tesch, reporting to the General as ordered, here are the requested items, Sir. I would like to apologize sincerely to the General. I meant no intrusion into the General's business or private life, Sir."

J.T. softened and said, "No offense taken, Major. You were following protocol and orders as directed. I have no problem with that. And if you ever want to try another command, let me know. The 17th could use an officer that accepts responsibility for his actions and doesn't try to blame others. In the future, I would be happy to write a letter of recommendation for you, should you decide you need one."

The Major was quite surprised because he had expected another lengthy ass chewing from the General. Now he understood why this officer had been promoted to General.

"Thank you sir, I appreciate the offer and will bear that in mind next year when I am up for rotation."

"You think about it Major, the DSF could use men like you. Dismissed." With that, he closed the door and placed the stack of transcribed recordings and video discs on his bed. A smile crept across his face. He was sure that the word would get around fairly quickly that the General was a good officer but didn't put up with any bullshit.

Heather knocked on the door before entering, looked around the room, searching for anything out of place. She hated the thought of being spied upon and vowed to herself she would discuss it at length and make sure J.T. understood her feelings.

"Honey, I'm here. You ready for lunch?" She asked.

"I'm right in here, just finishing up. You ready for lunch?" He responded.

"I need to talk to you for a minute." "OK, sure, what's on your mind?"

"I don't like living, having to worry about always checking to see if I am being spied on or not," Heather complained.

"I understand. If it will make you feel any better, I have already addressed the issue. Not going to happen again. I was looking forward to telling you about the ass chewing I gave the Colonel. Bet it is going to be a long time before he lets me see his face. I actually had a good time doing it too. A little justified righteous indignation mixed in with a large portion of not getting a chance to unload on someone for a long time. Actually, it felt good, cathartic. I have all the recordings and transcripts they obtained from our surveillance. The Colonel understands that he will no longer be the commanding officer of this or any base if he decides to reinstate any monitoring of me or my group. Hope that helps to allay your fears, sweetheart," J.T. responded.

"Wish I could be there to give him a piece of my mind. I wanted to unload myself."

"Let's get to lunch. Ass chewing gives me an appetite."

"Remind me not to have you chew my ass unless it's in bed."

"Roger that, wilco. Let's go."

They walked hand in hand to the officers' Mess for lunch. After they were seated, J.T. leaned over and kissed her gently.

"Before everyone gets here, I have something to ask you to do."

"Like what?"

"I want you to go talk to the section chief that handles the alien corpses and see if he had anything to do with studying them when they were living. I need to know if they did any studies on alien brain waves and if so, get copies of all that they have and any interpretations that go along with the actual tracings. Also, see if they identified the role each one had in the crew, need to know who the commander was and if his brain wave tracings differed from the other crew members. Then you will need to borrow the machine that did the recordings so we can do tracings of mine and Sean's brains. I am convinced the headbands are tied into the use and control of the computer on board and we need to see if there are any matching waves between the two of us and one of the aliens. May make the job easier on us finding a way to get the computer to release its' treasure trove of information," J.T. explained.

They ordered and waited for the other four members of the group to arrive and join them for lunch. After all the orders were taken, J.T. spoke to the group, informing them of what went on with the commanding officer that morning. When he had finished, he told everyone to be sure and check to make sure the devices had not been replaced. He then asked for an update from everyone.

Helen said she had finally gotten the reports that had been compiled about the propulsion systems of the spacecraft since day one. There, on one hand, was very little known about propulsion because no one had ever been able to see the propulsion system actually working so it could be studied. She felt that it would take three full days to completely read and double check the information contained within these reports. She asked if there was a plan to get these craft, even if just one craft turned on and the engines were ready to fly, so she could study a functioning machine.

Having said that, J.T. informed the group about his feelings concerning the headbands, being able to get the computer turned on, thereby getting every system in the craft running so it can be studied, understood, and recreated. There were questions from everyone, some directed at J.T. and others being directed at Heather. All the questions were answered to the best of their ability. They finished lunch and made arrangements to meet for supper, as well as deciding what recreational activity they would undertake. Heather said she was going to get the electro-encephalogram machine and bring it back to the room so she could obtain readings from everyone except Shannon.

She went on to ask Frank if he could write a program that could compare the tracings from the aliens and the group members. Frank said that he should be able to get that done before the end of the day. The group discussed things amongst themselves for a few more minutes before leaving the table. They were buoyed up by the knowledge that there was a solid, well thought out, reasonable plan in place to move things forward. J.T. returned to the suite he and Heather were staying in.

Despite the commanding officers' assurances, he searched his entire room, closet, furniture, and bathroom. He finally relaxed after finding no monitoring devices. He had a seat on the bed, waiting for Heather to return. Twenty-five minutes later, she came through the door pushing a cart with the device on it. She suggested J.T. take his shirt off and sit on the edge of the bed while she calibrated the device, put the electrode wires on the helmet, then putting the helmet on J.T.'s head.

When that was secured, she had J.T. lay down on the bed and then began the tracing. She put 3D holographic goggles on and began the different series of testing, flashing lights, visual scenarios designed to evoke a number of different responses. The whole test took twenty minutes. She undid the machine and called Sean and asked him to come by the room. The same procedure was performed on Sean as was done to J.T. This was followed by Helen and finally Frank, before he was trussed up and tested, told everyone he had finished writing the comparison program. When all was said and done, Heather said she would be back in a while and would meet them all for dinner.

She headed down the hall, made a couple of turns and arrived at the section where she had picked up the machine. She entered the area and began looking for the supervisor. When she found her, she asked where the alien tracings were, and the supervisor said she was in the process of obtaining the information but that she had to get permission from the area Chief who was busy at the moment. Little did she know that that comment was the wrong thing to say to her.

Heather stated, "You do know, that I am here on the orders of the Council and have been given authorization to have access to anything I require, don't you? The commanding officer nor your supervisor have the authority to deny me access to anything. I want those papers in the next thirty minutes, or the General will be back in the CO's office for the second time today. If the General has to go back in again to get cooperation from the employees of this facility, he will be removed as CO and retired in disgrace. Do you think he is going to deny me my request? He may decide that the person in charge here, that being you, is the wrong person to have in charge and he may decide to have you removed, since you don't seem to understand that no one refuses Council orders, period. Now I want you, personally, to get me what I have asked for right now. Am I clear?"

The supervisor turned two different shades of pale. She had never been spoken to in that fashion and was beginning to understand how much she had screwed up.

"Yes, ma'am, I'll get right on that. I'm sorry for the delay. I will be right back."

Heather thought of her conversation with J.T. earlier that day and understood how he felt unloading on someone that needed an ass chewing and a warm flush of pleasure washed over her. She hoped she hadn't flushed her skin. She didn't want them to see how much they had gotten to her. But it did feel good to throw her weight and power around, especially when people were trying to interfere with her getting the job done, and nobody was going to keep her from the task she had been assigned. J.T. will be amused when she tells him about it this evening.

It took the better part of two hours before the section chief returned with a cart stacked full of discs. At least she was not going to have to scan all the sheets in before the program could run and start giving them some usable information. On the chance, she asked if the discs were already in the computer and how she could access them if they were.

"Oh yes ma'am, these discs were inputted at the same time the information was put into the computer." She wrote down the directions on a sheet of paper and handed it to Heather.

"Thank you," Heather replied.

"No problem, ma'am," was the response. Heather packed up

her things, grabbed the cart, and pushed it down the hall to their room. J.T. was just coming out when he nearly collided with her.

"What do you have there?" he asked. Heather proceeded to tell him about the interaction with the section chief and how she found out she didn't really need all the discs. They had already been entered into the computer. With the directions the section chief provided her, she could access the results after she asked about it.

"I'm sure she wasn't going to volunteer the information until after I got in her ass," she said.

"That is always a consideration when you have to chew someone out. Next time you may want to try some sugar in your approach instead of jumping right to the ass chewing," was J.T.'s reply.

"Do have to admit that I was a little motivated by your description of your interaction with Farmouth," Heather responded.

"I rarely have to do that, and I wanted him to understand how upset I was with the invasion of our privacy, but I also wanted him to understand that we were not going to allow him to interfere with our mission, period." J.T. said. "I think we communicated in a very effective manner."

"Was there some way the team could be given a conference room, set up with computers etcetera, so that they would not have to do all the work in their bedrooms?" she asked.

"I'll see what I can do," he said as he left the room.

J.T. stopped by the X.O.'s office, spoke with the Major and made his request. The Major immediately made a call and then printed the room number and directions to an unused conference room. He then called another number and made sure that the computer system was turned on and operational and gave the person on the other end the names of the people using the system so that access could be granted.

"Major, that was the most efficient use of time I have seen by any officer in this complex. I will be sure to let the C.O. know about your service. Thank you," J.T. said.

The Major stood up, came to attention, with a smile on his face, and said, "Thank you, sir. If there is ever anything else you need, please contact me immediately."

J.T. returned his salute and thanked him for his offer. *Sugar does work better than an ass chewing sometimes,* he thought to himself as he left in search of the newly acquired conference room.

The inspection of the conference room was completely to his liking, and the location was pretty near their sleeping quarters. He stuck his head into the X.O.'s office and thanked him and then stopped by the C.O.'s office to tell him how pleased he was with the assistance the X.O. had provided. He then closed the door and took a moment to apologize to the C.O. about their interaction earlier that morning.

"I should not have come down on you the way that I did, and I apologize. I was just disturbed that all our privacy was being interrupted. I should have realized that in a facility such as this, visitors should expect to be under a 'watchful eye'. My mistake. It was nothing personal. Colonel."

With that, he extended his hand and gave the Colonel a firm, solid handshake.

"Well, I just wanted to compliment the XO on his efficient manner of dealing with my request and to clear up this matter.

You are doing a fine job running this facility. I sure wouldn't want a job like this myself." J.T. smiled, then exited the office.

He went back to the room, gathered up Heather and her cart full of info, and led her down the hall to the conference room. He let her in and showed her where everything was, then told her he was going to find the rest of the crew and send them to the conference room.

J.T. made the rounds and found everyone, told them where the conference room was located, and indicated that they should move their work to it. He stopped by the XO's office to ask him who he should contact about setting up coffee service for the conference room. The XO picked up the phone, spoke to someone and then turned to J.T. and told him the correct person will meet him at the conference room.

"Well done, Major. You know one day you should be given your own command and if there is ever anything I can do to facilitate that, please call me. I am serious. The DSF needs people that can take charge, decide and then see it through. You have all those qualities, and they should not be overlooked." J.T. extended his hand and gave him a solid handshake.

"Thank you Sir, I appreciate that and if I ever need your assistance, I will certainly contact you," the Major replied.

"Be sure you do," was J.T.'s response.

J.T. returned to the conference room and was met by the Mess Chief, standing by the door with a clipboard in hand.

"Chief, I am going to need a regular coffee service for six with whatever the baker has on the list for that day with pastries and rolls. We will need some tea bags also, as a couple of the women drink tea. They obviously have never been in the military," J.T. remarked with a little humor in his voice.

"Would the General like juice also?" the Mess Chief asked.

"Apple, orange, tomato, small amounts of each. There are only six of us and I would hate to waste anything," J.T. said.

"Aye, Aye Sir. By your leave, Sir," the mess chief requested.

"Dismissed and thank you," J.T. responded.

The Mess Chief turned and left with a smile. Had been a long time since any of the senior officer staff had been that pleasant with him, acknowledging his knowledge and expertise in his job, leaving him to do his duty without micromanaging his every move. The scuttlebutt about the General was true and accurate. Maybe some of him would rub off on the other command structure. Would make duty here a lot nicer, he thought to himself.

J.T. entered the room and greeted everyone. He passed along the idea that unless there is something you need to do specifically requiring you to go to some section of the base; it was his opinion that most of the work could be accomplished in the conference room. He pointed out that there were six computer stations, each with two screens and four huge screens on the rear wall that were accessible from any computer station. They all had been cleared to use the computer system and they would not be monitored or spied on from now on.

Heather sat down at a terminal and logged on, then started accessing the brain wave tests that had been done on the living aliens. She posted them on one of the large screens, then manipulated the other image to superimpose them on each other. There were differences in all of them. She set each one on a different screen and set about pulling up the tracings she had done the other day on J.T., Frank, Helen, and Sean. One by one she overlayed each tracing on an alien tracing, looking for any points of comparison. She noted that J.T. first had the most similarities, then Frank, then Helen, then Sean. She was surprised that all of them had some similarities, except Sean. She spent the next 2 hours reviewing each tracing until she was sure of her findings. She had made a few notes, then minimized the screens and went searching for data on how to improve the amount of brain waves, the amplitude, intensity and frequency of each.

Surprisingly, there was not a lot of research currently being done but, there had been a fair amount done just after WW3. She went back to studying those articles, making notes and writing down instructions. That evening's discussion about what had been accomplished that day was going to be fun. She knew exactly what, how and on whom she needed to work.

A few hours later, the rest of the crew made their way into the conference room, and each found a computer workstation for their use. J.T. called the meeting to order and had each person relate where they were at with their assigned tasks. He purposefully had Heather wait until the end, mainly because she was the only one of the groups, that had made any significant progress on their main task.

"OK Heather, the floor is yours," J.T. said.

"I have been going over the EEG tracings of the aliens. They were alive at the time the EEG tracing was done. There were a couple of issues. First, we have no way of knowing what the role of each alien was within the crew, since there was no effort made to determine status. I assigned the status of each crew men based on the tracing itself. Some of the tracings had markedly higher amplitude of certain brain waves, theta, delta and gamma, to be precise. This individual was most likely the crafts' commander. The other tracings had lower amplitude and were most likely subordinates. Second, we have no indication of the physical shape, amount, type and/or seriousness of any injuries sustained. When I reviewed the tracings of Helen, Frank, Sean and T.J, there were some differences noted.

"Helen, yours was the most compatible with what we have decided was the Commanders' tracing followed by Frank, then J.T. Sean unfortunately, you are not even close, I guess that is a good thing, not having a tracing similar to an alien."

That brought a little chuckle from the group, followed by a slight frown on J.T.'s face. "I have researched the available literature and found that there was not a lot of study on brain waves except from 2083 through 2096. A couple of interesting articles demonstrating exercises that showed improvement in intensity and amplitude in the brain waves. Those waves, we have noted, are in the aliens' tracings. So, I am setting up some activities that Helen, Frank and J.T. will be working on, one hour on and ½ hour off during the entire workday. This is almost double of what was done in the experiments. I am moving this right along because we do not have years to get things accomplished. Of the three of you, the one that demonstrates the greatest amplitude and intensity of the waves, we think, can communicate with the space crafts' computer will be the person we will use when we try headbands," she explained.

"What we will need to decide is what we want the computer to do if we are able to establish a link. The list I have composed is as follows: One, identify ourselves as humans, indicate the craft had crashed and the occupants did not survive. Two, ask it to scan our brains for our language communication. Three, inform it that this is how we will be communicating with it, and ask it to transform everything in to English. Four, find out how we can get printed schematics of power source, engine, computer, navigation to its point of origin, scanning, offensive and defensive weaponry, and protection. Five, scanning space for safe navigation and to help us decide which planets to explore. Six, communication over long distances. Does anyone have any other thoughts? Perhaps asking about hibernation vs suspended animation for long trips? But I thought we could get to that after we have everything answered and understood. Any questions, concerns, thoughts or suggestions?" she finished. She looked around the table, trying to read everybody's face, to see if anyone appeared to be confused.

J.T. spoke first, "Thank you Heather. I think what you have presented is very comprehensive and follows a logical progression. I think this is a great starting point and if, during the course of our little experiment, we may choose to change priorities on some of the points, or to add in new ones, as the situation dictates. I will remind all of you that using this technology is not without risk and if anyone feels that there is too much risk, please speak up. No one will be thought any less of or have any recriminations against them if that is their choice. Obviously, we do not have a lot of time to waste on someone that does not wish to participate in this phase. You are free to hold off on your part until such time as more is understood about what you will be facing. I want everyone to think long and hard about this and give me a decision tomorrow morning. In the meantime, I would like Heather to explain the exercises she will be needing us to work on. Heather."

Heather stepped to the front of the group and started to explain each of the five exercises, in detail. When she had finished, she asked if everyone understood what she needed them to do and if there was anyone that was not going to be able to do any of the exercises. Not getting any negative answers, she said she was finished, and the meeting was adjourned so they could all get something to eat.

During the meal, there were some simple questions asked like, would they all be in the same room for the exercises and were they going to be hooked up to any kind of machine or monitoring device? Heather replied that everyone would be wearing the EEG device along with a blindfold and earphones to limit any outside distractions. She reminded everyone that there were no right or wrong answers, just repetition, and their role was to concentrate on each exercise. These exercises were to be held for at least eight hours every day, with a thirty-minute break, after every hour. If one of them was making great progress when it was time to stop, Heather would decide if they should stop or continue until they reached a point where there was no further progress. She again reminded them that this was not a competition. It was more like going to the gym to see how strong they could get. In her heart, she knew they would all be trying to outdo the others. A little competition was good for results and the soul. If they were going to lift weights in the gym, someone could get hurt. With this kind of mental exercise, no one was going to break their brain.

Dinner went well as the conversation drifted from topic to topic, eventually getting around to wedding plans. That was the point when all the men present excused themselves and headed to the "O" club for a drink or two. While the women discussed dresses and color patterns, the men were discussing the suggestions and the sequence that was proposed. J.T suggested that language and communication be the best first thing, then to see about the other things, when they were able to see how well things were going before asking for the keys to the kingdom. He also suggested that they play a few things by ear, since they did not know if the computer was in contact with the home world. Revealing that earth was on its last legs may be something kept close to the vest. Sean did point out that if we were asking the computer to scan their minds, it may very well find out that information on its own. Frank suggested that if the computer did find out that information, they should not deny it because their civilization may, in fact, value honesty very highly and any attempt at subterfuge may cause the computer to enact some program that would self-destruct or worse yet, give them false information that kept the mission from being a success. After they finished their drinks, they all retired back to their quarters along with their women. After everyone got together, there was some small talk, then everyone went to bed.

The next morning, J.T. headed out to the gym for his daily workout. Then they all met for breakfast before moving to the conference room that Heather had already set up. They all took a seat and Heather started in, telling them about the exercises they would be doing, as she fastened the EEG monitoring helmets on each of their heads. She checked the monitoring module that had been divided into four quadrants, made sure each of the helmets was working and was relaying info to her monitor. Heather stood in front of them and again reiterated the plan for the morning. She asked questions and, finding none, told everyone to get started. One hour later, she told everyone to stop, they removed their helmets. Heather suggested everyone come and get a pastry and coffee/ tea and try to get their minds off the exercises. They all sat down and discussed how they felt doing the exercises. Each agreed that it was not as hard as they thought it was going to be but that, surprisingly, they commented on the amount of fatigue they were feeling. At the end of thirty minutes, the whole process started over again. The event was repeated, exactly the same for the next four hours. At the end of four hours, the group adjourned for lunch. When the meal was done, they all expressed a sense of being refreshed and ready to go back in and get to work. The afternoon was the same as the morning and before anyone realized it, it was time to finish the day and go to supper.

Heather thought that perhaps some form of recreation was appropriate for the evening, but the consensus was that everyone was just too tired, so she decided to postpone the plans.

CHAPTER
TWENTY

The next nine days were just a repeat of the first day.

On the morning of the 10th day, Heather stood before the group and told them that further work on the mental exercises she had given them would no longer be of any benefit. It seems that each of the groups had improved but plateaued as of the seventh day and showed no further improvement over the next two days.

She went on to give out the results, "Helen, you improved 23% to a total of 49%, Frank, you improved 32% to a total of 47%, Sean, you improved 30% to a total of 41% and J.T. you lead the field with a 42% improvement to a total of 61%. So, it looks like you are going to be the one to try the headband first, followed by Helen then Frank and then Sean. There is something to be said for family genetics, I guess," she said.

"Thank you, Heather, for the effort and work you put into everything. I feel confident that we have approached this in a logical, precise, and scientific method, instead of just diving in and seeing what happens. I am going to speak with the CO and invite him and all the section heads and chief scientists to the testing. I think we should use the vehicle that the headset was part of. Does anyone have a different opinion? OK then, let's have breakfast and then I am going to speak with the CO. I think everyone should attend that meeting. Afterall, you all were part of arriving at this point and you deserve credit for that," J.T. said. "Right now, I am starved, so let's eat."

The group headed to the Officers' Mess and proceeded to eat better than they had for the whole time they were training for the headset task. Gathering everyone together, J.T. led them to the C.O.'s office. He stepped up to the receptionist and asked her if it was possible to have a few moments of the Colonel's time for a very important meeting. The receptionist nodded, picked up the phone, spoke briefly then hung up and looked at J.T.

"General, the Colonel will be right out," she said.

A couple of minutes later, the Colonel opened his door and invited everyone in.

"Good morning, General. I am at your service. Please, come in. What can I do for you?" Colonel Farmouth said.

"Colonel, please have a seat. What I am about to tell you, if it works out, is going to revolutionize this command and change the function of the base. My group has determined that the headbands worn by the alien crewmembers were not badges of rank, but devices that allow telepathic contact with the vehicles' computer control. We have studied the records of brain wave tests taken on the aliens that were alive and compared them to our own EEG's. They are quite similar and after 7 days of doing mental exercises that were designed to increase the waves that were prominent in the aliens' tracings, we are ready to proceed to the next phase of testing, which is actually attempting to mentally connect to the controlling computer to see if we can get it turned on and to start getting it to release its' technology to us."

J.T. continued, "I will need to have all section heads, chief scientists and techs to be present at the testing. We will be using the last craft obtained because that is the vehicle that the head-bands came from. If all goes well, we will be able to activate all of the vehicles we have in the storage areas. The possibilities are huge. We can get access to technology that will allow space flights at greater than light speed, multi-functional computers activated by thought. Knowledge of other civilizations and knowledge about the origin of the universe and the impact other civilizations had on this planet. I think 1000 hours is a good time to start and that will give everyone a chance to get all of their equipment together, set up and ready to record different aspects of what the vehicles are capable of," J.T. finished.

The Colonel had a look of total disbelief on his face. He was slowly beginning to understand what was about to happen at his base, to his command. Thousands of thoughts ran through his mind and it overwhelmed him.

It took five full minutes, before he was able to speak, and then he said, "Are you sure this is going to work?"

"I have no reason to think that it won't, after reviewing all the evaluations, studies, testing and discussions, this theory has never been tested, if you think about it, the aliens that lived here, never talked. How did they communicate with each other? Had to be either sign language or telepathy. No one has ever tried to communicate with sign language, and to my knowledge, no one has ever tried headbands for anything. I really believe we are on to something." J.T. said. "I can tell you something else Colonel, if this works out, we will be building an interstellar spaceship here. After the test, I will need a secure visual connection with the Council of Elders. Part of that conversation will be private, but part of it you will need to keep yourself available for," J.T. said. "I will see you at 0945 tomorrow for a pretest briefing," J.T. finished.

"Aye, aye General," was Farmouth's response.

The group was waiting for J.T. He took about 20 minutes to relate the conversation with the Colonel and the set up for the next day. When he relayed the discussion about sign language and mental telepathy, they all looked like the lights had just gone on and now a lot of things made sense. J.T suggested they take the day off, because if everything goes the way he hoped and suspected it would, tomorrow was going to be one of the most significant days in human history. His entire family was going to have a place in history that no one else could ever have… forever.

The rest of the day was spent relaxing, first with a small bowling competition and then an early evening movie before everyone retired to their room for other more romantic interactions.

Nobody slept well that night. The anticipation kept everyone jacked up. Even after all the love making, members of the group trickled down to the Officers Mess, grabbing a cup of coffee and donuts or other pastries. They all sat down at the table, looking at each other. The significance of the day was beginning to sink in. Up to that time, this whole endeavor, from the time they were asked to join the group, to the moment that the decision had been made to tryout the headbands, things had seemed like a dream and now they were about to do something no human had ever done, make intellectual contact with an alien race. The intensity was nearly overwhelming and mind-blowing, to a point.

J.T. spoke up and said, "We need to decide whether we are going to try one headband or three headbands at once. Obviously, since there are three headbands, it is reasonable to assume that the computer is capable of handling the input from three different headbands at once. I have no way of knowing if one headband will allow the computer more of an unfettered approach or if three gives a better overall chance at allowing the computer to choose which headband was going to make a connection. Thoughts anyone?"

The debate began and was bantered back and forth for the better part of twenty minutes. It all came down to J.T. making a command decision. There would be only one headband used. The group accepted the decision, as they had with everything else. They had complete trust in their leader because he was usually always right.

At 0930, J.T. finished putting on his uniform, turning to look at Heather as she slipped into a pale blue silk blouse, covering her breast from his appreciative stare.

"Put your eyes and tongue back in your head sweetheart, and your head out of the gutter. You have some important things to do today. We can get in the gutter together after everything is done. I am sure you will be fine. Help me zip up, please."

J.T. stepped over as Heather turned around. He cupped her

ass and gave it a little squeeze, then zipped her skirt up to the top. She turned, and he gave her a warm gentle kiss, squeezed her butt again and then headed for the door on his way to the C.O.'s office.

The Colonel rapidly stood and came to attention when J.T. entered the office.

"As you were Colonel. Everything set up and ready?" J.T. asked.

"Yes Sir, I took the liberty of having the base PIO and her crew present in there to record the event," Farmouth replied.

"Good idea Colonel. The secure link with the Council ready?"

"Yes Sir."

"Then let's get on with making history, shall we Colonel?"

"Aye, Aye, Sir."

The two of them left the office, the Colonel leading the way. The pace was quick, indicating the urgency of the situation. They stopped by the quarters assigned to the group and had everyone follow the Colonel as they made their way to the area where the spacecraft were stored. When they arrived at the portal, there was a crowd milling around with a low-pitched murmuring that could be heard. The murmuring stopped as the Colonel and the rest of the unit walked up.

"Ladies and gentlemen, please enter the area of the space-craft so we can begin. Thank you."

With that, the doors opened, and all the attendees filed into the area and looked for a place to stand so they could see the *show*. Once inside the Colonel stepped up to a microphone and began his remarks.

"May I have your attention please. Thank you. I would like

to take this moment to thank everyone for attending what may turn out to be a momentous occasion. I am now going to turn the microphone over to the General."

He stepped aside as the crowd applauded.

"Ladies and gentlemen, honored guests and fellow scientists. This is a memorable day, and I would like to thank all of you for attending. My name is Brigadier James T. Coulter. The members of my team are Dr. Helen Coulter, Dr. Frank Coulter, Major McCann, Mrs. Shannon McCann, Dr. Heather Dunkirk. One of the things we have been tasked with is trying to create an interstellar spacecraft. We have been at this base for 12 days and we have come up with something that apparently had either not been thought of or tried. We noted that the group studying the aliens were never able to communicate with them, nor was there any evidence that the survivors communicated with each other. We decided they had to be using either sign language (which there was no evidence of) or telepathy which we humans were unable to prove.

"Assuming they were using telepathy, how were they able to pilot their vehicle? One of the things we noticed was that they all had headbands on. Reviewing the reports, it was postulated that these were signs of rank among the crew members. The headbands were more thoroughly examined, and we thought that perhaps they were used to connect the crewman to the craft, most likely the computer. That prompted us to review data obtained from the aliens, specifically brain wave tests. These were then compared to brainwave tests done on the members of my group.

"We were surprised to note quite a few similarities between our EEG's and theirs. This was further investigated by Dr.

Dunkirk. She reviewed the available literature, found some references to being able to boost certain brain waves via specific mental exercises. Members of the team spent the better part of 10 days doing the exercises. Subsequent EEGs indicated that certain brain waves were improved to the point where they came very close to approximating the tracings of the aliens. Based on that evidence, we are going to test the headbands and see if we can contact the computer in the craft behind you. We have several things we need from the computer, the first one being turning everything on, power source, engine, computer memory.

"We will also attempt to figure out a way to hook their computer to ours so we can obtain things like schematics for engines, the type of power source needed to run this craft and navigation to their home planet. So, with that said, I would like you all to man your machines and begin to record whatever aspect of the evaluation of the spacecraft you are involved in. Wish us luck! thank you for your participation."

J.T. left the stage and the group followed him to the entrance into the spacecraft. He stooped over and slowly eased his way inside the craft. Since he was going to be trying what was assumed to be the commanders' headband, he decided to sit in the commanders' chair, thinking maybe this might be a require-ment of the computer, that the individual using the headband had to be seated in this particular seat. Heather slipped into the seat to his left, holding the headband in her right hand. He mentioned the issue of sitting in the commander's seat and it being necessary to get the headband to connect with the computer. Heather asked him if he was ready to start to which he replied, "Let's get the show on the road."

She handed him the headband, and he slowly slipped it on moving it so the stones were in the same position that they were on the alien commanders' head. Once it was in place, he leaned back and started going through the exercises Heather had given him. He relaxed, and on one level, felt more relaxed than he had ever felt before. He then noticed a tingling sensation circumferentially around the skull and he could tell it was getting more intense. It reached a point at which it started to feel uncomfortable. He was tempted to remove the headband, but since it wasn't really a pain; he felt he could tolerate it a while longer. Suddenly there was a brilliant white flash of light inside his head and he began to make out dials, graphs, and controls in his mind.

In his mind, he heard a mechanical voice saying, "Welcome General James T. Coulter. I am CAIIP 4th generation. I have scanned your mind and understand most of what I have scanned. Some things will need more explanation. I have been aware of your species' attempts to understand and study this craft. Apparently, they were not intelligent enough to figure out basic communication. Where are the crewmembers currently located?"

"How do I refer to you?"

"You may refer to me as computer."

"Computer," he thought, "the members of the crew of this craft did not survive the crash of this vehicle. Can you tell me what happened?"

"Yes, there was a failure of a component that handled control of vehicle movement and at the speed we were traveling, replacing the component took too long and we were unable to correct the problem before striking the mountain."

"Obviously there are many questions to ask but first, is there some method that we may connect our computer system directly to you so that answers to these questions can be seen by a number of our scientists, like your energy and power systems, engine schematics, scanning and navigation schematics and readouts.",

"First, your computer will need one hundred billion terabytes of memory to be even partially compatible. There is a port on the left side of the main viewer where a connector may be attached."

"Will someone need to be in contact with you constantly to get the information to flow?"

"It is not required for constant contact to be maintained, but it can be beneficial. There can be things that need clarification on your side, and someone would need to know what to ask."

"I have three other members of my team that will attempt to contact you. Is that acceptable?"

"Yes."

"I am going to remove the headband now."

"Goodbye General James T. Coulter."

"Goodbye for now, computer,"

J.T. reached up and slipped off the headband.

Heather was sitting there next to him, and she asked, "Is there something wrong? You just put the headband on."

"I was in contact with the computer, had a conversation, asked questions and got answers, all inside my head. Pretty cool on one hand and a little weird on the other. The computer scanned my brain, knew who I was and also insulted the other humans working on the spacecraft as not being very intelligent because they had not figured out how to communicate with it."

"Did the computer tell you what happened?" Heather asked.

"A component went bad in the part of the navigation unit that steers the ship and before they could replace it, they hit the side of a mountain," J.T. replied.

"J.T. how could that be? You only had the headband on for less than 30 seconds before you pulled it off," Heather asked.

"I should have expected that a computer that can be connected to three different minds at once would be capable of scanning my mind in a little under five seconds, make changes and adaptions and still be able to answer questions. I am going to put the headband back on and ask the computer to turn things on so we can prove we have connected with the computer. Why don't you bring in Mom and Dad. We will see if we can get them connected with the computer."

Heather climbed out and motioned to Helen and Frank. "Come on in, we are going to get the two of you connected to the computer."

The group maneuvered their way around, found their seats, sat down and waited for J.T. to speak. J.T. started telling them what to expect from the moment he started until he removed the headband to break the link.

"There is no need to speak. All you have to do is think about what you want to say, and the computer will do the rest. Everyone ready to start?"

Helen looked at Frank and said, "In for a penny, in for a pound."

Frank looked at her, turned to J.T and Heather and said, "Let's get going."

Heather helped them situate the headbands properly, then stepped back and waited. J.T. already had the headband on before Heather finished and things inside the cockpit started happening. Instrument panels lit up. There was a soft hum that was audible outside. Heather tapped on J.T.'s shoulder to get his attention. He leaned over to her, and she suggested that he move the craft one or two feet off the ground, just to prove actual control over the vehicle. A few moments later, the craft lifted two feet off the ground and hovered, unmoving. After five minutes, the craft returned to its original position.

J.T. removed his headband, whispered to his mother, "Power supply, engine design" and to his father "Computer construction". He got out of the commander's chair and stooped to step out of the craft. There was a hearty round of applause and loud cheering as he stepped up to the microphone.

"I guess we were right! Connecting to a computer created and constructed by an alien race was amazing. There was no hostility, no negative interaction in either of my contacts with the computer. It told me how it happened to crash. This may sound bad, but it is a little comforting to know that the aliens are not perfect. They are not here to conquer or invade, they are here merely to see how the human race is progressing. They have been here intermittently since the human race was at the caveman stage. In my contact with the computer, I did not take time to investigate the thousands of questions that need answers. The safety of mankind was the primary concern I had when questioning the device.

"Rest assured, I will be getting those questions answered as soon as more pressing ones have been answered, such as what the power source is that propels this craft, what type of engine are they using, where is their home planet, how long did it take to get here, can they go faster than the speed of light, is there things like worm holes or other space anomalies that we are not aware of, things like that. Currently, my mother, who has a PhD in nuclear engineering and physics and my father, who has a PhD in computer engineering and mathematics, are still in contact with the computer and will be getting as much information as they can absorb. The computer told me we would need a computer with a hundred billion terabytes of memory in order to handle a download from it. Not being a computer expert, I have no idea whether we have one of those or if we are even capable of constructing one.

"I have ordered the shipboard computer to keep all systems on but not to take any other orders from anyone other than myself or members of my crew currently in contact with it. That concludes my remarks and unless you have questions to ask that I have not addressed, we conclude with the day's event. Thank you for coming. If there are any questions that any of the section chiefs would like to have us ask the computer, please type them out, being very specific and forward them to Mrs. Shannon McCann, my information and communications chief. I will attempt to get answers for you."

With that, J.T. stepped down from the podium and made his way over to Colonel Farmouth.

J.T. said, "I do not have to tell you that this event was ultra-high secret, top security and anyone leaking it will be dealt with immediately and severely. I need to speak to the Council, and I want the video that has been recorded available to show them."

"Aye, aye Sir. Follow me, please, General," Colonel Farmouth said while extending his right arm.

"Hold on for a second, Colonel," J.T. went over to the

entrance to the craft, stuck his head in and gave Heather a couple of instructions before returning to the Colonel.

"OK, we can go now. Just wanted to give Dr. Dunkirk a couple of instructions before I left the area."

The secure communications area was 10 minutes away by walking, and there were three separate security doors, two fingerprint scanners and two retinal scanners to go through, before they were allowed entrance. The communication technician pushed several keys on the keyboard and the face of the Chief Elder came into focus.

"General Coulter, I trust you are well and have some news for the Council."

"Yes Sir, I do. I have just finished being in contact with the computer that is in the latest alien spacecraft we have, the one that crashed nine months ago. Quite an interesting occurrence. First, I will state that they are not here to invade or conquer. They have been visiting Earth since we were cavemen. I did not ask if they had interfered with our evolution. This craft came to be in our possession because they had a navigational component failure and before they could replace it, they hit a mountain. As I told the group that was in attendance, it's nice to know that they aren't perfect. Currently, my mother and father are still in contact with the computer. I asked it what we would have to do to be able to download information from them to us. The answer was a computer with at least one hundred billion terabytes of memory. Since I am not a computer expert, I do not even know if is possible to build or if one even exists at this point."

"Elder Vandenhoff is the current reigning council member in possession of information like that, so I will forward that question to her. What was it like, being in contact with an alien machine?" Frank Easton asked.

"It was moving and awe-inspiring. Once I was in contact, things moved incredibly fast. It was almost as if my mind was being read, before I was able to formulate the questions. I did inform the computer that its crewmembers did not survive. My initial contact with the computer was less than 30 seconds, although it seemed markedly longer. The computers' designation was CAIIP4, which stands for Computer, Artificial intelligence, Ion Powered, 4th generation. Makes me think that we have a long way to go.

"My main question right now is, where are we going to build my spacecraft? My suggestion would be here in Area 43. There would be a few things to move in like manufacturing equipment to build the components. Perhaps we could get them from the Space Center or the Dome of Houston. One of my next questions for the computer is going to be what the materials are that compose the outer shell of the craft. I am absolutely certain they are composite material that can resist conditions found at faster than light speed. We will need to find out what composite materials they are and if they are available here on earth. I have some videotapes of this morning's event that I am going to roll now. Please set your station to record."

J.T. sat back and watched the recording for the first time. It was pretty impressive when the exterior lighting came on and the craft rose and hovered, unmoving for 10 minutes. The camera panned the area, getting the faces of the attendees, recording the astounded look on everyone's face. The recording finished and the Chief Elder came back on and again congratulated him on his success.

J.T. said, "Just to let you know, I am ready to start construction on the spacecraft. As soon as I can get some more information, I will be ready to submit plans to the Council."

"Thank you General. You have lived up to the Councils' expectations so far and we will be in touch with the answer to the computer question." The screen went blank.

"I need to get back to the spacecraft to see how the group is doing." J.T. said.

"Yes Sir" was the response.

Ten minutes later, he was standing at the door to the spacecraft. Helen and Frank were still inside attached to the computer. He stepped back inside, slipped into the chair and put the headband back on. The connection was almost instantaneous.

"Welcome back General. What can I help you with?"

"Please describe the makeup of the outer shell of this craft." The computer went into a detailed description of the composite material until J.T. had to tell it to stop. He then asked for the recipe of the components. He reached inside his pocket, retrieved a scratch pad and began writing notes, composition ratios and names of elements he was unfamiliar with. Some of them were not on the periodic table and he had to ask where they were obtainable from. One of the main components was only available, in this solar system, on Earth's moon. Mining on the moon had been suspended for the last two years as not being worthwhile. J.T. made notes to contact the moon and see how soon they could get a goodly supply sent back to Earth. Helen and Frank were starting to look worn out, so J.T. tapped them both on the shoulder and when they looked at him, he drew his hand across his throat. Within the next 10 seconds, they both had disconnected from the computer.

They both were really dehydrated and mentally drained. Next time they interacted, they would be sure to have food and fluids. After everyone had eaten and perked up a bit, they all sat down and started to talk, all at once.

J.T. raised his hand and said, "One at a time, please. Mom, you are first." Helen started in and both J.T. and Frank nodded their heads each time she mentioned something similar to what they all had experienced. She then said that the computer started giving her information about the power source for the craft. She was only able to remember some parts of it because the information was coming to her really fast. It seems that in this solar system, there were only two places where the substance they used as fuel could be found. The Van Allen Radiation belt and Titan, one of Saturn's moons. J.T. said that he understood and in the future they all were to have a lot of paper and plenty of pens and pencils.

They were also going to have to tell the computer that they were not aliens and the flow of info had to slow down so they could understand it. J.T. decided to call it a day. He returned to the secure call center and put in a call to the Council to request mining on the moon. That evening over dinner, they all discussed what they had been through. The enormity and significance of what they had been through that day finally started to sink in. They had done something that had never been done in all recorded history. Their names would forever be attached to this moment. In the future, their names might even be revered.

None of them had ever thought about this moment. They

had signed on, because their son/brother had asked them to help him save the human race and find some place to start it over again, not making all the mistakes the world had made the first time around.

They dined on a meal fit for a king. Lobster and steak, Caesar salad and Baked Alaska. They almost did not have a chance to eat, with all the well-wishers and those that wanted handshakes and to get pictures for posterity. That night, there was no romantic celebration. They were all too tired.

CHAPTER
TWENTY-ONE

The next six weeks were a repeat of the twelve-hour days they had just finished. The only break for J.T. was when he had to stop working so he could fly Heather back to Dome 17 to take care of a number of things with her employment and to get set up to do her portion of the Quest, which was sorting out people, seeing if they would be interested in joining the colony, getting them tested for genetic diseases and then if they were willing, get genetic therapy to correct the defects that had been found. This was an attempt to keep the colony members from starting a new colonized planet having illnesses and diseases that would require the colony to devote resources to healthcare, hospitals, diagnostic centers and a pharmaceutical industry. J.T. wanted to limit the need for medical services to acute care and not chronic disease management. He had no way of knowing if their new home would have the raw materials needed in order to manufacture medications.

J.T. managed to stop by the Unit and say hello to his old

command. They had heard about what had gone on with the alien spacecraft and were eager for news about this straight from the horse's mouth, so to speak. That took the better part of the day. It was really good to see his troops again, and he was a little surprised as to how much he missed his men. He mentioned some bare issues about his current assignment and managed to mention he was going to need 75 troops as part of the colony, mainly for protection and policing issues. He told them he would be taking written requests once the application form had been developed and completed. He also mentioned this was going to be for single people. No married or single parent families would be allowed on the mission, at least at first. Second flights would depend on what the new planet held in store as well as how long the trip took.

Almost the entire unit volunteered. He was overwhelmed with the response and told everyone there would be notification when he was ready to make personnel decisions. As he got ready to leave, he was inundated by troops, all wanting handshakes, a personal word with him and even a few of the old timers who wanted a hug. J.T. was so moved by the display of affection from his old troop that he had to wipe a couple of tears from his eyes as he left the Unit offices.

Heather herself had an almost identical day at the hospital. The handshakes, hugs and well wishes occupied most of her day. She managed to make an appointment with the Chief of the medical school for the next day. She had planned to enlist his help in obtaining a set protocol for testing and treatment using med students to help. She also wanted to discuss using III on Mr. Horner so he could have the education necessary to sit for the med school boards. It was her opinion that he had demonstrated enough medical competence through 25 years of practice, that he would be more than qualified to be a physician, if he just had the required book learning.

The next day, when her appointment time with Dr. Hendricks came around, she had J.T. call the unit and requested Mr. Horner to accompany her to the meeting, not informing him of the subterfuge she had planned. She greeted Dr. Hendricks with a warm, genuinely affectionate hug.

"Doctor, I would like to introduce you to Mr. Horner, the Dome 17 Unit medic and the Village of Coulters' Family Practice provider. He has been practicing medicine for 25 years. Mr. Horner, this is my mentor and head of the Medical School, Dr. Hendricks.

"A pleasure and an honor to meet you, Doctor," he said, extending his hand.

Dr. Hendricks shook his hand with both hands and said, "The pleasure is all mine. Dr. Dunkirk has told me a lot about you, and I must say I am quite impressed."

"Dr. Dunkirk is too kind," was his reply.

"When she speaks about a colleague, she is rarely kind but is always accurate and honest," was the return reply.

"Tell me why you did not go to medical school 25 years ago and instead chose to go to a PA school?" he asked.

"I would have to say impatience and finances. I found that I could be paid to learn to be a PA, as well as being able to go in to practice in two years, instead of 11 or 12 years for med school and residency. Plus, it was a time when the country had a lot of military problems and I felt a need to volunteer, something I have never regretted. Being assigned to General Coulter's command, allowed me to provide healthcare to Coulter, a small group of people, which was the reason my profession came in to being, being able to help a wonderful group of people who would have had a difficult time getting healthcare. It has provided me with a chance to positively impact their lives and make things better for all of them," he replied.

"Well, from what I have heard, you have acquitted yourself quite well. Your approach to domestic violence is quite unique albeit very effective." Dr. Hendricks remarked.

"Would you like to be a doctor, after all these years?" he asked. "Yes sir, I would. But at my age, the time in school, along with my duties to the unit and the village, would be difficult to pull off without having to give something up and I am just not ready to do that," was the reply.

Dr. Hendricks turned to Heather. "I agree with you Dr. Dunkirk, and you have my support and approval. Mr. Horner, this was your med school enrollment interview. You answered all the questions perfectly. I think you would make a wonderful physician. Dr. Dunkirk, would you fill in Mr. Horner? I will meet you in my office for the rest of our appointment. Mr. Horner, meeting you has been a true pleasure and you have renewed my faith in my profession, having dedicated individuals rendering care to those who need it, without regard to self or financial gain. My dear, I shall see you in my office in say 15 minutes?"

Heather responded, "I'll be right there."

Horner spoke up asking, "Will someone please tell me what the hell is going on? I'm kind of in limbo here."

Heather's answer was, "Doc, shut up until I finish then you can ask questions, OK? I think you have what it takes to be a doctor and what I am planning is to do to you what we did to

J.T. while he was in the tank. We are going to implant the entire curriculum of this med school while you are sleeping over a two-day period. When you are done, you will be given the med school final exam, and when you pass it, you will be a physician. You will not need to do a formal residency; you have been doing it for the last 25 years. You need to be a doctor. Mankind needs you, and your skills and compassion. Now you can ask your questions."

"Was I gonna get a chance to voice my opinion? Seems like you have already decided for me. Do you realize this may remove me from the Unit? There is no billet for an MD, only for a PA and a corpsman. Maybe, I was not ready to give up on my Unit. You never asked me and on one hand, that pisses me off. You are going to be married to the General, not me. On the other hand, I am truly flattered that you think enough of me and my skills to set something like this up, asking me first or not. My answer is if you think I am good enough, then I will give it my best shot."

Heather breathed a sigh of relief. She had never considered the fact that he might say no. Another lesson learned about men in the military, she thought.

"I'm sorry, I just thought it was something you always wanted and since you helped keep the General alive until I could get my hands on him, I thought it would be a nice thing to do for you."

"It was, but on major life things, there are only three people I let do that, whomever is signing my paycheck, whomever I am married to or whomever I am sleeping with, and you don't fit in to any of these categories. Having said that, thank you very much for the opportunity."

Heather shook her head and replied, "You are welcome. I have to go finish my meeting with Dr. Hendricks. I am sorry for making the assumptions I did. I had no right to do that. Please forgive me."

"Nothing to forgive Doc. You were just looking out for me, and I appreciate it. I will make you proud," he replied. Heather nodded with a touch of chagrin on her face, turned and started down the hall. Doc called after her, "You are gonna let me know when all this is going to happen, right?"

"Yes, I will," she responded over her shoulder. The meeting with Dr. Kendricks took another two hours or so and after she finished, she thanked him for his decision on Doc Horner.

He dismissed it with a flip of his hand, "It was a no-brainer. Usually, I must decide if the candidate is really serious about going into the life of medicine and what that requires. They don't usually figure that out until the end of the second year and by then there is a lot the school has invested in them. With Mr. Horner, he has more than demonstrated his commitment and that he has no illusions about what is going to be asked of him. No-brainer," he said with a shrug of his shoulders.

"I have to discuss some things with the Council, and I will be back in touch so we can move forward," Heather replied. She gave him a brief hug, excused herself, then left the Deans' office. Once in the hallway, she made a call to J.T. so she could update him. She also said that she had something that needed to be discussed at home, where it was private. J.T, told her he was about done and asked if she wanted to go out to dinner or have him cook.

"That's a no-brainer after all that time eating in Area 43, a nice romantic dinner is what I crave," she purred.

"Your wish is my command, m'lady. I will see you at home in say, 30 minutes?"

"I will be there with bells on," was her reply. She hung up and as she headed out, she started to get a *dreamy look in her eyes*. It had been a month and a half since she and J.T. had made love. She just couldn't bring herself to get intimate, after she found out about all the bugs in their quarters, even after J.T. had spoken to the responsible parties. Dammit, she was really horny.

It had been years since she had the feeling of needing to mate with anyone. She could hardly wait until they finished dinner. A long, soaking bath with candles and some chilled wines. Then she was going to turn in to her own version of a porn star. She was sure that J.T. would be *up* for it. She knew she was already.

The ride home was uneventful as she saw J.T.'s car in the driveway. She noticed her heartbeat speeding up a little. The smells that hit her as she walked through the back door made her mouth start salivating. As she entered the kitchen, the aromas intensified. J.T. turned and handed her a glass of white wine with rivulets of sweat running down the side of the glass. She took a good swallow, set the glass down on the granite countertop of the island, turned to J.T., went into his arms, molding and pressing her body suggestively, tilted her head up to receive his kiss, long, lingering, sincere with a promise of much, much more later.

"How was your day, sweetheart?" she queried.

"Fairly routine, actually. It was good to see the guys of the unit. What was so important that you needed to speak to me privately?"

"I introduced Doc Horner to Dr. Kendricks, dean of the med school today and after a few minutes, he told Doc that he had passed the med school interview with flying colors. The issue was that I had not told Doc about any of my plans. He was a little pissed, to say the least. One of the things he mentioned, and this was what I wanted to ask you about, was that Doc said that if he went ahead with my idea and he did become a MD, he would have to leave the Unit because there were billeting issues. Currently, a unit the size of yours was only billeted for a PA and one corpsman, and if he were a doctor, they would have to transfer him to another unit. Doing that would interfere with his duties to the people of Coulter and all the friends he had at Unit 17. Is that right? Would he have to transfer somewhere else? I was just trying to help him get to where he should be. He would make an outstanding Family Physician and since we have proved III can input information rapidly, hooking Doc up for two or three days then giving him the same exam you got and bingo he would become a physician."

"He was correct about billeting. There is only an allowance for one PA and one corpsman, for a 75man unit. The billeting requirement for a MD is a unit of 125 men. They get a MD, one PA and two corpsmen. I'll investigate what I can do now that I am a General and all."

"Would you? That would be wonderful if you could fix this. I know it's my fault, but, in defense of myself, I am a civilian and have no knowledge of the inner workings of the military, or at least knowledge to navigate through the military bureaucracy yet. I will learn it by the time I am a general's wife."

"I understand and I am sure we will be able to keep Doc at Unit 17." Heather jumped into his arms and kissed him thoroughly. "Now, let me finish supper, then we can have some time for us, okay?" he asked.

"So, what's for dinner, Chef?"

"Scallops Carbonara with some steamed broccoli and fettuccini. Didn't have time to make desert."

"Guess I will have to be desert, if that's okay?"

"Was going to suggest that was a perfect way to end a meal and start a romantic evening."

"Guess we both have the same thing in mind."

"I'm sure we do." J.T finished setting the table, Heather lit the candles and picked up a bottle of a dry, white wine. She handed it to J.T. who worked at pulling the cork.

"Losing strength, big guy?" she joked.

"I have had this bottle for a few years. Guess the cork just dried out a little," he remarked.

After a little more work, the cork came out, intact and dry, as predicted. Heather took a little sip and pronounced it drinkable while J.T. finished plating the dinner. They sat down, said a prayer and dove into the first home cooked meal in nearly two months. There wasn't a lot of conversation, but there were a lot of passionate stares floating back and forth across the table. Heather finished first, told J.T. how fabulous it was, finished her glass of wine and poured another, came around the table and gave him a very sensual kiss and told him to give her ten minutes before coming into the bathroom.

J.T. nodded and proceeded to clear the dishes. Taking them into the kitchen, he rinsed them off and put them in the dishwasher, along with all the pans he had used making supper.

He checked the kitchen, made the coffee for the morning, turned on the dishwasher and then made his way to the bathroom. The room was darkened except for the glow of four candles, strategically placed. Heather was sitting in the tub, holding two glasses of wine. He was struck by the sight of her perfect pink-tipped breasts protruding up, covered by suds from the bubble bath she had prepared.

"Get out of those clothes mister, and get in this tub. Don't make me wait."

He didn't, and she was thrilled as well as being thoroughly pleased.

———

Heather rolled over and stretched languorously in between the silk-sheets. It had been a long while since she had been screwed that well. Things had started out romantically, but then somewhere along the line it had turned into a purely physical screwing. She had forgotten how good a physical screw felt. She didn't care for it all the time, but every now and then, it hit all the spots just right. As she tried to get out of bed, there were a number of muscles that reminded her that she really shouldn't go 7.5 weeks without sex. It was a good type of ache, and it even got her a little stimulated. Maybe she could get a quicky in when J.T. got home. She decided to sit in a hot bath and relax for a little while. She had dozed a little when she heard the door slam.

"Sweetheart?"

"I am here in the tub. Come join me."

"Be there in a second." He entered the bathroom, shedding his workout uniform as he walked until he was naked, standing in front of her.

"Glad to see everything looks fine. I was thinking of putting it to use in a few minutes. Helps work out the kinks," she purred.

"Great minds think alike," was his reply as he stepped into the tub.

An hour and a half later, they both rolled out of bed. J.T. mentioned he needed to go back to the Unit for a bit and Heather mentioned she needed to go to see the Council to update them and to see if they had any thoughts that would be of benefit for her part in the operation. J.T. said he would meet her for lunch before the Council meeting. He also had a few things to discuss with the Council.

"See you at 11:30 am at the Wine Cellar, OK?" he asked.

"You sure you need to go?" she asked as she dropped her towel, posing seductively.

"Yes baby, I have to go. Gotta see a man about a PA request from my fiancée."

"Well in that case I understand," she replied.

J.T. headed to the Unit and his meeting with Colonel Stein. Stein had been his XO for quite a while, and he liked as well as respected him both as a man and as a Unit commanding officer. His greeting was warm and genuine.

"General, what can I do for you?" he asked.

"When we are alone, stop with the General stuff OK? We've been through too much to get into military formality when we are by ourselves, all right?"

"Sure thing J.T."

"On to my reason for a visit. My fiancée, Dr. Dunkirk has, behind my back as it were, had arranged something, that if it works out, Doc Horner will end up a real MD, complete with degree and a license. Both you and I know you and the Unit are billeted for one PA and one corpsman. My concern is that if Central Command hears about it, they will transfer him out of the Unit. I do not have to tell you how the unit will react to Doc leaving. Most of those guys have been treated by Doc for more than 10 years. They have confidence that Doc can do his job and keep them alive. You understand what that means to organizational efficiency, not to mention morale. What I am proposing is to keep Doc in the role as a PA until his enlistment is up. I know that this means you must stick your neck out, but I think you realize that this is what is best for the unit and for Doc. No one needs to know that when they call him Doc, he really is."

"I do not have a problem with this. Just make sure that Doc never officially tells me he really is. What I don't know, I can't do anything about."

"I knew I could count on you. He only has two or three more years until he qualifies for retirement at 25 years of service."

"Glad I could help, and I know this meeting never took place."

"Thanks Max, I really appreciate it and I won't forget either. You and the wife will be getting invitations to the wedding, but I would like to have you as one of my groomsmen, if you would do me the honor." J.T said.

"It would be an honor, J.T. Just let me know where and when," Max replied.

"Only if you let me know if you have a mission around that time. I'm kinda out of the loop with the Quest thing."

"By the way, congrats on the spaceship thing. Heard about it through the grapevine."

"To tell you the truth, my suggestion was just a wild guess that turned out better than I ever anticipated. It was really strange yet exciting to have an experience being mentally in touch with an alien-based lifeform. I am looking forward to next week when I start round two. I will keep you posted."

"Thank you. I appreciate that." J.T. rose shook hands and told the Colonel he knew the way out. As he departed, he told Max to have a good day.

As he was leaving the building, he took a moment to call Heather and let her know he was headed to the restaurant, and he would see her there.

The restaurant staff was pleased to see the General and his lady and seemed to go out their way to make sure that everything was perfect for them. J.T. noticed the subtle change in things but decided not to comment about them to Heather. That lasted about five minutes when Heather remarked on that same issue. All was understood when the manager and the executive Chef both came to the table, apologized, but then asked if they could have a picture of the people that had finally communicated with alien visitors. J.T. was seriously pissed that they were aware of the accomplishment but did his best not to show his displeasure. Four pictures later, they were finally left alone long enough to order their meals.

J.T. excused himself and stepped outside to place a call to Sean, asking him to notify the CO that there was a leak on his base and to convey his serious displeasure with said leak. He hung up and decided he needed to also address things with the Council that afternoon during his meeting with them. Heather had already decided what she wanted to eat and had to wait until J.T. finished his phone call, sat down and had a chance to look over the menu.

He asked her what she was having and decided he would have the same. After the waitress left, he turned to her and told her what had happened with Colonel Stein and what Stein had said. He told her he had not told Doc, and to keep what had transpired quiet and, if she saw him before he did, would she please tell him to keep his mouth shut concerning him becoming an MD. Heather was really pleased with the news and thanked him for helping get her out of her inadvertent problem situation. J.T. smiled and said he was happy to help since Doc had saved his life and tangentially helped him to meet his future wife.

Besides, he agreed that Doc was best served by getting his MD. Think of all the people he would help, how he would be able to benefit multiple communities, so all in all, a win-win situation. They continued the conversation, touching briefly on wedding plans as well as the project they were currently knee-deep in. The meal was delicious as usual, and they departed. Both were headed to the Council building for their separate but together meeting with the ruling Council members. J.T. decided that Heather would go first and so informed her, since he had a lot more things to discuss than she did.

The Sergeant of The Guard met them at the door, snapped to attention, rendered a perfectly crisp salute, and awaited the return salute, before saying, "Good afternoon, General. Nice to see you again. Hope all is well, Sir, and good afternoon, Dr. Dunkirk. Always lovely, as usual. Wonderful to see you again."

J.T returned the salute and replied, " Thank you, Sergeant. You are looking well and 4-0, I might add."

"The Council expects no less, Sir. thank you," the sergeant responded.

"Thought about my offer?" J.T. asked.

"Yes Sir, I have, but at this time I will need to decline. I still have 11 months on this assignment, and I never leave a job unfinished, Sir."

"Best answer I have heard today. Anyway, offer still stands as long as I am alive. Let me know when you are ready."

"Aye, Aye, Sir" was his reply as he opened and held the door.

"Carry on," was J.T.'s response.

J.T. held Heather's hands firmly but gently as they made their way down the long hall to the Council's conference room, where the door was opened and held by another squared away trooper, at attention, also rendering a crisp, perfect salute.

"Good afternoon General, Dr. Dunkirk. Please take a seat. May I offer you something to drink? Coffee, tea, water Sir?"

"Black Coffee for me."

Heather replied she would like some tea with sugar.

"Aye, Aye, Sir, Ma'am. The council is running a little late, so there will be a bit of a wait. Is there anything else besides the beverages I can get you?"

"No, Corporal, the beverages will be fine, thank you. It would be easier if the Council were a bunch of privates, wouldn't it, Corporal?"

"Yes Sir, my thoughts exactly Sir, unfortunately that is just a wish, Sir."

J.T. and Heather both chuckled, "Yes, it is, Corporal, carry on."

"Aye, Aye Sir."

They entered the conference room and took seats in the middle of the conference table. two minutes later, the Corporal opened the door and allowed the steward to wheel in a coffee service cart. The steward parked the cart at the end of the table, placed a napkin and a cup of coffee in front of T.J., and a napkin and a cup of tea along with a spoon and a bowl of sugar in front of Heather.

"Will there be anything else, General, Ma'am?" he asked.

"That will be all, thank you."

"Aye, Aye, Sir." J.T. took a sip and remarked that it was some of the best coffee he had had in a long time.

Heather remarked that she had never had this kind of tea and would like to get some for her personal stash. Ten minutes later, the door at the other end of the conference room opened and nine members of the ruling Council of Elders entered. J.T. stood and came to attention. Heather started to get out of her chair but J.T. restrained her with a gentle hand on her right shoulder.

"At ease, General. Great to see you again, in person this time. Dr. Dunkirk, wonderful to see you. Radiant as usual," said John Holmes, the First Chief Elder.

"The Council has been looking forward to this meeting with great anticipation, mixed in with a large helping of hope."

J.T. spoke up and said that he thought that Heather should speak first since he had a number of different things on his agenda.

"Very well, Dr. Dunkirk, you have the floor."

Heather began by indicating she had made arrangements with the Dean of her med school in Dome 17 to undertake the process of genetic testing and subsequent genetic therapies and treatments. What she needed from the Council was subjects. She felt that they should be between 22 and 28 at the oldest, exceptions made for applicants with exceptional skills. She also felt that the pool should be about 10,000 people and that would allow things to be narrowed down to between 6000 and 7500. She felt that it was going to take four to six years to get the spacecraft built and tested before leaving Earth on its voyage.

Not knowing, at this time, how long it was going to take to get to the new world, people picked would age and could become injured or killed through normal daily living. The thought of putting selected candidates immediately into hibernation would cut down on unexpected losses like car accidents and unforetold illnesses. She would need the Council to obtain applicants by their various means and reach into the population of the Dome cities. There was a brief discussion amongst the Council members present concerning her proposals and needs. In the end, the First Chief Elder told her they would send her their discussions and suggestions within the next week.

Then it was J.T.'s turn to speak. He stood up and began,

"Elders of the Council, I have a number of items on my list. The primary one being that I was just semi-accosted in a restaurant by the manager and executive chef, asking for pictures of the first man to have contact with an alien race. I have instructed Major McCann to inform Colonel Farmouth, CO of area 51 and 43 and for him to determine who or how this information was leaked to the general public. I would strongly suggest that the Council start investigating the possibility of a leak here."

There was a strange look on the faces of the Council members, almost as if he had just insulted them.

"My next point is obtaining the Vladerium from the moon. This along with titanium and aluminum, is the element that is needed to make the shell of the spacecraft able to tolerate faster than light speed in space. When can we expect to get the supply chain from the moon to Area 43 started?"

There was no response from anyone.

"The next point is the Iribadinium. This is the substance that provides the power to the spacecraft. According to the computer, the two locations in this solar system where this can be found is the Van Allen Radiation belt and on Titan, one of Saturn's moons. For us to move forward with this project, I must have these elements. I suggest that I try and take one of the spacecraft we have at area 43 and go get the Iribadinium from the Van Allen belt. I can fashion a scoop, attach it to another space vehicle and go up and pick up as much Irbadinium as I can find and return it to area 43. I would rather not have to set up a shuttle, running back and forth to the moon to pick up the Vladerium and bring it back to area 43, but I can if I must."

This time there was an answer from the Council.

"It has taken time to get the moon mining operation running again. We are awaiting their acknowledgement that they are running. They would like a number indicating how much ore they are going to have to make available for the job. Once we give them that number, they can tell us how long it will take to have everything ready for shipment. General, can you give us that number?"

"Yes, I can. 11 tons raw weight."

"Elder Brooks, can you please transmit that number to the mining colony on the moon?" First Chief Elder Holmes requested.

"Yes Sir," was the reply.

"General, the Council has no problem with you piloting an alien spacecraft to harvest the substance you need for propulsion. By the way, have you developed any thoughts on how you plan to propel your spacecraft?"

"Yes, I have. I intend to use the propulsion systems currently present in all the alien spacecraft at area 43. I can see no reason to reinvent the wheel. It is evident that the race that originally built these craft are not coming after them to return them to their planet of origin. Therefore, by rite of salvage, these craft now belong to us, and we intend to use everything in all these crafts to help our project to reach fruition. That should cut five to ten years off the time it would normally take, to make something new, test it, modify it for long-term use, then put it inside the ark. Right now, the main issues are fuel for the Ark, and materials to construct the exterior shell of the craft.

"We know for a fact that the shells of the craft we are in possession of have proved they are space worthy and tolerant of faster than light speeds, for prolonged periods of time. We have no further testing to do. We have the benefit of long term, actual, real life, use. We could not have asked for anything better other than to come upon a fully built and functioning Ark, ready for us to stock, board and take off in. And, as we all know, that has not happened, nor is it likely to."

The members of the Council huddled together, murmuring and occasionally gesturing, discussing the information they had just been given.

Later, the Chief Elder stood and addressed Heather and J.T.

"The Council has decided to accept both of your ideas and you have our complete support. Dr. Dunkirk, you will be receiving communications from us within the next few days. Once that is at hand, you may proceed with your plan. General, we are in complete agreement about your plans, philosophy, and thinking patterns. You have again reinforced the correctness of our choice for the man to lead the Quest. You will be receiving notification from us within the next week as to when you can expect the ore arrivals from the moon, when the equipment for smelting, manufacturing and fabrication will arrive. That should allow you to plan a start date for the construction of the Ark. You may go into space to obtain fuel for the arc at your convenience. I can assure you that there will be an investigation into the possibility of a leak here at the Council. We will notify you of the findings of that investigation. Please leave the name of the restaurant with the Sergeant at Arms at the door as you exit so this can get looked into as soon as possible. Is there anything else, General?"

"No Sir, not currently. Thank you for your time," J.T. replied.

"It is we who thank you, General. Carry on." With that the Council all stood and followed the First Chief Elder as he departed the room.

J.T. stood, extended a hand to Heather as she pushed away from the conference table, and said, "That went well, don't you think?"

"When were you going to tell me that you were going into space without me?" She questioned.

"I'm sorry, that was a spur of the moment thought, trying to get the importance of my position across," he replied.

"So, you are not going into space?" she pressed.

"Yes, I am going into space, most assuredly. You are welcome to come with me," was his reply.

"What if I don't want to go into space?" she asked.

"Then you can stay on Earth. Does that mean you will not be coming along on the Ark?" he asked.

"No, of course not. I just wasn't sure I wanted to go into space on a small flying saucer that's all."

"Personally, I think you would really like it, but it is up to you."

"I never said I wasn't going up into space with you. I just was trying to find out if you were serious or not," she responded.

"Just think, we can be the first to create the 1000-mile-high club," J.T. suggested.

"Your mind is always in the gutter," was her reply.

"I am trying to make up for lost time. Besides, look at whom I would be in the gutter with."

"Nice recovery, pervert," she responded, slapping his upper arm.

"Look at the time, dinner out or at home?"

"What do you have at home?"

"I'm sure I can find stuff to whip something up."

"Then let's eat at home."

"Works for me. Home it is."

They headed out of the building and down the street, a casual stroll, holding hands, window shopping and just being lovers, enjoying being with each other. They got into the car, set it for home, then set back and relaxed for the drive. Reaching the house, they noticed a fair-sized crowd gathered outside, milling around on the lawn. The crowd separated as they pulled into the driveway. Then they started pressing against the car, almost to the point of J.T. and Heather not being able to get out of the car. J.T. Stood up to his full height, squared back his shoulders and in a loud and clear voice,

"What the hell are all of you doing on my lawn without my permission? You all can just go home. I have no intention of allowing this assembly to continue, again without my permission. Please leave my property!"

"We just want to hear what it was like with the aliens. We gonna be invaded or taken over?"

J.T. noticed, out of the corner of his eye, he saw a television crew setting up and a reporter pushing his way through the crowd, trying to shove a microphone in J.T.'s face. J.T. grabbed the microphone, wrenched it from the reporter's hand, unplugged the cord and then handed it back. He sternly told the reporter.

"Get off my property or I will put you off personally."

"People have a right to know about this," the reporter said.

"Says who?" was J.T.'s response.

"We are the media. We have a right to know about things."

"Again, and this is the last time I will say this, GET OFF MY PROPERTY RIGHT NOW or else. There is no law that says you have a right to trespass and force a microphone in my face and demand that I answer your questions. Oh, oh, now you've done it. The cavalry has arrived and unless you want to physically get hurt, I suggest you haul your ass off my property."

The reporter turned around and saw four DFS 17 personnel carriers pull in and 40 troopers poured out and began pushing people off the lawn.

"General, do you want these people to leave your property?" the staff sergeant asked.

"Yes, staff sergeant, please remove these people. Try not to hurt them unless they resist. Are we clear, staff sergeant?"

"Aye, aye, Sir. 17 listen up. Remove the civilians from this property. Use force only if someone resists physically. Move out."

Within minutes, the front lawn was empty, and no one was injured. The reporter was handled roughly, but that was because he resisted, continually repeating the press had a right to get at the truth. The troops showed extremely good self-control and restraint. The reporter obviously did not realize the relationship between the troopers and the General. If he had, he would have bundled up his equipment and left. Instead, he was physically lifted by 3 troopers and when he yelled, "Let me down," he was summarily dropped to the ground, bruising his ego and his ass. He jumped up off the ground and acted like he was going to go back to the property he had just been removed from.

One of the large lance corporals stepped in front of him and said, "You do not want to do that sir. You would force me to hurt you, rather badly, I might add. This is my general's property, and we will do anything to protect it, him and his family. Are we clear sir?"

The reporter thought about it and decided that retreat was the better part of valor and walked off.

J.T. and Heather were watching the cleanup from inside the house behind the curtains. J.T. and Heather looked at each other when he said,

"I need to make a phone call."

He reached into his pocket and pulled out a business card, looked at the number then dialed it on his phone.

"This is General Coulter. I do not know if you are aware of what has happened but there was a disturbance outside my home, where a large group of people wanted me to discuss what has happened at Area 51. I was rescued by troops from DSF 17. There weren't any casualties, but one persistent reporter pushed his luck and was firmly dealt with but not injured. Think the Council needs to make an announcement about the discovery. Just thought you should know. Thank you Sir."

Then he hung up. Heather looked at him quizzically, waiting for him to give her information.

"They are drafting a statement at this minute. The Chief Elder apologized for us having to go through this, and that they were in the process of dealing with it."

"Doesn't help us trying to get into our own home without being accosted," she said.

"I can get a security detail to escort us if that would make you feel safe."

"No, I am just pissed that people feel they can barge onto someone's property demanding answers, with no respect for the people they were accosting," Heather complained.

"Feel better now? How would you like your ribeye? I am having mine medium rare. Thought I would steam some asparagus and some mashed potatoes with green onions. Do you need a sauce or gravy?"

"Everything you just said sounds great, no gravy. Would you like some wine, red or white?" she asked.

"Red would be fine," he said.

"Did they say when the statement would come out?"

"I assume it will come out tomorrow with the morning news. So, if there is work you can do at home, tomorrow would be the day to do that. Or you could go to the hospital and see some cases. The news people would not be allowed to follow you into patient's rooms." J.T. remarked.

"We could spend the day in bed doing you-know-what. I'm for that," she purred.

CHAPTER
TWENTY-TWO

The next morning at precisely 4:15 am J.T. was up and dressed in his workout togs, slapped Heather on her exposed bare ass, kissed the top of her head and then headed out to do his daily workout routine. He looked around with a trained eye, looking for anyone trying to ambush him for a story. He saw the TV van a block down the road. As he backed out of the driveway, he could see the van starting up.

He called the duty officer on call and asked him to set up an intercept and gave the OOD an address and a time frame of 15 minutes then backed out of the driveway and drove past the van, forcing them to U-turn in the middle of the road. They tried to catch up, but J.T. kept a good distance between him and the van, driving around until the intercept got set up. He got a signal from the intercept team showing they were set and waiting. J.T. headed for the spot and kept an eye on the van the whole way. As he went around the corner, the trap was sprung and the van was boxed in. He stopped his car, jumped out and pulled the driver's side door open, pulling the driver out and on to the ground. Holding him there with a wrist lock, J.T. asked him why he was following him.

The answer was, "Because I was told to."

"By whom?"

"My employer."

"And that is who?"

"The Herald."

"What were they looking for?"

"Anything they could use against you so you would give an interview to them exclusively about the aliens."

"Who told you to do this? What's his name?" J.T. applied more pressure to the wrist lock, eliciting a rather painful moan.

"Winston Heath, editor-in-chief." J.T. released the pressure on the lock, but kept hold of him.

"I am only going to say this once. Got me? You will have nothing further to do with any kind of surveillance or intelligence gathering of me, my family or anyone involved with the Council. Are we clear on this? If I catch you doing anything of the sort, let's just say they will never find your body and it will be very, very painful before you are allowed to die. As far as the people present right now, this meeting never happened. There is no record of it, so if you want to take a chance that I am bluffing, just make sure all your affairs are in order. Understand?"

A nod of the head and J.T. released his wrist. "I would suggest you look for other employment. I will be speaking with Mr. Heath a little later this morning. You can tell him if you like, it will make no difference in the outcome."

With that, J.T. helped him off the ground and then, after he had got back into the van, shut the door.

One of the men of the security detail came up to the window and said, "Like the General said, this meeting never took place. The General is a sincere, honest and truthful man. If he says you won't survive messing with him, you won't. I guarantee it. Now get out of here."

There was a screeching of the van's tires as it raced away from the curb. J.T. turned to the detail and said,

"That was very well done. Good job! You have my sincere thanks and appreciation."

"It was nothing General. In fact, we don't remember seeing you at all today. Have a good day, Sir." They both saluted and drove off.

J.T. proceeded to the Unit so he could do his daily workout. When finished and had showered, he stopped by the ET (electronics) shop to have a word with the staff sergeant in charge.

"Good morning, Sergeant Franklin," he said. The sergeant jumped up from his chair and came to attention. He had started to salute but was waved off by J.T.

"How have you been? Have you completely recovered from the last mission?" J.T. asked.

"I am well, General, it was just a little scratch, and it's fine now."

"It was hardly a scratch sergeant. I had to personally call the surgeon that repaired your arm. Just glad you are back to full duty."

"Thank you, General. Be sure to give my regards to Dr. Dunkirk next time you see her. Tell her she does good work, Sir."

"Be happy to. You are right, she does great work. I need to

borrow a couple of pieces of equipment for a couple of days. I need a scrambler so I can have an unrecorded conversation with someone, and it is not going to be pleasant for him, but I do not want it recorded. Also need something that would scramble any type of visual/video recording of me with this individual. Do you have anything like that I could borrow for a couple of days?" he asked.

"You are in luck Sir, just got in a couple of all-purpose scramblers. Supposed to work on audio as well as video. I saw the demo of them but have not had a chance to actually try it out."

"Well sergeant, let's set up a little short test run while I am here. That way, I will know if it works."

"Roger that Sir. Just give me a few minutes and we can see how it goes."

"Mind if I have a cup of coffee?" J.T. asked.

"Be happy to get you one, Sir."

"Sergeant, when it is just you and me, we can skip the Sir stuff OK.? And I think I can get my own cup of coffee. After all you are a staff sergeant and not a private," J.T. said.

"Pot's over in the corner, on the table. Cups are on the wall."

"Thanks" J.T. filled a cup from the pot and had a seat while the sergeant set up the equipment.

"This is some excellent coffee sergeant. Where did you learn to make such a great cup of coffee?" J.T. asked.

"I learned it from my mother. My dad was career military, and he taught her, so she passed it down to me."

"Well, you tell her for me that this was one of the best cups of coffee I have had in a very long time."

"I will, next time I see her."

"Are we ready for the test run?"

"Yep. Just look at me and say a few things." J.T. started rambling and a couple of minutes later, the sergeant told him he could stop. He went over to the audio/video recording, rewound it and when he hit play, there was nothing on it and no sound.

"Guess it works pretty well, Sir."

"Sure does, and I thank you for the test run.

I will get this back to you in a couple of days."

"No problem General. See ya later, and be sure to mention me to your wife."

"That I will Staff sergeant."

J.T. put the device in his pocket. It was only as big as a thumb drive and headed out to the car for the drive back home. He was sure to watch for someone following him, but fortunately, there was no sign of a tail. When he got home, Heather was just getting out of the shower, so he stood there leaning against the wall, staring at his fiancée.

"Get a good look big guy?" Heather questioned.

"I could stand here and look at you all day long. Magnificent. Absolutely perfect," was his reply.

"Nice recovery. How has your day been so far?" J.T. started at the top and went over everything.

"Do you remember Staff Sergeant Franklin, of the militia?"

"He was the one shot in the right wrist and arm, 7 hours of surgery. Looked great when I was done. Why do you ask?"

"I saw him today, and he mentioned you and asked me to tell you that you do good work."

"Well, wasn't that sweet. Why were you seeing him?

"I was getting a scrambling device to take with me when I go visit the editor for the Herald. I am going to get up in his face and make him some promises that he will pray never come true. That should stop all the harassment we have been getting about the aliens and all," J.T. stated.

"Are you sure that you will not get in trouble?" Heather asked.

"That was the whole point of the scrambler. There will be no evidence except his word against mine," J.T. stated.

"You sure you need to do this?" she asked.

"It is the only way to get them to stop pestering us," J.T. responded.

"Well, okay, if you think it is necessary. Can you drop me off at the hospital on your way to the showdown?" she asked.

"Sure, and it's not a showdown. It's just a one-sided meeting where I talk and he sits there and shuts up, except to say things like, yes, Sir, I'm sorry Sir, and it won't happen again, Sir," he said.

"Hope that it works out for you. Get me a cup of coffee and let's get on the road," Heather requested.

J.T got her the coffee and headed out to the car. The drive to the hospital took all of ten minutes and he was back on the road headed for the Herald office building. Sitting in the car, he turned on the scrambler and put it in his pocket. Getting out, he smoothed his uniform, put his hat on, and headed for the front door. There was a security guard inside the door, so J.T. asked for directions to Winston Heath's office. He was directed to the 9th floor where he simply followed the signs. Pushing open the heavy walnut door, he stepped up to the counter and spoke to the secretary that came over to help him.

"General Coulter to see Mr. Heath. I do not have an

appointment, but I am sure he will see me," J.T. replied.

"Please have a seat and I will check with Mr. Heath," she said.

J.T. nodded and moved over to a leather covered couch, taking a seat and getting comfortable. He reached into his pocket and turned on the scrambler. A couple of minutes later, the secretary returned and directed J.T. to Mr. Heath's office door. J.T. knocked once, then entered, not waiting to be invited in.

"What can I do for you, General?" he asked.

"You can get rid of the people tailing me, sitting outside my house and the crowds you managed to get riled up enough to trespass on my property and accost me and my fiancée," J.T. said rather loudly and forcefully. "I have already dealt with the man you sent to tail me. He will be looking for other employment."

"General, you don't understand. You are at the center of the largest news story of the century. People deserve to know about it," Heath said.

"Says who?" was J.T.'s reply.

"Well, that would be me as the editor-in-chief." He replied.

"Wrong answer. No one died and made you boss or God, so from my point of view, you have no right to send people out to harass me or my family or friends. If you persist, there will be serious consequences, quite painful I might add, or perhaps even worse. This is your one and only warning, and it is more of a promise. If you do not cease and desist, let's just say no one will ever find your body. Are we clear?"

"You can't do that. There are laws that prohibit that kind of thing," was the pitiful reply.

"Try and prove it Mr. Heath. You won't be around to press charges and there is no proof that I have made these statements. You would best be served to follow my instructions to the letter. That way, we both will know where we stand. If you think you can proceed down the path you are currently on, there will be consequences, believe me. Do not forget what I have done for more than twenty years. I am very good at a lot of things and causing death is one of those. It is up to you. I have stated my case and told you what will happen if you persist. I hope you have enough brains to choose correctly. I can find my own way out. Good day Sir," J.T. stated in his most commanding voice.

J.T. picked up his cap, set it properly on his head, pivoted on his heel, and strode purposefully out the door.

Heath sat down at his desk, reached into the bottom drawer and brought out a bottle of scotch. He poured three fingers and drank the whole amount down at once. He sat back in his chair and pondered what he had just been told, then he opened the second drawer and took out a tape recorder. He smiled to himself thinking, just who did this uniformed blowhard think he was, coming into my office and threatening me with death if I continued to try to get something on the General that would make him give me an exclusive interview. A smirk crossed his face as he pushed the rewind button. When it rewound, he thought to himself, I will show this ground pounding grunt who the fuck he was dealing with. He pushed the play button and listened. His face drained of all color and his heart started pounding, his hands started shaking. The tape was blank. He had lost.

Suddenly, his whole world started crumbling as he picked

up the phone and made a call to his chief investigative reporter.

J.T. strode out of the building like a proud peacock. He stopped at the corner and thought it might be a good idea to bring the Council up to date without giving them anything that showed coercion and illegal threatening. He pulled out his phone and dialed the number from memory. When the Chief Elder answered, he quickly brought him up to date on last night's occurrences and his decision to have a private chat with the man behind it. To his credit, the Chief Elder did not ask for any details, merely listened. When J.T. had finished, the Chief Elder paused, then said he thought that a press conference might be in order and he thought that J.T. should be at the Council Building at 3 pm., dressed appropriately, ribbons, no medals. He would not be required to make any comments other than the whole thing was classified and no one there, other than the Council, was cleared for that information, therefore, he had nothing further to contribute.

As a good military man would respond, J.T. said, "Aye, aye, Sir."

After the conversation was finished, he called Heather to let her know he was going to be on TV later that day. He also called Sean to see if there was any progress in the investigation into the leak. There was a negative response to the question, which he half expected. His response to Sean was to keep up the investigation. Before he hung up, he brought Sean up to date on everything including the proposed space flight to the Van Allen Belt to obtain fuel, the fact there was going to be a news / press conference that afternoon to tell everyone the long and short of it concerning contact with an alien culture. He also told him about Heath and implied the things he had said to him.

Sean's response was, "Did you threaten him?"

J.T.'s response was, "We effectively communicated cause and effect of persistent behavior, and I left the meeting feeling as though he completely understood my position. I also used an audio/video scrambler, so there was no record of the meeting, of which, I might add, he had no knowledge. I'm sure that pissed him off when he checked his recorder and found out there was no evidence of the meeting."

Sean broke into a deep belly laugh, picturing the look on Heath's face when he found that fact out.

"I can only imagine, as I was not in the room when that happened," J.T. said. He asked Sean to make sure his mom and dad were getting ready for the space flight, which would occur a day or two after he returned. He said goodbye and put the phone away as he arrived at his car. He got in, buckled up and headed off to the Council Office.

Upon his arrival, the Sergeant of the Guard met him at the front door, saluted, and then directed him away from the lobby where news people, cameras, and reporters were starting to gather. After a series of turns, he entered an auditorium where several Council Elders stood milling around. Elder Vandenhoff walked over to J.T., extended her hand and shook his.

"I wanted to take this opportunity to ask you about your interaction with the alien computer. Could you please tell me about it?" she asked.

"Elder Vandenhoff," he started.

"Please call me Janet, General."

"Janet, I am J.T.," was his response.

"On one hand it was fascinating. It spoke to me, telepathically, in English and from what I could tell, it completely scanned my mind and asked questions as though we had known one another for years. Surprisingly, it was not aware that the crew had perished. It did not seem to have a problem when I asked about downloading info like schematics of the computer and propulsion system design. That was when I asked what we would need to accommodate a download from it, and it told me the number I relayed to the Council. At no time did I get the impression that there was any hostility, thoughts of conquest, or a sense of a desire to destroy the Earth. There were several items I needed to obtain soonest about the composition of the hull and fuel for the propulsion system, that I did not have a chance to ask about the aliens, I did get the impression that they had been visiting Earth for more than 10,000 years. I did not have a chance to explore whether there was any interspecies breeding or the like. It is fairly evident that they occasionally lent a helping hand so to speak, but not to the point of taking over human society."

Janet said, "I would like to give you a set of questions to ask and explore with it the next time you link up. If that would be okay with you?"

"I do not have a problem with that. I will be leaving in two or three days, so if you could get them to me, by the time I am ready to leave, I will do my best to get you your answers," J.T. responded.

"Thank you, General. I look forward to hearing from you next time you are here in Dome 17. Please do not try to send me answers via any type of communication device, I am sure you are aware of the possible leak here. I would not like this information leaked to the public or our enemies. I am sure you understand," she explained.

"Yes, I do ma'am. I look forward to getting you the answers you are seeking," J.T. replied.

At that moment, the doors to the auditorium opened and the hoard of news and media people pushed and shoved their way into the room, each jockeying for the best position to hear and record the announcement. The Chief Elder motioned for J.T. to join him on the stage.

He began, "Ladies and gentlemen of the media, I want to thank you for taking the time out of your busy day to attend this announcement. One week ago, Brigadier General Coulter, acting under Council orders for a classified Quest project, managed to contact a computer taken from one of the aliens' spacecrafts we had secured. This is the first-time mankind has ever communicated with an alien race. The only information I am going to release will come from General Coulter. With that, I will give you General Coulter."

There was a loud round of applause, complete with whistles and inaudible words and sayings, none of which J.T. understood, as he approached the microphone.

The Chief Elder shook his hand, leaned in and whispered, "Not hostile, not here to conquer and been here before, that's all."

"Aye, aye Sir." J.T. stepped up to the microphone, raised both of his hands indicating everyone could stop clapping, quiet down and pay attention.

"Thank you for that applause. I have a couple of remarks. Number one, they are not hostile. I am not sure how long they have been coming here but they have been visiting since we were at the caveman stage. They are seeing how the human race is progressing. They are not setting up things to take over planet earth. Any other information that has been obtained is classified."

J.T. raised his voice and spoke as a commander of troops would speak, "AND WILL NOT BE DISCUSSED. PERIOD! That concludes my remarks. Thank you for attending this briefing. There will be no further briefings on this matter, as it will remain classified for a very long time. If the Council feels there is something to be disseminated, they will call a press conference. I will caution all of you that think classified materials can be disseminated at your whim, there will be severe penalties for said dissemination. Do not make the mistake of challenging either me or the council. You will regret it for a very long time. Please do not test the Council or me. The result will be very unpleasant. Good day."

J.T turned and stepped back to his original position, allowing the Chief Elder to take over the microphone.

"I think the General has been quite clear in his remarks and he is correct about what will happen if people ignore these comments. Since we are NOT taking questions, good day. The Sergeant of the Guard will show everyone the way out. There was a voice in the back of the crowd that called out, "How many aliens are there?

J.T. stepped up to the microphone and said, in a very loud and clear voice, "What part of the English language did you not understand? Was it No or questions? Sergeant, escort that particular idiot out personally."

"Aye, aye, Sir," was his response.

The sergeant grabbed the reporter by the elbow and muscled her out the door.

He whispered into the reporter's ear, "You must be some

kind of stupid. I personally am glad you are not in the service or life as you know it would be over. My suggestion is you write a very sincere apology addressed to the General here at the Council building and then let it go. Do you understand me?"

"Yes, I understand," was the response.

The Chief Elder came over, extended his hand and shook J.T.'s.

"You handled that quite well, I think. Similar to Mr. Heath, I would assume," he said.

"I was a little more colorful with Heath than I was here, but only because they were recording, and I was not able to erase any of it," J.T. replied.

"I understand now. I should have realized that you bear a close resemblance to a man who lives his life like a chess player, always five moves ahead."

"Helps, if you must go into combat, also. If you are not five steps ahead, a lot of people including yourself, can end up dead," J.T. replied.

"Yes, I can see that happening. Again, I would like to reiterate the Councils' pleasure with our decision to have you in charge. You have our complete confidence and support. Please, and I am serious about this, contact me with anything you need," the First Elder said.

"Yes Sir, I will and thanks for the vote of confidence. I could use three smelters and five fabricator systems at area 51 in the next two weeks. I must be able to start construction as soon as the ore comes in from the moon. When I get back to area 43, I plan to run my sketches through the alien computer and see if it can come up with any changes that may make construction easier, faster, safer or sounder than what I have come up with.

Who knows, it may be able to improve the design and cut down on fuel consumption, navigation, communication and defense because it has already been through the actual flight. It might have made the trip more than once," J.T. pondered.

"General, I have an appointment in seven minutes, so I must run. I will get started on your requests ASAP. Good to see you again. Good day."

J.T. stepped down off the stage, seeing the Sergeant of the Guard.

"Good job General, these media folks have no manners, and it was very pleasing to see them put back in their place."

"Sergeant, can you get me out of here? Since I came in the back way, I have lost my orientation."

"Right this way, General. I'll have you within twenty-five yards of your vehicle. Should keep the ambushes down to a minimum."

"Thank you, Sergeant. Remember my offer."

"Yes Sir, I will for a very long time."

"You do that. Now let's go. I have a dinner meeting with my fiancée I will not miss."

They walked down a long hall, made a right and a left, and then stopped in front of a non-descript door. The Sergeant punched in a code on the keypad next to it and the door unlocked and cracked open. The Sergeant pushed it the rest of the way open, indicated to J.T. to wait a minute then stuck his head out and looked around then waved J.T. out. Five minutes later, J.T. was driving towards downtown to his favorite restaurant. He called Heather and asked her to meet him there in thirty minutes.

CHAPTER
TWENTY-THREE

The next morning, after his usual morning workout, he got home and showered. Heather was sitting at the breakfast table having a cup of coffee as he walked by and headed for the bathroom. She followed him into the bathroom with a cup of coffee for him. He took the cup out of her outstretched hand, took a big gulp, then stepped into the shower. She took her robe off and joined him for an affectionate shower. J.T. asked her what was on her schedule for that day, and she said she had a few patients to see later in the morning, then she was free. He mentioned that he had a few phone calls to make, and he would be happy to make lunch for her if that sounded like something that would interest her.

Her response was that she would see how the morning went and call him when she was done, and they would discuss lunch then. J.T. responded OK and finished up showering before taking the washrag away from her and starting to wash her back for her. His hands strayed a little south, and she grabbed his hand and asked him what he thought he was doing. His answer was that he was washing her back, to which she replied that he had not asked permission to wash other parts of her body. J.T.'s response was that hadn't felt he needed to ask permission. She turned around, released his hand, and said that he should make sure he didn't miss anything.

His response was "I won't." She leaned back against him and said that she also had a front that needed washing too.

"May I?"

"I would be pissed if you don't, and be sure not to miss anything."

"Yes, ma'am." 25 minutes later they were toweling each other off. Heather went into the bedroom to get ready for work, whereas J.T. slipped on a robe and went back into the kitchen for another cup of coffee. He called out to Heather and asked her if she wanted a refill.

She replied, "No, not right now."

J.T. took his coffee in to the den/office, grabbed a phone and dialed Sean's personal phone number.

Sean answered, "Yes Sir, how's it going back home?" J.T. took a few minutes to recant the whole Heath issue and the Council's coming out press conference. When he had finished, he asked Sean if he had a paper and pen handy. When Sean replied he did, J.T. started giving him a list of things he needed to do. The first being to discuss with Colonel Farmouth where they were going to build the spacecraft, and where were they going to put the smelters and fabricating equipment that the Council was going to be sending in the next two weeks. J.T. impressed Sean's brain that he did not want there to be any delays in getting things up and running because they had not decided where things were going to go.

Next, he asked Sean to tell Helen and Frank to ask the computer to run a complete diagnostic scan of all parts necessary for space flight, including the amount of fuel currently available. He also wanted them to ask if it was possible to add an external tank that would be big enough to harvest a lot of Irbadinium, as much as we can find in the Van Allen belt. "We may need to take a few ore carrier type tubes to the moon to get a supply of Vladerium flowing so we can get the manufacturing process started on the exterior hull," he said.

"Next, I want Helen and Frank to find out how many of the alien spacecraft we have access to are able to fly at least to the moon and back more than once," he stated.

"I will be arriving at your pos on Thursday, this week. We will meet two hours after I arrive. Oh, yeah, if there are problems with the spacecraft being able to fly, I want an answer as to when the repairs will be complete. That about covers it. Are there any questions?" J.T. asked.

"No Sir. If any pop up, I will contact you soonest," was Sean's reply.

"Talk to you later, Sean. Be sure to continue to search for bugs. Our interaction with that alien computer was discussed with me in a restaurant here in Dome 17. Not sure if the leak has been plugged. Tell mom and dad, they can give me a call personally if there are any questions. I want to thank you for all you are doing. Couldn't have done it without you or Shannon. Give everyone my love," he said.

"Give our love to Heather, would you? I sure am glad she's

gonna be in the family. I'll talk to you later." Sean said then hung up as there were several things he needed to address.

J.T. got up and fixed himself another cup of coffee. Returning to the den, he sat down and got comfortable, turned on his computer and pulled up his sketches of the spacecraft he had envisioned 10 years earlier. Over the next couple of hours, he made several design changes. He saved them to the computer file and then called his father. Frank answered his call on the 4th ring.

"Hello son, how's things going?" Frank asked.

"Hey dad, have you spoken with Sean yet today?" J.T. asked.

"Why yes, just about an hour ago. I have not had a chance to connect with the computer. I was planning on doing that after lunch."

"Well, I was wondering if the computer had any method of being able to read input from someone else other than by the headbands?" J.T. asked.

"I believe it has a scanning mode, although I have not attempted to use it," Frank replied.

"I am sending you a file with my spacecraft design. I would like to have you scan it into the computer, ask it to review it and make suggestions on any changes that it thinks would adapt the design to long distance, faster than light speed, space travel, better. Heather and I will be flying in on Thursday so you can update me at the same time as you tell me about all the things Sean has already asked you to do. Is mom there?" J.T. finished.

"Yes, she is sitting across the table from me. Wanna speak to her?" Frank asked.

"Yes, if you don't mind. I will see you Thursday," J.T. responded.

"See you Thursday. Here she is." Frank said, just before he handed the phone to Helen.

After a short pause, Helen said, "Hello dear. To what do I owe the honor of you deigning to call your mother?"

"Mom, I was just there a few days ago, and I have been incredibly busy since I got back," J.T. whined then continued by going through everything that he had done over the last few days including the press conference and his dealings with Heath.

"I assume you have spoken with Sean, and there were a couple of things I wanted to add to my requests that you ask the computer. One of them is can we use more than one of the alien spacecraft engines in one vehicle.

"Number 2: would having more than one engine change standard fuel consumption rates outside the amount that would normally be used by two separate engines, and would we be able to make the trip to their home world without having to refuel. Next, would there be a need to have separate computers to run each engine or can one computer handle that function. Lastly, would it be more efficient to have one computer for scanning, one for navigation and one for the engines? Also, as I have already told dad, Heather and I will be flying in on Thursday."

"Tell Heather that Shannon and I have a few suggestions for the wedding. We are all so pleased she is joining the family. Glad you were smart enough not to let her get away. Love you son, see you soon." With that she hung up, just as J.T. was saying "Love you guys too."

J.T. pulled the file he had just put away and for the next hour, he drew several designs with 2, 3 and four engines, then put the sketches away and forwarded a copy of the file to his dad.

Heather called and said she had a couple of hours off, so whatever J.T. wanted to do was fine with her. J.T. suggested she come home for lunch and he would fix something for her. He went to the kitchen and started searching for something to make. Perhaps he would make her a Monte Cristo sandwich with some blackberry jam made in Coulter. He reached into the refrigerator and removed the smoked ham and aged cheese, all of which were made by hand in Coulter.

Making the egg wash for the bread, he added some nutmeg and cinnamon. The homemade bread was perfect for this dish. He warmed the griddle but held off on the butter, another Coulter product, until she walked through the door. He had a bottle of Moscato chilled and opened so it could breathe. Its sweetness was perfect for the savoriness of the sandwich. He poured a glass, turned to the back door and leaned up against the island. 30 seconds later, Heather breezed into the kitchen, took the glass from his hand, put a deep sensual kiss on his lips, then took a sip of wine.

"What's for eats?" she asked. "Monte Cristo sandwich, courtesy of the folks of Coulter. All the ingredients were made there." He turned to the griddle and put some butter on it, swirling it around. He began to make the sandwich, finally reaching the egg wash. He put the first slices of bread in the egg wash, then on the griddle. He put cheese, then ham, then cheese and topped it with another dipped slice of bread. After letting one side cook to a golden brown, he flipped them and while it was cooking, he got plates and silverware and a serving cup for the blackberry jam. When the cooking was done, he put the sandwiches on the cutting board, made two diagonal cuts in each sandwich, put them on a plate with a cup of jam in the center and set them on the table. Heather sat down with her partially empty wine glass, looked at it, noting the fragrant, oozing, gooey, melted cheese, then at J.T., then back at the wine glass. J.T. took the hint and got the bottle of wine, refilled her glass, and then took his seat. Heather attacked the sandwich with a gusto J.T. had never seen from her before. Heather could not believe how good the sandwich tasted. A small light bulb went off in her head. This was how J.T. managed to get the Coulter industry such a good price. The products they made were so superior to commercially made products, she had a hard time believing they were made in a small village back in the woods.

"Can you make me another one?" she asked.

"Here, finish mine," was J.T.'s response." J.T. pushed his plate across the table to her. It still had half a sandwich on it.

"You're sure? Thanks," was her answer.

"Please," he said. Heather snarfed down the half of his sandwich quite rapidly.

She pushed back, drained her glass of wine and said, "That was the best sandwich I have eaten in ages. I can see why Coulters' products are in demand and command a good price."

"So how was the morning?" he asked.

"Saw three consults, and I checked in with the Dean of the med school about the genetics program. They have made a goodly amount of progress on the screening protocol for the potential colonists," she explained.

"Excellent. I spoke with mom and dad about some things and they both sent their love and congratulated me on finding such a perfect choice," J.T. related.

"Oh, wasn't that so sweet! Remind me to thank them in person next time I see them," she commented.

"Oh, and mom said she and Shannon had some wedding thoughts to share with you when we get back there."

"Did she say what they were about?" she asked.

"No, just that they would talk with you when you get back. Did anything come up today, from anyone, about the alien stuff? Did anything come up that will keep us from leaving Thursday?" he asked.

"Not that I am aware of," was her answer.

"Good, how about we go out this evening? Movie, bowling, bar hopping, what do you say?" J.T. suggested.

"Might be nice to go to a couple of bars and have a drink or 2." Heather responded.

"Well, let's get cleaned up, changed and head out to O'Malley's Pub. They have wonderful Shepard's pie, some wonderful Irish Whiskeys and draft Guinness to start," he said.

J.T. slipped on a pair of jeans, loafers, a button-down, blue shirt and a tweed jacket. Heather put on a pair of very tight jeans, sneakers and a beige cashmere V necked, sweater and a light pale blue windbreaker.

J.T. spun her around, looked her up and down and then said, "Those jeans make your ass look marvelous."

"Really, kind sir? I didn't know you were an ass man. Could have sworn you were a boob kinda guy." was her playful reply.

"Well, when faced with the complete and total package of my fiancée, I can be an ass man on Monday, leg man on

Tuesday and a boob guy on Wednesday, then I can start all over."

"I love you," as she melted into his arms for a long, deep kiss. Kissing her back, he did reach around and grab her butt.

"Later, stud. Let's go."

"Yes, dear," was his response. "We can go, but your rear end still felt fabulous," he whispered in her ear.

She slapped his arm and said, "Outside big guy." Off they went. They walked into O'Malley's pub and found a couple of seats that were away from the rest of the crowd that was already there after work. The server came over, handed them menus, and asked what they wanted to drink.

J.T. said, "Jameson's neat and a pint of Guinness. Honey, what would you like?"

"Black and tan, pint, please." spoken confidently.

J.T. raised an eyebrow and commented, "I learn something new about you every day."

"What, that I have drank in bars and tried different things before you? I happen to like black and tans, as long as they are made with Guinness and Harps," she replied. The waitress returned with their drinks and asked if they were ready to order.

Heather said, "I will have the lamb chops medium rare, and a side of boxties and cabbage."

"I will have the Shepard's pie." J.T. replied. The couple sat back, sipped their drinks and traded discussion back and forth about a number of things when a slightly intoxicated man bumped into the table and slurring his words, asks J.T. if he was the guy on TV talking about the aliens. J.T. opted for the higher road and did his best to ignore the man.

In a much louder voice he said, "Hey, I'm talkin to ya! Ain't you the guy on TV talkin' about aliens?" J.T. realized this was going to end badly as he stood at least five inches taller than his antagonist.

"Yes, sir, I am, and I am here to have a drink and something to eat with my fiancée. We would appreciate it if you respected our privacy and kindly left us alone," J.T. said in a smooth voice, without the tone he normally would have used.

"You don't wanna talk to me? What, am I not good enough to talk to?" punching his finger into J.T.'s chest.

"Sir, I am attempting to be polite. I have no desire to talk to you. If I did, I would have come over to the bar and pulled up a chair and started a conversation. Since I didn't, I think it is evident that I do not want to talk to you. I think the manager of this pub is standing behind you and is going to ask you to leave. I suggest you do so before something happens that everyone will regret," a tone of annoyance was beginning to show in his voice.

At that moment Skip Johansen stepped up to J.T.'s side and said, "Is there a problem General?"

"I hope not Skip, I was telling this gentleman that I had no desire to talk to him and he seems to be hell bent on talking to me," a medium helping of annoyance in his voice.

"Hey buddy, I would suggest you leave this man alone before you get really hurt. He doesn't want to talk to you, so go back to the bar, have a drink, and leave this whole thing alone. Really. It's not going to end well for you," Skip cautioned.

The man acted like he was going to return to the bar, but instead he tried a haymaker sucker punch thrown at J.T.'s head. Heather was watching, and she never saw J.T. move but the man's head suddenly crashed into the table then slid to the floor, unconscious.

Heather got down on her knees and looked the man over and said, "Skip get an ambulance. Did you have to do this?" she asked a little upset.

"Two things. One, he tried to sucker punch me and two, he isn't dead, which means I must be slipping, because if you were not here, he would be," J.T. said in a calm, clear voice.

Skip jumped in and said, "He's right, ma'am. That is what he has taught us for fifteen years. People should end up dead in any fight. That way they don't come back to attack you later. That is why our unit didn't lose anyone for fourteen years. General, you did good, Sir."

"Thanks Skip. Make sure he gets taken care of," J.T. requested.

"Aye, aye Sir," was the automatic response.

"I would like to have my dinner, if that is okay with you, dear?" J.T. directed his comment to Heather.

"Thanks Skip, I owe you again," Heather said.

"No ma'am, you don't. It is an honor to help when needed," Skip replied.

Skip and the pub manager helped the man off the floor and escorted him to the front of the pub. Two waiters immediately came over and wiped up the table, reset the chairs and then scurried to get new napkins and silverware. The manager came over with a drink tray and replaced all their drinks and their waitress delivered their food order. The manager returned and profusely offered his apologies and explained that the tab would be taken care of. J.T. thanked him and apologized for causing a disturbance. He then asked that the police be called so that an accurate accounting of this event is on public record. The manager said he would do that at once. As J.T. and Heather started to eat their food when the manager came up and looked apologetically at J.T. and asked if he could ask a question about the aliens.

J.T. put his fork down and said, "Sure, ask away."

"You said, they were peaceful, and had been coming to earth for 10,000 years to see how we were doing. Are we related to them?"

"You know, the whole thing was so different from anything I have ever experienced that I did not think to ask that question. They have very little physical characteristics in common with us so my guess is that they have not involved themselves with our race. I think they have helped along the way with basic technology, like the wheel, internal combustion engine, the transistor, the microchip, but I do not think they have mated with humans. There are a gazillion questions that need to be asked but right now there are other priorities that come first. I'm sorry if that doesn't completely answer all your questions. Just know, I have the same questions and hopefully, I will get the opportunity to ask those questions and be able to get the answers that I can share with everyone. I do not know if or when that will happen, but I will do my best to get those answers for mankind."

The manager extended his hand and gave J.T. a hearty handshake and then shook Heather's hand also, thanking them for taking the time to answer his question.

As he walked off, Heather asked him, "Why didn't you just talk to the obnoxious man instead of brushing him off?"

J.T.'s answer was simple, "He was looking for an argument

and maybe a fight. I tried being polite and respectful but, if you noticed, that made no difference to him, even when I indicated to him, he was not going to like the outcome. There was no way this interaction was going to be stopped any other way. It's what happens when some people drink and get some liquid courage. They do things they normally wouldn't. Can I have a bite of your boxtie? I'll trade you a bite of my Shepard's pie," he asked.

"OK, deal," she replied, "This is really good, the gravy is to die for."

"I know. This boxtie is superb. Must come back here and each of us will order what the other had this time," J.T. suggested.

"That sounds like a deal." As they finished up, Skip came over and J.T. extended his hand.

"How does it feel, boss, to be the only man in the world to communicate with extraterrestrials?" Skip asked sincerely.

"Skip, I'll tell ya. If I would have known all the bullshit that was going to happen, I would have had someone else do it."

"General, you were the perfect choice. You are an honest, honorable, truthful man. I do not know of another man that could handle the job and do it with honor, poise and dignity. It was an honor and a pleasure to serve under you and if you ever need anything I would hope that my name would pop to the top of your list, and you would call upon me. I would have saluted you, but obviously neither of us are in uniform so allow me to shake your hand," Skip requested.

"Skip, I promise you your name will be the first one I think of. He extended his hand and gave Skip a heartfelt handshake that turned into a hug. Heather stood and gave him a kiss on the cheek as well as a good hug. Skip stood at attention until J.T. and Heather exited the pub. As soon as they stepped outside, two police officers approached them.

"General, I need a moment of your time to get your statement about the altercation that resulted in the injury to Mr. Roy Fitzhugh. J.T. gave them a clear, concise account of everything that occurred, including the attempted sucker punch and his response to it. At this point, the other officer came at J.T. from the side and tried to hit him. For the second time that night, there was an injured man lying on the ground and he never saw J.T. move. The senior officer was also caught unawares by the officer's move and J.T.'s response.

He stepped back and tried to decide what to do, J.T. stepped up to him and said, "If that was a test, to see if I can take care of someone trying to hit me, I guess you have an answer and you need to take your partner to the hospital to get treated. By the way, if there is any kind of media about this officer's injuries, and my name gets mentioned, you personally will rue the day you met and messed with me. I guarantee it. You have my statement. Good night, Officer."

"But I am not done," the officer protested.

"Yes, you are." J.T. took Heather's elbow and walked away, heading for their car.

"Wanna go to another bar for a nightcap?" J.T. asked.

"You are way too much excitement for one little woman to bear. Let's go home," Heather said sarcastically.

On the way home Heather said, "Is going out in public always going to be this way, beating people up, dressing down police officers, having people fawning all over you?"

"Gosh, I hope so. Makes for great memoirs," he replied.

"When are you going to find time to write your memoirs?"

"With you by my side when we are old and gray sitting by a fireplace rocking in a rocking chair," J.T. waxed philosophically.

"You must be talking about your other wife because, as they say, I will be shot in bed by a jealous wife," Heather responded.

"And where will I be?" J.T. queried.

"Gone by then, I assume," she said.

"Thanks, I would hate to have all the media attention," J.T. mocked, "I will keep that in mind."

CHAPTER
TWENTY-FOUR

He parked the car and went into the house. Heather asked J.T. to get a double Baileys on the rocks for her, while she got out of her clothes and into something more comfortable. J.T. poured them both a double Baileys on the rocks and went into the den and switched on some soft romantic music. He sipped his drink and relaxed, for the first time in a while. He had almost dropped off when he felt some soft lips graze his. He looked up and saw Heather dressed, in a Navy-blue lingerie outfit, accentuating her breasts and her butt. She grabbed her drink and took a very large swallow. She set the glass down and then straddled his outstretched legs grinding and scooting herself around, getting comfortable and situated. J.T. started to respond. He then looked around. Heather asked him who he was looking for and J.T. responded that he was keeping watch for a jealous wife. Heather playfully slapped his shoulder.

"She doesn't know I'm here, so you are safe," she said comfortingly.

"Thank God, I thought maybe I'd get shot mid-stroke," J.T. said, feigning worry. "Hard to concentrate with that hanging over my head."

"Hard is the operative word," she said, as she kissed him with a really intense sensual kiss throwing in a little additional grinding for good measure. He asked her to stand up, which she did pushing off on his upper thigh and groin. She then posed seductively. J.T. asked her to turn around very slowly, which she did better than any stripper on a pole. J.T. responded appropriately and he sure did stare, like a thirsty man at a glass of ice water. She stopped when her backside was directly pointed at him, muscles tight causing her buttocks to sit high and proud. *Yep, that was the finest ass he had ever seen.* He crooked his finger at her, calling her to him and she came. He was her man now and forever. She would always come when he called, willingly and immediately.

They both woke up at the same time the next morning and they both decided to work out together. Neither of them had anything scheduled so they spent most of the morning cleaning the house, doing laundry and catching up on the things that went undone while they were in Area 43. They decided to go to lunch over in Coulter believing that they would be shielded from pushy individuals like they incurred the other night at O'Malley's Pub. As they walked out to the car, a police cruiser was parked at the end of the driveway, effectively blocking them from leaving.

The two officers that got out of the cruiser started walking up the driveway. One was in uniform, with the rank of Captain and the other was in a suit.

"General Coulter? I am Captain Samuel Forrester, and this is Detective William Sloan. We would like a minute of your time because we have a few questions about the events of Tuesday night at O'Malley's."

"Very well, ask away," J.T. said, already getting annoyed.

"Could you go over the events as you recall them?" Sloan asked.

"I answered these questions, that night, to the two officers that interviewed us. Do you have questions other than what I have already answered? If not, then I see no reason to continue to have this conversation," J.T. stated quite firmly.

"Well Sir, there are questions about you assaulting one of the officers."

"Would that be about the officer taking the report or the one that attempted to hit me unprovoked?" J.T. said exerting more control over his response than he thought he needed to.

"The officer you injured." The captain asked.

"Ask your question," J.T. responded.

"Did you strike the officer that was injured?" the captain continued pressing the issue.

"No, I did not strike the officer in question," J.T. stated.

"Can you explain why he was injured."

"Yes, I can."

"So, explain."

"I was defending myself from an unprovoked attack." J.T. stated.

"Why were you the subject of an unprovoked attack?" Sloan asked.

"You will have to ask the officer," J.T. responded.

"We did, and he said you were confrontational and out of control and when he attempted to get you calmed down that was when you assaulted him."

"First, I had no interaction with that officer. He was six feet away from me. Second, I was not confrontational. I answered all the officer's questions with a civil tongue, normal tone of voice in a conversational level of volume. Do they have any evidence to support the accusation?" J.T. started going on the offensive.

"We have the two officer's words and account of the incident," the captain stated.

"Any recordings, audio or video of this alleged assault?" J.T. stated, pressing the offensive.

"None that we have at this time, was his response."

"Then it is their word against mine and the lady's, so if you do not mind, move your car so we can go about our business," J.T. finished with the officers.

"We may want you to come with us for further questioning," the captain said.

"I am not going anywhere with you. I have said all that needs to be said, so, unless you are going to arrest me, and if you are, you better have more than you currently have or when I finish with you and the department, you will be unemployed, and the department will be paying me a lot of money, for a very long time. So, what's it gonna be, huh?" J.T. stated with his usual command voice.

"We will be keeping an eye on you," Sloan said.

"You need to do a better job of training your officers. They are unprofessional and stupid to boot. From what I have just witnessed, stupidity seems to run wild through this department. I will be sure to mention it to the Mayor and the Chief Elder of the Council at my meeting with them later today. Now please move your squad car."

Heather was impressed with how well he kept his anger and his tongue under control. She was shaking a little from the whole intensity of the situation. J.T. mumbled under his breath about what an asshole the cops were.

"You sure were cool and calm back there," Heather said.

"I was struggling just a bit there at the end. They were starting to get under my skin," J.T. explained.

"Do you think it is over?" Heather asked.

"Probably not. I need to stop by O'Malley's on our way out of town. I want to see if they have an outside security camera that might have caught the action last night."

"I hadn't thought about that. You are a constant source of amazement, you know?" she replied.

The drive to O'Malley's only took a few minutes. As they walked up, hand in hand, J.T. pointed out two outdoor cameras. He released her and strode into the pub. The manager came over, immediately recognizing him, and asked him if there was anything he could do for him. J.T. explained what happened last night outside the pub, then asked if he could get a copy of the security disc from last night. He also mentioned that the police may be stopping by asking about everything that happened last night. J.T. told him to just tell the truth about what happened and not to worry, since no one did anything wrong.

The manager excused himself and went off to the back room to get the copy of the disc. Five minutes later, he returned, handed the disc to J.T. and apologized again for the events of last evening. J.T. assured him that there were no hard feelings, and that the food was excellent, and the service was great. He also let it slip that they would be coming back in the near future. J.T. walked out to the car, got in and headed off for Coulter. While the drive wasn't long, it was quiet and beautiful. He was going to miss this place and made a mental note to remember the fall weekend commitment.

———

Coulter was alive with green grass, colorful flowers and trees in full bloom, providing shade in strategic spots. There were a couple of dogs running around and the occasional cat sunning itself. There was the smell of cooking, heavy in the air as a few of the menfolk came out of the community house after eating their noon meal. They headed back to the different areas where they worked.

J.T. and Heather walked hand in hand to the door and opened it.

As they stepped inside, he said in a loud booming voice, "What's a man gotta do round here to get somethin' to eat?" As the ladies looked up from what they were doing.

Janice stood up with a full-face smile and said," depends on if they got their chores done. We don't feed lazy folk."

At that point, everyone stood and hurried over to give both of them hugs, kisses, handshakes and pats on the back, along with very warm, affectionate welcomes and greetings. J.T. and Heather were dragged, pulled and pushed into the room as everyone gathered around to hear what they had to say.

"Colonel, what brings you here? Anything wrong?" Janice asked.

"It ain't Colonel no more, Janice. He's a General now." Sara said.

Janice got a horrified look on her face saying, "I'm sorry, I didn't mean to offend you."

J.T. stood and said, loudly, "Ya'll don't have to call me General. J.T. is fine with me, after all, we are family, aren't we?"

Ralph stood, wiped his face with a napkin and said, "we done heard about them aliens you talked with. We gonna have ta fight 'em?"

There were murmurings running through the group when J.T. said that maybe someone ought to go round up as any of the folks as they could find, so he would only have to say stuff once. Meanwhile, could he and Heather please get something to eat as they were a mite hungry. They were semi-pushed into chairs, and within two minutes, there were plates with fried chicken, green beans, mashed potatoes with plenty of chicken gravy and biscuits pushed in front of them, and a very large glass of sweet tea for each. They both dove in with a ravenous vigor that surprised both of them. 15 minutes later, J.T. pushed himself back from the table and loudly belched, then apologized for it and followed that up with sincere compliments to all who prepared the day's fare. When he finished speaking, he looked around and realized the whole village was gathered around them.

"OK, everyone, grab a seat. I am going to answer questions but, please believe me, you will have more questions than I have answers. Let me start off by saying that I did not talk to a living alien. I communicated with a computer, with artificial intelligence. They do not talk like we do. They communicate with telepathy and the use of a device that looks like a headband. We communicated with thoughts. So, who wants to ask a question?" Ralph raised his hand and asked if they were here to conquer us.

"No, they visit to see how we are doing. Are we developing correctly? They have been coming here for more than 10,000 years.

"Where are they from?" Sara asked.

"I was in contact with the alien intelligence for about 30 seconds. I was not in contact long enough to ask many questions. This is all the information that I was able to get. I have some things to share with you and believe me when I say this. If what I am about to share with you ever gets out, the Council will retract the offer of the Quest. I have been offered a Quest. That Quest is to build a spacecraft and travel to another planet, taking colonists with me. Right now, I am just at the beginning of the project. I came here today for a couple of reasons. One was to tell all of you what was going on and to assure you that the DSF 17's twice yearly visits were going to continue, although I may not be with them every time and second, to get a good home cooked meal."

That brought a good-natured laugh along with a few "Darn rights, and you ain't kiddin's." The next questions were what was to be expected.

"Were you afraid? Did it mess with your head at all?" J.T. answered them truthfully and honestly. He decided that some of the more technical points were beyond their abilities to understand and were better left unsaid. The ladies that made lunch brought them dessert, blackberry pie and homemade vanilla ice cream. The womenfolk gathered round Heather asking her lots of questions about the wedding plans. Heather surprised them all by asking if it would be OK to have it in Coulter, outside, either late spring or early fall. She was not sure what she wanted. From the response she received, you would have thought that she had just given everyone there a winning lottery ticket.

All the ladies crowded around her, asking a myriad of questions. J.T. just sat back and allowed her to enjoy the attention. He was happy that the town had accepted her as unconditionally as they had. He never really expected anything less from the townsfolk. They had such good hearts. An hour or so later, J.T. indicated to Heather that they needed to go and get back home so they could get ready for tomorrow's flight back to Area 51. It took Heather the better part of 15 minutes to hug everyone and to hear everything each one had to tell her.

Heather was beaming the entire ride home. She chattered on the whole way home, going on and on about all the suggestions the women had given her.

She looked at J.T. and said," I can't believe how many of the women told me I had to make sure I gave you all the luvin' you wanted. I wonder why they said that?"

"I would guess because of the way they were raised, that it was a woman's responsibility to keep her man satisfied. Probably because that was the main reason for divorce and infidelity. You, my love, have nothing to worry about," J.T. explained.

CHAPTER
TWENTY-FIVE

As they pulled into their driveway, two police cruisers pulled in behind them. J.T. got out of the car and walked back towards the cruisers.

The occupants of the cruisers exited and surrounded J.T. "Is there something I can do for you, officers?"

"You can turn around and put your hands behind your back. You are under arrest." "For what, may I ask?"

"Assault on a police officer in the performance of his duties,"

"You sure you want to do this?" J.T. asked.

"You planning on assaulting me? I wish you would try. I don't take kindly to people assaulting my officers."

"Who are you?"

"Captain Wilkes, Division commander."

"Well Captain, when all of this is done, if you still want a chance to try me, you are welcome to bring it on. You are making a huge mistake, and it is going to cost you dearly."

"Are you threatening me, mister?"

"That's General to you, asshole." Heather got out of the car as she saw J.T. get handcuffed. She hurried over to where he was standing.

"What's going on?" she asked.

"Nothing, dear. Just another officer on the take. Please make a copy of the stuff we got on our way to Coulter, then call Skip, give it to him and ask him to come to the police department. May wish to call the Chief Elder and update him. Got all that?" he asked.

"Yes, dear," she replied.

"You think the Council is going to save you? General," the Captain said with disdain.

"They don't need to. They are going to end your career. Thank you very much." Heather retrieved the disc from the car, grabbed her phone then went in to the house. J.T. was placed in the car and they left the driveway on the way to the station. Heather got inside the house, made the copy of the disc, called Skip and told him what had happened and where she was so he could come and get the copy of the disc. She then called the Chief Elder and brought him up to date. He thanked her for the call. Heather sat down and was trying to make sense of all this. There was a knock on the door. Heather looked out the peephole and not recognizing the person on the other side, took three steps back and called out, "be right there". She quickly went into the den and grabbed J.T.'s handheld recorder, made sure there was a tape in, and it was working. She went to the door, acting like she was finishing getting dressed.

She opened the door and said, "Can I help you?"

"Maybe you can," was the response. "My name is Winston Heath. I am the editor of the paper."

"So, what?" she said with a lot of disdain in her tone.

"Did I just see General Coulter taken away in handcuffs?" Heath asked.

"What is it you want?" Heather said with an increasing amount of irritation in her voice.

"I had wanted an interview, but this is much better." Heath was positively drooling in anticipation of a story that would put General Coulter in a very bad light.

"You need to get out of this house right now. There is not going to be any interviews," Heather stated with newfound strength in her voice.

"Well then, I will just have to report what I have seen." Heath commented.

"Go right ahead and report whatever lies you wish. No one is stopping you. Now get out."

"You sure?" he said, with some incredulity in his voice.

"Get out or I will call the police," Heather threatened.

"Very well. Good day." When he turned to leave, Skip was standing in the door.

"Is there a problem, Miss Heather?" Skip asked.

"I am trying to get this man to leave, but he seems reluctant to go," she explained.

"Do you require assistance getting out of the door because I am more than happy to give you a hand sir," Skip said with his intense voice.

"No, I am capable of getting out of the door," Heath replied.

"Then why have you not left yet?" Skip asked.

"I was waiting to see if the lady changes her mind."

"He needs a hand Skip, he obviously does not understand English, even being an editor." With that, Skip grabbed Heaths' wrist, twisted it so it was bent up behind his back, grabbed his collar with the other hand and muscled him out the door, throwing him to the ground.

Skip looked at him, laying on the ground, and said, "I think you have decided to screw with the wrong people. I would strongly suggest you leave it and them completely alone. Are we clear?"

Hearing no answer, he lifted him up, got right up in his face, and said clear as day, "You sir, are one dumb son-of-a-bitch, you know that? Either that, or you must really like pain and suffering." He lifted him up, then let him fall back on the ground. He then took out his phone and called the police.

"Please send a car to this address, as we have a trespasser that refuses to get off private property. Yes, we will press charges. Thank you." Skip said.

Skip hung up and looked at Heather. A couple of minutes later, a squad car arrived and Heather happened to notice that these were the same two officers as she had seen at O'Malley's Pub. She called Skip over and took out her phone and started recording the officers' interaction with Heath. She told Skip that these were the same two officers that had assaulted J.T. outside the pub.

"Skip, just watch everything they do. There's something fishy going on," she explained.

The officers came up to Skip and said, "Sir, this man says you assaulted him."

Skip responded, "The homeowner had requested this person get out of her house because she felt threatened. When he refused to leave, she asked me to help him get out of the house.

I asked him to get out, and he refused, so I helped him get out of the door."

"He says that you did not give him a chance to leave."

"He's lying. We have him recorded." Heather stepped up and played the recorded occurrence for the officers to hear.

They looked at Heath and said, "Winston, I think you had better leave the premises. They have proof and you don't this time. Nothing we can do to help you. Ma'am do you wish to press charges?"

"Yes, I do." was Heather's reply.

"Winston, you are under arrest for trespassing. Turn around and put your hands behind you. Sorry, we can't help you this time."

Heather looked at both of them and said, "what did you mean by that? Sorry you could not help him this time?"

"Nothing, nothing at all." Heather was glad she had not turned off the recorder. She looked at Skip and whispered,

"I think that Heath is controlling or paying these two. Please be sure to pass that on to J.T. when you see him."

"Yes ma'am, I will," was Skip's response.

Skip went out to the car and headed to the police station. He arrived 20 minutes later and parked the car. When he went inside, he looked around for some kind of directions when an officer stopped him and asked him what he was doing there. When he mentioned General Coulter, the officer took him by the elbow and led him down to an office he would never have found, even with directions. Skip knocked on the door and then entered the room. J.T. was sitting on a chair in the corner. Sitting at the desk was the captain that had arrested J.T.

"Who are you?" he asked.

"Skip Johanson, Sergeant Major DSF17," was the reply. "Who are you and why are you holding the General?" Skip demanded.

"I am Captain Wilkes, Division Commander," was his answer.

"And a 4-0 idiot," was thrown in by J.T.

"You ain't making your case any easier," the captain said, looking at J.T.

"General, I have a copy of the stuff you got this morning," Skip said to J.T.

"What's that, Johansen?" Skip looked over at J.T. with a quizzical look.

"It's okay, Sergeant Major. Let him have it. I have the original, so it doesn't matter if he destroys the evidence," J.T. said.

"What evidence is that?" the captain said in a derisive tone.

"The evidence that proves your officers are lying and on the take. A copy of a security camera outside O'Malley's Pub that recorded the entire interaction that night. Sergeant Major, please contact the Chief of police and ask him to come down here for the showing. Remember how I told you that you were making a mistake and that there would be a reckoning? Well, that time has come. Not all suspects are guilty or liars. You aren't very good at telling one from the other. Get the Chief down here now," J.T. commanded.

Twenty minutes later, the Chief and his deputy Chief entered the room.

J.T. stood, extended his handcuffed hands, and introduced himself. "I am General Coulter. I am in the process of being arrested and booked on a phony charge with no investigation by Captain Wilkes. I have a video recording of the event from the outside security camera of the establishment, a recording that Captain Wilkes never looked for nor even considered might have existed, indicating he is not fit for the rank of Captain.

"You are welcome to watch it. It will also show that at least two of your patrol officers are on the take from someone, most likely Winston Heath, managing editor of the newspaper. He is pissed at me because I refused to give him an exclusive interview concerning my interaction with extraterrestrial life. My fiancée has a recording from a couple of hours ago where the same two officers came to my house, when she asked Mr. Winston Heath to leave the property, he refused and she had to enlist the aid of Sergeant Major Johansen, the man sitting right behind you, to physically remove him. The recording captures the officers telling Mr. Heath that they could not help him out this time."

The deputy Chief put the disc in a player and turned on the player. All three of the officers sat and watched as the disc showed the unprovoked attack on J.T. and the speed with which he was dispatched. J.T. stopped the disc and struck his arms out.

"Get these off me, now," J.T. commanded.

The Chief nodded and the deputy Chief reached into his pocket and took out a handcuff key and removed the cuffs. J.T. rubbed his chafed wrists and put them through some range of motion exercises.

J.T. then spoke out. "Now that I have proved my position, I expect all paperwork alluding to my guilt to be turned over to me. I no longer trust the police to act truthfully or honorably. Next, I expect some severe discipline of Captain Wilkes, and an appointment in the gymnasium with him. I also expect the two officers involved to be charged and incarcerated. Next, I expect you to start investigations using outside investigators to see how deep the corruption goes. Next, I want Winston Heath arrested and convicted. Next, I am going to advise the Chief Elder of the Council. He may have things he also will require done before things are over. Am I clear, Chief? If not, I will be happy to repeat things until you are crystal clear. I have spent over twenty years protecting this dome and the people in it. I would hate to think I should have been protecting them from you and this police force."

The Chief had never been dressed down, in front of subordinates, in a manner that made him feel completely incompetent.

All he could say was, "I am sorry for the way you have been treated and I think the things you outlined will be started on, as soon as we are through here. I am a little unclear about the gym thing, though."

"I promised him I was going to kick his arrogant, ignorant ass from here to next week. He seems to think he can bully suspects or others that he has interactions with, and I am going to knock him down a couple of notches and probably hurt him a bit. He will still be able to find work when he heals up, but not in law enforcement," J.T. said.

"I told him this would happen, and I am a man of my word. Just ask my troops," J.T. stated.

Skip threw in his two cents saying, "The General has always told the troops the truth regardless of whether or not it made someone feel bad. He has always kept his word on every single thing he has ever promised the troops and I have served under him for 19 ½ years."

J.T. finished his comments by saying, "Set the appointment for 0600 hours. I will be there. Captain, I expect to see you there. Do you understand me?"

J.T. stood, pushed the eject button so he could retrieve his disc and then he was followed closely by Skip, who held the door for him.

As they left, Skip turned and said, "I sure am glad I am not you. Things are gonna get ugly and painful. From what I can see, it needs to."

On the way out to the car, Skip said, "General, I have to say that I am glad you unloaded on them. Makes you wonder how many people have been screwed by the department but never had the power to do anything about it until they messed with the wrong guy. Now maybe we will get this cleaned up."

J.T. turned to him and said, "Thanks Skip, for all your help today and in the past. You have been a loyal and true friend, and it has been a real pleasure to have you as part of my team. You will be expected to be one of my groomsmen once the boss has told me when I am going to marry her."

Skip chuckled and even blushed a little.

"I would be honored, Sir. At least she is smart enough to know what is going on. She's a keeper, Sir."

"That she is Skip, that she is. Let's get out of here."

The drive home was relatively quick. J.T. shook Skip's hand as he got out of the car and walked to the back door entrance to the house. Heather met him right inside the door with a hug and a very tender kiss.

"Are you alright? Is it over?" she asked.

"I am okay, and it won't be over until tomorrow morning,"

he replied. "Excuse me, I need to make a quick call. I'll be right back." He walked into the den, pulled out his phone and dialed.

"Skip, I need you to be present tomorrow. Get a video camera, sniper rifle with red dot scope and a silencer. I want you at the gym at 5:00 am, up high, with complete vision. I do not trust the captain. I halfway expect him to bring those two cops, either with him or setting a trap, waiting for me to enter. I want everything recorded. Keep me always covered. Thanks."

Heather was standing at the door, listening to the whole conversation. After he had hung up, she entered and came up behind him and hugged him.

"So, what's going on?" she asked.

"I am supposed to meet the captain tomorrow morning in the gym, where I promised him I was going to kick his ass. I showed the video to the Chief of police and told him that if he did not clean up his department, I would share things with the Chief Elder and the Council. I was just covering my bases," he responded.

"You are not going to get hurt *teaching him a lesson*, are you?" There was genuine concern in her voice.

"Sweetheart, I do not trust them, so I am taking precautions. Try not to worry."

"I can't help it. I just worry that something unplanned will happen, and everything you are trying to do will be for naught," Heather said.

"I sure as hell don't want to give up my dream, but I do have principles, that I am not about to set them aside either," J.T. said. "What do you want for supper? I am starved."

"How about a steak, salad, and some veggies?" Heather asked.

"Sounds wonderful. I'll get the grill going. Pick whatever veggie you want and put it in the sink for me to wash and prep. There is some salad in the fridge, so all that needs is to be plated. Do you want some sweet potatoes?"

"That sounds wonderful," was the quick response.

J.T. took out a couple of sweet potatoes, washed them off, and popped them in the microwave. The grill was heating up nicely and would be ready for the ribeye's he had taken out of the meat keeper. Heather had chosen asparagus, so he washed it and put it in the drainer. He seasoned the steaks with his own seasoning mixture and put them on the grill. He cut the asparagus stems off, set them in the steamer, put the lid on and set the timer. J.T. loved marking steaks with a diamond, as he rotated the steaks, at the three-minute mark, Heather had filled the salad plates, added croutons and set out three different salad dressings, set the table and got cloth napkins. The asparagus was done as were the sweet potatoes. The smell of the cooking steaks wafted its way through the kitchen and into the dining room, causing Heather's mouth to salivate. J.T. walked into the dining room carrying a platter with the two steaks on it, still sizzling.

She asked if he would like a glass of red wine and he replied, "Merlot would be nice."

"One Merlot coming up," was her reply.

J.T. finished carrying the veggies and sweet potatoes into the dining room, setting them on the maple dining room table. They each helped themselves, said grace and clinked glasses in a toast to themselves, then dived in on dinner. There wasn't a lot of conversation during dinner. They were both too busy eating since neither had eaten all day. After a satiating meal, they took their glasses of wine and went into the den to relax.

Most of the conversation was about the things that were going to happen over the next thirty days, specifically, harvesting the Irbadinium from the Van Allen Radiation belt and possibly a quick trip to the moon to get the mining of Vladerium as well as bringing back a good size load so the refining process could be started, as a first step to making the outer hull of the spacecraft. He pulled his diagram of the spacecraft up on the computer so Heather could start to wrap her mind around the concept and get to start critically thinking about the craft.

Heather was seeing the design for the first time and was a little overwhelmed by the amount of thought and effort that J.T. had put into drawing and designing a craft of this size, complexity, and functionality. *My admiration for my man keeps growing day by day. He continues to amaze me. Our future is going to be a really wild ride.* She leaned over and gave him a hug and a kiss on the cheek.

"I had no idea what this was going to look like. This is mind-blowing. It's kinda hard to wrap my head around the enormity of this project, and it was all done by you. I am amazed and blown away by what I am seeing," Heather said with a bit of awe in her voice.

J.T. responded matter-of-factly, "This is just a jumping off point. I am not sure what the final product will look like. I have asked Dad to run a copy of all this through the computer in the spacecraft and to ask it to suggest design changes it would recommend based on its knowledge of space flight, engine performance, mission, and functionality. I haven't even shown you the interior design layout of the entire ship. There are 23 floors in the middle of the ship, that will house living quarters, mess halls, gyms, libraries, medical facilities, armories, workspaces, laboratories: 15 tube-like structures, 300 feet long, 50 foot in diameter. Each tube is going to have something different in it. They will be internally divided into three floors. They will house hibernation units, livestock, crops that will be grown while in space. Water, oxygen. Equipment for farming, seeds, trees, livestock waste to use as fertilizer."

"Smelting and metal working area to be able to repair the ship, in the event that there is a need to repair the hull of the ship inflight. Some of them will be purely for storage of several pieces of equipment. There are going to be spaces for a complete second computer system that is not going to be connected to the main computer system, unless it is needed. It could be connected to the ship's main computer system in the event of damage or an emergency, and at least 10 miniature nuclear reactors, five or six of which will be online at any given time. The others will be reserves or used for the ship's weapons and force field systems. The hand drawing of this ship is 225 pages long, that includes air systems, electrical systems, computer systems, water systems, waste detoxification systems, personal storage areas, crawl spaces", he said. "If I printed it out, it would take more than a week to go through everything."

"That is why having the alien computer review it and make changes should make things much easier," he continued. They sat there for another hour before J.T. indicated he needed to get to bed since he needed to be at the top of his game tomorrow morning. So, after cleaning up the kitchen, making coffee for the morning, they both went to bed.

CHAPTER
TWENTY-SIX

The alarm went off at 4:15 am, J.T. had already been awake for ten minutes. He dressed quietly, kissed Heather on the forehead, and made his way out to the car. He called Skip and made sure he was going to have a communication device on him, so J.T. could be apprised of the situation inside the gym before he entered. J.T. stopped at the unit and went into the locker room to change into the clothing he would wear to the gym. He also decided to wear the newest issued body armor. The body armor was very lightweight, and resistant to most of the caliber of bullets used by police as well as being resistant to knife attacks. J.T. was surprised by how light the material felt. He hoped that the captain had again underestimated whom he was dealing with, and that would give J.T. a huge advantage. J.T. stretched himself out, went through a couple of katas to relax, focus, and limber himself up in preparation for his interaction with the captain. He got out and got in the car and drove himself to the gym, where he was supposed to meet his opponent.

He scanned the parking lot and noted that there were no other cars other than his.

Guess the captain backed out of the challenge, he thought. "Skip, status report. Over."

"Skip here. At this point I see no bad guys inside the gym. Got the whole place to myself. Over."

"Roger, stay put. Will give him a few more minutes. Over," J.T. said.

"Wilco."

J.T. walked over to the gym door and stepped inside the gym. He turned to the right and started flipping switches on the bank of switches located there. He squinted as he looked around the open area, trying to see if there was anyone there. From the other side of the gym, in a darkened corner, came a voice J.T. recognized.

"I didn't think you had the balls to show up. I want to thank you for all the trouble you have caused. I am going to enjoy this. May have lost my job, but whipping you really good, will soften the blow a bit, I think."

"Step into the light if you dare, and let's get started. I have more important things to do today," J.T. challenged.

The captain stepped out into the light. J.T. noticed he was keeping his left arm behind him.

"You need some kind of a weapon to take me on? Bring it on. Just remember the old saying, 'you better be able to use whatever you bring to a fight, cause, if you can't, it'll get taken away from you, and you will get beaten with it'. You are a big, fat bully that is used to pushing people around, using your position as a police officer to make people do what you want. Guess what? you picked on the wrong guy," J.T. spat out.

J.T. continued to advance on his opponent, causing the captain to start backing up. That was the wrong thing to do. It makes you a backpedaling pedestrian, not a combatant. J.T. was pleased to see this happening. He continued his careful, guarded advance, watching for any hint of a trap or a sudden assault move. He heard in his ear, "You have movement in the shadows to your right, over." J.T. kept his focus directed at the captain but did note the movement to his right.

"I kinda figured you were gonna bring help. Get your attack dogs out in the open so I can see them."

The police officer that had attacked J.T. outside the pub moved out of the darkened corner and into the light. J.T. noticed that there was more movement in the same corner and called him out too.

"Now that all the cowards are out where they can be seen, bring it on," J.T. again challenged.

J.T. looked at the first cop and said, "I guess you didn't get enough the first time around. I won't be as easy on you this time."

There was a prolonged moment of hesitation in the first cup, which allowed J.T. to strike first. He was thinking of the rules of street fighting a self-defense instructor had taught him back when he was just 20 years old. Strike first the hardest, the fastest and don't stop until the opponents can't fight back. J.T. snap kicked him in the stomach, causing him to bend over. He stepped in and hit him in the back of the neck with an elbow strike while raising his knee, hitting him in the face as the neck blow drove him to the floor. He lay on the floor, out of the fight.

"J.T. spun and returned to his original position, advancing on the captain. The second officer rushed from the area behind the fallen officer. J.T. planted his right leg, kicked straight into the left knee. There was a sickening snap that was audible. The forward motion of the assault immediately stopped as the knee buckled, unable to support the weight of its owner. J.T. grabbed a handful of hair, lifting his assailant's chin and punched him right in the throat. Not enough power to crush the windpipe, but enough for him to know his part of the fight was over.

J.T. made sure he was down by kicking him in the groin. A sixth sense told J.T. to duck at that second, and he did as the baton passed right through the space that his head had just occupied. J.T. pivoted and launched a two-handed eye strike, gouging at the captain's eyes. There was a roar of pain from that strike, along with a lessening of the grip on the baton. J.T applied a reverse grip on the baton and exerted his full strength and weight on the grip. There was a snapping of several bones in the left hand and forearm. He took the baton and struck the captain on both shins, breaking both tibias, causing him to drop to the floor. J.T. dropped to a knee and drove a straight punch to his rib cage, breaking ribs. He then drove a second blow to his solar plexus, taking all the wind out of his sails.

He leaned over the captain and whispered, "I could have killed all of you and I would never have been prosecuted because I have a man videotaping all of you and it is clearly 3 to 1. I told you, you fucked with the wrong man. As you limp for the rest of your life, you will remember the ass whipping I just gave you and your clowns. I suggest you move somewhere else where they don't know you. I can do this to you again if I need to, and don't ever forget it."

"Skip, come down, we are leaving," J.T. commanded.

"Roger, wilco."

Skip came down the ladder and walked over to where they were all laying. They saw the video camera and his sniper rifle.

J.T. looked at them and said, 'You are lucky none of you brought a knife or gun today. You would have died where you stood, all of you. Skip, let's go. I'm hungry and I am buying."

"Aye, aye General."

CHAPTER
TWENTY-SEVEN

After they were all done having breakfast, Skip and Heather cleaned up the kitchen while J.T. went in and took a shower. When he was done and dressed, he came out into the kitchen and reminded Heather that they were flying to Area 51 in an hour and a half. Heather excused herself to go finish packing. That left Skip and J.T. alone.

"Skip, if you have any issues from this morning, be sure to call me ASAP. Do not try to deal with it on your own. Do not allow them to take you to the police station for any kind of questioning. Be sure to watch out for Heath. He has money, no scruples, a long memory, and a vengeful nature. I am serious. Leave him to me if the situation arises. Are we clear on this?" he asked sternly.

"Aye, aye General," was Skip's reply.

"Heather, are you ready to go? We are supposed to be taking off at 1100 and I still have preflight to do before we can leave."

"I am ready right now. So, let's go," was her response. J.T.

gave Skip a hug and Heather gave him a kiss on the cheek. They all exited the house and got into their cars.

Skip went on his way while J.T. and Heather went on theirs. 15 minutes later, they arrived at the airport, parked the car and were met by the airplane crew chief who showed them to the dressing rooms, where they got into their flight suits. J.T. went out with the crew chief and started the preflight checklist on the outside of the plane. He then boarded the plane and did the cockpit preflight. The crew chief stowed both of their suitcases and then helped Heather get situated in her seat, which in fact was an ejection seat. She put on her helmet and the chief hooked up the oxygen lines and checked her face mask. The chief went forward and double checked J.T.'s ejection seat, oxygen hook-up, gave J.T. a thumbs up and indicated that as soon as he got the door closed, J.T. could start the engines.

Within 10 minutes J.T. was sitting at the threshold of the runway awaiting clearance for takeoff. The tower gave him clearance and reminded him he had to use computer approach and landing at Area 51. J.T. acknowledged the instructions and radioed he was on the way to cruising altitude of 60,000 feet. Two hours and fifteen minutes later, J.T. was contacted by Groom Lake control. He switched on the computer at the frequency they sent him and let go of the yoke and throttle. The computer executed a perfect approach and as soon as the wheels touched down, the computer disengaged and J.T. completed the landing.

He followed the Jeep on the runway with the blue flashing light and was directed to a covered aircraft parking area. The airman doing the directing signaled him to shut off the engines and a crew chief came up to the aircraft and attached the ladder, opened the storage hatch, and unloaded the suitcases. He helped Heather climb down the ladder, then popped to attention and saluted until J.T. stepped down and returned the salute. A Captain came up and offered to carry the suitcases, but J.T. declined. They were shown to a golf cart that would carry them to the entrance that was closer to the quarters they had been assigned on their previous visit.

The whole clan was there when they walked in and there was a round of hugs and kisses when Sean said they had asked the mess Chief if they could eat a little later than usual because the General was due in around 1400. The Mess Chief was more than happy to oblige the General. The word had gotten around that the General was a good, down-to-earth kinda guy who only expected people to do their jobs correctly and didn't have any time for micromanagement and nitpicking bullshit.

They all walked into the mess and took their seats. The Mess Chief entered and handed everyone a menu and made sure to give J.T. his menu and welcomed him back and told him he had been missed. J.T. thanked him and said it was nice to be back. The family all made their orders and sat back waiting for J.T. to bring them up to date on everything that happened while they were back at Dome 17.

J.T. went through the press conference, the going to the pub and having to deal with a drunk asshole, about being assaulted by the police officer (unprovoked he might add), the being arrested for assaulting the police officer, having to deal with the newspaper editor who bribed the drunk and the police officers because he wanted to have leverage in order to get an exclusive interview for which he was blown off and the arrest by a Dome police Captain that was also on the take from the newspaper editor, as well as the ass whipping he had given that captain just that morning.

"But, other than Mrs. Lincoln, how was the play?" That brought a chuckle from the crowd. Helen asked J.T. if he had gotten hurt this morning, to which J.T. replied "Of the four people in the fight, the captain had brought a couple of men to be sure that I was taught a lesson, but after all was said and done, a number of them would remember this morning every time it rained," he said. Helen said she didn't understand, so Frank had to explain that there were a number of broken bones that they had suffered because they did not know who they were messing with.

"I also showed the Chief of Police a video of them attacking me and me defending myself and I told him if he didn't clean up his department including firing the captain and the two officers that I would personally tell the Chief Elder and the Council how he was running his department and that charges should be filed against all 3. Also, they should have their police credentials revoked. But enough about all that. How are things going here?" J.T. asked.

Helen started in and said that she, "had instructed the computer to run a full pre-flight engine scan. This was done, and it found a few minor things that I instructed it to fix. Fuel status is such that there is enough fuel to fly in space for about 10 days. It also said that it has a built-in scoop to use when it needs to get fuel when in flight. Apparently, there are latches and other fastening areas that are retracted during normal flight. I did not ask what the max load was the last time I interfaced with it. Sorry."

Frank started with, "I managed to get the computer linked

with the one we created from everything the Council sent us. Before you ask, it has already been converted to the metric system, including all the specs for everything in the craft. The setup computer has CAD ability. The only issue I have is that there is no way to scan anything into the alien computer. It does not have that capability, nor does it have any intention of changing its programming to accommodate human beings' needs. It was quite clear on that."

"OK, thanks Dad," J.T. replied with a suppressed smile. He then looked at Sean, waiting for his update.

"I have checked with the CO, and he has an unused area that has plenty of power and can accommodate the fabrication of parts of the ship, including the smelting process. The only issue is where we are actually going to assemble the spacecraft. We have areas where we can build components, but there is nowhere we can put the whole thing together, plus having the ability to allow the finished product to take off. The manufacturing areas do not have access to the outside world like the areas the current alien craft are housed in. The designers of this base did not think that far ahead. They thought they had already considered and addressed everything with the current design," Sean said.

J.T. stood and looked over at the group. He was really pleased and proud of everything that had been done in his absence.

He said, "I want to thank each of you for all you have accomplished. It has laid the foundation for the next step in this mission. I have a couple of questions. Number 1, Anybody have any ill effects being connected to the alien computer? And second, how long were each of you actually in contact with the computer?"

Helen started first. "I just noticed I got very fatigued after, oh say, maybe, 30 minutes in the beginning. I mean fatigued, to the point I needed a two-hour nap. I was gradually able to work up to two hours of computer time yesterday without the need for a two-hour nap, but I did have to lay down and close my eyes for an hour."

Frank said, "That goes for me also, but I was able to get to three hours before I had to stop and rest. Otherwise, the only thing I am noticing is that I think a lot more clearly. Things come to me quicker. It's almost like my brain has been cleaned, dusted, and vacuumed out. I don't think I am forgetting anything, but definitely clearer headed."

Helen remarked, "Now that you mentioned it, dear, I would have to say that I feel mentally sharper and more focused as well."

"OK, but no one is feeling any negative side-effects, is that correct?" J.T. asked. They both answered that they had not noticed anything negative.

"Good. Here's what I have planned and need to accomplish soonest. Sean, please contact the Council and get the status of the moon mining operation. Try to get some kind of idea as to when we can expect the arrival of the first load of the Vladinium. That way we can be sure to have the refining process up and ready to start as soon as it arrives."

"Mom, please check with the computer to see if all the repairs have been completed and find out if we must make any adjustments to the craft to have human passengers, oxygen, toilet facilities, food, etcetera. And how much of the Irbadinium the scoop and storage tank can hold, and how long would that amount allow four or six engines to fly in space before needing to refuel."

"OK," was her reply.

"Dad, I am going to need you to run an electrical cord inside the spacecraft and set my laptop up in there. What I am going to try to do is look at each page of my design while I am connected to the craft's computer and have the computer get the info from my brain. Then the computer can digest it, correct the designs with the knowledge it has about interstellar space flight and faster than light velocity experience, then print out the new design and specifics for construction on the CAD of the new computer you just built. Before you do anything in the spacecraft, please be sure that there is a large supply of blueprint paper available and in the CAD, so there are no glitches when the computer in the spacecraft is ready to give us answers. Would hate to have to do all this twice cuz we were not prepared."

"Sean, please find out if any of the engineers that had anything to do with the construction of Area 43 are here, so we can see what it is going to take to construct a place where we can assemble the UDASS SEEKER. I just named the ship," J.T. said. "Of course, we will need to be able to take off from that spot. It will need to be completely enclosed so it can be worked on 24/7/365 regardless of the weather. There will need to be attached storage facilities and housing, employees' mess. We should be able to access the bases entertainment and gym facilities. We will worry about the crews after everything gets designed and supplies are ready to go. In the meantime, we can do things like making the pieces of the ship, getting it ready for assembly. So, go."

"Shannon, I need to have you keeping track of everything on paper. You are the glue that holds everything together, so I don't want you thinking that everyone else is more important than you. That's not true. This is a team effort, and EVERYONE plays an integral part, and no one is irreplaceable or indispensable, or better than another. Never forget that, OK? So, start taking copious notes. The Council is going to want to know what is going on, so remember that when you forward your notes to them, OK?" J.T. said.

Shannon had not heard that J.T. felt the way he did and was taken aback.

Heather looked at J.T. and said, "I can see why you are in command. you don't miss anything. You think of everything, and leave no stone left unturned. I am really impressed. Now what do you need me to do?"

"While I am in the craft hooked up to the computer, you are going to be hooked up to the computer to see if there is any medical information you can get that we may be able to use, like gene therapy. OK?"

"Really, you really want me to interact with an alien computer?" she asked incredulously.

"Yes, I do. Before you get hooked up, I need to have you write down your questions, and have paper and pen available to write down answers. Try not to think of them as aliens. It may be taken as an insult and then they may stop helping to pay us back for the insult. Understand?" J.T. said. Heather nodded her understanding and agreement.

"Let's get back to the room, get settled, then head over to the spacecraft and get linked up," J.T. said.

Heather nodded and together they got up from the table, exited the officer's mess and headed down the hall to their quarters. When they arrived, before he opened the door to their suite, J.T. put his index finger to his lips.

He moved alongside Heather and whispered in her ear, "don't enter and don't speak until I tell you it's OK."

He entered the room and started searching, checking the lights, decorations, the entire bathroom, where he found one bug, then he searched the bedroom, bed, bedside tables, chairs and dresser, where he found a second bug. He also found a video camera lens in the clock face on the wall. He stepped outside the room, showed her what he had found and then waved her in. Out loud he said,

"Let's get everything put away and get back together with everyone else before we head down to the spacecraft."

Heather responded, "OK, I'm gonna change into something a little looser, since I am going to be sitting for a while longer."

So off she went to the bathroom. J.T. got out of his khakis and into a set of fatigues. He put the bugs and video camera in his pocket. They headed out the door and down the hall when J.T. stopped and excused himself and said, "I'll be back in a few minutes," and walked off.

He made his way to the CO's office. As he entered, he told the secretary to have the XO come to the Colonel's office. He knocked on the door and entered when he was told to come in. Colonel Farmouth immediately stood and saluted.

"General, welcome back. I heard you had returned. Sorry I did not meet you at the ramp."

"Relax Colonel, I am not here about military protocol. I have asked the XO to join us. There is a real problem here and we need to get to the bottom of it and get it corrected immediately."

There was a knock at the door and the Colonel said, "enter."

"XO reporting as requested. Nice to see you again General." J.T. reached into his pocket and pulled all the devices he had found in his quarters. He looked at both of the men standing in front of him.

"I thought that I had already addressed this issue, yet as soon as I get back, I find my quarters were re-bugged. Colonel, I believe that I told you, just before I left, that there was a leak here. Now I am wondering whether or not there is an espionage problem. Clearly, the issue has not been addressed. As of now, anyone that came within 100 yards of my quarters is to be polygraphed and if that test is not 100% clean, they will be interrogated using chemical methods. Are we clear on this? When I got to Dome 17, I had people asking me what it was like talking to aliens. This was before the press conference. I want to know how this information left this base before I did. Am I clear? Find out who did this ASAP. If you can't tell, I'm pissed. Get to it. Dismissed,"

He turned and walked out the door, slamming it behind himself. The CO and XO were both pasty white and had cold sweat running down their faces. Neither could remember the last time they had their collective asses chewed by a General. They both understood that if this was not corrected as soon as possible, both would be transferred to bases, in the middle of nowhere, that had no prestige being associated with being assigned there. Basically, the end of their careers. J.T. was still fuming when he arrived at the section where the spacecraft was being housed. He apologized to the group without going into everything, but he did pull all of them together and told them to check their rooms for bugs and video cameras again and to bring them to him if they found any.

Obviously, this information upset everyone, but they quickly put it behind them and got back to the job at hand. J.T., Heather, Helen, and Frank all entered the spacecraft. J.T sat in the central commander's chair, Helen to his left and Frank to his right. Heather stood just behind J.T. Frank handed J.T. his laptop and J.T. logged in to his file that had the spacecraft design in it. Once he was signed in, He picked up the headband, placed it on his head, adjusted it and set back and tried to clear his mind and relax. Within five seconds, there was a tingling sensation in his temples that intensified for just a few seconds, then there was a sense of calm.

Then, the voice inside his head said, "welcome back General Coulter. It has been a while since you were in contact. I hope you are well."

J.T. replied, "Yes it has. I am well, thank you. I have a task that I need your assistance with. You have a vast array of knowledge concerning spacecraft design, propulsion, interstellar travel, faster than light speed, and spacecraft composition, that I do not have. I have designed a spacecraft that is based on knowledge and information from the limited actual experience of our own space program. I will look through the designs, you may obtain the information from my mind, then design a spacecraft, with all specifications, from which we will be able to construct a craft, that we can attempt interstellar space travel in, with the highest likelihood of success.

"Please use a design that incorporates both four and six engines from the spacecraft we already have here from previous crashes. By the way Helen Coulter requested a complete preflight scan and correction of any discrepancies found. Has that been accomplished?"

"Yes, General that has been done. This craft is ready for flight. May I ask where the intended destination is?"

"The Van Allen radiation belt. We will be going there to harvest Irbadinium. How much is this vehicle able to harvest and return to earth?"

"Approximately 200 kilograms."

"How many engines will that power and for how long?"

"Six of our engines at 80% output for two of your years."

"Is that enough to get us to your home world or will we require inflight refueling?"

"It will either require a larger amount being harvested, approximately two kilotons, or a refuel about 69% of the way there."

"For this upcoming flight, will there be any accommodations necessary for a human flight crew?"

"The atmosphere composition will need to be adjusted to support human existence. The computer replied.

"Please start making those adjustments now," J.T. ordered.

"Very well. Completed."

"I am about to visually scan my spacecraft designs. Are you ready to accept this information?" J.T. queried.

"Standing by."

"Beginning now." J.T. looked over each page slowly to not miss the subtlest detail.

"Am I scanning too fast or too slow for you?"

"You may scan faster. I will inform you if you need to slow down."

"Speeding up." J.T. started moving faster through each page of the design and in a fairly short time, he had completed scanning the whole design.

"When you have completed your changes to the design, you may export that information to the CAD section of the computer we have constructed per your recommendation, so we may print out the blueprint," J.T. said.

"Done."

"Can you tell me where your home world is?"

"Terra Prime is located in the Tau Centauri system, 4th planet from the star. It has a twin of Terra Prime, Terra Prime 2, which is located on the exact opposite side of the star. The two planets never see each other, ever, unless it is from a spacecraft. The civilization from Terra Prime split into two factions, one that revered science, arts, intellect and the other felt that militarism, conquest and domination were the civilization's destiny. They destroyed each other. Those from Terra Prime chose to branch out into the universe to seek out new civilizations and to help whenever the new one seemed to be going down the wrong road. We have been successful in saving quite a few civilizations."

"Did you include the formula for the exterior hull in the designs?"

"Of course."

"I'm hoping to go on the harvesting mission in 24 hours. I assume you will be able to pilot and navigate this mission?"

"Yes, General, I am programed for all of those functions."

"Signing off, turning this headset over to Dr. Heather

Dunkirk. She has never been in contact with you, so please take it easy on her."

"Of course, General." J.T. took the headband off and stretched his arms out to the side. How long was I in contact with the computer?" he asked.

"A little over 43 minutes," Heather replied.

"Felt longer," J.T. commented.

"Heather, please have a seat in this chair," patting the head-rest on the chair he just got out of.

"Put the headband on. There will be a tingling over your temples that will slowly increase for a few seconds, then it will dissipate. Identify yourself and tell the computer how it is to refer to you. Just speak normally inside your mind. The computer will do the rest. Do you have your questions and material to write down the answers?" J.T. asked.

"Yes, I do," she replied.

"Just try to relax. It is not going to try to take over your brain or make you into something you are not, so don't worry. OK?" J.T. said, trying to calm her fears and concerns.

"Ready," Heather said with a bit of tentativeness in her voice.

Heather sat in the chair for the first time and was a little overwhelmed which, fortunately, passed quickly. She slipped on the headband and tried to relax. She was a little surprised at the intensity of the tingling she felt in her temples, but was reassured when she felt J.T.'s hand rest on her shoulder and give her a little squeeze.

"I am Dr. Heather Dunkirk; you may call me Heather."

"Hello, Heather. It is very nice to meet you. What can I do for you?"

"I have some questions about medicine and therapeutics.

Do you have access to information applicable to humans or is your database only for the race or species that piloted this craft?"

"I have access to medical information, diagnostics, therapeutics and laboratory testing for 73 different species, including humans."

Heather took her list of questions from her pocket and began asking them and writing the answers down on her paper material. There seemed to be an endless stream of information (which surprised Heather because a lot of what she was told and shown, she understood). She thanked the computer for the information and told it she would be back soon for further discussion. She slipped the headband off her head, stretched, and yawned and asked J.T. how long she had been in contact with the computer? 37 minutes was the answer. She was really surprised because she thought it had been a couple of hours at least.

J.T. looked at her and said, "The whole thing was pretty awesome and amazing, wasn't it?"

"I had so many preconceived ideas about what it would be like, and none of it panned out the way I thought it would," Heather responded.

"The information given to me is going to change how we address genetic therapies.' The computer mentioned using 'piconites," which are similar to nanites but much smaller and are able to accomplish many things that the nanites are unable to do, simply because they are too big to get to where the issue was located."

"Let's exit the craft and let Helen and Frank get back inside to make any last-minute changes needed for the flight tomorrow evening. I want to check in with Sean and see how things are progressing on the moon side of things."

They left the craft and as they walked to the conference room, Heather continued ruminating over the experience she had just had. She also noted the fatigue that everyone had commented on. They entered the conference room and were pleasantly surprised to see that everyone was there. They all noticed that Heather was going on and on about the computer, so J.T. had to tell her that she needed to let everyone else get a few words in edgewise. Heather got a hurt look on her face then realized that she was rambling on and apologized.

"That's OK dear," Helen said, "We've all had the exact same feelings. It's really quite amazing, isn't it?"

Heather looked at her and said that they could talk later, after work. Helen nodded agreement. J.T. nodded and asked Sean if he had found any bugs or other spy devices. Sean produced a listening device, as did Frank. J.T. took possession of all of them.

He said," Sean, what is the status of the mining on the moon?"

"Sir, they have approximately 10 tons ready to be transported, but nothing to transport them in. I was told that a shuttle system was being set up to deliver four tons every 7 days and that is the fastest they seem to be able to get the ore here."

"Mom, see if we can devise some sort of system to attach four, two and a half ton cylinders to the outside of the craft we have been using so that when we head to harvest the fuel from the radiation belt. We will head to the moon, fill the cylinders and then stop at the belt on our way back to earth. They can continue with the current plans, but we will be able to move forward with 10 tons of ore that we can start refining. You will need to check with the computer to see if that is possible and where we put the retaining structures so that it will not interfere with the in-place system for harvesting from the belt. Dad, have you checked the CAD section of the computer for the design changes recommended by the computer?"

"No, but I will get on it right now," Frank said.

"OK, I must go back to the CO's office and give him the two other bugs. We'll meet here in an hour." J.T. said and then walked off down the hall towards the administrative office section, where he would find the CO's office.

As he entered the outer office, he looked at the secretary and said, "Call the XO and have him report to the CO." He knocked on the door then entered, not really waiting for permission to enter. Two minutes later the XO entered and stood at attention.

"As you were," J.T. commanded. He walked over to the XO and dug the two bugs out of his pocket and handed them to the XO.

"Are we any further in the investigation?" he asked.

The XO responded, "I have a few things in the hamper, just waiting to see what they produce. I have set up a motion sensitive camera on the doors to all your quarters. If anyone enters to replace these, we will get him on camera. I would suggest that you put them back where you found them, but do not reattach any wires. I want the guilty party to notice they aren't working and return to the scene of the crime, so to speak, to either replace them or see why they aren't working."

"What if he has a jamming device that will keep your device from recording his image?" J.T. asked.

"Possibly, but he would have had to sneak it on to the base

and that part is pretty hard. I will set up a similar device over the storeroom where all these devices are kept, and I will be personally inventorying every surveillance device we have on the base. We will just have to see how things go. As far as the interrogations go, I will be starting them tomorrow at 0800. I had to wait until then because a number of personnel do not start work until then and I did not want to compromise the investigation by starting and then having to stop and wait for people to come in to work. Didn't want to give anyone a 'heads up' if you know what I mean."

"Very well. Colonel, anything else to add?"

"No, Sir, the XO seems to be on top of things."

"Be sure to polygraph your secretaries. They are privy to a lot of information that flows through your offices." J.T. said.

Colonel Farmouth spoke up and said, "my secretary has been with me for years and I trust her."

"I don't care Colonel. Sleeper spies sit dormant for years until there is something to pass on. Same goes for you XO. Have your office swept for bugs, by yourselves, not enlisted or anyone in the officer corps. Try to maintain the normal personal interactions you have daily with your secretarial staff. No sudden changes and do not exclude them from meetings they would normally be required to attend. Until we correct the leak and determine how extensive it is, we can't afford to tip our hand. XO, your office was made aware of the bugging issue by me when I made my first complaint a number of weeks ago. Do you recall mentioning anything to anyone about me finding more bugs since my return? If your secretary wonders why you have been summoned by me to the CO's office twice in a couple of days, tell her I have given you a special task to accomplish in a short period of time but do not tell her what. Ask her to pull all of the files of the current qualified pilots stationed here. Tell her nothing else. Understood?" J.T. said in his command voice.

"Aye, aye, Sir."

"Dismissed." The XO came to attention smartly, pivoted on his heel with a near perfect about face and departed the room.

"Colonel, I am going to be taking one of the alien craft for a spin, so to speak to the moon and back with a stop off in the Van Allen radiation belt to harvest ore that these spacecraft engines use for fuel. When I return, the ore that I will be returning with will need to be refined, so if there is anyone you need to inform, please have them contact me personally. When I return from this trip, I expect to have almost all the polygraph interviews completed. You will immediately incarcerate anyone who does not pass or who has questions about the test. Are we clear?" J.T. said quite sternly. He wanted the Colonel to understand how seriously he was taking the leak.

"Aye, aye, Sir," was the response.

"Carry on and good day, Colonel. I have every confidence this matter will be handled." J.T. said.

"Yes, Sir, thank you for your confidence, General," the Colonel said.

J.T. executed a perfect about face, and left the CO's office. As he was making his way back to the conference room, J.T. got lost in thought. He was concentrating so intensely he walked by the door to the conference room and if Sean hadn't seen him walk by and called him, he would have kept on walking. Feeling a little chagrined, he walked back to the conference room and entered.

Everyone was present, and Frank took the opportunity to speak first.

"I have checked with the computer and had it extend the scooping device and inspected its storage area. It is really quite spacious. If we leave these extended, then we can see where the storage cannisters can be attached. The size of the containers will fit, and each will carry 2.5 tons and there are going to be four of them."

Helen said, "When I talked with the computer, it indicated that the spacecraft could carry six total cannisters without issues. It also indicated that the headbands were interchange-able, with the different crafts that are in storage here. I did ask if the ship had the capability to recreate the headbands and it indicated that it could except for the emeralds, rubies, and sapphires that adorn the ban. Apparently, the size, color, and shape of each must be precise and it printed out the require-ments and measurements."

"Did you ask if it had to be natural or could they be manmade?" J.T. questioned.

"I did not think to ask that question, but I will next time I am in contact," Frank answered.

"Did it tell you what else it would need to make more headbands?"

"Yes, titanium, aluminum, silicon and tungsten. It would take about two hours per headband. It said that all the computers on the crafts that are here are capable of making the headbands. It was part of their basic programming. Kind of a safety thing in case the headbands got damaged, lost, or destroyed," Frank explained.

"Well then, I guess we had better get started making five

more headbands, at least. Please be sure that you get the exact amounts needed for each headband. What I think we will need to do is to have each of you get in a different craft, get a diagnostic scan run and anything that needs repairing, fixed and get at least three spacecraft ready to fly by the end of the week.

"Sean, you need to contact the fabricators and get them to make 24 storage containers. The CO is going to get me the files of the most qualified pilots here in area 43, and once we have 3 craft ready to fly, we will start shuttling back and forth to the moon one craft a day. They will all follow the same procedure. The first flight will carry four cannisters, every flight thereafter will take six to the moon and return with four, leaving two to get filled and ready for the next flight. Each flight will stop in the Van Allen belt and harvest more fuel. I expect to start processing 50 tons of ore per week, and we will store the fuel in some of the spacecraft so that we will not be flying. Any questions? Heather, when we get a headband made, you will be able to use the computer for more research, in one of the crafts that will not be flying. Is that, OK?" J.T. asked.

"I was just about to ask that very question," Heather replied.

"Will the headband be interchangeable with which ever spacecraft I am using?" she asked.

"I believe all the headbands are interchangeable with any of the spacecraft. The next person that links up can ask, OK?" J.T. said. It was Helen's turn to update the group.

"Last time I linked in, I went through everything I could think of concerning carrying the ore back from the moon. The only significant issue is that if you are carrying more than four containers, it changes the method, speed and a couple of other things with re-entry. Surprisingly, weight does not seem to matter. Only changing the configuration or the shape of the craft is what is important and brings other factors into consideration. The computer seemed to think that more than four full containers was not a good idea," she explained.

Sean spoke up and told the group that the ore refining equipment would be in within five days, and there was a specific area that had access to the outside, allowing for the spacecraft to fly the ore to within 10 yards of the equipment. There was also an area set aside for fabrication. It was 25 yards from the refined ore storage area. There were still negotiations going on about the construction site. Regardless of where the construction site is located, it will take at least 18 months to complete before construction on the actual craft can begin.

J.T. immediately suggested that they could put together components together and store them until such time as there was a place to do the final assembly. That should keep the construction time of the actual craft to a bare minimum. He was thinking that they should be ready for departure in 4.5 years, give or take. He also said the first voyage was going to be to Titan, one of Saturn's moons because according to the computer it was a source of fuel that was very extensive, enough to power the craft to the home world where the computer and the aliens originated. J.T. withheld the information about the world being in the constellation of Tau Centauri.

Heather said she was glad to get a time frame considering she had to get 2000 people screened and then correct any with genetic illnesses and they had to finish their education so that they would be productive, fully functional members of the colony. It would be between five and seven years before a complete crew of colonists would be ready to board the spacecraft, be put into hibernation or to take their places as active crew members of the spacecraft. The length of time they would be crew members would depend on how long the actual flight would take. The plan J.T. had was to divide the cruise time into thirds that would allow everyone aboard to be in hibernation for 2/3's of the cruise and awake and working $1/3^{rd}$ of the cruise. It also meant that he was going to have to get to work on the hibernation process.

That thought reminded him to ask the computer about the hibernation process that was used by the crew of the current spacecraft. With that help, and the work of Jacques LeClerc in Belgium, he should be able to get a prototype built and get some volunteers to try the prototype out.

"Shannon, please have the top two pilots on the list plus their RIO's report to the conference room at 1500 today, General's orders." J.T. said.

Shannon voiced her understanding and moved over to the phone to get started. J.T. looked at Frank and Helen and told them that the first flight would be in 48 hours and would be a flight of three craft.

J.T and the rest of the crew headed to the officers' Mess for lunch. The lunchtime banter was good natured, comical and the meal passed quickly. J.T. adjourned lunch so they could get back to the conference room. J.T led the exodus from the Mess and walked down to the conference room.

When he opened the door and entered the room, he heard the familiar "Attention on Deck" sounded by the first officer that saw the general as he entered the room.

"As you were." J.T. responded. "Take your seats, gentlemen. I am General Coulter. I have asked you here today to ask a few questions and make some decisions. Is there anyone here who is NOT currently cleared to fly?"

The response was a universal "no sir".

"Is there anyone here that has applied to the astronaut training program?" J.T. asked.

There was a universal "yes sir".

"Why were you not chosen? I want to hear from each one of you individually," J.T. ordered.

"Sir, I am Lt. Colonel Norman Tolliver. I was declined due to my age."

"Sir, I am Major Steven Roosevelt. I was rejected because of insufficient time in service."

"Sir, I am Capt. James Franklin, I was rejected because of recurrent sinus infections and balance issues."

"Sir, I am Capt. Lewis Mitchell, I was rejected because my advanced mathematics grades were 0.2 of a point low."

"Are any of you still interested in space flight?" J.T. asked.

There was a resounding "yes sir" from all present.

"In a few minutes you will be taken by Dr. Helen Coulter, PhD Nuclear engineering, and Dr. Frank Coulter, PhD in advanced computer engineering. They are going to take you to your space crafts, help you get linked up with the computer and get familiar with your craft. What you are about to be told is ultra-top secret and not to be repeated to anyone under penalty of never being heard from again. Are we clear?" J.T. stated rather forcefully.

"Sir, yes sir!"

"Very well," J.T. started, "gentlemen, I have been tasked to build a spacecraft that will take a group of humans on an inter-stellar trip to set up a colony in another world. I have managed to learn how to connect with the computer that controls these space craft that we have had here for the last century. At this point, please understand, you will not be flying these crafts, the computer will. You will be taught to input commands to the computer. The computer will decide if it is going to follow your input or not. Things must be this way because these craft are incredibly sophisticated and are capable of flight maneuvers you have only dreamed of.

"All of them have flown at faster than light speeds and interstellar distances. You jet jocks, all have a streak of 'push the envelope' and 'I am indestructible attitude', if you are in possession of these attitudes, you will leave them at the door, and if you can't, you are dismissed without prejudice. Am I clear? Is there anyone here that wishes to back out for any reason?"

There was only one man that raised his hand, and that was Major Roosevelt. "Sir, none of us are leaving. When do we get started?"

There was a general nodding and positive murmuring from the group. "Since I am given to understand, there is a unanimous acceptance from the group, I will continue with the briefing. Each pilot and his RIO will be flying two missions per day, five days a week. You each will fly one of the alien craft, each will have six containers attached, three per side, to the moon where the mining colony is located, where these containers will be removed. Four of them will be filled with ore and reattached to the craft. You will then lift off headed to the Van Allen Radiation belt, where you will harvest material that is used as fuel for the spacecraft. You will land on earth and that will be offloaded. Then the four empty cannisters will be reattached and readied for the next flight. There will be four cannisters left on the moon that will be filled while the next flight is inbound."

"The ore is very specific to the construction of the outer hull of a faster than light speed, interstellar vehicle. Apparently, this ore is critical to this project. The other material, which will be used as fuel, we will stockpile for future use and clear up the VARB. These flights will continue until there is enough ore here on Earth that we can manufacture an entire spacecraft, plus have enough that we will be able to make and carry onboard enough replacement hull plates in case of inflight damage. The moon has a huge amount of this element. We are just having to speed up the delivery of it, until the regular service flights can ship us the amounts of ore we will need. With reference to fuel, the computer informs us that two kilograms of fuel will power 42 flights back and forth to the moon, so as you can see, you will be flying for at least 6-7 weeks before we will need to refuel.

"The computers have all been instructed to conduct preflight scans and to list discrepancies and show proof of correction. They have adjusted the intra-craft atmosphere to accommodate humans. You will wear a space suit, donning the helmet especially when you are landing on the moon and having the transfer of the ore containers, just in case of an accident and damage to the spacecraft."

"Each of you will be wearing a headband that will allow linking with the computer. You may also use verbal language, although the computer will already have read your mind and completed your request before you would actually be able to speak. Oh, by the way, there are no sticks, rudders, or throttles. This part is very important and will get you grounded in nothing flat, pending a disciplinary hearing that could result in your dismissal from the service. You will not exceed 3/4ths light speed, no exceptions. ¾ light speed should get you to the moon in two minutes. Jumping to light speed would require you to immediately get out of light speed in 2-3 seconds, thereby overshooting the moon by coming very close to Mars. It would also be hard on the craft and, since we are just learning about these vehicles, if you break one, a) you will probably die and b) we might not be able to fix what you have broken. Am I clear on everything? Anyone have any questions or not understand the mission, or the mission parameters involved?" J.T. finished speaking.

"Mom, Dad, take your charges with you and get them broken in. Gentleman, there is a tingling sensation in the temples that intensifies while linking up with the computer. Keep your hands off the headband and just relax. Try not to have negative thoughts about the aliens or the craft. Would hate to have you offend the computer, causing it to decide, it was going to teach you a lesson, understood?"

"Aye, aye, Sir," the group replied.

"Dismissed," J.T. said.

"Ten-hut," came the command.

"Carry on."

The men stood at attention then followed Helen and Frank as they led them down the corridor to the area where the spacecraft were stored. Three hours later, they all got back together, and the pilots could barely stay awake. After a quick debriefing, they headed off for a sleep. Helen looked at J.T. and said "They are gonna be fine. They took to it like a duck to water. Just gonna have to get them a little more time with interfacing with the computer so they don't get so tired. They will have to fly in shifts, one of them out, one of them back, until they have a lot more hours under their belt. That has to be a 'no discussion rule', James."

"Yes, ma'am" was the reply.

"That sounds like a stellar idea," he agreed.

"You are making puns now?' Helen replied.

"Obviously not good ones." J.T. responded.

"At least you are trying. I am very impressed with the way you are handling things, the amount of thought and planning you have done for the whole project. The Council was right to offer you the Quest. I do not know of anyone that could pull it off, except you. Your dad and I are so proud of you. So is Shannon, even though she would never tell you. It's a sister thing." Helen said.

"I know mom, I try to tell her that I appreciate all she does for this project. Do you think she would like to go on the first manned, alien vessel, moonshot flight with me?"

"I think she would be ecstatic, honored, and pleased! Be sure to ask her soon so she could brag a little," Helen replied.

That night at dinner, when the whole crew was present, after everyone was done eating and enjoying a cup of coffee, J.T. stood up at the head of the table and indicated he had some things to say.

"Sean, what is the status on the construction of the ore cannisters?

"There are 13 of the needed 16 for the first three flights ready, and the rest will be done by noon tomorrow. They will continue to make another 16 when they have finished the amount needed for the upcoming flight."

"Mom, are there any mechanical issues with any of the craft we're going to be using?" he asked.

"All three of the craft have run self-diagnostics, and any inconsistencies have been corrected, or so I am told. I will say this, that since these craft were built on another planet, we do not have anyone here on Earth that is actually qualified to take anything apart, repair or replace it, then reassemble it to make it functional and safe. I understand we do not have a lot of time to get people trained and up to speed, neither do we have the manufacturing ability nor the machinery to fix something if it were to break. I believe the craft are safe to fly but I would like to take one or two of the older craft and start learning to take them apart, replicate them, then replace the parts into the engine, and see if we can get it to fly. This is going to be necessary before you take a spacecraft to another world. So, I would like to make that my focus, after I get back from this outing," she said.

"Dad, anything to add?" J.T. asked.

"I would echo Mom's points, substituting computers for the mechanical components she referred to. In your spacecraft design, we will need to insert actual physical controls that a human can take charge of and actually drive the ship. The computer has been really helpful and so far, it has been accurate, but do we know if there is a program imbedded in its core that activates when instructed to return to the mother planet if any creature other than the original flight crew in control of the computer? We will need to build a similar computer that we write the programs and applications for. It should be as close as the ones currently in the alien crafts. I think that would be the area that my services would be best served."

"Shannon, would you have a problem going on the first flight to the moon in my craft?"

Shannon was caught completely off guard and shocked. She was not sure she had heard correctly.

"Did you just ask me to go along on the upcoming flight to the moon and back?" she asked incredulously.

"That was the question, yes?" J.T. replied.

"Of course, I would love to go. I just thought that there was no reason for me to be along, so I wasn't going to be asked." she remarked.

"Shan, you may not realize it, but you have one of the most critical parts of this project. You keep track of everything, you keep records of everything we do, say and plan. Without you, there would be no history of one of the most important projects ever undertaken by the human race. I can't think of anyone I know that I would trust to have that job. That's why I gave it to you."

Shannon started to tear up and then broke into a sob. She had no idea that J.T. felt that way about her. She thought he had given her the job just so she had something to do.

"Thanks bro, I'd love to go along," she replied between sobs.

"Sean, I have given you the jobs I want to be sure will be done right. You have always been able to manage and motivate people to get things done, manage problems with an ability to fix problems quickly with intelligent suggestions that are simple and easy to follow. You are going on the flight, in one of the other crafts. Each craft only has room for three occupants, so you can choose one of the other crafts. Dad, you will be in one of the other crafts as well. I want everyone to be extra observant of the entire process, take copious notes especially as to how the landing on the moon, offloading of the ore cannister, reloading the cannisters and take off goes. Same thing with the takeoff and unloading of the cannisters when we land back on earth. These are the areas we are most likely to have issues. The plan is for my craft to leave first, the second to leave 45 minutes later, and the third to leave 90 minutes after my departure. These times will fluctuate, depending on how fast the mining company can fill four cannisters, reattach them to my craft and then allow for me to lift off without having to dodge the next incoming craft. Same with landing back here on Earth. Last, thing we need is to crash two of the craft that can fly. It would set everything back years, years we do not have. Heather, you will go with me on the second flight."

J.T. continued, "Sean, I need to know if the people on the ground have a plan to load and unload, then move the cannisters out of the way and empty them out and get ready for the next flight. Tomorrow is the only day that we are going to have three craft flying routes. After tomorrow, we will fly two sorties in the morning and two in the afternoon, five days a week. We will also need to have some way to empty the scoop storage unit on each craft and store the harvested fuel from the VA Belt then move it out of the way before the next launch." Sean replied,

"I will check on that, make a plan of action, and get back with you before close of business tomorrow. I will try to get a schedule of spy satellite overpasses so we can schedule unobserved launches and landings also."

"Excellent, I hadn't thought of the satellite issue. OK, let's adjourn and everybody get a good night's sleep. The next couple of days are going to be busy and hectic." J.T. finished his comments.

Shannon came around the table and kissed him on the cheek, and gave him a big hug. "I had no idea you felt that way. Thanks for telling me. I will make you proud," she said.

"I never doubted that for a moment. If I had, I wouldn't have given you the job," J.T. remarked. Helen came over and it was a repeat of Shannon with the cheek kiss and hug.

"Nicely done, James, very nicely done," she said.

Frank shook his hand and clapped him on the back. "We got this son, no worries," Sean came over and shook his hand and said, "I appreciate your trust and confidence in me. I will not fail nor let this project down."

"I know you won't. You never have failed in any job I have ever given you," J.T. said.

"Heather, let's go to the room. I'm tired." Hand in hand, they walked down the corridor to their quarters.

J.T. slept in until 0600, completely missing his morning workout. He had other things on his mind. After his shower, he wrapped a towel around his waist and sat down at the table provided and looked underneath just as a matter of habit. He noticed a listening bug taped under the corner nearest the wall. He pulled it loose and then proceeded to go over the room, with a fine, toothed comb. There were two other bugs that were found and each one raised his boiling point. Heather got out of bed and J.T. put his fingers to her mouth and then showed her the listening device.

She nodded understanding and then said, "Good morning sweetheart." She kissed him convincingly.

"Did you sleep well?" he asked.

"I slept well for the first time in a long time. It surprises me because of tomorrow. I should be really cranked up but strangely, I feel really calm," she answered.

"I'm starved. Let's go get breakfast." Heather suggested.

"Lead the way," was J.T.'s response.

They headed out to the officers' Mess and were shown to the table where the rest of the group was already congregating. Before he sat down, he showed everyone the three bugs he had found in his and Heather's quarters. He sat down and issued instructions to everyone to search their quarters as soon as they were finished with breakfast. If they found any more bugs, they were to bring them to his room. He asked the Mess Officer to bring a phone to the table. After it was plugged in, he called the XO's and CO's office and asked them both to meet him in his quarters in 30 minutes. J.T. then ordered eggs, bacon, hash browns, orange juice and a pot of coffee. Heather doubled the order but wanted scrambled eggs instead of sunny side up like J.T. had ordered.

10 minutes later, the food arrived and J.T. wolfed down his food, frequently checking his watch. Heather put her hand on his forearm and told him to go to his meeting. She would meet him in an hour. J.T. breathed a sigh of relief and then Heather noticed a complete change in J.T.'s face and demeanor. There was anger in his eyes, and she was glad she did not have to deal with him for at least an hour. By then, he should have cooled down. J.T. took a cup of coffee and headed back to the room. The CO and XO were standing outside the door to his quarters. Both men snapped to attention as J.T. approached.

He looked at them and said gruffly, "As you were." He

opened the door and walked in, leaving the door open for them to follow.

They both entered the XO closing the door. Colonel Farmouth said, "why are we meeting in here, General?" J.T turned to him and said, "because the two of you have demonstrated an inability to solve a simple espionage problem." He dropped five bugs on the table. "This is the third time me and my crew have had their quarters bugged and both of you seem to be incompetent and inept in figuring out who is doing this. I really should call the Council and tell them the two men in charge of this ultra-secret facility can't find a spy or spies. You realize that if I do contact the Council, it will be the end of your careers, along with a lot of personal disgrace. The only thing that could maybe change my mind is you telling me that you have a suspect or someone(s) in custody. Care to enlighten me?" he asked.

Both men were white as a ghost. They knew J.T. was not kidding. They also knew their careers hinged on what was said next. The XO started first.

"General, I have performed approximately 75 polygraphs and have uncovered no abnormalities. A review and inventory of the devices used has not shown any inconsistencies or errors. I have personally installed a hidden camera focused on the doors to each living space. We can see a man in standard coveralls wearing a hat with no identifying features entering the rooms but can never see his face. There are no other identifying features we are able to detect. Frankly Sir, I am at a loss as to how to proceed, Sir."

The CO spoke next," my secretary has been polygraphed and was exonerated. Other than the usual traffic of divisional and battalion commanders in my office for routine meetings, there has been no one else in my office. I have a camera set up to record the room, and no one has been in my office except the cleaning staff, and they have been polygraphed and videotaped during their work assignments. There was nothing there that indicates anyone is bugging my office either, Sir." J.T. looked both in the eye and held their gaze for a very long second.

"Very well. XO, when you looked at the tape, was the man wearing gloves?"

"I believe so Sir," was his reply.

"What about boots?"

"They looked like standard issue combat boots, Sir."

"I will need some florescent radioactive tracer powder. What I am going to do is spread some on the floor and on the furniture throughout my quarters, as well as my crew's quarters, just before we leave for our flights tomorrow. When this dirtball realizes that we are going to be gone all day and most of the base is going to be occupied with the launch, recovery or just plain observing the whole thing, he will try to replace these bugs. I am hoping he will get the powder on his boots and clothes. You will then be able to track his movements. If he tries to change clothes or boots, he will get the powder on his hands and since it must wear off and can't be washed off, we will have our perp. Any questions?"

"No Sir" was the immediate response from both officers.

"Dismissed. XO, try to be unobserved when you get me the powder, OK?"

"Aye aye, Sir."

"Needless to say, this issue has to be resolved soonest. Please bring the powder to me in the Officer's mess this evening. I will disperse it tomorrow morning as we leave the room. This is the last shot. If this doesn't work, I am obligated to notify the higher-ups." J.T. turned on his heel and left the room. He ran into Heather a little way down the hall.

"You all better now?" she asked. "I haven't killed anyone, but I am not far from the line. I have been in the CO's office with the XO three times now, for implanted espionage devices and they still have not locked the perp up yet. I have a plan and I will discuss it at dinner, but I do not have a lot of time before I have to notify the Council of an espionage problem in area 43 and 51," J.T. vented.

They turned right at the corner and headed for the conference room. Everybody there was hard at work in their own area of responsibility. Heather continued to the area where the spacecrafts were housed. She picked up the craft she had used before, entered, and sat in the commander's chair, put the headband on and connected herself to the computer. She set her writing paper and pens out and began to explore different aspects of medicine therapeutics and diagnostics that were available. She set her watch timer for two hours and 30 minutes.

J.T. called his dad and asked him to bring the computer-generated changes to his spacecraft blueprints to the conference room so he could peruse them. He then called his mom and asked her to bring blueprints of the engines and her thoughts and ideas about miniature nuclear reactors to power several the different ship systems. They spent the first 10 minutes searching the conference room for surveillance devices. They found four bugs but no video devices. J.T. wrote all instructions on paper and passed them around for all to see and read.

There was a lot of paper shuffling and a lot of non-specific comments like "that's an interesting change, wonder why they did that? And where's page 4?" J.T. made a motion across his throat to get everyone to stop talking.

He said," Heather has gone to the spacecraft to see what info she can get about hibernation and/or suspended animation. I have a call in to Mr. LeClerc. I am going to see when he can be brought here for further research. Of all the things I think need the highest priority, it's hibernation. After all, 3/4ths of the colonists will be asleep for years and having a safe, easily reversible process was paramount to the success of the project. Waking up replacements, then getting the group coming off one or two-year tours, to sleep quickly and safely, thereby having a smooth and seamless transition.

J.T. also advanced the thought of III for everyone while asleep. That way, the newly awakened crew would already be up to date and current, that would allow them to immediately take over their jobs with a minimum of glitches. J.T. instructed Helen to set up a repair manual for the ship's engines, and Frank was instructed to do the same thing for the computer system. He dismissed everyone and told them he would see them for supper.

Heather was amazed by all the info she got from the computer. A lot of it was going to make her job much easier, and it was going to help J.T. to be successful in the project to spread humanity through the cosmos. She headed for the conference room to join the crew. Before she could get to the conference room, she managed to run into the crew headed for the officers' Mess for supper. She could hardly wait to tell J.T. As they entered the private dining area, J.T. turned to everyone and put his index finger to his lips. He pulled out a piece of paper and wrote, *look for bugs everywhere. No talking!'* and showed it to everyone. They all nodded understanding. One by one, they started looking at everything and under everything. They turned up two listening devices. They were removed and five minutes later, the XO showed up, carrying a paper bag. Nothing was said as he handed it to J.T.

He snapped to attention and said, "By your leave Sir?"

"Carry on Major."

"Aye, aye Sir." He handed the devices to the XO as he turned to go. J.T. turned to the group and said "I will explain during supper. Let's get seated and order cuz I am starving. Chewing ass always gives me an appetite."

They all grabbed their usual seats and started looking over the evening menu. Heather was unusually bubbly as she sat next to J.T.

She leaned over and kissed his ear and whispered," it was a great day, and you will never guess what I found out today, from the computer."

"You have information about hibernation and long space flight," he responded.

She slapped his shoulder and complained, "I hate it when you ruin surprises."

"I'm sorry honey, it just slipped out because it made sense," he explained.

"We will discuss this later," she responded with more than a little irritation in her voice.

"Yes, ma'am."

J.T. tapped his water glass with his fork, getting everyone's attention.

"In case you haven't noticed, he began, "we have a spy problem. The CO and XO have been investigating, but to this point, they have not found the culprits. To that end I am going to try something. I have a powder here that only three people know about. Me, the XO and the CO. I am going to sprinkle it in each of our quarters, in areas where it will get on people that brush against it. That way, we can track this criminal. Meanwhile, be sure to check your rooms for bugs any time you have been gone for more than an hour. I will stop by after everyone has left the rooms. I am going to dust the area. Be sure to make your beds before you leave for the day.

This is very important. There should not be any reason for anyone to be in the rooms while we are gone. Put the 'do not disturb' signs on the doors. Call me from your room when you are about to leave. One way or another, we will catch this spy. Now, let's enjoy supper. Tomorrow is going to be a huge day for everyone involved." J.T. finished.

10 minutes later the appetizers were served followed by either the salad for some and soup for others, and finally the entree. Quite a variety: seafood (Scallops, shrimp and lobster), steak and chicken; along with asparagus, potatoes, either au gratin or baked. The dessert was chocolate mousse with a raspberry coulee. There was fresh Blue Mountain coffee from Jamaica and a snifter of 100-year-old Courvoisier. Everyone was stuffed and very satiated when all was said and done. J.T. stood and reminded everyone that they should be ready for breakfast at 0630 and he wished everyone a good night.

J.T. rose at his normal time, 0415, and headed for the gym

for his daily workout regimen. He had been markedly less faithful to this regimen since coming to area 43. He felt, deep in his heart, that his non-adherence to his regimen was contributing to his missteps concerning the espionage problem. He felt that without his workout routine; he was not able to think things through, carefully, clearly, thoughtfully and completely. Well, starting today, that was going to change. He was going back to what had always worked for him, through all the years he was part of and commanding a military unit, protecting a hub of civilization, as well as he and his men had done, for more than 15 years. He would not continue with a routine that did not keep him at his best with razor sharp thinking and a clear-headedness he was used to having, and desperately needed it back. He got back to his room in time to join Heather in the shower.

She noticed how buffed he was as well as how badly he needed a shower. She purred appreciatively as she soaped his muscular torso from head to toe as well as the fun parts too.

"Glad to see you working out again. I like the results," she cooed.

"Thanks babe, you are still pretty hot yourself. He could feel that her ministrations were causing him to react, and he said, "keep that up and we will miss breakfast."

"That a promise or a threat?" she asked.

"It's a guarantee my love, a solid gold guarantee," was his reply.

"Wish I could call your bluff, but everybody is going to be waiting for us at breakfast. So, pick up the pace stud," she said as she rinsed off, kissed him briefly before grabbing a towel and stepping out of the shower stall. J.T. rinsed off, grabbed his towel and followed Heather out of the bathroom, toweling himself off. He watched the movement of her ass as she walked to the dresser and started to get dressed. *And smart too, I did good*, he thought to himself.

He stepped over to his side of the dresser and slipped on briefs, socks, and a flight jumpsuit. The flight suit was a little snug after his workout, but eventually conformed to his physique. He slipped on some spit shined flight boots and laced them up snuggly. The phone on the bedside stand rang, so J.T. answered it.

It was Helen. She said, "Your dad and I are about to leave for the mess. You said to call."

"I'll be there in a moment mom," J.T. responded.

He turned to Heather and said, I'll be right back." He grabbed the bag and slipped it inside the flight suit, and walked out the door. He looked up and down the hall and seeing no one, stepped over to his parents' quarters, tapped on the door and then entered before anyone saw him. Once inside the door, he made his way to the desk and sprinkled some of the dust on the lampshade and the whole phone, including the underside.

He then turned to the bed and dusted the dust ruffle all the way around, then the fronts of the pictures on the wall and the clock on the wall, and within the clock radio on the desk. He instructed his mom and dad to hang the sign on the doorknob, and as they all left; he sprinkled more of the dust on the floor and inside of the door. They headed off to the mess and J.T. returned to his room. Heather had just finished putting on some makeup and finished zipping up her flight suit. The phone rang again and this time it was Sean.

He left and went to their room and completed the same

routine he had just done in his parents' room. Shannon and Sean left, put the sign out on the doorknob and after they left, J.T. finished his task of preparing this room. He checked the corridor and left the room, heading back to his room. As soon as he returned, he asked Heather if she was ready to go to breakfast and she replied she was.

So J.T. started doing the same things in their room that he had just completed in the two other rooms. He hung the sign on the outer doorknob and finished dusting every surface he thought the spy might brush up against. He ushered Heather out of the door and dusted everything on his way out the door. Satisfied that he had laid the trap as best he could, he now had to wait to see if he was successful.

Breakfast at the mess was the usual, but J.T. noticed that his appetite was up and he attributed that to his re-initiation of the workout regimen. He decided to indulge himself and double ordered a fully loaded omelet, hash browns and double bacon with OJ and coffee. He sat back and ate slowly, savoring each bite. He loved to cook, but breakfast was his absolute favorite meal. He began a discussion about the upcoming flight and asked Sean if everything was set. Sean replied by listing everything that was ready, including all the transportation tubes and they had been attached to the different spacecraft.

The craft were running preflight assessments. And the other flight crews were in preflight and waiting for him to brief them. J.T. smiled and the only thing that went through his mind was *a well-oiled machine*. He finished breakfast and slugged back his coffee. He got up out of the chair and motioned to the rest of the group to follow him.

The other four members of the mission were waiting

outside the conference room J.T. and the crew had been using. They all snapped to attention as J.T. approached.

"As you were, gentleman." J.T. said as if he had been saying that for a long time. "Please come in and grab a seat." As they all made their way to find seats, there was a quiet knock on the door. Sean stood and answered it. It was a senior messman with a cart of coffee, tea, juice, and pastries.

"Would you thank the Mess Officer for his kind consideration? That will be all." J.T said.

The response was a typical "Aye, aye, Sir." from the messman. After the door was closed, J.T. started in with the morning's briefing. Sean stood and gave the weather and vehicle status report.

J.T. started in with, "This is going to be a historic day in the annals of mankind. Never before have humans piloted an alien spacecraft, much less used it as a delivery truck. Ms. Shannon is handing out a sheet of paper that has the moon base coordinates on it. It also has places for you to enter time of liftoff, elapsed time of flight, time of unloading and reloading, time of flight to the Van Allen belt, amount of time spent harvesting and time of touch down back here at area 43. I can't stress the following things: 1) These crafts are capable of faster than light speed. You are not, I repeat NOT, to fly faster than 3/4th light speed. You are not to try maneuvers just to 'see what she can do'. Are we completely clear on this point?"

Heather noticed the change in the tone of his voice immediately. He was very clear, and she knew he expected complete obedience. "Sir, yes Sir," was the unanimous response.

J.T. continued, "no human has ever flown faster than light speed. I do not wish to find out that by going to light speed, we activate some internal computer order that automatically returns the craft to the home world. You would not survive the trip, which means we would lose good, qualified, well-trained crew members and in addition one completely functional spacecraft. The other info we are keeping is so we can efficiently plan repeated sorties and get as many in each day as we can. The materials you will be bringing back from the moon are a necessary, major, vital component of the hull construction of an interstellar space craft we will be building right here in area 43.

"The second function, the harvesting of an element only found in two places in this solar system, The Van Allen belt and Saturn's moon, Titan. It is the only fuel that alien engines use. We are going to build a large secure stockpile so there will be plenty available for the craft we are building. We will be going to Titan with the spacecraft after it has been built, as part of the shakedown cruise, before we actually load up with crew, colonists and everything we will be taking on the voyage. I should not have to remind you to stay mentally alert and focused. Remember, there are no controls for you to take over to actually physically fly these craft. It is all thought controlled. There will be no acrobatic maneuvers. The containers you will be hauling are secured to the craft but are not physically part of the craft. Acrobatics may weaken the attachments which might cause them to dislodge, thereby affecting the control and flight of the craft. Can't afford hotdogging or trying to prove whose is bigger, understand?"

"Aye, aye, Sir."

Sean then stood and finished his part, telling them a radio had been installed so they could contact the moon base and area 43. He gave them the frequencies and suggested that they start at the top of the list, then drop down to the next one for subsequent calls. The crew voiced understanding. He also reminded them that they needed to contact the tower, as they were ready to land. He then indicated that Sean needed to inform the tower to shut off the defense system when a spacecraft is about to land. The computer system in area 51 could not handle the computer system in the spacecraft and would be burned out if that was tried. J.T. spoke up and said that flight two would depart 50 minutes after he left. If for some reason, it was taking longer to fill and reattach the cannisters, they should orbit the moon following the line marked by the front and back side of the moon, at an altitude of 5000 feet.

Asking for questions and getting none, J.T. dismissed everyone with a "Safe flight, enjoy yourselves."

Everyone headed out to the areas where the spacecraft were being held, joking amongst themselves, trying to relieve the stress of the moment. As they walked by their assigned craft, the crews peeled off the group until J.T., Helen and Shannon were left. When they reached the craft, J.T. turned to Shannon and asked her if she had ever put one of the headbands on. She replied she had not, so J.T. proceeded to give her the tutorial on what to expect and to try to focus her attention on the flight and if anything came up that she was not sure about, she was to tell the computer to transfer it to him. The crew chief helped her to get into her space suit, hooked the supply tubes to the suit, and showed her to her chair.

As she got situated, they handed her the headband and showed her how to put it on. Helen was also given personal attention by her crew assistant. She only needed help with the suit. She was comfortable getting into her seat and the assistant hooked up all the supply hoses. She had worn the headband a number of times before, so she went ahead and put it on, connected herself to the computer, then ran down a checklist of things she needed to ensure were working.

She then inputted the coordinates for the moon base, verified them with the computer, then leaned back and relaxed. J.T. got into his suit, had help attaching the tubes, got settled into the chair and reached for his headband. He looked over at the other two crewmembers, satisfying himself they were set and prepared for flight. He slipped the headband on, adjusted the fit so it was a little more comfortable, then connected himself to the computer.

"Welcome General Coulter. I hope you are well." The computer asked.

I am well, thank you. Helen, Shannon, are you guys ready? he thought. Helen's thoughts came through forceful and clear while Shannon's thoughts were weak and very difficult to understand.

Shannon, you must put more effort into your thoughts. They are quite weak and difficult to understand. Copy?

I understand. I feel like I am shouting, came Shannon's very weak voice.

Try to clear your mind and relax. You do not have to fight the computer. It is not the enemy. It is a tool. Use it like one, J.T. explained.

Roger. A couple of minutes later, Helen and J.T. heard a much clearer and stronger answer.

How's this? Shannon asked.

Both J.T. and Helen responded, *perfect.*

Everyone set? J.T. asked.

Roger, from Helen.

All set, From Shannon.

"Computer, slow liftoff, and gentle acceleration to an altitude of 150 miles, then hover at that height until a complete systems' check is complete. Them proceed to the coordinates already inputted." J.T. reached for his arm rest and flipped the transmit button to the radio.

"Area 43 this is Coulter one. We are taking off now. Will report before heading to moon base 1. Over."

"Roger, Coulter one. Safe journey." There was a sensation of a moving elevator pushing everyone into their seats. The suits compensated and kept all the crew comfortable.

"Altitude 150 miles achieved. System check in progress. Fuel reserves 99.5%. Cabin integrity intact. Scanning out to 500,000 kilometers, all clear. Projected route free from objects. Amount of space debris calculated at minimal. Shall we engage star drive?"

Engage at 50% of light speed. Bring us to within one mile of the programmed coordinates. J.T. thought.

"Acknowledged. Expected flight time 2 minutes 45 seconds. Engaging now."

There was a slight sensation of being pushed back in their seats that seemed to dissipate within a few seconds.

2 minutes later the computer said "Arrived as per instructions. Currently hovering at one mile altitude. Moon base directly beneath us."

J.T. pushed a few frequency buttons and then depressed the send button. "Moon base 1, this is Coulter 1. We are directly above you at one mile altitude. Awaiting permission to land. Over"

"Coulter one, Moon base 1. Begin slow descent at 500 feet/min. Hold at 100 feet in hover. over."

"Roger wilco. Beginning descent now at 500ft/ min. Will hold at 100 feet per instructions. Over"

"The computer said, "beginning descent at 500ft/ min, will hover at 100ft." a few minutes later, the computer said, "Hovering at 100 feet."

"Moon base 1, Coulter one at 100 feet."

"Coulter one, Moon base 1, extend landing gear and descend to land at your discretion. Over."

"Roger. Computer slow descent to landing per your programming," J.T. ordered.

"Roger."

60 seconds later, "landed, engines shut off. Flight efficiency 96.89%. No damage sustained, fuel expenditure nominal. Reserves left 99.20%."

"Computer unlock the ore cannisters and allow them to be removed, filled and reattached." It took 39 minutes for four of the six cannisters to be unloaded, filled, then replaced on the spacecraft.

"Coulter, Moon base 1. You are cleared for launch at your discretion. This came off clean as a whistle. Safe trip home."

"Moon base 1, Coulter one. Give your guys a job well done in this historical undertaking. Be sure to send me everybody's name, so they can be mentioned and acknowledged in the official record. Coulter one departing, Coulter two should be here in about 15 minutes. Out"

Computer same departure protocol as for leaving earth. Engage.

J.T. thought. *At altitude. System check, all systems working in normal parameters. Fuel reserves 99.19%.*

"Engage star drive 50% of light speed, target, Van Allen belt, scan for deposits of Irbadinium and set course to position craft to harvest said deposits," he ordered.

"Computed. Systems engaged. Flight time one minute 50 seconds. Adjusting trajectory for harvesting run."

"Engage." They could feel the slowing down and tilting for a turn. There was a slight rumble and whine while the harvesting scoop was extended and locked into place. There were three or four fairly minor bumps as the craft made a scooping run. There was a turn and a repeat of the scooping run.

"Harvest complete. Storage bay filled to 98% capacity," the computer informed J.T.

Very well, set course for area 43, slow descent through atmosphere, normal landing procedures per your programming, J.T. thought.

"Wilco."

"Area 43 Control, Coulter one. Ready to land. Cannisters will need hosing before detachment from the craft."

"Roger, Coulter one, you are cleared to land. Hosing units standing by. Welcome back. Well done."

"Coulter one on final approach. Thanks. Out,"

The computer said. "Landing gear extended. Touchdown in 10,9,8,7, at three it stopped counting and everyone in the cockpit felt the craft touch down.

They expelled a collective sigh and then noted how tired they were feeling, in addition to feeling relieved that they had in fact been to the moon and back and survived.

BOOK II

THE ADVENTURE BEGINS

CHAPTER
ONE

J.T. undressed and jumped into the shower following his own recommendations. The shower did exactly what J.T. had expected it to do. He briskly towelled himself off, shaved, and slipped on a fresh jumpsuit complete with his stars on the collar points. Checking himself in the mirror, he squared his shoulders and headed out the door. He strode down the hall with a purpose, and it was noticed by everyone he passed; they all seemed to stand a little taller, walk a little straighter and demonstrate a little more pride in themselves. He entered the officer's Mess and was escorted to the private dining room. While walking to the back of the mess, he told the steward that there would now be 2 more people added to the group. The steward merely nodded, then went off to make the addition to the table as well as fixing the General his three fingers of Tullamore Dew. Over the next 20 minutes, the crew slowly made their way in and took their seats, ordered their drinks, and relaxed from a busy day at work. Sean entered, bringing the two elders with him. Heather, Helen, and Frank pulled up the tail end and finally seated, got their drink orders, and got comfortable. J.T. stood and looked over the group.

"I want to introduce the two new members of the team. First Chief Elder John Holmes. He will be working on the ship's force field and shielding system. Elder Janet Vanderhoff is joining us to help Frank with the computers. John, Janet, this is Dr. Helen Coulter, Ph.D. nuclear engineer, who works on the spacecraft engines; Dr. Frank Coulter, Ph.D., computer engineer, works on the computer system in the alien craft; Major Beth Kendall, mechanical engineer, and metallurgist working on the manufacturing and construction of the spacecraft. Major Roger Tallant, advanced weapons specialist, designing weapons that will provide protection and security to the ship. Jacques LeClerc, he is our hibernation specialist. Major Sean McCann, the X.O. and project manager. Shannon McCann, is our archivist and historian. You both know Heather Dunkirk, MD, in charge of the health screening of the colonists and treatment of any genetic defects found. Normally this is the time when everyone gets to report on progress in any of their projects, any problems, and any need for help.

"Roger, you start off."

"I am developing three different types of weapons, a sonic weapon, a laser and anti-matter torpedoes. There are still some glitches that I am working on, and I have yet to get enough time with the alien computer. I am sure there are answers there; I just have to know what questions to ask." Roger sat down, somewhat defeated.

"Beth, You're up."

Beth stood and said, "I have put the finishing touches on

Jacques' hibernation chamber. Tomorrow, we will give it a test run. The smelting operation is up and running, going 24/7, spot checking that the process is right on the money. We are building the external hull sections first then we will start in on the tube sections. The interior components of the craft will be constructed last, even though we are building from the inside out, because the smelting process will have to be redesigned, mainly because the metallic composition of the interior structure is markedly different than that of the hull."

"Helen, your turn."

Helen stood and began, "We have completed one whole engine, and we are trying to figure out how to test-run it. The amount of power it will produce is making it difficult to figure out how to anchor it, then light it off, and run it up to full power. We have followed the computer's design specifics to the T, and I am 85% sure it will function as expected and as it is designed to, but I would still like to try it out before I make more engines. I don't want to waste the resources or time."

"OK, Frank, you're up." Frank just spoke from his seat.

"As I have said before, the alien computer has a self-repairing mechanism, and until I can find out how to bypass it, I am not able to remove any of the computers from the space-craft. Janet, I believe that was the reason for enlisting your assistance. Have you had the opportunity to review the data I sent along with James?"

There was a quizzical look on most of the team's faces. They had only heard J.T. referred to as J.T. or General, and they were unaccustomed to hearing him referred to by his first name.

Janet said, "I have reviewed the data, and I think I may have an idea as to how to get around the issue. We can get started first thing in the morning."

"Well then," J.T. said, "let's order dinner and enjoy the meal and the company.

Sean, I will need to have you notify or remind if you will, Colonel Stein that Coulter's weekend is in 2 weeks, which reminds me. We will be taking a two-week vacation starting the week after next. It is the fall, and the bi-annual volunteer week is scheduled for those that wish to attend, so I would like to have all the projects advanced to a point where we can stop work on the project and go help the Village of Coulter. This is not mandatory by any means, but it is fun, and it helps out a group of people that are some of the finest people on earth. Heather, you will need to screen all of them as potential second-round colonists."

John Holmes raised his hand and asked what this was all about. Sean stood and, for the next 10 minutes, explained the whole scenario about the creation of Coulter and the DSF unit 17's involvement in helping the community in the spring, so they could get ready for the summer and in the fall, so they could get ready for the winter.

J.T. said, "Do you remember the pig roast after the awards ceremony? Those were the folks from Coulter. The Unit gives them a hand, hunting wild game so their meat lockers are restocked. It also helps keep the wild game from overpopulating, as well as allowing the Unit to build something other than having a life where all they do is destroy people and things. It's a worthy cause, and these are really great folks."

"Sounds like a lot of fun. I'm in."

"I don't need to remind everyone that this mission is still

classified, so watch your mouths. None of the Coulter folks will be going on the first flight of colonists. I am going to do all I can to have a second flight, and they will be on that one. They are just the kind of people that should be part of building a new home world for the human race."

The Chief Steward came in and delivered another round of drinks and walked around the table getting each person's orders. He informed the table that the entrees would be served in 20 minutes. After he exited the room, the conversations started, and all of the team members were interested in getting to know the new team members. The 20 minutes zipped by, and the steward was back, serving the meal.

The conversations died down so everyone could eat. About halfway thru the meal, the conversations started back up. Everyone seemed to be meshing together well, and that made J.T. feel more sure of his team. After the meal was done, the decision was to let everyone decide for themselves what they wanted to do for entertainment. Janet and John decided to go back to their respective rooms as they both were still tired. The rest of the group decided to go to the O club for a drink. All in all, the group had a good evening with each other; the laughter flowed easily, and the love there was obvious.

The group broke up around 2130, and J.T. was surprised to see Beth and Jacques retire into the same room. Made him smile that, in some small way, he had a hand in getting them together. He hoped it worked out for them. He took Heather by the hand and retired into the room for some intimate personal time.

The next morning, everyone met for breakfast as usual. J.T. handed out instructions to all the crew members. He also reiterated to Janet and John the rules and warnings about computer use. He also suggested that Janet and Frank use a separate craft.

"Janet should have no more than one hour this morning, followed by a rest period. She may have another hour in the afternoon, followed by a rest period. The next day, computer time will depend on her response today. Do not press the issue; we have already had one team member that did and spent a couple of days in the hospital. I would rather not have to go thru that again. Am I clear?"

"Yes, Sir," was the response from both of them. John would be in the conference room unless he was going to need some time with the computer.

"So, everyone needs to get moving. We have a long way to go."

ABOUT THE AUTHOR

Steven "Steve" Horne, a veteran and Family Practice Physician Assistant, now enjoys his retirement in the serene environs of Rapid City, South Dakota. Steve's journey began when he graduated from Cassopolis High School in June 1970 and soon after, he responded to the call of duty by enlisting in the U.S. Navy in July 1970.

Steve's military service was highlighted by his tenure on the USS Newport News (CA148) from 1971 to 1972, a pivotal period during which he participated in the Battle of Haiphong Harbor. This fierce encounter is remembered as the most substantial naval battle of the Vietnam War, cementing Steve's courageous spirit. Following his tour of duty in Vietnam, Steve served at the Naval Hospital Orlando before undertaking a two-year tour at the esteemed Great Lakes Naval Station. His time in the Navy culminated with independent duty at Beachmaster Unit 1, situated in the iconic NAB Coronado Island.

On leaving the military, Steve transitioned into the medical sector, securing a coveted spot in the Physician Assistant Training program for the Federal Prison System, based at the Medical Center for Federal Prisoners in Springfield, Missouri. However, life took an unexpected turn with the untimely death of his first wife, leading him to resign and relocate back to Orlando. In search of a fresh start, Steve pursued a new path in the culinary arts, enrolling in the respected Chef's program at Mid-Florida Tech.

A fateful incident at The Marriot Hotel, where Steve was honing his cooking skills, thrust him back into the medical world. Called upon to assist in a medical emergency, Steve successfully resuscitated a fellow employee who had fallen into a seizure and stopped breathing. This life-altering moment sparked his realization that his true calling was in medicine, with his cooking talent reserved for intimate circles.

Reinvigorated, Steve applied to the University of Central Florida (UCF) and secured his Associate's degree. With renewed determination, he progressed to the University of Florida's Physician Assistant (PA) Program, not only graduating in 1986 but also earning the distinct honor of being elected class president.

Upon graduation, Steve devoted himself to family practice, gaining extensive experience in several practices throughout Orlando. The year 2000 marked a new chapter as he relocated to Atlanta and joined the team at North Atlanta Primary Care. Steve served the Cumming, Georgia community with unwavering commitment until his well-earned retirement in 2019. Today, he looks back on a rich, multifaceted career that blended service to his country, commitment to the medical profession, and a passion for culinary arts.